"Jennifer Deibel's debut is rich in atmosphere, family mystery, and sweet romance. Her love of Ireland and her years spent there shine through in her depictions of characters and setting. Her vibrant descriptions make me want to visit the Emerald Isle myself. A gem!"

Julie Klassen, author of *The Bridge to Belle Island*

"Journey to the Emerald Isle with *A Dance in Donegal!* With an authenticity born of having lived in Ireland herself, the author deftly paints a lush landscape, colorful customs, and memorable characters with personal journeys of their own. Certain to appeal to fans of historical romance, this impressive debut marks Jennifer Deibel as an author to watch. I can't wait to read what she writes next."

Jocelyn Green, Christy Award–winning author of *Veiled in Smoke*

"Set against the backdrop of romance, beauty, and a firmly held faith, Jennifer Deibel's debut paints a lavish portrait of Ireland's Emerald Shores. *A Dance in Donegal* is a reader's dance with the beauty of well-threaded words, a storied Irish hamlet, and a vintage-inspired journey worthy of turning pages while cozied up by an old, stone fireplace. Fans of Catherine Marshall's *Christy* will want to clear room on their favorites shelf because this one's earned a place alongside!"

Kristy Cambron, bestselling author of *The Paris Dressmaker* and *The Butterfly and the Violin*

"The misty air of Donegal will seep into your soul just as swiftly and surely as the characters do in Jennifer Deibel's debut novel. Jennifer clearly knows and loves Ireland, and she fills every scene with vivid description and lilting dialogue. *A Dance in Donegal* is a romance, to be sure, yet there are secrets to uncover and a tender spiritual journey at its heart. Pour a cuppa and curl up with this gem of a story."

Liz Curtis Higgs, *New York Times* bestselling author of *Mine Is the Night*

"Jennifer Deibel's debut is a hallmark of atmospheric and immersive writing. Her obvious passion for Ireland is a deft brushstroke against a lush green canvas. Featuring a strong heroine and themes of resilience through adversity, this lovely and impeccably researched debut is a treatise on belonging and the many facets of home. Unabashedly romantic both in setting and in tone, *A Dance in Donegal* firmly establishes Deibel as a must-read author for fans of Kristy Cambron, Jennifer Delamere, and Sarah Ladd."

Rachel McMillan, author of *The London Restoration*

"Rich in atmosphere, deep in meaning, and sweet in nature. Jennifer Deibel's *A Dance in Donegal* captivated me. Moira's courage and compassion and Sean's solid strength make them endearing characters, and the supporting characters were both flawed and charming. I truly loved this story."

Sarah Sundin, bestselling and award-winning author of *When Twilight Breaks* and the Sunrise at Normandy series

A DANCE IN DONEGAL

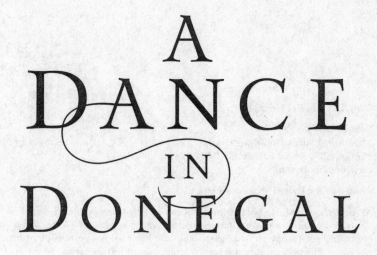

A DANCE IN DONEGAL

JENNIFER DEIBEL

Revell

a division of Baker Publishing Group
Grand Rapids, Michigan

Published by Revell
a division of Baker Publishing Group
PO Box 6287, Grand Rapids, MI 49516-6287
www.revellbooks.com

Printed in the United States of America

Library of Congress Cataloging-in-Publication Data
Names: Deibel, Jennifer, 1978– author.
Title: A dance in Donegal / Jennifer Deibel.
Description: Grand Rapids, Michigan : Revell, a division of Baker Publishing
    Group, [2021]
Identifiers: LCCN 2020019533 | ISBN 9780800738419 (paperback) | ISBN
    9780800739638 (hardcover)
Classification: LCC PS3604.E3478 D36 2021 | DDC 813/.6—dc23
LC record available at https://lccn.loc.gov/2020019533

This is a work of historical reconstruction; the appearances of certain historical figures are therefore inevitable. All other characters, however, are products of the author's imagination, and any resemblance to actual persons, living or dead, is coincidental.

Scripture used in this book, whether quoted or paraphrased by the characters, is taken from the King James Version of the Bible.

The Ballyeamon Cradle Song, found on page 79, is a traditional Irish lullaby. The author is unknown.

Published in association with Books & Such Literary Management, www.books andsuch.com.

21 22 23 24 25 26 27   7 6 5 4 3 2 1

To the Author
of the Greatest Story

And for Seth—my real-life
dreamy handyman hero

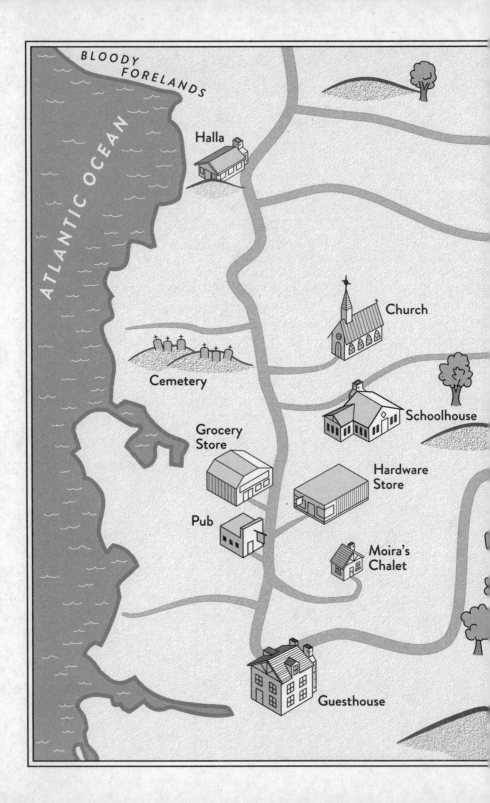

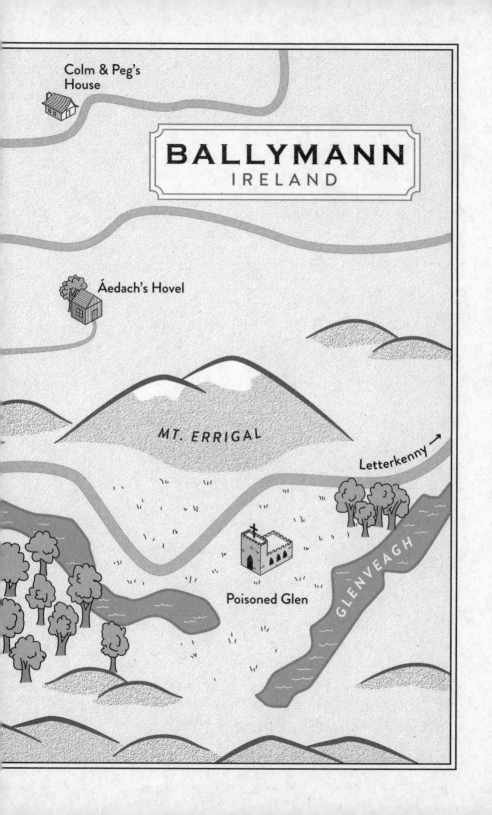

CHAPTER 1

BOSTON
OCTOBER 1920

The grandfather clock downstairs chimed the hour, its clangs all too reminiscent of the funeral bells presiding over Mother's service just yesterday morning. Silent tears slipped down Moira Doherty's cheeks—each one punctuated by the unforgiving *clang, clang, clang.*

I never did care for that clock.

Moira's gaze fell on the street below, though she truly saw nothing more than blurry figures and blotches scurrying in the rain. Her burlap travel bag lay forgotten on the bed, surrounded by all the trappings of her impending overseas voyage. Moira feared if she returned to packing, she would find herself hurling each item in anger, rather than carefully rolling and placing them in the bag for her journey—a journey she was no longer sure she wanted to take.

How had it come to this? Only weeks ago life was simple and good. Moira, having just graduated from Boston Normal School, was set to begin her teaching career not far from the brownstone where she grew up. Her mother was alive and well, and Moira was content to daydream about someday embarking on a grand adventure to see her mother's homeland. Today, life was drastically different.

Thunder rumbled across the sky, sending a chill down Moira's spine. Hugging her shawl tighter around her shoulders, she turned to the bed and travel trappings strewn across it. Heaviness weighed her down like an anchor. Neither able to continue packing nor clear the bed for sleep, she shuffled to the tufted chair near the fireplace and slumped into the seat.

The flames danced hypnotically in the grate, drawing Moira into their spell. No thoughts flitted through her mind as she absently watched the fire. Time released any grip on sense or logic, and she gave herself over to the trance as the flames slowly died. Her eyelids growing heavy, Moira rested her head on the quilted back of the chair and let her lids fall closed.

"Goodbye, Mother," she whispered into the darkness.

༺✦༻

The explosion rocked the building, and Moira shot up in her seat, gripping the armrests so firmly she feared the fabric would tear. Beads of sweat dotted her forehead and dropped in dark stains on her shawl. She struggled to catch her breath, and she clutched one hand to her chest to quell the pounding underneath.

Rain pelted the windows, lightning split the sky, and another peal of thunder shook the room.

"Not an explosion," she spoke to the room and gulped. "Thunder."

Falling back in the seat, she wiped her brow with the hem of her shawl. Chills crept up her neck as the details of the dream floated to the forefront of her mind.

Mother.

The door to her bedroom squeaked open, and dusky-haired Leona entered. "Are you alright, Miss? I thought I heard you cry out."

Leona looked at Moira with an expression of sadness and sympathy. A look Moira had grown to hate in the short days since Mother's passing.

"Yes, Leona." She pasted on her most authentic-looking smile. "I'm fine. Thanks for looking in on me though."

"Of course, Miss." She bobbed her head before scurrying to the window to draw the drapes. "It's a frightfully awful storm tonight, if I say so. I've not seen one like this in years."

Moira straightened her shawl once more and poked at the embers in the grate. "Goodness, it sure is."

Leona finished her task, then came to rest a hand on Moira's shoulder. "Are you sure you're alright? You're as pale as a white rose, and despite the chill in the air, I can't help but notice the perspiration on your face."

Sighing, Moira measured the loyal housekeeper. Leona had proven to be an invaluable help and comfort these last weeks. She, more than most, would likely understand. "It was a dream," Moira began at last.

"A dream?" Leona's brow furrowed.

Moira motioned to the stool across from her, and the woman sat down.

"I saw a far green country with hills rolling on for eternity. Waters crashed upon the shore, and when the sun shone on the hills, they glistened like emeralds."

"Ireland." A small smile dawned on Leona's face.

Moira nodded. "I can only assume so. It was breathtaking— like nothing I'd ever seen before. It felt so familiar, yet I know I've never been to this place."

Leona knitted her brows together and leaned over to place more coal on the grate. "Interesting."

"Indeed," Moira continued. "But then, out of nowhere, pewter clouds darkened the sky and fog as thick as I've seen closed in around me. In the distance, I could just make out the figure of a woman standing on a hillside. I squinted to try and make out her face, but it was too dark, and the fog too thick. But I could see her skirts blowing in the wind."

"That sounds . . . eerie."

"It was, and yet I felt compelled to press on. In a flash, the scene swept forward and I found myself standing right behind her."

Leona scooted forward on the stool, her eyes as wide as saucers.

Taking the cue of Leona's interest, Moira continued. "I extended a trembling hand to tap the woman on the shoulder, but before I could touch her, she turned around." Moira squeezed her eyes shut and took in a slow, steady breath. Her heart already quickening, she could feel the sweat pricking the back of her neck.

"Well, who was it?"

"It"—Moira paused—"It was Mother."

"*Tsk!*" Leona wagged her head. "Oh, you poor dear. That must have been shocking."

"Yes, truly, it was. But more than that, it was the look in her eyes." Moira turned her own gaze back to the fire, searching for the best way to describe the haunting look she'd seen on her mother's face. "She looked . . . terrified. And sad."

"Goodness, I wonder what that could be about?"

Moira slowly raised her eyes to meet Leona's. "That's not the worst of it." Her throat tightened, and she suddenly wished she hadn't shared the dream. Not because she worried about Leona's reaction but because she wasn't sure she could get through the rest of the telling.

"Oh, sweet Moira." Leona rested a hand on Moira's knee. "It might ease your heart to share the burden." She offered a kind smile, and compassion shone in her eyes.

Moira sighed and rubbed her palms up and down her skirt, drying and warming them at the same time. "She looked me square in the face and said, 'Save me, Moira. Come to Ireland and save me!'"

Leona's jaw fell open. "But—"

"I know." Moira shrugged.

"It's as if she was trying to tell you—" Leona stopped short and shot her eyes to meet Moira's. "Never mind."

Moira furrowed her brow but, eager to be done sharing her dream, chose not to question what Leona was referring to. "Before I could ask her what she meant, she disappeared. And that's when I woke up."

"No wonder you were so upset when I came in."

The two sat in silence for several minutes before Leona turned her attention to the window. "It seems quieter out there." She stood and made her way across the room to the window. On the way, she kept her eyes on Moira's clothes and travel bag on the bed. "So, you've decided to go?"

Moira's shoulders rose and fell. "Maybe. I don't know."

CHAPTER 2

DECEMBER 1920

Moira's burlap bag sat in the corner. Though packed and ready for travel, a layer of dust had settled across the top. It had been three months since Mother's passing, and still Moira had yet to decide about the offer her mother had presented just months before she died.

Though she had always dreamed of seeing her mother's home village of Ballymann, Ireland, what her mother had asked Moira to do was simply too much. Moira poked at the fire in the grate and returned to her window. Her perch in her second-floor room had been a favorite and hallowed place ever since her childhood. She had spent hours gazing out at the world below, crafting stories in her mind about the people who passed by. Now though, the timeworn sill was no longer a place of solace and comfort. It was her place of melancholy.

"Begging your pardon, Miss"—Leona's voice shattered Moira's reverie—"but we've a telegram from Ballymann."

Moira's gaze remained glued on the street below.

"Moira."

She turned to find the housekeeper's face compassionate but resolute.

"They need to know," she urged. "They need an answer."

Moira nodded. "Yes, yes. I know." But she *didn't* know.

"Today," Leona added softly. "I'll be in the parlor when you come to a decision." She hovered at the door another moment and then disappeared into the hallway.

What on earth had possessed Mother to recommend Moira for such a task? Moira tried to remember the conversation when Mother had told her the news.

Noreen Doherty had sat in an overstuffed chair in the living room of her brownstone, overlooking Massachusetts Avenue. A funny sort of smile flirted with the corners of her mouth, and an unfamiliar emotion swam within the woman's eyes.

"Moira, dear, I have some wonderful news from home." She gestured for Moira to take a seat on the matching chair across from her. "Do you remember when I told you that my old teacher from Ireland, Miss McGinley, had passed on?"

Moira nodded slowly, not sure where her mother was heading with the conversation.

"Well, I didn't tell you because I didn't want to get your hopes up unjustly." The dignified woman paused. The amber light from the setting sun set her silvery gray hair alight.

"Tell me what, Mother? You're worrying me."

"Oh, darling, there is nothing to fear." She smiled. "Did I not say I had wonderful news? You see, when I learned of Mrs. McGinley's unfortunate passing, I wrote to the parish and recommended that you be the new teacher in Ballymann." She grinned more broadly and sat back in her chair, clearly pleased with her surprise. Yet her eyes held something that unsettled Moira.

"So?" Moira swallowed hard. "What did they say?"

Her mother had stared out the window behind Moira for a moment. Something akin to wistfulness, or regret, reflected in her eyes. "I'm told the parish leaders were reluctant."

Moira knitted her brows but remained silent.

"But," Mother continued, "Lady Williams insisted upon you being the one."

Moira sat, dumfounded, with her chin practically hanging in her lap. "What? How? When did—?" Unbidden, a rumble of laughter bubbled up and tumbled out of her mouth.

"I know, I don't deny I was shocked as well." Mother clasped Moira's hand. "I'd had some dealings with Lady Williams . . . before."

"Before?"

"Oh . . ." Her mother had faltered. "When I was younger."

Moira nodded but something niggled at her gut that there was more than her mother was telling her.

"At any rate, Lady Williams was quite insistent that you come. I don't pretend to know why she is so interested in you, but I'm grateful." A warm smile spread across her mother's face and she pressed Moira's hand.

"Oh, Mother, thank you! But"—she swallowed—"it's so far! I can't leave you here."

Mother's smile faded a little, but her eyes still held their gleam of excitement. "Moira dear, I'll be fine. This is the chance you've always dreamed of, is it not?"

Moira had pressed her lips together. She leaned forward and swallowed her mother in a hug. The two of them sat and rocked for the longest time, just mother and daughter.

Though Mother's speech had been encouraging, it had yet to convince Moira to leave everything she'd ever known, voyage across the seas, and settle in a foreign place with foreign people.

Moira had all but decided not to go when the dream began haunting her. When it first occurred that stormy night in October, Moira hoped it had been born of the toxic mixture of grief and fatigue. But as time pressed on, the dreams not only continued but grew in frequency and intensity.

Though the specific details changed from night to night, each dream took place in Ireland, and concluded with Mother pleading with Moira to come to Ireland and save her.

Moira had discussed the dreams at length with Leona over the past three months. The same question vexed both women: How could Moira possibly save her mother if she was already dead?

"Oh Lord," Moira whispered, not sure if it was a prayer or exclamation, "I don't know what to do." Adding to her apprehension, word had reached America of the "War for Independence"—Ireland's fight for its independence. Donegal seemed a sweet respite from the heart of the fighting, but the idea of traveling to a war-torn country unsettled her.

Mother's words echoed in her mind, "Save me, Moira! Come to Ireland and save me."

Moira squeezed her eyes shut and slumped to the floor, exasperated and exhausted. "I don't know." She sighed. "I just don't know."

And thine ears shall hear a word behind thee, saying, This is the way, walk ye in it, when ye turn to the right hand, and when ye turn to the left.

The words floated into her heart, and Moira opened her eyes to scan the room. "Could it be?" She raised her eyes to the ceiling. "Could it be that simple? Are You asking me to go to Ireland?"

A sense of confirmation took root within her.

I will never leave you. I will never forsake you.

Moira stood and a shaky breath escaped her lips. She brushed off her skirts and returned to the window. What, truly, did she have to lose? Father had passed away when she was a child. Mother was now gone. With no siblings, no other close relations nearby, and no husband, there was nothing tying her down to Boston. She had always wanted to see Ireland, walk the streets her mother had walked, and experience the culture, the food, and the community firsthand.

Could she really do this?

"Leona," Moira called, heading for the door, a smile spreading across her face. "Start a telegram, please."

CHAPTER 3

Moira had always longed to see the places of which her mother often spoke with nostalgia and longing. She wanted to smell the sweet aroma of the burning *peat* and hear the crashing waves beating upon the rocky Irish shores. Why had her mother never made a return visit? Moira would never know.

Standing atop the cliff now, gazing at the valley and the angry waves of the Atlantic pummeling the rugged shore, excitement and longing withdrew into the wings as fear and doubt waltzed in and took center stage. The circumstances of her life were barreling ahead like a steam locomotive, but she preferred the gentle rocking of a horse and buggy.

Moira scanned the horizon, letting her eyes linger, taking in all the sights that until that moment had lived only in her imagination and her mother's memories. Smoke rose from the chimneys of the bungalows below. The salty, almost sweet smell of the churning North Atlantic stirred her exhausted spirit and ignited her hopes.

In the dead center of the valley, looming in stark contrast to the welcoming scene of farms and flowers, a gray stone building stood with a tower jutting high into the air. The church. As she took in the sight, the magnitude of the gift of grace that had been extended to her overwhelmed her. Were these soon-to-be new neighbors locked in the catacombs of moldy tradition? Or did they enjoy this same grace from her heavenly Father? *Let it be so, Father. Let it be so.*

The wind bullied her, carrying with it whispers of secrets and mysteries yet untold—but the gales were not alone in their intimidation. Acrid thoughts butted close to her, hissing doubt and confusion with each whip of the salty air.

She hadn't fully realized the storm's ferocity and the wind barreling in from the sea until a gust ripped the woolen scarf from her neck. She snatched it just before it flew away for good and tucked it deep into the front of her jacket. Earlier in the day, the slate-gray clouds on the horizon had caught her eye, but she hadn't expected them to reach land so quickly.

Once again, your wandering mind has led you down a shaky path, Moira Girl, she scolded herself. *If you're going to reach your lodging before the torrent, you must leave now.*

Sighing, she clambered back into the seat of the carriage. Moira flicked her wrists. The shadowy brown horse responded to the tap of the reins and resumed the trek down the path toward the village.

Driven by the wind, mist stung Moira's face as the horse plodded steadily into the valley. It changed to a drizzle before finally evolving into heavy, fat raindrops. She was traveling on what she assumed to be the main road, though it looked little more than a back alley. Small, humble bungalows with whitewashed walls and thatched roofs lay scattered here and there along the hillsides. Just off the road to the right was the local pub, where the silhouettes of four hunched figures drinking their pints drew her gaze. The scene appeared warm, quiet, and inviting.

To her left stood the local market shop, closed for the night.

Though much smaller than she had anticipated, the town—with its dainty cottages, glowing windows, and sleepy little streets—hosted a cozy atmosphere, even in the midst of the storm. Anticipation wound up her spine and into her heart. This place, despite the cold and wind, felt like home. Up the road, a few more darkened buildings lined the street. At the horizon where the road began to bend, an orange light flickered in the night.

"Oh bless! Please, God, let that be the guesthouse." A sigh of relief welled in her chest and spilled out with a flutter of her lips. The horse nickered and quickened his pace, jaunting down the muddied path with energy Moira hadn't seen in him since they'd set out three days prior. "I guess you're glad for this trip to be over, too, boy?"

The flickering beacon welcomed Moira. Her pulse raced as she headed toward the building.

The horse startled. A dark shadow emerged on the side of the road. The horse flew as fast as his pounding hooves would take him, narrowly missing the shadowed figure. Already coated in thick, wet mud, the wooden wheels refused to grip the rutted path. Moira jolted into the air, then fell back on the wooden seat with a thud. The carriage skidded side to side. She gripped the reins, tugging to no avail. Tipping and lurching, the carriage threatened to flip with each bump. Rain mixed with tears blurred her eyes and her heart pounded in her ears.

With one final, desperate tug at the reins, she veered the wagon to one side of the road. The horse skidded to a halt with a whinny, his hooves slipping in the mire.

The shadowed man stomped toward the rig, head hunched low against the elements. "Whoa, now! Watch yourself before you kill someone, includin' ye!"

Moira spun about in her seat to face the man standing off to the side of the road, her mouth agape.

"Ya won't last long around here drivin' like ya own the place, so ya won't!" the man scolded. He was naught but a shadow shrouded in dark and rain, but Moira could just make out the figure snatching the hat from his head and running a hand through a thick mop of hair, shaking his head in disgust.

"Probably English," he growled as he turned and stormed away.

"I'm terribly sorry!" Moira called after him, but it was too late. The wild winds tore the words from her mouth.

The figure disappeared into the downpour as Moira righted herself in the seat and urged the horse on toward the light.

A woman stood in the doorway as Moira pulled up to the modest, two-story home. "Mrs. Martin?"

Joy glowed from the woman's smile. The smell of strong black tea and fresh-baked Irish brown bread wafted out of the open door behind her.

The woman rushed to Moira's side. "Aye! Oh, I'm so glad ye're here!" Mrs. Martin called over the storm. "I was ragin' when I saw the storm coming, and I was worried to death you'd not make it. Thank God ye're alright! Come in, now, pet, come in! My Owen'll see to yer horse."

An older gentleman bustled around the corner and unhitched the horse. Shifting his feet impatiently in the mud, the animal made it clear he was ready to get out of the rain as well.

Mrs. Martin sang out a command to the man in what didn't sound like words at all. Moira knitted her brows together.

"I'm sorry to be speakin' the *Gaeilge* in front of ya when ya don't have a word of it, do ya?" She chuckled. "That's what most of us speak around here. Ye'll catch on soon."

Moira blew a puff of air. "I'll certainly try." Doubt clouded her voice as she followed her hostess indoors. As they entered the house and the warmth of the turf fire enveloped her, thoughts of letters, Gaelic, and languages vanished as longing for hot tea and a comfortable seat stole every ounce of her attention.

"The sittin' room's just there." Mrs. Martin motioned to the left. "Give me yer bags and sit ye down. Ye must be wrecked." The woman scooped up Moira's bags and scurried off.

Moira studied the room. The trappings of a charming but unpretentious home greeted her. Small tables stood at either end of the couch. A long brown sofa with a blanket her mother would have said was "made for the frosty nights of an Irish winter" beckoned her. Moira's icy toes squirmed inside her boots as she stared at the inviting fire.

A work of needlepoint—The Lord's Prayer in both English and another language—hung over the mantel.

That must be Gaelic.

Moira ran tender, reverent fingers over the strange-looking jumble of letters and accents. A smile spread across her face at the precise detail of the stitching.

Mrs. Martin returned carrying two teacups, a kettle, sugar, milk, a few biscuits, some piping-hot brown bread, and a dish of butter, all precariously yet perfectly balanced on a decorative tray.

"Have a seat, darlin'. Would ya like a little cuppa?" the spry old woman asked, setting it all down on the table.

"Yes, please." Moira sighed. The idea of tea brought relief to Moira's tired bones. "Mother made sure I knew the value of a good cuppa."

Mrs. Martin chuckled. "She always did enjoy her tea, so she did." Her shoulders quaked with quiet laughter. "Shall we sit?"

The woman sat in one of the chairs nearest the fire and proceeded to pour the tea. Relief washed over Moira as she lowered herself into a padded seat, taking the hot cup offered to her. The heat of the turf fire embraced her like flannel. It was such a gentle heat, so unlike the harsh coal fires she'd grown up with in Boston. She closed her eyes for a moment, allowing the soothing warmth to comfort her weary body.

"Ya must be wrecked after that long journey. Traveling all that way by yerself? 'Magine! Were ya not scared at all?"

"It wasn't too bad. Mother, in her wisdom, had places arranged before she passed for me to stay each night, so I wasn't alone in the evenings. But, yes, I am exhausted. I didn't expect the trip to be so cumbersome. I'm glad to finally be here." She stole a sip of tea before Mrs. Martin could ask her another question.

The two sipped in comfortable silence while Moira watched the fire in the grate. The flames seemed to grab a partner and reel around like the High-Cauled Cap—Moira's favorite Irish dance. Mesmerized by the scene, she fought to keep her eyelids from drooping.

"Well, I'll not keep ya up tonight then." The old woman drained her tea in a gulp. "Come on up the stairs and I'll show ya yer room. I'll have breakfast ready in the mornin' for ya. You'll need your strength for those wee ones, won't ya?"

The last sentence tumbled out in a curious chuckle. Unnerving. Either the woman was implying Moira was not going to do well, or she was in for a surprise. But Moira was perfectly confident in her training and ability to teach the local children all they needed to know and more. At least she had been, until about an hour ago when she first gazed at the village and doubts rose like the tide.

As if reading her thoughts, Mrs. Martin murmured, "I

know one or two wee ones who take the energy of this whole village and more."

Is she talking to me? Or herself? Moira took a final sip of her tea before abandoning it to follow her hostess. As they ascended the stairs, black-and-white images in ornate frames looked on them with solemn faces. Did they, too, know what lay ahead for Moira? Were even pictures in frames concerned about her naivete?

This new job—which had once been an innocent idea of adventure in her mind—was beginning to weigh Moira down. A daunting task lay before her, and she wondered if she had made a colossal mistake.

She followed her hostess down a short hall.

"Now, here we are, love," Mrs. Martin chirped.

The door creaked open, and Moira caught her first glimpse of the room that would be home until the teacher's chalet was ready.

Lit only by a gas lamp, the room looked homey—just what Moira had envisioned for a rural Irish guesthouse. The roof was so slanted she could hardly stand upright near the window. A bed lay in the corner, covered with a thick duvet and a pillow so flat it practically blended into the mattress. On a low stool in the corner, a portly cat lay curled, his tail flapping lazily. He lifted his head toward Moira as he licked his nose, then returned to his napping.

After a heavy blink, Moira mustered a smile and turned to her hostess. "Thanks very much, Mrs. Martin. It's perfect, just lovely."

She gestured to the snoozing feline. "Don't let Benny there bother ye. Feel free to shoo him from the room. Now, if there's nothin' else you'll be needin', I'll be on my way, then." With that, Mrs. Martin quietly closed the door.

Moira yawned and set about getting the room ready for the night. Her two large canvas bags seemed to weigh a thousand pounds as she moved them near the bed. She decided to unpack properly in the morning, too tired to bother with it tonight.

What couldn't wait, however, was a good face washing and running a brush through her hair—three days out in the elements was a lot to take for a city girl. Her hands, clumsy with fatigue, rummaged through her satchel until she found her brush. Sitting on the stool by the window, she swam in the memories of all that had brought her to this place.

Her mother's stories swirled in her mind, and she wondered what the future might hold for her here. It had never occurred to her she would be asked to come to Donegal to replace the beloved schoolteacher who had passed away just last year.

The chance to teach brought Moira to life and filled her soul like nothing else. Having worked hard at her training, she was eager to impart her newly acquired wisdom to the spit-shined faces of the boys and girls in her charge. The only question had been where and when.

Six months ago, when word reached Moira's mother that her childhood teacher had passed away, she had put Moira's name in for the replacement. Now, after a dizzying flurry of preparations, Moira was here, in the village she had always longed to see. Though she felt no more prepared than when she first received the news.

Moira spotted a washbasin next to the door and brought it and a towel over to the chest of drawers beside her bed. Cool, clear water splashed from the pitcher into the basin. Raising her weary eyes to the mirror above the wooden chest, she gasped. No wonder Mrs. Martin had been so concerned for her! Black curls that had been neatly tied back in a low plait now stood out several inches from her head. Disheveled locks of hair roamed wherever they wished. Her face bore brown splotches of dried mud. What a sight she was! Her thin frame was swallowed up in a sea of clothing.

One by one she removed the layers of waist jacket, woolen sweater, and cardigan. "There." She blew out a long breath. "That looks more like the Moira Doherty I know. Now, let's take care of that dirty face. It just won't do to have a teacher dirtier than her pupils, now will it, Benny?"

Benny stood, hopped on the bed, circled twice, and lay down with his woolly back to her. She smiled at his indifference and leaned down. Cupping both hands in the basin, she splashed water onto her face. One hand groped for the towel next to the basin. When her chilled fingers found it at last, she snatched it and buried her face in the rough but warm material.

The smoky mirror now showed something much more to her liking. Her cheeks bore a rosy hue from the slaps of wind and cold. Her pale green eyes, although exhausted, danced with anticipation.

Pressing a hand to her stomach, she willed the nervous flutters still. The next few weeks might leave her emotionally splattered with mud like the splotches she'd washed from her face. But Moira swallowed her nerves and straightened with resolve. Her faith would hold her steady. Time to cease fretting. The bed was an invitation to rest, and she intended to take it.

She plodded across the room to one of her bags and riffled through it. Muscles aching and head heavy, she moved as if in a fog. She clothed herself for sleep, hanging her dress on a bent nail on the door. After draping her jacket and sweater over the back of the low chair in the corner, Moira padded across the floor and eased herself into bed.

Oh, good heavens above, it may as well have been made from all feathers and fluff for as good as it felt to her weary bones. The covers that tucked under her chin soothed her.

Moira adjusted her position and winced as the wooden furniture groaned and squeaked.

The silence that followed should have been welcome. Instead, it screamed in her head. Unlike the endless commotion on the streets of Boston, the utter lack of noise overwhelmed and unnerved her. Each occasional creak seemed a siren, every groan of the wooden floor a gong. She whispered a prayer for peace and settled deeper into the covers, her eyes already closing.

Chapter 4

Blue light, soft and bereft of heat, seeped through the square window on the eastern wall. Tucked as snug and deep in the covers as she could get, Moira tried to block the bite of the morning chill. Her senses awakened as she stirred and stretched. She inhaled deeply, wishing morning away as the damp Irish air filled her lungs. Musty and earthy, it was like breathing in the scent of an old book.

"Maybe a few more minutes," she whispered to herself and snuggled farther into the cocoon of the covers. The warmth of the duvet blocked the callousness of the wool blanket.

Just as her body settled back into the comfort of the mattress, a quiet tap sounded at the door. Moira's eyes peered out from under the duvet. A slice of golden light swept across the floor as the door opened.

"Are ya awake, pet?" Mrs. Martin whispered.

Moira squinted at the light from the hallway.

"You've already slept half the day away." Her hostess chuckled.

Moira sat up and stretched. The clock downstairs chimed eight times.

Half the day, eh? A smile spread across her face. "Morning, Mrs. Martin. I do need to get an early start today."

"Would you be havin' yer breakfast now then?"

"Yes, that would be lovely," she said through a yawn. "I'll be down shortly."

Mrs. Martin slid the door closed and her footsteps scurried downstairs. The aroma of rashers, sausage, bread, and that distinctive strong black tea wafted through the draft of the closing door. A rumble gurgled in Moira's stomach. She pawed through her bags and found the other dress she had packed.

Moira smiled at the garment. "Hello again, old friend." Although slightly more formal than her traveling dress, the light-blue frock seemed as appropriate for a walk in town as a visit to church. Thankfully it had not gotten wet in the torrent the night before. The one she had worn on her journey was still dreadfully damp and would not do for her first day in town. She dressed quickly, splashed water on her face, straightened her hair, and headed downstairs for her feast.

The food was already set on the table when she arrived, but it was still piping hot. As she sat down, Mrs. Martin came around the corner with a fresh pot of tea and some toast with melted butter. Moira didn't know where to begin.

"I can't remember the last time I had a good fry." Moira eyed the array of dishes, delighted to find them just like the ones her mother had made on occasion.

Mrs. Martin laughed. "'Tis one of the things we do best, eh?" She set the toast and butter on the table and returned to the kitchen.

Though tempted to shove it all in her mouth at once, Moira exercised restraint and reached instead for a single piece of toast. Every few minutes Mrs. Martin passed by the open kitchen door in a blur, followed by a cacophony of clanks, thuds, and clinks. Moira wasn't sure what kept her hostess so busy. Since she was the only guest in the house, Moira figured the workload would be rather light.

Unable to contain herself any longer, Moira dug into the many dishes set before her. The food delighted Moira's every sense. The sausage, cooked to perfection, popped when her teeth sank into the skin, and the inside burst into juicy goodness in her mouth. The rashers, salty and tender, were delectable, and the eggs didn't run a bit.

Warmed to the core by the delightful ambrosia, the morning chill melted away into a lovely glow. Refreshed and ready to face the day, Moira worked to rein in her excitement. Anxious to get out and see the town in the daylight, meet some of the locals, and gain her bearings, she gathered up her dishes and carried them into the kitchen. Owen and Mrs. Martin stood next to one another at the basin, chattering away in Gaelic, with the occasional burst of robust laughter punctuating the conversation. As he leaned over to grab the next dish, Owen bussed Mrs. Martin's cheek.

They're married!

"Where shall I put these?" Moira asked.

Mrs. Martin whisked around, a shocked expression on her face. "Ya needn't be pickin' up after the meals, child!" she scolded. "Thanks for the thoughtfulness though. You can just set them here next to the press."

Moira did as instructed, setting her dishes down on the large wardrobe, then stepped into the hall. Relief energized her like a fresh breeze as she donned her coat and slipped out of the house. A twinge of guilt niggled at her belly for not telling her hostess she would not be attending Wednesday mass. It would have been the polite thing to do, but she wasn't sure the woman would understand. While Moira was unfamiliar with the way things were done in this parish, she suspected the service would be officiated entirely in Irish, and she wasn't sure she was ready for that.

That's not the real reason and you know it.

Reluctant as she was to admit it, even to herself, she

couldn't ignore the feeling of unease that had nagged her while overlooking the church the day before. Usually places of worship inspired exactly that from her heart—worship. Yet for reasons she couldn't explain, the sight of the church that day left her uneasy—whether from the unknown of it all or something else, she didn't know. She turned her thoughts to the scenic landscape surrounding her.

Walking aimlessly, Moira wandered down a narrow road— no more than a footpath, really—and found herself atop a small knoll overlooking the rugged Atlantic Ocean. She could imagine no better place to spend time in prayer and contemplation than on the boulder she found about half-way down to the sea. She sat and adjusted her cloak more tightly around her shoulders. Closing her eyes, she took in all that was unseen.

Waves crashed on the shore, uttering secrets her heart could not yet discern. Tender sea grass rustled in the wind. The pungent, heady aroma of salt, earth, and air filled her lungs. Filled her heart.

I know the thoughts that I think toward you. So audible was the voice in her heart that her eyes jolted open to see who was speaking. Nothing stood before her but the vast expanse of rugged terrain and sea. She closed her eyes again, listening.

I am with you. I will never leave you.

She breathed in deeply, as if trying to inhale the message itself, to make it a part of her very being. Uncaring about the passage of time, she sat still in that place—in that hallowed outdoor sanctuary—neither moving nor thinking.

"Well now, what have we here, *a thaisce?*" a voice rasped.

In one swift motion, Moira was on her feet, staring face-to-face with a strange older man. His right shoulder drooped lower than the left, and his back was hunched. His eyes, gray and clouded with age and—she supposed—drink, stared far more intently at her than was either welcomed or appropriate.

"I'm sorry, s-s-sir. I'm sorry if I intruded on your land."

"Oh, *ná bac le sin*, lovey—don't ye worry aboot tha'. The land belongs to the Laird alone." His voice was thin and tinny. Moira was convinced a hearty sneeze would rend his vocal cords in two.

"Ya oughtn't be sittin' alone outside wit' yer eyes clamped shut like 'at. Ya never know who might come up an' snatch ya away." He wagged his head. "Ye're the spitting image of yer mammy, ya know."

Moira furrowed her brow. *He knew Mother?* Before she could ask him, a wheezy laugh escaped his lips and they curled into more of a snarl than a smile. One obstinate tooth poked through the man's thin, cracked lips. Lunging toward Moira, he reached out and clawed at her sleeves, his laugh evolving into a bone-chilling cackle.

Startled and horrified, Moira clutched her skirts in her fists and ran as fast as she could toward the main road. The man's terrifying laugh chased her on the air. Her feet hastily traversed the rough terrain, her shoes stumbling over stones. It was as if an evil banshee had risen and chased away all magic from this mossy land.

Moira plunged ahead, not bothering to see if she was being chased. Her toe caught on a root, and she hurtled toward the cold ground, blackness washing over her as the man's hollow laughter echoed in her ears.

⚬∽⊙∾⚬

Moira lay in a dazed heap, her knee throbbing. She had hardly a second to wonder how long she'd been lying there when a pair of strong, calloused hands grabbed her arms and lifted her in one smooth motion. Moira fought against the grip until she saw who held her.

Not the older, cackling drunk. No rheumy eyes. These eyes were as green as the emerald shores. And they searched hers.

"Miss? Are you alright?" His masculine voice was drenched in concern and confusion.

She wriggled free from his grasp and fought to gain her bearings and make sense of what had happened. The beach lay behind her, and the main road stretched just beyond this new mystery man. She remembered where she was.

"Miss!" His voice snapped her back to reality. She noticed the light stubble scattered over the jawline of his young, tan face.

She wiped her eyes with her sleeve and turned to run back to the Martins' house. Once again, however, the stranger's strong hands grasped hers and brought her around to look him square in the eye.

"Are you okay?" His words were measured and calm but carried an air of authority that settled her nerves in the most peculiar way.

"Please, pardon my clumsiness. I'm fine, thank you." She gave him a weary smile and brushed the dirt from her skirts, careful to avoid her aching knee.

"Ya won't last long 'round here if ye constantly run into folk." He winked as a deep laugh rumbled from his belly.

Moira started to chuckle, then flinched and pressed her lips together. She narrowed her eyes to reduce his features to a mere silhouette.

If it isn't the welcoming committee from last night on the road. Annoyance shot through her veins and she balled her skirts in her fists.

"Well, it appears I won't last long around here no matter what I do." She sniffled. "And thank you very much for the kind and hearty welcome last night. Fear not, I'll do my best to stay out of your way, good sir." With a whip of her once-styled plait, she turned sharply on her heel and headed back toward the guesthouse.

"Wait! What happened?" he called after her, but she refused to stop.

She glanced behind her as she took marked steps, attempting to retain what little pride she had left. The stranger's eyes were fixed on her, and his hand worked the back of his neck.

Once back at the Martins', Moira burst through the door, tears clogging her throat. Fear, pain, and embarrassment vied for control as she bolted up the stairs and sank onto the bed. Blast it, if she wasn't weeping tears at the rate of last night's rainfall! She heard the door open with a creak. As gentle as a spring rain, a hand rested on her back.

"Oh, *peata*, what's wrong? Are ya okay?" the older woman crooned softly.

Moira took a deep, shaky breath, willing herself calm once more, not knowing where to begin. She absently wiped her nose with the back of her hand and turned to face Mrs. Martin.

"I was down at the seaside," she began, not quite sure how much to divulge about what exactly she was doing there, "when this old man came up behind me. He started telling me I should be careful—that someone could snatch me away. Oh, I don't know. It gave me such a fright. He had the most horridly wicked laugh, I thought for sure I was face-to-face with Lucifer himself."

"Och! That sounds just like yer man Buach." She practically spat the name.

"B—Boo-ac?"

Mrs. Martin's head bobbed. "Buach O'Boyle. *Tsk.*" Mrs. Martin inhaled sharply and continued. "Ya needn't worry about him spiritin' ya away. The man can barely lift his pint. And lift it he does, mm-hmm." A blunt nod punctuated her statement.

"But why would he say such things? He doesn't even know

me! What joy or sport could he get from frightening a young woman?" She closed her eyes, trying to recall what else had transpired with the man. "And then he said something about my . . . my mother."

"Aw sure, it makes no sense to nairmull folk like you an' me. But ya wouldn't be hearing folk sayin' 'Buach' and 'nairmull' in the same breath, sure ya wouldn't." Mrs. Martin's stare drifted somewhere far off. "Some say his mind left him years ago, along with his wife. Other folk say he sold his very soul to the devil. And pay ye no mind to what he said about yer mum. He says more than should be heeded."

So, I wasn't so very far off, after all. It was strong drink that fogged his eyes. Moira winced at the thought and tried to drum up some compassion.

"Doncha be feelin' too sorry for that dairty ol' man. He mightn't be able ta take ya away, but he can do his fair share o' worm-toungin'." She patted her hair and tucked a wayward strand back in place. "For a man what's said to have lost his mind, or have one foot in hell, folk sure do listen to what he has ta say. 'Specially if it's to do with . . ." Mrs. Martin's voice trailed off.

"What? To do with what?" Moira insisted. "And what did he mean about my mother? Does he know something about her?"

Mrs. Martin only shook her head, her lips pressed into a firm line. "No, lass. I've said mair than my share already. You just steer clear of ol' Buach. I have yer word, have I?" She arched her brows in a no-nonsense manner.

Moira searched the woman's face. When there was no hint of more information, she resigned herself to obedience. "Yes, ma'am. I promise."

"Och! Ma'am's fer old ladies and schoolmarms." The woman's eyes widened. "Oh. Heh heh. No offense, peata, no offense." The woman chuckled as she headed toward the door.

Despite her fright and a gnawing sense of doubt plaguing her gut, a smile played on Moira's lips. "None taken, Mrs. Martin. None taken."

"*Anois*, come ya down the stairs and I'll fix a nice cuppa and bit o' toast, eh?" She stopped in the doorway and turned back. "And by the way, if ye're to be stayin' 'round Bally-mann, ya can call me Bríd."

With that, the pair headed down the stairs for tea and happier talk, with Bríd still chuckling at her inadvertent slip of the tongue the whole way.

CHAPTER 5

The next day dawned clear and cold with a blanket of white frost covering the earth in a veil of diamonds and stars. Moira had awoken earlier than usual, with her nose an icicle and her toes numb despite being buried deep within the folds of her duvet.

Although February was technically spring in Ireland, northwest Donegal was holding on to the last of winter's chill with a firm grip. She dressed quickly to minimize her exposure to the cold and damp.

Once again, as though summoned by Moira's thoughts alone, Bríd appeared at the door with a jug of steaming water. "'Tis far tew cold a morning to be washin' wit'out a bit o' steam," she stated with a dramatic shiver.

A thousand needles bore into Moira's fingers as she plunged them into the hot water. The shock gave way to sheer bliss as the warmth radiated up her chilled hands. Relishing every last ounce of heat, she lifted cupped handfuls to splash her face, wishing she could fit her entire body into the small basin of steaming water.

She dried her hands and face quickly, and deftly assembled her hair into a long plait that she wrapped around the crown of her head. Stubborn black ringlets fell around the nape of her neck and her temples.

"Ah, well." She sighed at her reflection in the murky mirror. "Perfection belongs to the Lord alone, right?" She gave herself a curt nod in agreement and headed down the stairs.

After another hearty breakfast, Moira prepared to explore the village a bit more and visit the schoolhouse for the first time. Feeling compelled to let her hosts know her plans for the day this time, she stopped at the doorway. "Thank you again for breakfast. It was delicious. I'm heading out to see the town today, hoping to get into the schoolhouse and set a few things up before next week."

"Will ya be back for lunch, then?" Bríd asked.

"Yes, that'll be lovely."

Moira stepped outside and took a deep breath. There was a freshness in the air she had never felt in Boston. It rejuvenated her spirit. It was like inhaling pure life with every breath.

Just past the entrance to the guesthouse property, the road curved and headed east. Isolated bungalows stood scattered along the winding dirt road. Fields of bog, bordered with rustic rock walls, lay like a patchwork quilt between barns, sheds, and whitewashed homes that gleamed in the morning sun.

She sensed something familiar about this place. Although she had never been here before, she could almost describe what was around each corner before she got there. Though unexpected, she welcomed the perception of familiarity.

Even with peace washing over her, the muttered statement Bríd had made about the schoolchildren the first night rolled like a stone deep in the pit of her stomach.

The day-to-day language of the village was Gaelic. Bríd had said so herself. Why, then, would they hire a young, English-speaking *American* teacher? Surely there were more experienced, more qualified, Irish teachers.

Moira came to a road that ran perpendicular to her

current path. About thirty yards down stood a single-story building with pebble-smacked walls and a tin roof. As she got closer, it reminded Moira of a flower box topped with a slanted lid.

Small windows lined the long walls. Soggy, hand-drawn pictures, paper cutouts, and other educational paraphernalia littered them, alerting the community of the children's activities. *That must be the schoolhouse.* Moira smiled with quiet satisfaction. She had only finished her teacher training in October and had not yet been given a chance to put her skills to work. Pushing her doubts aside, she felt anticipation overwhelm her, and she ran, childlike, to the door, pushing it open.

Inside, the humble building smelled of pencil lead, damp paper, and glue. She sighed.

The pupils' desks sat in tidy rows, each with a pencil atop, waiting for its owner. Moira strolled beside the back wall and ran her fingers along the large bookshelf that stood there. The shelves bowed with the weight of the collection of literary works. A large blackboard hung on the front wall. The teacher's desk sat kitty-corner from it, allowing her to see all her pupils in one sweeping glance.

Moira was so lost in thought, all else around her faded away. But a metallic click told her she was not alone.

CHAPTER 6

Sean McFadden stood outside the schoolhouse, memories of beloved old Miss McGinley—who was like a grandmother to him—swimming in his heart. Having spent countless hours after school with the teacher, poring over old books and discussing their favorite authors and stories, he had developed a close relationship with the older woman. Once finished with school, Sean would stop by during the day, as he had time, to help out with whatever he could. Whether it was lighting the fire or reading with the young ones while Miss McGinley presented a more challenging lesson to the older students, he was eager to do anything that would make the sweet teacher's day easier.

He had returned to Ballymann in January after completing his apprenticeship in Donegal Town. Other than being outdoors all day, he had never really enjoyed thatching, but his uncle had arranged for the opportunity. As there had been no other option for him after completing school—other than joining the country's fight for independence—he'd had no choice but to accept it. Although he had enjoyed his time in Donegal Town, he had been anxious to return home and settle down in the quiet seaside village of his youth. When he saw a strange woman walk into the school, he had to investigate. *Must be the new teacher,* he thought. He approached slowly but followed her inside.

Having had such an affinity for his childhood teacher, he had a right to be protective of the school she had run and felt compelled to ensure her replacement was someone worthy of the position.

The woman before him now looked at the classroom as though it were her own. Tenderness shone on her face, as if she were admiring a work of art rather than an old, musty schoolhouse.

He closed the door behind him, flinching as it latched with a click.

The woman jumped and whipped around to face him. His stomach dropped as he stood face-to-face with the woman from down near the beach. He wasn't sure what on earth he had done to earn such a vehement response to his help yesterday, but she sure hadn't hesitated to inform him of her annoyance. It both irked and delighted him.

Unencumbered by fear, her beauty was even greater than he'd remembered. The woman's eyes grew wide. Sean pressed his lips together to keep from laughing.

"Ya won't last a second 'round here with nerves like that, now," he taunted. *Nice one, eejit.* Although he fancied himself as known about town for his roaring sense of humor, Sean usually saved sarcasm for his better acquaintances. Yet when his eyes had met hers, her simple beauty shook him so deeply, he'd blurted out the first thing that popped into his head.

The woman glared at him. She didn't seem to appreciate being startled or the way Sean enjoyed her discomfort at his presence.

"Let's hope these wee ones have a few more manners than to be sneaking up on people." She planted her fists firmly on her hips and narrowed her eyes.

"Whoa, now." He held his palms up as though soothing a wild horse. "Why do ya spew venom on me? Is that yer customary response when someone comes to yer aid?"

"It *was* you that night on the road, wasn't it?" Her eyes narrowed again, and he suspected if her hands weren't in fists they would be trembling. "Is it *your* customary response to hurl sarcasm and insults to a young lady struggling with her rig? Is that how this village welcomes visitors? God help us all if the rest of the village has manners like yours!"

Sean took a step back, shocked by her vehemence but equally charmed by her stance and the way the bridge of her nose crinkled when she scowled at him.

"Really, Miss? You're speaking to me of manners? Don't ya know any better than to be gallopin' full speed ahead in the dark o' night—in the middle of a gale, no less? Manners, ya say? *Humph*! If ya don't know how to handle a cart and pony, don't drive one." He crossed his arms over his chest in his best imitation of obstinance. Part of him wanted to smile at her. But as feisty as she was, she'd probably think he was taunting her. Part of him hoped she did.

Sean let a smile tip his mouth. He was who he was, after all, and she was a snippet of a lass from America who couldn't drive a wagon to save her life. "And I suppose where ye come from, it's perfectly polite to run off when asked a question?" He jutted a thumb toward the view of the shoreline out the window.

Her face flushed and she chewed her lip. Her gaze fell to the floor, losing a bit of its determined sparkle.

Remorse rushed through Moira from top to toe. Overwhelmed by the desire to swallow her harsh words, she softened her stance and stepped forward with her hand extended—a gesture of peace. No matter how he had treated her, she had no right to respond in kind. Her mother's voice echoed in her mind: *When someone seems bent on making your life miserable, heap coals of kindness on their head.*

"Maybe we could . . . start over?" She cleared her throat. "I'm Moira—Moira Doherty. I'm sorry if I was rude just then. It seems I'm still recovering from the long voyage over and balancing my anxious thoughts about starting my new role here."

The man extended his hand and shook hers gently, lingering in the hold just a second too long.

"I'm Sean McFadden," he said. "So, either you're the new schoolteacher or you're the oldest student in Donegal." He chuckled while rubbing the back of his neck absently. Moira wondered if the action served to soothe his nerves.

"Your observational skills are very keen. I am indeed the new teacher. While I'm thankful they've given me the week to settle in, I admit I'm anxious to get started. I have so much planned for the wee dotes," Moira said.

"Ah, yes the 'wee dotes.'" He imitated her American twang and gave an exaggerated nod. "They're *wee dotes*, alright. You just tell 'em that if they give ya any trouble, *Muinteoir* Sean'll be after 'em. I'd be derelict in my duties if I let them run off the new girl in town."

Sean's eyes locked with hers and he winked. Heat seeped across her cheeks. Why was she so shaken by this man? Until a moment ago, he'd done nothing but give her a hard time. He'd practically insulted her. And now she was blushing?

"Well, it was lovely meeting you, eh, *John*, was it?" Like a precocious schoolgirl, she pretended not to remember his name. "And thanks for the help yesterday, but I'd best be off."

Sean blanched and blinked hard. "Well, yes, it was my pleasure." He removed his hat and swept it in an arc as he bowed low, a mischievous smile playing on his lips. "And the name's Sean."

Satisfied that her playful blow had hit its mark, Moira headed for the door, her footsteps echoing in her ears. The blast of the fresh breeze stung as it hit her flushed cheeks. The door latched and relief washed over her once she could no longer feel the man's gaze boring into her back. Life here was certainly going to be more interesting than she had expected.

You'd better steer clear of Mr. Sean McFadden, Moira Girl. The last thing you need is some lad distracting you every time you turn around.

Heading down the main road, she stopped to admire the sea view once again.

You're a long way from Boston.

She loved the city life, to be sure. With a skyline like no other, the buildings of her hometown mingled together to make an impressive work of art. However, the streets around the city were muddled and so terribly crowded with people, carts, and traffic.

The seaside here was secluded, quiet, grand. The view stretched for endless miles, making Moira feel very small. The magnitude of it all stirred her soul to life. And humbled her.

She turned right onto the main road and continued north, taking in what appeared to be the center of Bally-mann. She passed the pub she had seen on her way into town. That night in the storm and wind, it had appeared inviting and alive. In the quiet light of morning, however, the run-down building looked every bit as aged and hunched as the figures in the window had.

Just beyond the pub stood the market—a small, square building with whitewashed walls and double doors at the main entrance. Fruit and vegetable stands were being rolled out into the sunshine. The aroma of fresh delicacies from the bakery wafted on the gentle morning breeze.

A few people were beginning to mill about the town now. Moira was keenly aware all eyes were on her. Even the buildings seemed to have eyes and ears straining to see the newcomer and hear if any gossip had yet begun to circulate as to her identity.

You're being paranoid, Moira Girl. I'm sure they all have better things to worry about than your life history. She plastered a shaky smile on her face and continued on her self-guided tour.

The road carried her past the market, up the line of the coast, and around two S-shaped curves. The rolling hills, the churning sea, and the endless fields dotted with white sheep presented a feast for her eyes. Moira struggled to pay heed to the path upon which she was walking rather than gazing at the immense, ever-changing view.

A sharp rise loomed before her. She took a deep breath. Body still sore and joints aching from weeks of travel, trudging up the hill proved quite difficult.

She finally reached the crest and was rewarded with yet another spectacular view.

To the west, the land gradually sloped and ambled down to the tumultuous waves of the Atlantic, framed in wispy, rustling sea grasses. Ahead of her lay the rolling hills atop which sat her viewpoint from the night she'd arrived in town.

Scanning the scene, Moira pictured all the details from her mother's stories aligning with the shapes on the maps she had studied in preparation for her journey, and she immediately recognized the unique landscapes greeting her. The red beaches of the Bloody Foreland loomed in the distance. Toward the east rose the pinnacle of Mount Errigal peeking over the top of the quaint valley where sporadic houses, hemmed in by farmland and sheep pastures, nestled among rock walls and gorse bushes. The smoke from turf fires hung close to the hills and blanketed the valley in a sweet, earthy-smelling fog.

It was clear she'd reached the end of the town center. Continuing on would take her farther into the remote edges of the community.

"Where's the village hall?" she asked the wind. Moira's favorite stories were the ones her mother would tell about the old village hall; how everyone in town would gather on cold nights and heat up the thatched building with their dancing, laughter, and *craic*—better known to those in the States as fellowship.

For twenty-three years, Moira had heard her mother's tales, and dreamed of seeing the place with her own eyes. But for all her wanderings that day, she hadn't found it. Its absence left a story-shaped hole in her heart. While the road beckoned her ever onward, sensibility won the argument for the time being. "You'd best not get lost today, there's much work to be done yet. Back to the schoolhouse with you now," she told herself.

As she started down the hill, grateful for the ease of walking in agreement with gravity rather than against it, her thoughts were both nowhere and everywhere. Ideas, questions, and uncertainties pirouetted in dizzying circles.

What if this is a horrible mistake? What was I thinking, coming all this way, alone? Who am I to think I can take over an entire school's instruction? What if . . . ?

From somewhere deep within, a quiet voice echoed, *For I know the thoughts that I think toward you, saith the* Lord, *thoughts of peace, and not of evil, to give you an expected end.*

Once again, the words allowed a sense of peace to settle over Moira's heart. She might not know what the future held, but she knew the One who did, and she knew of His love for her. Lifting her chin and walking confidently back toward the center of town, she offered a prayer of thanksgiving.

At the sound of a twig snapping behind her, she whipped

around and searched for the source. The breeze through the trees seemed to whisper her name. But no matter where she looked, no culprit could be seen. The hairs on her neck crept upward, and she had the inescapable feeling she was being watched. Willing a neutral look back on her face, she turned and hastened to the schoolhouse.

Chapter 7

"Whar's yer head, lad? You've been thatchin' that same strand of straw for nigh half an hour!"

Colm Sweeny's voice sliced through Sean's thoughts like a hot knife through butter. Sean flinched at his superior's tone and chided himself.

Aw, japers! That woman had gotten into his head and was going to be the death of him. Fancy a woman like that drifting into town with the lofty idea she could teach the children. She had not an idea what it was to live here. Her and her American ways. "Eh, sorry, Colm. I was . . . thinkin' 'bout the best way to carry the thatch 'round the corner of the eaves on the gable end."

Liar.

There was no point letting Colm in on the truth that a wee gal from a far-off land had piqued his curiosity. Sean knew Colm already fancied him a flirtatious lad, so there was no point in trying to explain that for some reason it felt different this time.

"The gable end, ya say? Mmm." Colm's gray head bobbed and he returned to his work, though not before Sean caught a hint of a gleam in the chap's eye.

Not much slipped past Colm. He was older than Sean by a score and seemed wiser even beyond that. His weathered skin, barely shielded by his flat cap, was thick as leather and as brown as milky tea. He held more respect from the community than was due his station.

Sean set about working on the next section that needed securing. It was a brilliant day for thatching. Although the calendar showed *Feabhra*, the sun was shining like the middle of July, and the breeze gently led the tattered ends of the bales of straw in a jig as they waited to be thatched. Sean took a deep breath, energized by the chill that filled his lungs, and glanced up at the top of the roof.

He grimaced. Over the straw he could see a lithe figure walking down the hill toward the market, skirts bouncing blithely in the breeze.

Miss Moira Doherty. Sean, feeling every bit the schoolboy, ducked his head, lest he be seen. *Why are you hiding, man?* Had he offended her with his good-natured ribbing? He hoped it hadn't ruined his chances at friendship with the girl.

Aye, friendship . . . or more.

"*Tsk!* Don't be such an *amadán*," he muttered under his breath as he returned to his thatching, trying not to wonder where she was going.

❧

Moira would not let her run-in with a silly lad like Sean McFadden further deter her from completing her tasks for the day. There was plenty of work to be done to ready the schoolroom for classes on Monday, and it was already midmorning. If she had any hope of starting instruction ahead of the curve, she had no choice but to venture back, whether Sean McFadden was there or not. She set a determined pace to the schoolhouse, but as she neared, her confidence began to wane.

She scanned the area before entering the schoolhouse.

The strange noises meeting her ears had to be merely the wind in the bare branches of the birch trees. The heavy door groaned in protest as Moira tentatively opened it, listening for anyone inside. A quick glance around the room answered her question.

Ah, alone indeed. Thank God.

She cautiously closed the door, and then laughed at herself for being so childish. Taking a deep breath, Moira once again surveyed her surroundings. At the front of the room near her desk stood a fireplace—the room's only source of heat. Next to it sat a basket of turf and a small shovel for removing the ashes.

Having grown up in the city, she had never laid eyes on a brick of peat before but had heard her mother describe them. Walking about town that morning, she had smelled peat's uniquely sweet and earthy aroma and couldn't help but bend down now to take a closer look.

Roughly cut briquettes lay neatly stacked in the basket. She lifted one out for further inspection, running her hand over the packed dirt. Handfuls of dry grass, twigs, and moss jutted in all directions, poking her soft skin.

Although the morning held plenty of chill, she'd not waste the fuel today. *Better to save it for school days.* Returning the peat to its place, she brushed the dirt from her hands and stood to face the pupils' desks.

The imagined faces of her students, round and ready to learn, floated across her mind. Running her fingers over the top of each desk, she slowly walked up and down the rows while whispering a prayer over each child.

Bless him with health. Let her find joy in this room. While the students' names were still unknown to her, she dearly loved each one. Her mother would have said that to be the sign of a true teacher. Was she?

Her attention turned to her own desk, and she crossed

the room to take her seat. Her posture more that of a queen than a teacher unsure of herself, she sat tall, as if the mantle of responsibility had been freshly placed on her shoulders. The desk before her wasn't the shined oak or mahogany of a barrister or wealthy landlord but the rough-hewn desk of generations of teachers before her. She'd prayed over her students. Now she whispered a desperate plea of her own.

The rest of the morning passed quickly as she arranged books, removed outdated projects and materials from walls and shelves, and organized what few teaching materials were provided in the room. Tomorrow she would return with her own effects to finish getting ready for the first day of school. Sunday would be spent resting, reflecting on Scripture, and praying, as she had done every week in Boston with Mother. This time she would be alone. As if on cue, the church bells tolled in the distance.

The morning had flown. Bríd would be waiting, as would lunch. Moira was grateful the guesthouse was not far, and she prayed the Martins had not waited to partake of their own lunch until her arrival. Moira grabbed her skirts and flew home.

Her gait slowed to a measured walk as she approached the house, fighting the urge to burst through the door with deepest apologies for her tardiness. On the doorstep she noticed a small bunch of white flowers.

"How lovely!" She stooped to pick them up, raising them to inhale the sweet scent before entering the house. Her hostess rounded the corner as if she had been perched there the entire time Moira had been gone.

"Well, hello, peata. Ye're just in time for a bit of lunch. I'm only after finishing the bacon."

Moira loved the way the last word rolled off of the old woman's tongue. *Bee-con.* The strong Donegal accent was quite different from the ones she had heard from immigrants in Boston, watered down and thinned out over time and life in a melting pot of cultures and languages.

"Good afternoon, Bríd. Are you sure—"

Before Moira could finish, Bríd's eyes widened. She snatched the flowers from Moira's hand, spit on them, and threw them out the door. "Where on earth did ya get those? Ya didn't pick them yerself, did ya? Don't ya know if ya pick white flowers from a thornbush and bring them home, ye'll die?" Desperation swam in Bríd's expression.

"I—" Confusion swirled in Moira's mind. "I found them on the doorstep. They're such lovely flowers, I thought I'd bring them inside."

"Ye found them on the doorstep?" Bríd chewed her lip. "Well, pay ye no mind, lass. Pay ye no mind. Just . . . stay away from those flowers, aye?"

Moira nodded.

"Now, what were ya wantin' to ask me?" Bríd plastered a smile on her face.

Moira swallowed, dizzied by the rapid change in subject. "I just wanted to make sure I wasn't late for lunch."

"Oh!" Bríd chuckled. "A'course ye're not late!" She headed for the kitchen. "Lunchtime 'round here is one o' the clock."

Moira filed that piece of information for safekeeping. *At least you've not been rude to yet another person your first days in town, Moira Girl.* She pushed thoughts of manners and flowers out of her mind and hurried upstairs to tend to her ablutions, then returned just as quickly to take her place at the table. No sooner was she seated than an overflowing plate bearing a pile of chunky bacon sandwiched between two slices of thick, crusty bread was set before her. Seared tomato halves and a dollop of mashed potatoes accompanied the sandwich. The bacon looked more like ham steak than the streaky bacon she was accustomed to at home.

The hearty meal filled her with warmth as she savored the saltiness of the bacon against the cool of the bread and creaminess of the potatoes. *If I'm not careful, I'll be visiting the local seamstress to have my dresses let out after just a week of Bríd's hospitality!*

The muted thuds and clanks coming from the kitchen told Moira her hostess was busy cleaning from the afternoon meal and likely making preparations for dinner. She stared at the closed door to the kitchen. Her shoulders slumped. Although she understood the work in a guesthouse was never done, she had hoped Bríd would join her for lunch and provide insights into her new community.

As if overhearing her thoughts, the woman appeared in the doorway. She began to clear Moira's dishes and paused to ask, "Did ya find yer morning productive, peata?"

"Oh yes, quite. Thank you. I took a stroll through the town center and up the hill near the church. Then I spent the rest of the morning in the schoolroom cleaning and organizing. There is a good bit more work to do, but I feel much better having seen the school and getting some preparation done."

"That's lovely, dear, just lovely. Did ya meet any of the local folk while you were out?"

"Oh, well, yes." She shifted in her seat. "While I was in the schoolroom, a young fellow came in. Nearly scared me to death, I was so lost in my own thoughts. A young man by the name of Sean, I believe. Sean McFadden?"

"Well, I am sure ye'll be meetin' a good number of folk over the next few days."

Bríd's voice was steady and matter of fact, but Moira detected a twinkle in the woman's eyes when Moira mentioned Sean. Then again, maybe she was imagining things.

CHAPTER 8

The tranquil, soothing power of a simple cup of tea always took Moira by surprise. The company of a friend didn't hurt, either, of course.

In Ballymann less than a week, Moira felt a true bond forming between her and Bríd. A friendly cuppa and chat filled her with renewed peace as she sat with the woman on Sunday evening.

"Yer chalet is nearly ready for ya, peata," the woman said before taking a bite of toast.

Moira's jaw fell open. "Already?" She wiped a napkin across her mouth.

"Aye, it's a wee bit earlier than we expected, but a woman needs her own place, doesn't she?" Bríd prattled on about curtain styles, cooking over a turf-fired stove, and ways to make a new house a home.

Moira, however, struggled to turn her thoughts from snapping twigs, Buach, and his cackled threats—the memory of his clawing fingers haunted her more and more of late. She longed to ask Bríd more about what the old man might have meant about her mother, but she couldn't manage to eke out the question. She didn't want to press Bríd too much too soon and push her away. Feigning interest in the woman's stories, Moira dutifully sipped her tea. When the teapot had been sufficiently emptied and the conversation fell to a natural lull, Moira excused herself and headed to her room.

She scanned the humble chamber, attempting to sort through the melting pot of emotions churning within. The prospect of finally starting her own life and making her own home sent flurries of excitement to her heart. Yet a pang of sadness rang deep as well. The seed of doubt that had planted itself firmly in her gut days earlier sprouted at the idea of living alone.

Would she ever feel truly settled? Could she care for and protect a house, even a tiny chalet, in the manner needed? Would it ever truly feel like home?

Home.

The word dallied in her mind, swirling and swaying like a leaf on the breeze before finally settling silent and heavy on her heart.

It had been days since she'd truly thought of her home across the water in Boston. Until now, anytime thoughts of home or family threatened to surface, Moira tucked them away. There was too much to do to get bogged down with nostalgia and loneliness. But now, sitting alone in her small room in the top corner of the guesthouse, the memories were too great to suppress.

Overcome by the magnitude of the task before her and the sense of loss for all she had left behind, Moira wilted onto the bed.

❦

Surrounded by a fog not unlike the one she had seen from her perch the day she arrived in Ballymann, she could neither see nor feel her feet.

"It's too much! I can't do this!" she called into the abyss. Her voice bounced and echoed around her, though no walls contained her. "I don't know what I am doing. I can't speak the language. I'm all alone. Do you hear me? Alone!"

I will never leave you. I will never abandon you.

Moira spun about, the fog encompassing her more and more with each breath.

You look at the path before you and your eyes rest upon the obstacles. I will be with you, whispering the way, where you should turn, to the right or to the left.

Once more, Moira searched for the source of the voice. As she turned, she suddenly found herself sitting up in bed. Beads of sweat covered her forehead, her heart beat wildly within her chest, and she panted for breath like a horse just across the finish line.

The dream unsettled her. It was a dream, wasn't it? How could such powerful words both encourage and frighten? Dusk shrouded the room in shadow and still she sat.

Exhausted from an emotional day and looking ahead to what promised to be another trying day as she began school the next morning, Moira wrapped herself in the soft comfort of the duvet and tried to rest.

❧

Moira stood in the open doorway of the school and stared into the silent room, bathed in the silver-gray light of pre-dawn. Had she eaten breakfast? Washed her face? Not one recollection of that morning remained in her mind.

God, give me strength. A shiver ran down her spine—from cold or nerves she couldn't say, but it was enough to shake her into action. As she inhaled deeply, the aroma of dust, musk, and days long past filled her lungs. The fragrance filled her heart and mind with a new sense of purpose and confidence. She strode resolutely across the room to her desk and readied her things.

Confident she had allowed herself plenty of time before the students arrived, Moira busied herself arranging papers and looking over lesson plans and notes scribbled in the margins of well-worn pages.

Church bells shattered the early morning silence. Moira startled, knocking over a box of beads at the interruption of the bells' insensitive peal. The beads she'd planned to use in a sums lesson later that morning bounced and rolled on the plank floor.

"Och!" she screeched, scrambling to rein in the wayward beads, moving more like a newborn lamb clamoring to find his legs than a qualified teacher.

Still the bells tolled. "Good gracious me, I think they can hear you all the way in Boston!"

Three more clangs split the air. Hunched in mid-stoop, Moira froze. How many times had the bells tolled? *No. That cannot be the time.*

Alas, it was nine o'clock. The bells had beckoned the pupils from their homes, and they would be arriving any moment. Depositing the remaining beads from her hand into the box whence they came, she fumbled through her papers to find the roll sheet.

Caoimhe.
Deirbhle.
Cian.
Eoghan.

Her heart sank. "How can I greet them at the door if I don't know how to pronounce their names?" She banged a fist on her thigh. Why had she waited until now to look at the list? It would have been easy enough to ask Bríd how to pronounce the names, but it was no matter now. The students were on the way.

She steadied herself against her desk, bowed her head, and whispered a desperate plea. "Help me, Lord."

I am with you. The promise reverberated deep in her soul, bolstering her with a confidence she couldn't explain and had no business possessing. At that moment the door opened.

CHAPTER 9

Moira pasted a smile on her face, willing her lips to stop quivering, as she turned to face the door. "Good morning. Please, come in."

A timid face peeked around the edge of the open door, eyeing her inquisitively. "Marnin'," the child murmured.

"Please, come in, dear. There's no need to be shy. I'm Moi—eh—Miss Doherty. I'm very pleased to meet you."

Although she hoped to present an air of confidence and authority, Moira was just as nervous and scared as the wee face peering back at her. With marked steps, the child made her way into the room.

"I'm Aoife."

"I'm very pleased to make your acquaintance, Aoife. How old are you, dear?"

The child stared at her feet as she traced the line of a crack in the floor with the edge of her shoe. Moira watched the way the girl's auburn ringlets fell softly over her shoulders, refusing to stay in the plaited bun at the nape of her neck. Slowly Aoife's hand raised, and she held up five fingers, a rosy blush filling her cheeks.

"Five, is it? Well, that's a very important age. Tell me, Aoife, where are your classmates?"

Blue eyes, clear as Dunlewey Lake on a bright summer

day, met Moira's, and a mischievous smile played on the girl's lips. She turned and nodded at the door, then motioned ever so slightly with her finger.

Craning her neck to look out the window without being seen, Moira could just see the feet, skirts, and pant legs of a group of children.

"They're all outside, are they?"

Aoife nodded.

"Let me see if I can guess. They sent you in to check things out and see what kind of a monster I am. Is that about right?"

The girl's stance immediately relaxed, and she broke out in a grin and fervent nod.

"Well, I say we let them in and satisfy their curiosity, shall we?"

Aoife skipped lightly to the door and called out to her schoolmates, *"Tá sé ceart go leor, gach duine! Tá sí go álainn!"*

"Lovely, eh?" A voice drifted in from behind Aoife. "We'll see 'bout that."

One by one the children filed into the schoolroom. With girls curtsying and the boys tipping their hats, they each shuffled past the new teacher and made their way to their seats.

"Good morning, children. My name is Miss Doherty, and I'm sure you all know I've only arrived in town a few days ago," she began. "I am very excited to get to know each of you and see all the wonderful things we can learn together this year. Make no mistake, boys and girls, I don't expect to be the only one doing the teaching."

Pausing for effect and clasping her hands comfortably in front of her, she looked from pupil to pupil. Where fear and anxiety had sunk an anchor deep in the pit of her stomach just a few minutes earlier, inexplicable peace now reigned.

Moira clapped her hands together. "There is a whole textbook worth of things I can learn from you too."

The children shared furtive glances. Some eyes were wide in excitement. Other eyes were like windows open in the springtime. They seemed to be airing out mischievous thoughts of just how much they could teach this Yank—and how much they could humiliate her in the process. Moira dismissed the idea that any of her students might have it out for her, moved her mind to the task at hand, and asked the children to go around the room and tell her their name and age.

A young man stood up, shuffling his feet. He twisted his hat nervously between his hands and cleared his throat. "I'm Martin Ó Ghallchobhair, Miss. I'm seventeen and this is my final year in the school."

"I'm Eoghan Ó Baoighill, t'irteen years of age."

"Marnin', marm. I'm Caoimhe Ní Ghallchobhair, and I'm thirteen."

"Gallagher? So are you Martin's sister?" Moira probed.

The classroom erupted in laughter.

"Are ya really so daft? Do ya not know our history 'tall? There's many in our parish that have the same surname, but that don't mean we's all close relations. We're a nation made of clans. Sure you've heard o' dat before?"

The disrespectful remark dripping in sarcasm hit Moira like a punch in the gut. "Excuse me, young man, but that sort of talk will not be tolerated in my classroom. Tell me your name."

"Sure, if ye're so fit to be teachin' us, you should already know a bit o' the Irish now, yeah? Sure ye can find my name on the list and read it out. I don't hafta tell you an'ting."

A sickening burning rose to the back of Moira's throat. She swallowed it down, along with her hopes for a flawless first day. So torrential were her swirling thoughts, it was impossible to allow any specific one to float to the front of her mind. Her eyes roamed over the class list, neither seeing nor comprehending anything. Finally, her eyes fell on a name with a black dot next to it. *Áedach MacSuibhne.*

Before she could scramble together a scolding, a voice sliced through the silence of the room. "Áedach, you shut yer gob an' give Miss Doherty the respect she desairves."

Although mortified that she needed a student's help, Moira was secretly grateful for Martin coming to her rescue, and she made a mental note of how he'd pronounced the impossible name: AY-joc. Offering Martin a smile and slight nod of thanks, her cheeks warmed as Áedach's gaze rested on hers longer than was comfortable.

"Well now, Áedach," Moira began. "It would seem we have gotten ourselves off to a bit of a rough start. I propose we try this again from the beginning." She firmly straightened her apron, making sure she looked every bit the part of teacher.

She smiled and extended her hand, but rather than accepting her gesture of goodwill, the boy merely laughed caustically and slunk down into his seat. Although she knew this behavior needed to be dealt with, Moira decided it best to approach the lad privately later.

The rest of the day passed fairly uneventfully with a few activities designed to help Moira become better acquainted with her pupils, as well as the typical daily tasks of arithmetic, writing, and recitation.

CHAPTER 10

Moira's feet ached as she walked back to the guesthouse. She wanted nothing more than to stretch out on her bed in the room that had finally begun to feel a bit like home. With all the strength she could muster, she heaved open the Martins' door. Had it always been this heavy? Bríd appeared in a flash with breathless news for her lodger.

"Yer chalet is ready for ye, peata! Yer man is waiting to show ye 'round. Come now, we'll go have a wee peek and ye can take yer things over tomorrow. It's a blessing to have it done so soon, so it is."

Moira's head spun. "My man? Who? What?" *Surely she isn't referring to Sean? I barely said two words about him.*

Understanding dawned on Bríd's face. "Sorry. That's just what we say when we're talkin' about a lad without sayin' his name. I meant nothing by it. I was talkin' about the caretaker of the chalet."

Moira nodded as if that all made sense. Her mind moved like molasses, her body ached, and the impulse to both laugh and cry vied for control. She fidgeted with her fingers and chewed her lip nervously but couldn't help the smile that tipped the corner of her mouth as her mind stirred awake with anticipation.

Bríd's arm entwined with Moira's, and she whisked her out of the guesthouse.

☙⁂❧

Moira stood on the roadside gazing up at the tiny chalet. A neatly thatched roof slanted gently down over the tops of whitewashed walls. Two small square windows, trimmed in red, perched like eyes watching the goings-on down the street below. Between the two windows stood a bright red door, with the top half fully opened. She loved it instantly.

Behind her, Bríd was chattering on about one thing or another while fussily sweeping the path to the door with her foot. Once inside, Moira studied the room, falling more and more in love with her little home.

She walked over to a large wooden dresser and ran her fingers lightly over the open shelves on the top half, reveling in the roughness of the wood. A set of crockery, cream-colored with delicate blue flowers painted on the sides, sat proudly displayed.

Kneeling down, she opened the large doors that covered the two cabinets on the bottom of the dresser. Dust and years of musk wafted up, welcoming her to her new home. Moira imagined all the cups of tea and slices of hearty brown bread that would be shared with the friends she prayed the Lord would bring her.

To her left was a floor-level fireplace with a *footed* stack of turf waiting to be lit. Her eyes stopped on two tiny, three-legged creepie stools sitting near the hearth. She couldn't imagine how anything that slight and rustic could ever be a comfortable place to sit, cook, and share company with a guest.

"Och! They've let the fire go out!" Bríd's disgusted gasp interrupted Moira's thoughts.

"That's alright, Bríd. I imagine it wouldn't be safe to leave a fire burning when I won't be staying here until tomorrow anyway."

"Sure, peata, don't ya know that the soul goes out of the people of the house if the fire goes out?" Bríd bustled to the fireplace. "When we come tomorrow, I'll show ya how to use the embers of today's fire to light tomorrow's."

"I'd be . . . grateful," Moira stammered.

"*Never* let yer fire go all the way out. That's the way of the turf, ya know. Use every bit for as long as ya can. Sure, there's fires here in Gweedore parish that have been burnin' for a hundred years running."

The old woman clicked her tongue in annoyance and worked quickly to remedy the situation. Moira looked on, eager to learn the ancient tradition, still not sure why Bríd was so upset by it.

With the fire properly lit, the ladies finished their inspection of the premises. Just beyond the fireplace, Moira pushed aside a thin curtain and stepped into a small room.

A large bed with tall oak posts and a wooden canopy draped with canvas the color of milky tea stood opposite a chest of drawers, a jug, and a basin for washing hands and face. Over the door hung a strange shape woven out of reeds.

"I never expected such a grand bed," Moira said. "It's absolutely lovely."

"Grand's got nothing to do with it." The older woman chuckled. "Ya don't want any creepy-crawlies landin' on ya in the middle of the night, do ya?"

Moira stared at the woman blankly.

"Ye'll find most families here in Ballymann have beds like these, though most don't have the luxury of havin' the bed all to themselves. When ya live in a t'atched house, ya live in a house with critters, damp, and drips. The canopy bed keeps ya cozy and clean—and critter free." Bríd laughed.

Moira's eyes stretched wide, and she inspected the roof carefully. Visions of beetles, fleas, and mites filled Moira's mind, and she struggled to hide her dismay.

"Come on now, my girl. It's getting late and you need a good dinner, a nice cuppa, and an early bedtime. After all, it's a school night."

Moira groaned and then chuckled as she walked with Bríd, arm in arm, out of the chalet and into the dusky evening heading for home—and tea.

CHAPTER 11

That night, no matter how long Moira lay quiet with eyes shut tight, sleep eluded her. Despite her bidding them leave her until morning, a million-and-one ideas for her new home danced around and around in her head.

Earlier, fear had tightly wound around her heart about the unknowns of her little chalet. When she had finally seen how lovely it actually was, she found it difficult to bridle her imaginings.

Be still, Moira Girl. There's no need to lose sleep over a chalet. Her scolding did little good. Eventually, and far later than she would have preferred, sleep overtook her.

No sooner had she settled into the comfort of a dream than Bríd was knocking on her door, beckoning her to breakfast. Moira washed, dressed, and ate breakfast in the fog that inevitably follows a night full of hopeful dreaming, before finally making her way to school.

Never let yer fire go all the way out. That's the way of the turf, ya know. Use every bit for as long as ya can. Bríd's words echoed in Moira's head as she absently made her way to the schoolhouse.

"Good thing I paid attention to how she lit the fire in the chalet," she said. "I should get the turf going before the children arrive today."

Determined, Moira swung wide the schoolhouse door and marched straight to the fireplace. A basket full of the rough briquettes sat off to the side, ready for use. As she stacked the turf in the hearth just so, a terrifying thought plagued her mind, stopping her in her tracks.

The fire has long been out in this *house. What if the soul of this place, these children, has gone out with it, just as Bríd warned?* The idea chilled Moira's bones as she flopped to the floor in defeat.

I am the way, the truth, and the life, my dear one. Trust in Me, not a fire.

Closing her eyes, Moira allowed the truth to wash over her. Of course the state of a hearth and fire could never determine the soul of a person! And if these children, God forbid, didn't understand the love lavished on them from their Father above, she was going to let them experience it through her. Bríd was full of superstitions. As, apparently, were many in the village. But Moira would hold to the truth.

She returned to stacking and arranging the turf the way she had seen Bríd do the night before and set it alight. As she finished, the children began to arrive.

"Marnin', Miss," called one child.

"*Día dhuit,*" croaked another.

Moira half-turned and smiled at her pupils when there was a tug on the back of her dress. She craned her head around to see Aoife, who smiled sheepishly, waved, then ran to her seat.

"Good morning, children," Moira sang as she rose to her feet. "It's so lovely to see you all again today. Yesterday we spent a lot of time getting acquainted, so today I'd like to dig in and get some good work done."

As she spoke, the children's eyes grew bigger. Some of the students chuckled, some coughed, but most simply sat with mortified looks plastered across their face. Realizing something was happening behind her, Moira turned just in time to be enveloped by a cloud of thick black smoke.

"Och! Someone open the door!"

Moira ran to the fireplace, waving her arms madly to dispel the smoke. All around her, children coughed and gagged, flailing their hands in front of their faces or hiding their noses inside the tops of their jumpers. In the corner, Áedach laughed hysterically.

"Morning, a Mhúinteoir."

Moira stiffened. She turned toward the door. *Please, God, don't let it be . . .*

"Sean—er—Mr. McFadden! What brings you to the schoolhouse this morning?" She hoped the burning in her cheeks wasn't evident to everyone else.

"What brings me here?" he quipped, barely hiding a laugh. "Why, not much. Only that t'ick black smoke pourin' out from the door there, that's all."

Moira buried her face in her hands. "I really don't know what's wrong! I just learned this last night. Och! This is just lovely."

In three strides Sean was right in front of the fire. Moira was all too aware of his presence beside her, despite the fact her face was still buried in her hands. Through her fingers she saw Sean reach to put his hand on her arm, but he stopped short and lowered it to his side.

"Well now," he said gently, "let's just see what we can do about this, shall we?"

Moira lowered her hands and nodded, waiting to see what manner of sarcastic comment the man had prepared for her today.

Sean crouched in front of the hearth. "Ah, see? You've no kindling 'tall here. You need to put some grass or paper underneath the turf." He gestured to a stack of dried grass and hay in a smaller basket to the left of the fireplace. "And then your biggest culprit is you've not opened the flue inside the chimney, like this."

He turned a black iron lever jutting out of the left side of the chimney. Immediately, a rush of air sucked the smoke up the chimney, slamming the schoolhouse door.

"I see," Moira said, straightening her skirts. Deep down she was grateful for Sean coming to her rescue. But she restrained her gratitude to keep the mood dignified. Proper.

"Thank you very much, Mr. McFadden. I'm much obliged to you."

"And I'll remember that you owe me, to be sure," he replied with a sly smile and a wink.

Moira's face burned once more. There was no hiding it this time.

Sean brushed the soot from his hands, bid the students farewell, and left as suddenly as he had come in.

"Now, children, I think that's enough excitement for one day. If you'll all take your seats, we can begin."

The children shuffled around, wiped their desks of soot and ash, and found their seats. In the corner, Áedach still laughed.

CHAPTER 12

Fleecy clouds frolicked on the breeze like spring lambs, drawing Sean's eyes upward. Setting his flask of tea aside, he eased onto his back with a heavy sigh. The freshly thatched roof, coarse yet forgiving, cradled him as his thoughts joined the clouds in their gamboling.

It had been a long time coming, but he had finally come home. At long last he was in the place he had been pining for all that time he was away, working now with the best mentor a man could hope for. So why did he still feel so restless?

His eyes drifted from sky to sea. She was calm today, her skirts of waves swirling like a lace gown in a waltz. Despite the peaceful scene before him, Sean couldn't deny the angst churning deep within his heart.

"What's your secret, old girl? How can you be so at peace?" Sean's fingers found a loose strand of reed and brought it to his mouth. A familiar taste. Earthy. Rooted. Comforting. And a distraction from other thoughts he wrestled to untangle.

"Ya know, you'll never plow a field by turnin' it over in yer mind, lad." Colm raised both woolly eyebrows but light sparked in his eyes. He nodded to his apprentice and climbed toward the ridge of the roof. Sean was familiar with the old proverb. It was one of Colm's favorites when the lad was a little too restful for the man's liking.

"Why do I always feel like you're sayin' more than what your words mean, Colm?" Sean chuckled as he heaved himself to standing.

"Come, now." The old man's voice was reassuring. "Ya know that when it comes to work, I'm all business."

Colm always managed to have a twinkle in his eye, even when reprimanding. How was that? A smile played on both men's lips. Sean joined his mentor at the ridge of the roof.

"All jestin' aside, I canna help but notice ya seem a mite troubled of late. As though yer soul is in a wrestlin' match with *Fionn mac Cumhaill* himself."

"Aye," Sean murmured. He might as well have been scrapping with the legendary giant the way his thoughts bandied him about. How much should he tell the old man? The truth of it was, Sean felt deep down he was meant to do something truly meaningful with his life, and he wasn't sure how thatching was going to bring that to pass. Yet he loved and respected Colm and did not want to insult his life's work.

"I dunno." He shrugged. "I am so happy to be here in Ballymann. And I'm honored to be workin' with the likes of ye."

The twinkle returned to his mentor's eyes as he cleared his throat and shifted his weight, clearly embarrassed by the compliment.

"It's just that, well"—he paused, searching for the right words—"I'm grateful for the job, and to learn such an honorable trade. But deep down, I just want something . . ."

"More?" Colm finished for him.

Sean's gaze shot up to meet the old man's. Relief swept over him as he recognized nothing but compassion in Colm's expression. "Well, yes."

"Sit with me, lad."

Both men bent carefully to perch themselves on the crest of the ridge. Colm's large hand, calloused with time and hard work, rested on Sean's shoulder.

"A man's life is a high calling, to be sure," Colm began. "And the fact that ye're so moved to distress is a blessin'."

Sean's brow furrowed.

"A man who lives only for himself is a man with few convictions," Colm continued. "However, conflict is not absent from his life. On the contrary! That man's life is chockablock with the agony of constantly fightin' to protect his own."

Sean nodded slowly.

"But a man who lives according to a higher purpose"—Colm's finger pointed skyward as he continued—"that is a man whose life may, too, be overflowin' with conflict, but it's the fight to protect others. Surely, his calling is to do rightly, to love compassionately, and to walk respectfully with his God."

"I see," Sean replied, fearful his face belied his words.

"Ya see, lad, it doesna matter a lick if ye're a priest, a barkeep, or a thatcher by trade. When ya seek to love the Laird wit' all yer heart, soul, an' mind, and then seek ta love others selflessly, ye're a man who will make a difference in this world one pairson at a time."

Understanding dawned in Sean's heart. The old man had a knack for helping him see truth in murky waters.

CHAPTER 13

Moira sighed and flopped onto her back, lacing her fingers underneath her weary head. She wriggled her rump, trying to work a lump in the mattress to one side or the other and find a comfortable spot. She stared at the canopy above her, tracing every line and crease in the dingy canvas. The turf fire in the kitchen was slowly dying, filling the air with stale smoke that made her head ache.

After the mishap with Sean and the fire, Moira had struggled to regain composure with the class. Her bones ached with exhaustion, and she assumed sleep would come quickly. She closed her eyes and willed herself to rest, but no sooner had she released a deep breath than her eyes would rock open and the inner dialogue would begin again.

What in the world are you doing here, Moira Girl? You're in way over your head. You can barely keep a fire lit, let alone guide and direct a schoolful of children to a brighter future. Surely there's been some mistake.

Tears stung her eyes and spilled down her cheeks. There were no sobs, no rocking cries. Silent tears streamed, soaking her hair as she wept.

Why would Mother think I could do this? What would possess her to recommend me for such a task? She tried to recall the conversation when Mother had told her the news. But the thought of Mother filled Moira with an ache that threatened to swallow her whole. As she lay in the dark of night—tears soaking her face, her hair, her feather pillow—dread surrounded her like a lead cloak. She could scarcely breathe for the weight of it and struggled to keep her composure. Her eyes squeezed tight. Could she call up an image of her mother's visage?

Soft, gray hair piled high into a tidy bun framed a kind, bright face. Tiny wrinkles surrounded bright blue eyes shining with kindness and love. Suddenly her mother was there in the room with her. Moira reached out a weary, trembling hand to stroke her mother's precious cheek, only to find cold, dark air in its place.

She longed to hear her mother's voice with its velvety lilt, softened by time and distance from her homeland. Moira strained to remember that voice, devastated that she no longer could.

Despair flooded Moira's heart as the reality—and finality—of her mother's death sank in. She struggled to catch her breath. She would never see her mother again. Never hug her. Never hear her voice utter prayers over Moira or sing as she tidied the kitchen. No longer held back, violent sobs racked Moira's body. Her cries echoed in the tiny chalet. She didn't care who could hear.

"Oh God! Help me! What have I done? What were You thinking? Why did You bring me here?"

The lyrics of a song her mother had sung to her every night of her childhood floated into her memory. Deep in the recesses of her mind she could faintly hear the clear, high voice of her mother as she tenderly sang while rocking back and forth, back and forth. Moira's breathing slowed and the sobs abated. She pushed the woolen blankets aside and shuffled to the small, square window in the kitchen.

The shutters creaked open, and Moira stared into the dark, misty night. She shivered as the chilled air met her face, hot from grief and crying. The moon cast an eerie silver light over the village. Moira closed her eyes, took a breath, and began to sing.

> *Rest tired eyes a while*
> *Sweet is thy baby's smile*
> *Angels are guarding and they watch o'er thee*

Her voice, weak at first, grew clearer with every note. On the words with tones that hung long, she accented with runs of notes, adding to the ethereal comfort that accompanies an Irish lullaby. She continued, her voice growing stronger with each phrase.

> *Sleep, sleep,* grá mo chroí
> *Here on your mamma's knee*
> *Angels are guarding*
> *And they watch o'er thee*
>
> *The birdeens sing a fluting song*
> *They sing to thee the whole day long*
> *Wee fairies dance o'er hill and dale*
> *For very love of thee*

Moira sang until the anxious thoughts drifted away and home seemed a comfort before her very eyes.

⁓⤳෴⤳⁓

Sean lay in bed, mulling over what Colm had said to him on the rooftop earlier that day. Perhaps the old man was right. Could Sean truly make a difference, even as a thatcher, simply by following God and loving others sacrificially? His eyelids grew heavy. Though he had more to ponder, the promise of sleep lay thick upon him.

The night air seeped in through the cracked window above his bed. As Sean drifted toward sleep, he thought he heard the voice of an angel singing on the breeze.

CHAPTER 14

Clang! Clang! The church bells tolled, startling Moira awake. She tried to move but a shooting pain in her neck kept her still. Slowly her eyes focused on the fireplace. *Why is the fireplace in my bedchamber? And why is it on its side?* Her head and body ached, and her mind struggled to catch up. Gingerly she lifted her head and looked around, familiarizing herself with her surroundings.

"What in the world?" Confusion surrounded her like a fog. She sat in a chair by the open window in her front room. Dew covered the windowsill, her arms, and the crown of her head. She shivered from top to toe.

I must have fallen asleep singing! Her cheeks burned with embarrassment at her silliness. Images of home flooded her mind, surrounded by the familiar tune of her childhood. She remembered now.

The lullaby had done its job—it had put her to sleep. A peaceful sleep full of dreams of home and family, for which Moira was more grateful than she could express.

But to fall asleep in front of an open window and allow a chill to have its way with her had been foolish. She willed herself to stand and was by no means steady on her feet. Finally regaining her bearings and balance, she shut the window tight and tended to the fire before seeing to her breakfast.

The hot tea went down smoothly, warming every inch of her as she sipped. Although she had fallen asleep very late, she had somehow managed to wake up with plenty of time to eat a leisurely breakfast and fully prepare for the school day ahead.

"Thank you, Lord, for the church bells," she spoke to the ceiling.

The chills eventually dissipated as the fire crackled awake and the tea worked its magic from the inside out. Her bones ached. She prayed it was merely soreness from sleeping in such an awkward position. She could not afford to be ill the first week. Nor could she afford to let grief or pains overtake her better judgment.

After seeing to her morning ablutions, she opened the door ready to venture out into the new day, determined to face whatever challenges awaited with strength and grace. Her breath caught in her chest as the sheer beauty of Ballymann struck anew with full force.

The sun shone bright—a rare occurrence in Donegal in February—casting rainbows over the emerald sea. Thatched roofs, frosted with dew, sparkled like jewels on velvet. Each breath brought a potpourri of grass, dew, and the sweet scent of turf. Moira closed her eyes, took one final cleansing breath, and stepped resolutely out the door.

Whoosh! Her slick-soled boot met with the dew-damp stone of the threshold, and her bum landed firmly on the limestone.

"Oof!" Moira sat stunned for a moment before glancing around to make sure no one had seen her fall. "Well, so much for a graceful start to the day!"

Laughter bubbled up from deep within. Though she knew she must look like a fool laughing on the damp walkway, she couldn't stop. Before long, a rolling belly laugh drifted on the air over the sleepy town.

"I do believe it is going to be a great day, Moira Girl!"

Before rising to her feet, Moira noticed small white bits crushed on the stones before her. Several eggshells lay scattered on the path from her chalet. Some on the stones, pulverized from her fall. Others hidden under the bushes on either side of her doorway. Moira grimaced, searching for a reason they would be there, but no logical reason presented itself.

"A few eggshells never harmed anyone. At least they'll keep the slugs away."

Rising to her feet, Moira adjusted her skirts and brushed the dirt from her hands and backside. Looking around once more to make sure no one was witness to her comedic mishap, she started down the footpath to the main road.

She looked back for a moment and renewed admiration for her charming little home filled her heart. Passing the small market, Moira made a mental note to stop in after school. Busy thinking of a list of items she wanted to collect— tea, butter, flour, and bread soda—Moira barely noticed Bríd approaching before the woman was in front of her.

"Well, hallo, lovey. I missed havin' ya 'round last night." The old woman wrapped Moira in a warm hug. The pair rocked back and forth before finally releasing one another.

"It's so wonderful to see you, Bríd! I was just on my way to school. Walk with me?"

Bríd feigned a deep think before linking her arm in Moira's and heading off down the road with a lilt in her step.

"So, peata, how are ya findin' the chalet? Are ya keepin' the fire lit, now?"

Moira laughed. She had missed the company of her friend more than she'd realized. Her heart stirred at the realization that she actually had a friend.

"Yes, ma'am—er, Bríd—the fire is lit, and I've gotten a little better at using the embers. At least I think I have."

"That's brilliant, peata. Glad to hear it." Bríd eyed her. "You seem awfully chipper this mairnin'. All is right in the teaching world, I wager?"

Moira took a sidelong glance at the woman and smiled. "Yes, I'd say it is. A few growing pains still, but it'll all come together in time. This morning has been a comedy of errors."

The pair turned down the street where the school stood. Gravel crunched beneath their feet, and Moira wrestled with whether or not to tell Bríd about her little midnight serenade and waking up in the windowsill. While she dearly valued her new—and *only*—friend in Ballymann and wanted desperately to open up to her, she didn't know how Bríd would react. Would she think Moira silly? Would she deem her an unfit role model for the children of the parish?

"First of all, I slipped coming out of the house." She opted for the safe version. "I was quite the sight, I tell you. Then, I noticed a stash of eggshells scattered across the front walk."

Bríd stopped, her brows furrowed as she looked Moira square in the eyes. "Eggshells, ya say?"

Moira chuckled. "Yes, it was the strangest thing. I guess a bird must have nested in the bushes nearby. Or perhaps they came from the large oak south of the chalet." She paused, picturing the number and size of the shells. "Although, they seemed quite large for a nesting bird. They looked truly like hen's eggs. Quite curious."

Bríd rolled her lips between her teeth and then laid a hand on Moira's shoulder.

Silence stretched between them. Each second Bríd didn't speak was another brick on Moira's already weighted heart.

Bríd's eyes clouded.

"What is it, Bríd? What's wrong?"

Bríd inhaled sharply and forced a smile. "I'm sure it's nothin', peata. I'm an auld woman, prone to superstition. I'm sure everything's fine. Plus ya have the good Laird watchin' over ya. Anyway, I'd best be getting home now." She laid a kiss on Moira's cheek before giving her shoulder a gentle squeeze and scurrying off toward the main road.

"Keep yer fire lit, peata!" she called over her shoulder with a wink and a wave before disappearing around the corner.

CHAPTER 15

Three o'clock could not come fast enough for Moira's taste. At half-past two, the minutes had slowed to a crawl. Aside from a few well-timed pranks from Áedach, the day had passed with relative ease. The lumpy brown toad waiting in her seat after the lunch break was her personal favorite of the day. "How was Áedach to know I love toads?" she had asked the class. Snakes, on the other hand, were another matter entirely.

"Thanks be to God for Patrick driving all the snakes from this land," she muttered to herself while stoking the fire. Whether or not Moira believed the tale, the fact remained that no wild snakes existed on the Emerald Isle.

The day reached its lowest point when Moira took a large gulp of tea and was rewarded with a mouthful of soggy peat instead. She reminded herself to say an extra prayer for the lad during her evening devotions.

Yes, pray he survives the school year.

Moira regretted the thought as soon as it had formed but couldn't deny the nugget of truth buried in the sentiment. She had no idea how she was going to not only finish the year with her pupils having learned all they needed but also with her sanity intact, the way things were currently running with the boy. His pranks and outward disrespect were growing in frequency and severity. Clearly ignoring the issue served only to feed the lad's confidence.

You must address it, Moira Girl. But . . . perhaps tomorrow.

"Miss Doherty, why is yer feece so red?"

Moira jolted out of her reverie to find Aoife standing next to her, innocent curiosity floating in the child's eyes.

"What, dear?" Moira pressed a hand to her cheek. Roasting. "Oh, I must've been standing too close to the fire, sweetheart. I'm alright."

She couldn't very well tell the child she was flushed with embarrassment over her harsh thoughts toward Áedach. At least she hoped that's all it was.

The church bells began to chime, and Moira's head pounded in unison with each peal. The students, however, instinctively began closing books and dropping pencils, slate boards, and sticks of chalk in various containers around the room.

For once the chimes came to her rescue.

Taking advantage of the distraction, Moira said, "Very well, children, thank you for a lovely day."

Mostly lovely anyway.

"Be sure to eat a hearty supper and get lots of rest. I'll see you all in the morning."

Relief flooded Moira when the door closed behind the last child and their chatter and laughter faded into the distance. Not only had Bríd's odd reaction that morning left her with a strange sense of dread the rest of the day, a dull ache had taken up residence in the back of her throat. All she wanted was to grab the items she needed at the market and get home to a nice cuppa in front of the fire and then an early bedtime.

What a quirky little place. The till sat on a long, rough counter running the length of the back of the store. Various dishes bearing sweets and baked goods crowded each nook and cranny. Her eyes could scarcely take in all the canisters of tea, tobacco, and the few medicinal herbs available, as well as large sacks of flour, oats, and sugar, loading the floor-to-ceiling shelves behind the till counter. Moira could almost hear the ledges groaning under the weight of it all.

She meandered around the store, taking in each eccentric detail to keep like wee treasures deep in her heart. The scent of tea leaves, stale tobacco, and fresh-baked scones hung in the air. Moira's stomach growled and her mouth watered for a decent cup of tea. She fingered strange vegetables resembling white carrots, adding their earthy notes to the medley. She admired the odd towel or lace table runner scattered in among the usual groceries.

"I'll be right wit' ye, dearie," called a voice from behind a curtained doorway.

Moira craned to find its source.

A second later, a young woman with an apron at her waist rounded the corner. "So, now, sorry to keep ya waitin', dearie. What'll it be for yas?"

A wide grin broke across Moira's face upon seeing the woman. *She's young!*

Other than Sean, Moira had yet to meet another soul anywhere near her own age. The young lady's round face bore a rosy hue with a set of deep, welcoming dimples marking the center of both cheeks. Piercing blue eyes stared back at Moira, with eyebrows raised.

"So, do yas want anytin' or will ya just stand there and stare?" A hearty laugh rumbled from the young lass. Moira liked her instantly.

"Right. Sorry." Moira echoed the girl's laugh and stepped closer to the shopkeeper. "I was just so shocked to see someone my own age, I didn't know what to say," she offered in a stage whisper.

"Ah, right so! You must be the Yank—er—teacher."

Though Moira hadn't thought it possible, the young woman's smile grew even bigger. She skipped over to Moira, leaving mere inches between them.

She returned the girl's smile. "I'm Moira. Moira Doherty."

"Well, now, Moira Darrty, yas have a right good Irish name for a Yank, so ya do." The robust young woman grabbed Moira's hand and gave a hearty shake. "I'm Sinead. Sinead McGonigle. I'm pleased to make yer acquaintance, so I am."

"Yes, me too," Moira said. Though unexpected, Sinead's boisterous manner and bubbly personality refreshed Moira's spirit.

"Now, dearie, what can I get yas? I'm sure yas didn't come in here to chew the fat with the likes o' me."

"To be honest, the conversation is quite refreshing, even if it wasn't my main reason in coming to the market today." She shrugged. "It's been a bit lonely. I wasn't sure I would ever have a friend my age again."

She bit her lip. *Don't be so presumptuous.* Of course, Sinead had grown up here, and running the local market, she must be well connected. Perhaps she didn't need, or want, another friend.

"Oh, I don't doubt that, dearie. Northwest Donegal isn't exactly the social center of Ar'land." Another guffaw was followed by a snort. Sinead clapped a hand over her mouth, eyes wide.

Moira stifled a giggle. "Very true."

"Anois, what can I get fer yas?"

"Right. I'd like a small slab of butter, some tea, a half kilo of flour, and a hundred grams of bread soda, please."

Moira couldn't help but track Sinead as she collected the items. The discovery of someone so similar to her—yet so vastly different—revived Moira's hope of having some semblance of a normal life. She hadn't even realized that hope had withered in so many days of relative solitude.

Sinead scooped flour into a small canvas sack. Fine white dust floated up around her. "So, that's the last of it. This should be all yer messages."

Moira pressed her brows together. "I, er, messages? Did a letter arrive for me?"

Sinead jabbed a chubby fist on her hip and cocked her head to one side. "Wha'?"

The two stared at each other in silence for a moment, both clearly searching for what to say.

Moira broke the silence. "You said you had . . . messages for me?"

"Yeah?" Sinead gestured to the pile of groceries on the counter.

Moira turned her gaze to the items. "*Those* are messages?"

Sinead raised her eyebrows and nodded emphatically. Once again her throaty laugh shattered the air.

Moira found it useless to resist and added her own laughter to the mix.

"I see I have a lot to learn. Where I come from, messages are . . . well . . . *messages* from one person to another."

"I don't know about America, but here in Donegal, messages are the nairmull things you collect from the market." Sinead paused, crossing her arms over her chest. "Do ye have a word for that over there in the States?"

"We call those staples."

"Ya don't say? Staples?" Sinead wagged her head. "I t'ink maybe we should meet again soon for some language lessons, dearie."

"That's very kind of you. I do hope to learn Irish someday, but for now it's a bit overwhelming. You know, with me still settling into the school and whatnot?"

"I'm not talkin' about layrnin' the Gaeilge, dearie. I'm talkin' about our so-called common tongue. Yas need to layrn how to talk *our* English or you'll never survive."

Sinead's laughter again punctuated the conversation.

Moira gathered up her messages and headed home, chuckling now and again the whole way.

CHAPTER 16

Moira barely reached the table in her chalet and dropped all of her *messages* onto it. A moment longer and they would have crashed to the floor. She made a mental note to bring a basket to the market next time.

"Phew!" Breathless, she leaned against the edge of the table and shook her arms to release the cramps from carrying her load. When her breath had steadied, she turned her attention to the fire. It was burning but only just. She stoked the turf and added two briquettes.

Please let them take fire quickly.

Positioning herself onto one of the creepie stools, she stared deep into the red embers and allowed her mind to drift.

Tap, tap, tap.

Moira turned and stared at the door as though doing so long enough would allow her to see through it. She waited and listened. Nothing. She returned her attention—and her chilled fingers—to the fire.

The thumps that followed left no room for doubt. Moira pried her backside from the low, awkward stool and made her way to the door.

"Yes?" Moira said.

"I have a message fer yas!"

Moira swung the door open. "Sinead, welcome!" She stepped aside. "Please come in. What can I do for you?"

The effervecsent girl marched into the chalet and looked around. "Well, now, isn't this just fine and dandy? I've never seen the inside. We all figured there'd be a cauldron and broomsticks, wha' with the auld witch—er, *Miss*—McGinley havin' lived here." Bright red splotches climbed up her cheeks.

"Well, I'm no witch, I can assure you. Only creepie stools and books for me," Moira said, trying to hide her smile.

Sinead gave a sheepish shrug and her gaze fell to her feet.

"Oh! I nearly forgot." She shoved a package at Moira. "Ye left yer tea back at the market. I thought ye might be needin' tha' tonight, so." She smiled and her dimples reappeared in earnest.

"Good heavens, yes. I had been waiting all day to come home and have a cuppa. I would have been one pitiful mess had you not rescued me. Join me in a cup?"

Sinead pursed her lips. "Why not? I'm sure Mammy won't miss me for a while yet."

Moira hung the kettle over the fire and gathered the cups, milk, and sugar.

Sinead helped herself to a seat at the table, and the two women set about getting to know each other.

"Ya know, it mightn't be my place to say this, but ya really shouldn't leave eggshells lyin' about. If ya aren't sure what to do with 'em, bring 'em to me, and I'll feed 'em to our pigs."

"I know they're a bit unsightly, but I figured the rain and wind would take care of them soon enough. I'm not bothered by them." She shrugged. "Anyway, I didn't put them out there. I assume a bird dropped them or someone passing by did for some reason."

Sinead whipped her head up to meet Moira's gaze. "Wait . . . are you tellin' me tha' someone else put those shells there?"

"Yes."

"*Tsk!* I don't like that 'tall now, sure I don't. Don't ya know tha' eggshells are the preferred home of"—she shifted in her seat nervously and looked around before leaning in close and whispering—"the wee faeries?" Sinead knocked on the wooden tabletop twice.

"Fairies? Oh, how lovely!" Moira clapped her hands.

"*Shhhh!*" Sinead bolted to her feet. "I don't know what ye Yanks think, but here in Ar'land those t'ings are mischievous little devils. Always lookin' for ways to make life miserable for us human folk, so they are."

She searched the room with wide eyes, then took her seat again. Moira could feel the girl's breath on her neck as she whispered ominously, "If you didn't put those shells out there, someone is tryin' to bring the faeries to ye."

Moira's eyes widened and her mouth fell open. "Why?"

Sinead's shoulders rose and fell nonchalantly. "We're a people of blessings and curses. Not a witch-type sort o' curse but rather wishing their enemies ill. Ya know, 'May you have an itch but no nails to scratch with.' That sort of t'ing."

Moira stared at Sinead in disbelief.

Sinead continued, unaffected. "But if they don't want to get close enough to say it to ya directly, the best way to get the job done is to set the faeries on ya."

Sinead's voice was low and foreboding. The fire in her eyes unnerved Moira to the core.

"But why would someone wish me ill? What have I done to anyone in this town?" She huffed and slumped her shoulders.

"I don' know, dearie. But I'd say ye need to watch yer back and make sure ya say yer prayers. Saint Michael's yer man for that, so he is." She rested a hand on Moira's shoulder and gave a little squeeze. "I'd best be off now. I'm sorry to be the one to bring ill news."

Moira gave a weak smile to her new friend. "Good night, Sinead. And thanks."

Did she really mean that? Was she really thankful for the strange interpretation Sinead had given her?

She made her way to the bedchamber and pulled her small, worn Bible out of the dresser, searching for one of her favorite passages. Now more than ever she needed a reminder of who was truly in control, even when everything seemed to spiral into confusion. She thumbed through the worn pages, the smells of home wafting up from within, and finally landed on the book of Romans.

She read aloud: "'For I am persuaded, that neither death, nor life, nor angels, nor principalities, nor powers, nor things present, nor things to come, nor height, nor depth, nor any other creature, shall be able to separate us from the love of God, which is in Christ Jesus our Lord.'"

She clamped her eyes shut and clutched the book to her breast. "Please, God, let this be true in my life."

Deep within, strength began to build again. The more she rolled the words in her mind, the more peace settled in her heart.

God had brought her here, and He had a purpose in that. Moira wasn't going to let some superstition distract her from whatever it was God was going to do in her life and in this village.

CHAPTER 17

The following two days passed in a blur, with no major hiccups to mark them differently. At last, Friday dawned, bringing with it the promise of rest and respite from the mundane.

Mundane? A sour laugh escaped Moira's lips at the thought. In mere weeks, she had moved to a new country, into a new house, started a new job, and discovered someone might be wishing her harm. A far cry from her old life.

She tried her best to force the acrid thoughts from her mind. But the more she tried to shake them, the tighter they gripped her. Doubt. Disquiet. Regret. The toxic mixture seeped into every corner of her spirit.

The church bells began their toll. Their incessant knell sounded more like a death march than a call to worship. In the fog of fatigue and worry, she gathered her things and headed for the school.

The walk seemed inordinately short. She was not prepared to face the day. Ready to finish the day? Yes. But to start it? Not quite.

She took a deep breath in hopes that the frosty morning air would bolster her energy as she pushed the heavy oak door.

After dropping into the chair behind her desk, she cradled her head in her hands.

Lord, I need Your strength to get through this day. Please, God, help me.

"Ahem."

Moira gasped, catching herself just before falling off her seat. "Good grief, Áedach, you frightened me!"

A caustic sneer curled one corner of the lad's mouth. Moira's stomach fell at the sight of it.

Moira stood, forced a sugar-sweet smile on her face, and willed her voice steady. "What can I do for you? Did you need help with yesterday's writing assignment?" She clasped her hands behind her back lest he see them trembling.

"What can ya do fer me?" His eyebrows arched and his eyes widened. "What ya can do is know what it is *I* can do *to* ye." His sneer spread into a sickening grin as he placed one foot in front of the other, making his way toward her.

"Áedach." The firmness in her voice surprised her. "I think perhaps you are mistaken. You might want to rethink what you are doing." The large desk provided a welcome barrier between them. Moira gripped the edge of it.

"*Tsk! Tsk! Tsk!*" He wagged a filthy finger at her. "Ya need to be keerful how ya talk to me, Miss. Ya see, I know yer saicrit." A combination of giddy delight and power swirled in his ice-blue eyes. The hairs on Moira's arms stood as if stirred by a lightning storm.

Anger roiled in her belly at the audacity of the boy. Rather than air her ire, she mustered every ounce of patience she possessed. No telling what the lad was capable of. "I have no secrets, young man, and I'm sure I have no idea what you're talking about."

"*Psh!* 'Dats nonsense and ya know it. Watch yerself 'round me, Miss, or I'll spill yer saicrit to the whole of Ballymann."

He closed the distance between him and the desk. Pressing his hands hard onto its surface, he leaned forward until his nose was inches from hers. The stench of stale drink poured out on his foul breath.

Moira's breakfast threatened to come back up.

"I'll tell the priest hisself, so I will. Don't cross me, woman. Ye've been warned."

Áedach straightened to his full height, then clicked his tongue as he sauntered from the schoolhouse.

Curiosity tempted Moira to run after him, grab him by the shoulders, and shake whatever secret he thought he held.

How could I have a secret I don't even know about?

A deep breath did nothing to steady her nerves. Her teeth chattered. The room started to spin, and her stomach lurched. She bolted outside just in time to be sick in the gorse bush below the window. Mortified, she rose, thankful to see no one else around yet. Unsteady feet carried her back into the schoolhouse, where she attempted to focus on the day before her.

Áedach didn't return for lessons that day. And Moira was deeply grateful not to have to face the boy and his sneering gaze.

⌘

As the afternoon waned, the wind picked up, rattling the windows of the schoolhouse. The gorse bushes and maidenhair trees rocked violently in the tempest. Moira welcomed the dark weather. It mirrored her mood. If she couldn't vent her anger and frustration to the world, she was glad to let the world do it for her.

Walking home proved difficult, though, as the gale-force winds shoved her this way and that, threatening to toss her off the path. Ahead, the sanctuary of home beckoned.

As Moira opened the door, the wind ripped the handle from her hand, shoving her inside the chalet like a used rag. It took her full weight against the door to close it and secure the latch.

With shaky hands, she smoothed the tendrils of hair that had been blown across her face. Without caring about an evening meal, she stoked the fire, then collapsed on the bed, still fully clothed.

Sleep fell upon her swift and fierce, while outside the storm continued to roil.

Moira jolted awake. Disorientation whirled in her mind. The shutters on the living room window flapped in the maelstrom, slamming against the house. Rain splashed into the room and ran down the wall. She jumped out of bed and shrieked. Icy cold water covered her feet, with more pouring off the canopy over her bed.

"You can't be serious!" The torrent of the gales and percussion of the shutters on the house swallowed her voice.

She ran to the window. A branch must've broken through the glass. Moira grabbed a platter from the table. She placed it up against the hole in the glass and set a heavy book against it, praying it would hold.

One crisis averted, she returned to her bedchamber. The waterfall from the ceiling drew her attention. She gawked at the gaping hole in the roof.

What am I supposed to do with that?

She rushed to the press, snatched some towels, and tossed them on top of the canopy. Then she dragged a chair from the dining table to a spot near the bed.

Standing on the chair, she placed her hands on top of the canopy and hopped. Her upper body landed on the hard surface with a splat. Her midsection stuck on the edge leaving her feet dangling. With only flat wood and canvas under her hands, there was nothing to grab and pull herself up. Swinging her feet like a pendulum, she eventually built enough momentum to carry her legs up and over the ledge. She prayed it would support her weight.

Working as fast as her chilled muscles allowed, Moira shoved towels into the opening of the roof. The deluge slowed to a trickle. Then stopped.

"That'll have to do until morning." She scooted to the edge of the canopy. It hadn't seemed so high when she had climbed up. Turning onto her belly, she slithered off the edge. Her toes searched for the chair. Lying on top of a soaking-wet canopy, with her rump dangling over a chair she couldn't find, she chuckled in disbelief. Her body bobbed up and down with her laughter, causing her to giggle all the more.

How do you always seem to get yourself into these situations, Moira Girl?

At last, her toes found the chair, and she slid the rest of the way off the canopy.

The remaining towels in the press served as mops as Moira tried to sop up what water she could from the floor before fetching her nightgown.

"That's one good thing about sleeping in your clothes. At least your nightdress is still dry."

Bríd had been right about that canopy keeping out the damp. Though the top of it was soaked, the mattress was still quite dry.

Dressed in warm, clean clothes, with crises abated for the moment, Moira buried herself deep in the covers and waited for morning.

CHAPTER 18

At long last the sun peeked its head over the horizon. Moira pried herself from the covers and braced herself for the frigid, watery floor. *Thanks be to God.* Much of the water had dried up during the early morning hours. It left in its wake, however, a slick, frosty footpath. Traversing it to fetch her shoes from the press proved an unpleasant task.

As she fumbled about, her thoughts worked to untangle how to repair the damage. Disappointment settled in her heart as her dream of a quiet, relaxing weekend vanished amid visions of time-consuming—and likely expensive—repairs.

"Yes, Moira Girl, it looks like all work and no play for you this weekend."

She looked wistfully at the broken window. "But at least you won't be alone. You'll need to have experts help you. You'll need to find a tha—"

Images of Sean's eyes, green as the Irish countryside, filled her mind. Her hands drifted to her cheeks. Burning again. This time, however, she knew no fire was to blame.

She thought back to the first time she'd seen him, silhouetted in the gale that welcomed her to Ballymann. Drenched in rain, running a strong hand through his thick mop of hair, he'd been altogether enchanting—and infuriating. Her heart beat in her chest like a bodhrán driving a reel. She dreaded the thought of seeing him again. Or did she? He'd been such a dolt. Then again, he *had* come to her rescue at the beach with Buach. And again at the schoolhouse with the fire.

A deep sigh puffed from her chest. She shuffled to the mirror to set her hair and freshen her face.

You must present a tidy appearance to uphold your sense of professionalism.

She didn't believe herself for a second.

⁓

"Sean!"

Sean craned his neck to peer over the western edge of the O'Malleys' roof.

Colm squinted up at him.

"Aye?"

"I've another job for ye." The old man shaded his eyes with a hand.

"Land sakes, another one?" Sean dropped his head and muttered to himself through gritted teeth. He nodded. "Aye. I'd say it'll have to wait. We've got enough jobs from the storm last night to last a fortnight."

"Aye, we do." Colm cleared his throat. "Do ye not want to know who its fer, then?"

Sean stopped working and sighed. *Doesn't the auld man know there isn't time for chitchat? Sure, and if he's so worried about it he can go take care of it.*

Remorse filled him for the careless thought—along with gratitude that he hadn't shot it out of his mouth. He pressed his lips together and peeked over the edge again.

A goofy grin crinkled Colm's face.

"Who's it for, then?"

"Miss Doherty's chalet didn't fare too well in the gale last night. Tore a hole the size o' my foot in the poor girl's roof, so it did." He arched his shaggy eyebrows.

Moira? Unrest niggled his belly at the idea of her. Of course he would use any excuse to look on her fair face once more. But could he trust himself not to play the fool again—or worse, insult the poor girl, which he seemed to have a penchant for doing? Not to mention he'd have to endure more of her abuses in response to his every action. As much as he tried to stifle it, a smile spread across his face. He dared not look down at the old man again, lest his mentor see his delight.

He kept his head down, his hands busy, and called out, "I'll be there after lunch."

"Yer a good man yerself," Colm called as he headed down the lane. A faint chuckle wafted on the breeze as he disappeared over a hill.

⸙

The red door stared hard at Sean. Taunting him. Daring him to knock and not make a fool of himself in the process. He stood there for ages working up the courage while trying to figure out what to say.

Good grief, lad, it's not like you're coming to call on the girl. It's a simple business call. Just think of it as Old Man McGuire's house.

"Except Old Man McGuire doesn't have eyes like the sea on a summer's day," he mumbled. Just as he raised his hand to knock, the top half of the door flew open.

"I thought I heard someone out here!"

His breath caught in his chest. Moira's eyes sparkled even more than he remembered. *Steady, lad.*

"Sorry to beat you to the punch," she continued. "Someone has been skulking about the place lately, leaving little

. . . treats for me. I thought maybe you were the guilty party."
She shrugged and smiled.

How had he not noticed her dimples before?

"Not a bother, Miss." Could she hear his heartbeat in his
voice? "Eh . . . Colm said you had some damage from the
storm? I see the tree took offense at the chalet being in its
way." He nodded to the broken window and chuckled.

Eejit.

"Yes, it was quite the rude awakening. Please, come in
and I'll show you." She gestured toward the back room. As
he made his way back, he noticed she left the door open.

"The floor took quite a beating too." She swept her hand
in a low arc. "There was probably half an inch of standing
water in the bedchamber."

Was she blushing? "The floor looks alright, but we need
to address that roof." Sean's cheeks burned. After all, it
wasn't everyday he stood in a single woman's bedchamber—
a beautiful single woman, at that. No wonder she left the
door open.

Moira pointed to the damaged area, and Sean stepped
closer to take a better look. She remained in front of the
fireplace. The dim light offered no help. He needed to get
closer still.

"I need to fetch my ladder. I'll be back in a wee while."

Upon returning, he carried the ladder to the bedside
and leaned it up against the wood frame of the canopy. As
soon as he placed his full weight on the first rung, its feet
slid out from underneath him. The ladder fell over him
and nearly landed on his head, but it somehow hovered in
midair. He looked up to find a petite hand holding firmly
onto a rung and a cheeky grin on Moira's face.

"Well now, I suppose this makes us even?" she said.

Her laugh was like water over rocks. Sean stood and
brushed off his breeches.

"Well, yes, I suppose it does, Miss Doherty." Though sure his oversized smile painted him every bit the simp, he couldn't hold it back. "But I do believe you're about to owe me again."

Her face clouded.

"I can't be certain until I get a closer look, but it seems I'll be working my fingers to the bone to repair it." He let a wink slip.

A lovely shade of pink filled her cheeks and she ducked her head coyly. "If you say so."

The two stared at one another, swapping silly grins.

At last, Sean shook himself back to reality. "If you'd be so kind as to hold the ladder for me while I investigate things up there?"

The blush on her cheeks deepened, and she eyed the open door. "Yes, of course. We can't have you killing yourself before the job's done."

Sean started up the ladder, one shaky step at a time, his head spinning at the nearness of her. The heady fragrance of lavender that wafted up from her hair didn't help the matter.

Focus, lad. The roof.

Once atop the canopy, he surveyed the damage and made note of the needed supplies before descending. Thankfully the journey down was much smoother than the way up.

"I'll fetch the supplies and be back in a jiff. Colm will join me." He wanted her to know he cared about propriety and her reputation. It just wouldn't do for him to spend so much time alone in her chalet, whether she was there or not. Especially with the way tongues wagged in this village.

Moira dipped her head and smiled. "Thank you, Mr. McFadden. I'll be sure to have the kettle on when you both arrive."

CHAPTER 19

How long could it take to fetch thatching supplies? A sense of urgency for the men's return churned inside Moira, and she chided herself for it.

The kettle hung over the fire, ready to brew the finest cuppa in Gweedore. A small selection of tea cakes, biscuits, and brown bread lay in a flower-shaped pattern on a dainty platter.

Moira presumed Sean respected his mentor a great deal. Though a hand-trade, thatching was a highly respected profession in Ireland. She was determined to make a good impression.

Are you sure that's all it is?

Anytime Sean's name came up, those eyes floated in her mind, stealing her breath. Her attraction to the man made no sense. While she couldn't deny the ruddy thatcher was handsome, she barely knew him. And most of the time she had known him, he had infuriated her.

The argument is better than the loneliness, her mother's voice sang in her head. Moira remembered well her mother's oft-used phrase. Moira first heard it when, as a child, she inquired about her parents' playful, flirtatious banter. However, it then became a regular part of the reconciliation ritual after the more heated debates not uncommon to an Irish marriage.

She hated to admit it, but Moira certainly didn't mind the kind of "arguments" in which she and Sean had engaged. Her stomach leaped at the memory of the sparkle in Sean's eye when he had good-naturedly teased her about the fire in the schoolhouse. Then there was the ladder incident earlier today. Their eyes had locked, awakening feelings she didn't know were possible from a simple look.

She clicked her tongue and shook the image from her mind. The man was as irritating as wet wool. She couldn't let her need for companionship infuse affections where there were none.

A knock at the door interrupted her reverie. She pressed a hand to her abdomen and took a deep breath to steady her pounding heart. When she opened the door, Sean stood there next to an older gentleman. Not as old as she had pictured but certainly old enough to be her father.

"Miss Moira Doherty, I'd like to introduce you to my mentor, Colm Sweeny."

Moira dipped a shallow curtsy and Colm extended his hand. Moira accepted it. His sun-darkened hand immediately swallowed her small, pale one.

Standing a good six inches shorter than Sean, Colm wasn't a large man by any stretch. But his hands! Massive, solid, and strong. They were rough from years of hard labor but not overly coarse.

"The pleasure is all mine, Miss." Colm tipped his hat and smiled. The light twinkled in his eyes, setting Moira at perfect ease. He reminded Moira of her father—God rest his soul. She loved him from the start.

"Thank you for coming." She smiled. "I suppose you both will need to build your strength with a cuppa first?"

The men exchanged glances and Colm swiped his nose to the side.

"Sean, ya better not let this gairl get away. She's got her

priorities straight." A breathy guffaw escaped Colm's lips as he slapped his knee and strode inside to sit at the table.

Once again Moira's cheeks warmed. She decided to ignore the heated glance Sean shot his mentor.

Grateful for the distraction, Moira turned to prepare the tea.

The trio drank in relative silence. Colm devoured so many cakes in such quick succession, Moira wondered if the man had eaten at all in a week. Just as the lads were finishing their final sips of tea, footsteps came scurrying up the path.

Moira looked out the window. "How lovely! Bríd's just arrived."

Bríd's head poked in the open door. "Hallo? Anyone home?" A grin was plastered across her face.

The men uttered crumb-filled greetings, and Moira let her in, welcoming her friend with a warm embrace.

"I knew youse were comin' to fix the roof and I wanted to make sure things were done properly, like." She leveled a motherly glance at Sean first, then Moira.

Good grief, was the whole town going to involve themselves in this affair? Who knew a hole in the roof was so fascinating?

"How's the schooling, peata?" Bríd asked, helping herself to a pinch of brown bread.

"Yes, does Muinteoir Sean need to make any house calls to unruly students?" Sean set a mock stern look on his face.

Moira poured a cup of tea for the newcomer. How much should she reveal about Áedach's little rampage? Perhaps one of them would have some idea about what the lad could have meant with all the nonsense about secrets and whatnot. She decided to test the waters.

"It's going fine, mostly." She handed the tea to Bríd and leaned up against the windowsill. "Most of the children are lovely, and so eager to learn."

Colm leaned forward, placing his elbows on the table. "I notice ya say *moost* of the children. Moost isn't all, is it?"

A firm swat from Bríd displaced his elbows from the table.

Moira rolled her lips between her teeth, measuring how much to say.

"Well, Áedach—" A collective groan went up from her visitors at the mention of the lad's name. "He's been a bit of a scallywag from the beginning," Moira continued. "Nothing I can't handle, of course. But yesterday—"

Sean shot to his feet. "What? Yesterday what? Did that brute lay a finger on you? If he did, so help me . . ."

The group stared at Sean. Colm hid his mouth behind another slice of bread.

Sean's face reddened and he cleared his throat before returning to his seat.

Moira tried not to find his ire, and chagrin, adorable.

Bríd rolled her eyes at the younger lad. "What happened yesterday, peata?"

"Well, he was waiting for me in the schoolhouse when I arrived. He cornered me. He said he knows 'my secret' and threatened to reveal it to the whole village." She crossed her arms. "The peculiar thing is, I don't have any idea what he's talking about."

Bríd and Colm shared a passing look.

Odd.

"What did he mean?" Sean questioned, looking from one person to the other. "What secret?"

Moira shrugged. "That's just the thing. I haven't the foggiest notion! I've only just arrived. What scandalous affair could I have drummed up in such a short time?"

Another glance flashed between Bríd and Colm. He opened his mouth as if to speak, but at a shake of Bríd's head, he promptly clamped it shut again. At least, Moira thought Bríd shook her head. Perhaps her eyes were playing tricks on her.

The older woman sidled up next to Moira and laid a motherly arm across her shoulders. "Don't ya be worryin' about the likes of Áedach. I'm sorry if he scared ya. The lad doesn't know what he's sayin'."

Moira searched Bríd's face. Something akin to guilt or sorrow clouded the woman's eyes. Moira didn't know what to think. She looked at Colm, who was staring hard at a spot on the floor. Her eyes looked to Sean's, hoping to find some sort of answer there.

Sean's brow was furrowed, and a hand worked the back of his neck so hard she worried he would break the skin. Then he stopped and his gaze shot up to meet hers.

"You said this morn' that someone had been skulking about the place. Leaving you . . . treats?" From the pinched arch of his brow Moira gathered he was angry or confused. Or both.

"I didn't ask about it before," he said, "because I was too, eh, distracted. By the damage to the roof." His face flushed.

"Well, yes," Moira offered. "I've found eggshells scattered around the entrance to the chalet a few times. Sinead says someone is trying to send the faeries to hurt me." She shrugged and turned to stoke the fire.

"Perhaps it's that dolt Áedach," Bríd said a bit too quickly. "Maybe he's just tryin' to intimidate you with false claims of some saicrit and fake afflictions?"

Colm picked at a splinter in the table, keeping his eyes firmly planted below the gaze of the others.

"I don't know." Moira sighed.

Memories of her dreams floated to the forefront of her mind—visions of her mother entreating her to come to Ireland and save her. Could this be related to that? Moira resolved in her heart to find out.

Chapter 20

Seething anger spurred Sean as he worked on Moira's roof. The storm from the night before may have cleared, but the gale in his heart and mind had only begun. In his mind's eye Áedach MacSuibhne's smarmy, freckled face taunted him. The lad had always been one for shenanigans, but this time he'd gone too far.

How dare he threaten Moira! Oh, that boyo had better pray he didn't cross Sean's path anytime soon or he was likely to discover a swift fist to the jaw.

As his fingers deftly wove the straw, making the roof as sound as he was able, Sean rolled the day's events over in his mind again. His little tryst—nae, it was more innocent than that—his encounter with Moira that morning shook him. It had stirred something in him he hadn't known before now. He tried hard to ignore the school of mackerel that seemed to be swimming in his stomach at the thought of her smile, those dimples. A grin broke across his own face at the memory.

Just as quickly as it had appeared, his smile dimmed as he recalled Moira's expression as she told the harrowing tale of Áedach's affront. And her account of someone trying to bring her harm. The poor thing must've been terrified.

Sean had always assumed Áedach was capable of no real harm. In truth, the lad's troubles had been innocuous enough in the past.

I suppose someone like him is capable of just about anything if he believes he holds great power over a weaker person.

The sun sank toward the water. February was tricky. She lulled you into a false sense of spring but still held on to the bite and quickly falling nights of winter.

Sean finished the current section of thatch before gathering his gear. As he stood to descend from the roof, he stopped to watch the orange glow on the watery horizon. He vowed in that moment to watch out for Moira Doherty. And to protect her honor and reputation at all costs.

<hr />

The week flew by at breakneck speed, and before Moira could catch up, it was Friday again. Mist hung in the air, neither rising nor falling, coating the world in a fine dusting of diamonds. The excitement of the week before had settled into a peaceful determination to solve the mystery shrouding her.

Moira's prayers of late had transitioned from cries of desperation and incredulity to pleas for His will to be done in and through her. Last night, the thought had landed on her heart that perhaps God hadn't made a mistake in calling her here after all. Perhaps He had brought her here for this very reason, for this very time. That thought, coupled with the curiosity of how her mother might fit in to everything, opened the door for a sense of purpose and peace to settle over Moira. She had enjoyed her first uninterrupted night of sleep in over a week.

Today, with eyes clear and heart alight, she closed out the week at school and stepped into the weekend with hope.

Sinead had invited Moira to join her family on a trip to Letterkenny, the town just over the mountains, the next day.

Excitement nipped at Moira's heels as she made the short walk from the schoolhouse to the chalet. The mist kissed her cheeks, frosting them like a tea cake.

Sinead's invitation had come none too soon. Not only was Moira in need of a good dose of friendly companionship, but she also needed some new fabric to make another dress. The two frocks she had brought with her served her well, but in this damp Irish weather, they could take up to three full days to dry after being washed. And that was if the sun shone unabated. If the weather consisted of the soft, soggy days so common to Donegal, it could take even longer.

Once home and with the fire properly restored, she turned her attention to the small mirror hanging over the chest of drawers in her bedchamber. Smoothing a hand over the unruly tendrils curled up by the moist Irish air, she examined her features. Eyes green and bright stared back at her. Her cheeks held a becoming shade of pink and just a hint of sparkle from the mist remained.

How lovely it would be to find material in a nice shade of dark blue or a persimmon accent to highlight her eyes. The red in her cheeks deepened, but she couldn't deny it was important to her to find something becoming.

Thoughts of whether or not Sean would approve or appreciate such a garment floated across her mind. How irksome!

What value was it to spend time and energy pondering such things? True, it was important for a teacher to present a clean and tidy appearance. But Moira had more pressing matters to tend to—the mystery of her supposed secret and Moira's stealthy "treat" bearer being paramount.

She committed to focusing solely on solving the puzzle, her work at the school, and her relationship with God. She wouldn't allow distracting thoughts of Sean McFadden to cloud her mind any longer. While she hoped to fall in love and marry one day, it wasn't her reason for coming to Ballymann. With all that lay before her, letting her heart and mind get swept away by a fanciful crush seemed irresponsible.

A determined nod settled the self-dispute, and a sense of freedom rose in her chest—freedom and anticipation for her outing to see more of her beloved new home on the morrow.

CHAPTER 21

Tiny, frigid droplets held the atmosphere captive. A cap of dense clouds pinned the frosty, saturated air to the earth. Moira hugged herself against the cold as she made her way to the market to meet Sinead's family. What a dreadful day for a wagon ride.

An intense shiver shook Moira from her head to her feet. Despite the dismal weather, she was determined to enjoy the day. Quickening her steps, she wished she could somehow coax the sun from its hiding place.

"Ye look as though yer cat's had kittens wit' dat smile across yer face." Sinead's stout laughter burst through the mist like a lighthouse.

Moira's grin widened and she bounded down the hill to her friend. The two embraced and squeezed so tight Moira couldn't breathe. Their friendship was young but solid. Moira was infinitely grateful for the instant connection.

"Well, you know," she answered, "I thought I'd try my hand at controlling the weather with a happy heart."

"If dat works, soon we'll all be walkin' 'round beamin' like eejits."

Sinead hoisted a large sack and dropped it into the back of the wagon with a thud. "Ye'll be riding up on the seat there. Ma said we can't be havin' ye crumpled in the back like a sack of spuds." Sinead shrugged and pointed Moira to the top of two benches at the front of the rig.

"Will you sit with me?"

"Me? No, I sit in the back an' make sure nuttin' falls off. Plus, the lads get the preferred seatin' anyway. You know how it is, men're more important, so they are." Sinead's eyes rolled so far back in her head, Moira feared they might not return to their proper places.

"What lads?"

At that moment, a figure rose from behind the wagon, wiping his hands on a rag. He turned and froze.

"Moira! I—it's . . . er . . . hello." A funny little smile played on Sean's lips as he raked a hand through his auburn hair.

Moira's ears and cheeks burned as if she'd spent too much time in the sun. "Good morning, Mr. McFadden." She bobbed her head before turning her attention to a stubborn string on the sleeve of her coat. What was he doing here? Surely he wouldn't be joining them?

"Ma and Da said Sean could come along. Old Man Sweeny needs some supplies," Sinead offered as if reading Moira's thoughts. "No sense in two wagons making the journey when one will do."

"Sinead, are those sacks on the wagon yet?" A red-faced woman bounded out of the shop, hands in a tizzy twisting her apron. She was the spitting image of Sinead, only at least a score her senior. She caught a glimpse of Moira and stopped short. Her hands met in front of her mouth with a clap and a wide smile broke onto her face.

In an instant the woman was at Moira's side. A heavy arm landed on Moira's shoulder.

"*Céad mile fáilte, a leanbh!*"

Moira cocked a crooked smile and chuckled.

"A hundred, thousand welcomes, my dear! My Sinead

tells me ye're the new teacher. I am so glad youse are here, now! Come, let's get ye up into the seat and we can head off, so."

The woman offered Moira a hand, but Sean pressed in front of her.

"Ya don't have to do that, Mrs. McGonigle. Ye go see what's keepin' that man o' yourn." He smiled at Moira and extended a hand. "Allow me."

Moira blinked, internally rebuking herself for feeling every bit a giddy schoolgirl. She placed her hand in his and each nerve in her arm awoke. With the help of Sean's strong support, she made the climb to the seat without any trouble. She took her place on the far edge.

"Sinead, are you sure you won't join me?" Her eyes implored her friend to read her mind and sense her unease. "I'd quite like the enjoyment of your company on the journey."

"Nah, I won't," she replied, seemingly oblivious to Moira's agony. "I've got me own job back here. Ye just enjoy the scenery." *Was that a wink?* Sinead hopped up onto the back of the wagon with surprising ease and settled in between two large sacks of potatoes. The elder McGonigles took their places on the lower front bench. Sean, much to Moira's dismay, claimed the seat next to her.

A snap of the reins and the wagon jolted forward. Moira's knuckles turned white and ached as she gripped the front edge of the seat. Was it possible to crack a wagon seat with one's bare hands?

The rig rolled through the village, past the guesthouse, and followed the bend in the road, taking the passengers east. The peak of Mount Errigal loomed on the horizon.

Moira was keenly aware of Sean's presence. Heat radiated from his side and the subtle aroma of heather and musk sent her insides aflutter. She stared straight ahead, neither seeing nor hearing anything, trying desperately to think of something other than the man next to her.

Suddenly the wagon jerked and a violent bump vaulted Moira off her seat and over the side of the rig. Her arms flailed. All seemed lost when a steady hand gripped her wrist and a firm arm wrapped around her waist and pulled her to safety.

She heaved a sigh and brushed a shock of hair from her forehead with her free hand. She turned and met Sean's eyes, only a handbreadth away from her own. One arm was secure around her waist, the other held fast to her left hand. Never before had she felt so protected. She could have stayed like that for hours. Though she tried, she could not bring herself to let go.

"Are ya okay?" Sean's eyes searched hers. It felt like his question addressed more than the situation at hand.

She bobbed her head and cleared her throat. "Yes, I am. Thank you."

He paused as though making sure she wasn't going to topple over again. Once he seemed convinced she was steady, he released her and reclaimed his seat a respectable distance away. But his gaze remained steadfast on hers.

The warmth from his embrace dissipated. She missed it instantly—and scolded herself for the notion.

"Sorry about that, love." Mr. McGonigle turned his gaze to meet hers briefly. "These roads are a mite disheveled. Ye must keep a good hold as we go."

Moira nodded in obedience as the rig turned a corner. Her mouth fell open and her eyes widened to take in the spectacular scene before her. On their right lay a mirror of the sky. Dunlewey Lake, as still as glass. A valley stretched before them with towering rocky hills forming a bowl around a smaller hill standing center stage. A white marble church stood atop it, glistening even in the cloud-darkened mist.

"It's absolutely beautiful." Moira took a deep breath of fresh air. "It's unlike anything I've ever seen."

Mr. McGonigle turned, pride plastered across his face as though he himself was responsible for the scene. "'Tis the crowning glory in all of Donegal." He beamed. "There's no place in the whole wairld like our Poisoned Glen. There's not the likes of it to be found anywhere."

Moira frowned. "I can't imagine why on earth anyone would call this stunning place 'poisoned.'"

Boisterous laughter erupted from the McGonigle clan.

"No, no," Mr. McGonigle explained. "'Tisn't because the place is poisoned. It comes from the auld Irish."

"Oh?"

"You see, the Irish name for this place means 'the heavenly glen.' But the words for 'heaven' and 'poison' sound very similar. So when the Brits came"—Mr. McGonigle and Sinead hocked and spit over the side of the wagon—"they muddled the whole t'ing and thought we'd called this place 'Poison.'" Mr. McGonigle nodded. Apparently deciding he had explained sufficiently, he turned his back.

Sean and Moira exchanged a glance. He leaned nearer and whispered, "Clear as mud?"

Moira covered a hand over her mouth to stifle a giggle.

Sinead popped up from the back and added, "Doncha be encouragin' me auld man to tell his historical tales. He fancies himself a *seanchaí*. Once ye get him goin', ye'll never get him to stop."

The three younger ones laughed freely before the sights beckoned them once more.

Sean scooted just a bit closer to Moira and pointed out each of the mountains that made up the Seven Sisters of the Poisoned Glen. "That's Errigal"—he gestured to the nearest peak—"and there's Mackoght, Aghla More, Aghla Beag, Crocknalaragagh, Muckish, and that one over there?" He pointed and took a deep breath. "That one is Ardlough-nabrackbaddy."

Moira blinked hard and shook her head. "Well done, sir. That was quite a mouthful."

"*Tá, cinnte!*" Mr. McGonigle chimed. "Indeed!"

"I don't think I'll ever be able to pronounce those names, let alone remember all of them." What a rich and fascinating language Irish was turning out be.

Though they sounded less like monikers and more like the ramblings of her uncle when he'd had one too many pints down at the tavern back in Boston, the names weren't what mattered to Moira anyway. It was these people. This place. The beauty of the sweeping valley with its far green slopes and glistening slate mountaintops.

The group rode on in silence, enchanted by the allure of the Irish valley. As they rumbled on to the east, Sinead popped up once again and pointed out a narrow road that split off to the south before disappearing into a grove of trees.

"That there's the entrance to Glenveagh Castle." She wagged her finger in the air. "I suppose ye could educate us on that place better than we could you, Moira."

Confusion clouded Moira's mind and she pressed her brows together. "Why do you say that? I've never even heard of that place."

In the front seat, Mrs. McGonigle spun around and shot a fiery glance at her daughter. Moira turned to Sinead, who looked both caught and hurt. The mother and daughter stared at one another before Sinead acquiesced.

"Never mind, I must be mistaken." She huffed and flopped down to her seat in the back.

Moira looked at Sean, wondering if he had any idea as to what had just happened.

He was silent, bewilderment clouding his face. His eyes

were fixed on his boots, but his gaze was a million miles away as he chewed his lip.

Moira stared at the grove of trees as they rolled by, wondering what secrets lay beyond. Donegal held more intrigue than she had bargained for. And certainly more than she welcomed.

CHAPTER 22

The wagon rumbled over the crest of the last knoll on the edge of Letterkenny town. This vantage point rewarded travelers with sweeping views of the hill-kissed terrain of northwest Donegal. To the southwest, the spire from the cathedral jutted high into the air, bidding all who would to come.

Mr. McGonigle urged the horses away from the Port Road that would carry them to Derry and beyond. He steered them, instead, to follow the main road as it wound in a gentle curve toward the city center.

He parked the rig at the entrance to Upper Main Street, and the group disembarked. Each released groans as they raised their weary bodies from the hard wooden seats. A symphony of cracks and pops rang out from Mr. McGonigle's joints, followed by a look of sheer bliss. Though only a distance of thirty miles from Ballymann to Letterkenny, the journey had taken nearly three hours. The entire party was road weary yet excited for a day in town.

The men discussed their plans for the day's business, and the women calculated their route among the few fabric and dressmaking shops along the thoroughfare. The party agreed to reconvene at one o'clock for the midday meal.

"Ma must see to some barters for the shop. She's givin' spuds in exchange fer other t'ings we can't get back home," Sinead said, linking her elbow in Moira's. "That means you an' me have some time ta take in the sights."

After setting a time to meet Mrs. McGonigle at O'Toole's Textiles, the two girls set off for a stroll along the cobbled main street.

A potpourri of baked goods and fresh meats and the pungent, unmistakable odor of coal spouting from nearly every chimney in the city center mingled in the brisk air. People milled about, wearing everything from the rags of poor farming families to the finest fashions this side of Dublin. The city was teeming with life and energy.

Moira breathed a wistful sigh. "I forgot how energizing a city can be." She scanned the skyline, enjoying the sharp, geometric silhouettes of buildings against a hazy, smoky sky.

"Isn't it simply splendid, like?" Sinead agreed. "I love comin' to Letterkenny. There's just so much to see and do. And eat!" She pulled Moira toward a confectionery shop window. The two girls oohed and aahed over the decadent treats displayed on dainty trays and tiered towers, agreeing to return following the meal for some tasty afters.

As they continued strolling along the direction of Lower Main Street, enjoying the sights each window offered, Moira gasped and ran to the main display window at O'Toole's Textiles. Amid the bolts of vibrantly colored fabrics stood the most exquisite gown Moira had ever seen. The velvet bodice, a stunning shade of sea blue, hugged the form of the tailor's dummy down to a dropped waistline. From there the skirt flowed in a simple A-line that just brushed the floor. A ring of delicate lace in the softest shade of peach adorned the ends of the sleeves. A fine cream-colored cotton apron with peach rosettes completed the ensemble.

Moira grabbed Sinead's hand and gasped again. "Oh,

Sinead, isn't it lovely?" She clasped her other hand to her own chest, attempting to steady her heartbeat.

Sinead pressed a hand to her forehead. "Great Mary, is it grand!" She turned to face Moira and jerked her arm until their eyes met. "Ya hafta try it on, so. Oh, you'd be such a sight in it."

Moira shook her head. "I'd love to, but there's no way I could justify the money for a premade gown such as this." She gazed at the dress with longing.

"I didna say ya had to buy it, like. I only said ta try it on!" She grabbed Moira's hand and dragged her into the shop.

The woman behind the counter greeted them. "Good morning to ye, ladies."

"Hiya. My friend here would like ta try on that lovely blue frock in the window." Sinead grinned and shoved Moira front and center.

Moira offered a chagrined smile accompanied by a soft laugh.

"Oh, that's a lovely choice, so it is. I admire it myself. It's only gone up yesterday. And with your eyes, it should really be stunning on ye." The shopkeep rambled on as she removed the dress from the dummy and led Moira to the changing stall. She hung the dress on a hook and slid the curtain closed with a deft flick of her wrist.

Moira ran her fingers along the sleeve, reveling in the luxurious softness of the velvet. She had never owned a gown as lovely as this, and her heart ached at the sight of it. Taking care not to soil or tear the rich fabric, she dressed and tied the apron around her waist. Even without a looking glass, she already felt like royalty.

"C'mon now, are ye gonna show me or make me wait till I'm as old as me ma?"

Moira laughed and slid the curtain aside.

Sinead's mouth fell open, and her dimpled hands flew

to her cheeks. "Great Mary, ya look like the mistress of the castle!"

Moira's cheeks warmed, and she smoothed the flat of her hands over the apron again and again.

The shopkeep guided Moira to a tall mirror in the center of the store. She blinked at her reflection. Never had she felt so beautiful.

"G'on, now. Give us a twirl." Sinead pirouetted with a flourish.

With slow, marked steps, Moira spun. Keeping her eyes on the looking glass as long as possible, she admired how the dress hugged her form and flowed effortlessly as she moved. It was as if it had been custom-made for her. Movement in the street caught her eye. A figure was heading toward the shop.

⁓⁓⁓

Sean set a brisk pace to the textile shop. He was tasked with keeping the ladies abreast of the plan, and he didn't want to lose the table he'd booked for lunch in the process. Thankfully, he'd reached O'Toole's in record time. He could see the silhouettes of Sinead and Moira through the lace-curtained window before he stepped inside.

"Hello, ladies. I wanted to let you know—" The words caught in his throat as Moira spun to face him. All thoughts of business and timetables evaporated.

A captivating vision stood before him in a blue dress. Though it wasn't the dress that caught his attention. It was her eyes. He didn't know if it was because of the shade of blue she wore, or joy he hadn't seen in them before, but her eyes glowed like jade in sunlight. Why had he come here? What was he intending to tell them? All that existed in the world at that moment was Moira, standing there, looking at him, a beguiling smile gracing her porcelain face.

"Moira," he said at last, taking a step toward her. "You look . . . you look brilliant."

Moira dipped her head and looked up at him through dark lashes. "Thank you." Her voice was barely audible, and color kissed her cheeks. The two stood looking at one another, Sean grinning like a fool but unable to will his eyes to turn away.

Sinead's face popped up in front of his. He blanched.

"Yeah, she's a sight, isn't she? So, what're ya doin' in a shop for women, like?"

Sean stared at the grocer's daughter, stunned.

She stared back at him, an eyebrow cocked and foot tapping impatiently.

"Right. I've booked us a table at The Central Bar—but if we're to keep it, we must make haste. It's a bit earlier than we'd planned, but it's all they had." He cleared his throat, tipped his hat, and burst from the shop like a spring lamb, the cool air a welcome shock to his heated face. Grateful to be out of that shop, and out from under Moira's mesmerizing gaze.

CHAPTER 23

Located near the top of Upper Main Street not far from where the wagon was hitched, The Central Bar buzzed with patrons. Moira stared at the whitewashed building. The two-story inn and pub loomed strong and menacing with its black-trimmed windows. She wasn't entirely comfortable setting foot inside a public house—her mother's warnings about women and pubs echoing loudly in her mind. Yet other women came and went unbothered. And Mrs. McGonigle certainly didn't seem to mind. She had gone barreling into the place like it was the last ship to America during the Great Famine.

Moira stepped inside, squinting against the hazy darkness. The walls were paneled with dark wood, and a high counter, flanked on all corners with tall posts, stood in the center of the room. Mirrors lined the wall behind the counter, so the countless bottles of amber liquid appeared never-ending. A few figures sat at the bar in seeming world-changing conversations with the pints before them. A crackling fire in the hearth completed the cozy ambiance.

At the far end of the room, Sean motioned for the group to join him. They all took their places at the table. Within minutes, each was served a steaming bowl of soup. Moira inspected the creamy broth, filled with potatoes and leeks, before tearing off a chunk of the crusty brown bread that had been served with it. She dunked the bread into the hot ambrosia and delighted as the liquid soaked it. She lifted the bread to her mouth and closed her eyes to better savor the experience. Salty and creamy, the hearty soup satisfied her down to her toes—exactly what she needed after the long morning of travel and shopping.

The group enjoyed their meal and lively conversation as seconds of soup and bread were offered. Mr. McGonigle regaled them all with the tale of his excellent bartering skills, and Sinead recounted with great fervor the finding of the dress—and with great disappointment, Moira's refusal to purchase it.

From her seat at the end of the table, Moira was able to engage each of her new friends in conversation with ease, as well as take in the entirety of the room. Sean sat to her right, Sinead to her left, with the elder McGonigles beyond.

Sinead and her mother excused themselves to the loo while Mr. McGonigle—who now insisted Moira call him Paddy—made his way to the bar in search of a pint. Moira, intent on sopping up the last of her soup with the delicious bread, stopped mid-dip. The hair on the back of her neck stood up and her stomach sank with the sense that someone was watching her. She looked up from her dish and scanned the room. In the far corner, a lone figure sat in the shadows. Moira squinted to see through the darkness. The silhouette leaned forward, bringing his face into the light. Hard eyes glared at her, while aged lips nursed dark port from a glass.

Buach. Without thinking, Moira placed her hand on Sean's forearm.

Sean looked at her hand on his arm, and then to her face. He must've seen in her eyes the fear that was coursing through her, pushing her lunch to the back of her throat. "What it is, Moira? Are ya alright?"

Moira swallowed the bile in her throat and shook her head. "That man in the corner there."

Sean's gaze followed hers and landed on Buach, who was shuffling to his feet and heading in their direction.

"I see looks aren't the *only* t'ing ye have in common with yer mother." Buach's voice was thick with intrigue and drink. His steely eyes dropped to her hand on Sean's arm, and a crooked smile formed on the old man's lips.

Moira dropped her hand to her lap, bemoaning the brazen appearance of her innocent gesture. "I'm sure I have no idea what you mean by that remark."

Buach sucked on his wayward tooth. The *tsk, tsk, tsk* of it churned Moira's stomach.

Sean pressed his palms to the table and rose to his full height. "Ye've had too much to drink, auld man." His voice was calm, but anger flickered behind his eyes. "G'on now and find a place to sleep it off afore ya say something you'll regret."

Buach and Sean stared at one another. Neither man moved. Seconds seemed hours. Moira heard nothing but her heart pounding in her ears. By the rise and fall of Sean's shoulders, he was straining to control his anger. She looked from his shoulders to his face. His jaw worked back and forth, then he leaned forward until he was inches from Buach's face.

"I said get." He gave a slight motion to the door with his head. "And ye'll leave Miss Doherty alone. Or ye'll have me ta answer to."

Buach turned his full gaze to Moira, annoyance and fear spiraling in his eyes. "Yer mother's tale will come ta light sooner or later, peata. Then the whole of Ballymann'll know the truth about ye. I'll tell ye the same thing I did that day by the beach: keep yer eyes wide open." With a final *tsk* at his tooth, and a slight flinch when Sean crossed his arms over his chest, Buach turned and shuffled out the door.

Sean lowered himself to his seat and turned his attention to Moira. His eyes probed hers, his hand working the back of his neck just as she'd seen him do in her chalet. "Moira, I dunno what is going on here. And I want to ask ya, but I don't want you to think my asking means I doubt ya."

Moira nodded. "Go ahead."

"Do ye have any idea 'tall what everyone is talkin' about? Too many people have brought up this idea of a saicrit for it to be a complete bunch a malarkey. I just wonder if there might be a wee bit o' truth to it? Even a half truth?"

Tears pooled in Moira's eyes, and she willed them not to fall. "As true as the day is long, I have no idea what is going on." She rested her chin on her hand and allowed her mind to retrace the weeks since she'd come to Ballymann. "Buach mentioned my mother when he found me on the beach the first Sunday I was here."

"I remember that day well," Sean said.

"Then Áedach threatened to reveal my 'secret.' And I didn't like the look exchanged between Sinead and her mother when we passed by Glenveagh."

"I noticed that too."

"I came to Ballymann because Mother wanted me to be the teacher after Mrs. McGinley passed away. She had told me of her wonderful *céilí* dances in the village hall and the beauty of this land, but outside of that, she never talked about life in Ballymann. I don't even know what she did for work before coming to America."

The two sat in silence, chewing over the information. Finally, Sean cleared his throat and shifted in his seat. When he spoke, his voice was soft and kind, and Moira saw a hint of sadness in his eyes. "Do you think it's at all possible that . . ."

He shifted again and ran his hand through his hair. "Is it possible that this, this saicrit, has anything to do with yer mother doin' something wicked?"

Moira's heart ached to see Sean struggling so, wanting to be so tender with her. "I hate to admit it, but the same thought has crossed my mind." She sighed and nibbled on a rogue fingernail, deciding to keep her dreams to herself for the time being. "Mother was the most honorable, decent person I've ever known. But I can't help but wonder if perhaps that wasn't always so." She searched Sean's face and found only compassion.

"If she's anything like you"—he laid a hand on hers briefly—"I can't imagine anything unseemly about her 'tall. But I promise you now, I will help you uncover the truth, and I will stand by your side. No matter what."

Moira mouthed a silent "thank you."

CHAPTER 24

A sense of urgency hung in the air as the bedraggled crew began the journey home. The clouds had settled in, driving out the mist, bringing dense fog in its stead. The sun would not delay setting, removing what modicum of light cut through the fog. Everyone was anxious to make it over the pass before darkness fell fully upon the land. It was a precarious journey over Dunlewey Pass, with steep drops to the valley below mere inches away from the wagon's wheels. Every bit of light was needed to navigate the rutted path safely.

As the rig rumbled and bounced over the furrowed road, heading for the precipice near the peak of Errigal, exhausted silence settled on the group. A soft snore drifted from the back of the wagon. Moira turned. Sinead lay, sound asleep, spooning up against a bolt of lace her mother had traded the potatoes for. The heaviness of Moira's eyelids grew by the minute.

Paddy's voice broke the silence. "Say now, why is that wee cloud movin'?" He squinted and bobbed his head to and fro, obviously attempting to get a better read on a shape up ahead.

"Ya daft fool," his wife retorted, "that's no cloud. 'Tis a sheep!"

Sure enough, smack in the middle of the road stood an

obstinate Donegal sheep. The ewe stared at the wagon, chewing stubbornly. She offered a cursory *baa* before lowering her head to take another bite of the sweet grass growing between the ruts. She clearly had no intention of moving. Paddy pulled sharp on the reins and the horses nickered in protest. The wagon lurched to a reluctant halt.

Sean hopped down and ran at the sheep yelling and clapping. The sheep blinked at him and continued to eat.

Amusement and mild annoyance played on Sean's face. He shrugged and strode resolutely to the ewe. He scooped her up in one fell swoop and plopped her safe and sound on the hillside. She *baaed* once more while Sean resumed his place on the bench.

The gang chuckled and Moira breathed a sigh of relief as Paddy called "*Hya!*" to get the horses trudging along again, thankful he hadn't tried to steer around the animal. The steady plodding of hooves and the gentle rocking of the wagon were like a lullaby. Moira struggled to keep her eyes open. She needed to stay awake. For one, she didn't want to risk falling off of the wagon. Secondly, she had hoped to use the journey home to try to piece together what few tidbits of information she had learned about her mother's supposed secret. She needed to figure out this mystery to which the whole of Donegal seemed privy.

She straightened in her seat, facing the road, calling to mind what she knew so far. Her eyes, however, had different plans. They altogether ignored her attempts to keep them open.

⚜

What in the world could Old Man Buach know that could hold such power over a girl like Moira? Sean laced his fingers together then apart over and over as he thought. He was determined to suss out what Buach and Áedach were scheming. Sudden warmth radiated up his shoulder and arm, breaking his thoughts. The heavenly scent of lavender washed over him. He looked to the source of the heat. Moira leaned against his shoulder, eyes closed with lashes splayed over her alabaster cheeks. She was fast asleep.

He watched her for a moment, taking in the scent of her hair. His gaze traced the gentle slope of her nose. The soft breaths rising and falling. He averted his eyes and clenched his fists. *God, help me protect her honor.*

For a brief moment, he considered nudging her upright. For propriety's sake. But he hadn't the heart to wake her.

And you can't bear the thought of not having her so near you.

Sean knew what brewed within him was more than mere attraction for the lass. She was a beauty to behold, aye. But her gentle spirit and the grace with which she had handled the disturbing situations of late filled his heart with compassion. He was falling for the girl, and the harder he resisted, the faster he plunged.

From the way she had looked at him in the dress shop, it seemed perhaps she might also hold some interest in him. He hoped she might one day fully return his affection and this secret—whatever it was—wouldn't sever their chance at a life together.

A life together. Could he be so blessed?

❦

Moira awoke with a jolt. The wagon had stopped and footfalls on the road sped the waking of her mind. She rubbed her eyes.

Sean still sat beside her, eyes sparkling, a sweet smile on his face. "Mornin', sunshine. Well, evenin', I guess." He winked and her heart melted. Then realization dawned. She had fallen asleep against his shoulder. She clapped a hand to her forehead, mouth agape.

"I . . . uh . . . I . . ." Utterly mortified, words of explanation failed her.

"Easy now, pet." Mrs. McGonigle comforted her from the front seat. "There was no impropriety. Many a folk succumb to the lullaby of the Seven Sisters. Paddy and me were wide awake and yer man here was a perfect gentleman." She patted a compassionate hand on Moira's knee and turned to her husband, who helped her out of the carriage.

The tension in Moira's shoulders eased. If only the heat in her cheeks would dissipate with as much haste.

Sean lifted his hand and offered to help her down from the bench. She nodded and bent to place her hands atop his shoulders.

He held her securely at the waist and lifted her as effortlessly as if she were a feather pillow. He set her down and held her just long enough to ensure she was steady on her feet before releasing his grip. He then tugged on the brim of his hat, bidding her good night.

Moira, helpless to look away, watched as he disappeared into the mist.

CHAPTER 25

Áedach and Moira stood face-to-face in her classroom, a scant handbreadth between them. "You will not threaten me again." Moira's voice was firm and low. Her words deliberate. "I have nothing to hide. You hold no power over me."

The wiry lad licked his lips and scanned Moira from head to toe. Her skin prickled under the intensity of his leer.

"Oh, I'll be sayin' what'er I please, marm." The words dripped with rancor. "An' ye have no idea wha' kind o' power I hold over ye." He closed what small gap remained between them in the empty schoolhouse and raised his hand. It hovered just over her shoulder.

Her heart raced and no breath could escape her chest. Moira feared she might faint but refused to allow him the pleasure of seeing her flinch. Instead, she stretched her spine tall, steeling her gaze firmer into his. Seconds stretched into eternity as the silence hung around them like a shroud. He lowered his hand but traced the contour of her body in the air, unhurried.

Despite her best efforts, Moira shuddered.

"Perhaps we should see how far the apple falls from the family tree? See if ye folluh in yer mammy's footsteps, like?" He bit his bottom lip and leaned closer. Fearing he might attempt to kiss her, Moira lunged to the side, managing to free herself from his imposing stance.

"You spew venom and folly!" She hastened to the door of the schoolhouse and opened it. "I don't know what you hope to achieve with this lunacy, Áedach, but God will deal with you and your lying ways." She whipped her index finger toward the door.

A shadow smacking of fear flashed across Áedach's face. He stuffed clenched fists in his pockets and sauntered toward the open door, but a sickening smirk grew on his lips. He stopped in front of her.

Moira gritted her teeth and tightened her grip on the handle, prepared to swing the door into the lad's head should he try anything more than a passing nod.

"We'll see now, marm. We'll see."

Moira watched the bones of his spine sway through his threadbare shirt as he sauntered outside.

As Áedach's outline disappeared around the corner, movement across the road caught her eye. Sean.

His arms were laden with all manner of thatching gear. He watched as the troublesome teen departed before turning his attention to Moira, eyebrows raised.

"Are you okay?" he mouthed.

For the first time since the ordeal began, she released a full exhale and tension melted from her shoulders. No, she wasn't okay. When would this end? She wanted nothing more than to run to Sean. To let him shield her from Áedach and secrets and old men with stale drink on their breath.

But she couldn't. She had too much to do to let herself be distracted by a man. And if Áedach's insinuations held any truth, kindling any romance might well be the nail in the coffin of her newly sprouted life in Ballymann. She managed, instead, a weak smile and a slight nod.

Colm's voice carried on the wind, beckoning Sean. His countenance fell, and he looked at the tools and hay in his arms, then back to her. He stole a glance over the hill and took a half step toward the schoolhouse.

"Sean! *Déan deifir!*"

Moira motioned for him to go.

He shrugged, offered a silent "sorry," and dashed off in the direction of Colm's voice.

Overwhelmed by relief and lingering fear, Moira sank back onto the door and sighed. Was she willing to follow through with whatever warning she had just given Áedach? She had been clear that he wasn't to bully her any longer, to be sure. But what would she do if he did?

As deeply as she believed that neither Áedach nor Buach truly held any secrets about her mother, she couldn't shake one nagging question: *What if they do? And what if they're true?* Moira had to find out the truth once and for all, but getting the information would not be easy.

It was clear Bríd and the McGonigle family had at least some idea about what was going on. The only question now was, who would be most likely to divulge knowledge? Moira thought back over her encounters with each person.

From the beginning, Bríd had been an incredible support and help—a comforting mother figure, which Moira needed far more than she had realized. However, each time Buach or the secret came into the conversation, Bríd had dismissed it and shifted the subject.

Paddy, God love him, seemed blissfully ignorant of anything other than groceries and his daughter.

Mrs. McGonigle had been the one to stifle Sinead from saying anything further when they passed Glenveagh Castle on Saturday. It seemed unlikely she would reveal anything.

Sinead, however, seemed to know whatever it was Buach alluded to. She also seemed to assume Moira knew about her mother's history with Glenveagh—and whatever hidden meaning it might carry.

Nerves gnawed at Moira's stomach. She needed to get Sinead to open up to her but feared the girl would believe Moira only wanted to be her friend in order to glean information. Moira desperately wanted a friendship with this lass who brought such life and laughter into every relationship. She also couldn't stomach the idea of cultivating a bond knowing Sinead held knowledge that could prove hurtful to herself or her reputation.

Moira mulled over the delicate balance while she locked the schoolhouse door and turned to head for home. Just as she rounded the corner onto the main road, a breathless ball of skirts and hair flew across the street and grabbed on to her.

"Youse won't believe this, now. Wait 'til I tell ya." Sinead held up her index finger while pressing her other hand to her bodice, swallowing gulps of air. After a moment, she continued. "Mammy says ye can call over to us Sunday evening."

Moira stared at her friend and raised her eyebrows, waiting for the rest of the message.

Sinead only stared back, wide-eyed and grinning, bobbing her head up and down with glee.

"Oh, er, that's lovely, thank you. What time will you be expecting me?"

"What time will yew be expecteeng me," Sinead said, mimicking Moira by using a thick voice to disguise her accent. It was clear the girl was holding back laughter. "Ye don't hafta be so proper, Moira. It's me ye're talkin' to, not Mrs. McGinley. Pop 'round about five o'clock." Her dimples deepened and she gave her friend's cheek a tweak before bustling across the road once more.

Moira stared at her friend, dumbfounded but amused. She'd heard few people other than Sean refer to Mrs.

McGinley, the former teacher. The woman must have gained a reputation for propriety. That certainly hadn't been the reputation Moira had built with her flaws and foibles.

Though she hadn't had the chance to ask additional questions as to the occasion, she was grateful that someone was beginning to accept her in this village. Most people in town ignored her. Or at least they appeared to. But Moira noticed the lingering stares and heard how voices hushed to a whisper when she rounded a corner. Even her own students kept a polite distance when she saw them in the McGonigles' market or at the beach.

Life in Ballymann was proving to be far more lonely than she had anticipated, so the prospect of an evening with a family for which she was growing to care very deeply was salve for her homesick heart.

CHAPTER 26

Sinead had proven scarce following her spontaneous invitation at the start of the week. Moira had planned to broach the subject of her mother's connection to Glenveagh Castle when next she saw her, but her friend had remained unseen. That week had held its share of other disappointments as well, and Moira was anxious to see friendly faces. Despite the low points, the days had held blessings. Áedach had been blissfully absent from school the entire week.

Guilt gnawed at her for the thought. She brushed it away like crumbs from a plate.

As his teacher, Moira should have investigated his absence after the second day. But, truth be told, she was enjoying the quiet pleasure of a classroom without his barbs and threats too much to go out of her way to bring him back.

Forgive me, Lord.

She promised in her heart to investigate if his seat went unfilled yet again on Monday.

The thought of Monday widened her smile. A new start to the week meant the distinct possibility of seeing Sean. After the thatcher's silent and regrettable parting last week following her encounter with Áedach, Moira noticed that

Sean or Colm was always nearby when she arrived at school each day.

One day they were pruning hedges along the roadside. Another found them investigating a questionable section of thatch on the roof of the schoolhouse, though it looked as solid as could be to Moira's untrained eye.

She wondered if the men had taken it upon themselves to watch over her upon discovering Áedach had made a habit of waiting for her in the shadows most mornings. She secretly hoped so.

Grateful for caring friends, Moira gathered the freshly baked scones she'd made to take to the McGonigle family and made her way to Sinead's house.

Moira rounded the corner. Her steps slowed and her mouth fell open. Though it was a modest bungalow with gleaming white walls topped with a clean thatch and a door as black as coal, the house crawled with people. A group of at least two dozen more milled about the property. Smoke curled lazily from pipes. Stout laughter and the lilt of Gaelic conversations melded into a symphony of Irish delight.

Conversations lulled to whispers and feet shuffled this way and that as Moira approached. Men gave a slight tip of their caps but refused to look her in the eye. Women dipped shallow curtsies and mumbled, "*A Mhúinteoir*" as she passed.

"Hello." The word caught in her throat. She nodded in greeting and searched the open door for any sign of a friendly face.

"Moira! Ye came!" Sinead bounded from the bungalow, arms outstretched.

Relief rolled over Moira as she embraced her friend. "So much for a quiet family gathering, eh?"

Sinead's brow furrowed. "Wha'?"

"When you said to come over—"

"Oh, youse thought it would be just ye comin', did ya?" Sinead laughed.

Moira nodded.

"Ah, g'on, now. We gather every Sunday night for the craic."

Finally, a Gaelic word she recognized! "Well, let's hope the craic is mighty, then," Moira declared.

Sinead erupted into breath-stealing guffaws. "Ah, yer a good woman yerself, Moira Darrty." She wrapped a broad arm across Moira's shoulder and led her into the house.

The air inside was thick with smoke, heavy with a blazing turf fire and the heat of far too many bodies stuffed into too small a space. Moira pressed a hand to her cheeks, letting the chill from her walk pass to her already heated face.

Sinead made a few cursory introductions, but Moira was met only with gruff nods and averted eyes.

At her mother's bidding, Sinead scurried off to pour tea, leaving Moira alone in the sea of strangers. An older gentleman nursing a pint of ale was the only one willing to look at her. His face was dour and puckered—from age or a cantankerous personality, she couldn't tell. Moira thought his eyes, squinting in discerning slits, held a gleam that belied his grim expression. The same could not be said for the other parishioners.

Moira fought to hold back the tears stinging her eyes. Did the whole town believe her to be evil? Frustration mounted, and Moira began to think she preferred the loneliness of yet another night in her chalet to the hateful silence thrust upon her here. She had just turned to leave when a voice near the hearth caught her ear.

Craning to see beyond woolen-clad bodies and over a sea of flat caps, Moira caught a glimpse of familiar green eyes. Sean jumped to his feet, putting whatever conversation he was in to an abrupt end.

"Miss Doherty!" He waved and began to navigate the gauntlet of people, making his way toward her. Given the throng pressing in around them, he made it to her side with impressive speed. "How are you?"

Moira scanned the crowd before bringing her gaze back to his. She stood silent for a moment, trying to rein in her thoughts. Why must his eyes be so enchanting?

He inclined his head, brows raised, clearly awaiting her reply.

"Well, this is certainly not what I had in mind when Sinead invited me to call over tonight. Is the entirety of Ballymann in this bungalow?" A nervous laugh escaped her lips.

"Very nearly," he replied. "The McGonigles' Sunday gatherings are the stuff of Donegal legend. I know it's a bit overwhelming now, but just give it a chance. Ye're gonna love it, I promise."

Moira shrugged. "Perhaps. I just can't help but think everyone here hates me." She lowered her voice just above a whisper. "I feel like . . . like perhaps Áedach isn't bluffing. That maybe there is something dark in my past and everyone knows it but me."

Sean's expression was a mixture of compassion and comfort. "If yer mother was anything 'tall like you, there can be no substance to Áedach's—or Buach's—claims." He stepped closer. "And even if there were, it would have no bearing on yer own character."

Moira smiled. "Thank you, Sean. That means a great deal." Her arms ached to wrap themselves around him, letting him protect her forever. Instead, she twisted her fingers and forced herself not to get lost in his eyes. She was discomfited by the intensity of her feelings, and the swiftness with which they had gone from annoyance to attraction.

Thwap! Thwap! Paddy rapped his *shillelagh* on the doorpost. The crowd fell silent as bodies lowered onto creepies, chairs, and whatever empty spot on the floor was available, leaving a space no bigger than a two-foot square in the center of the room. Moira found a stool near the edge of the crowd, and Sean slipped to the back with some of the other men.

The host launched into a swift-spoken Gaelic greeting before turning attention to the dour-faced man Moira had noticed before. The gathering erupted into a rousing round of applause, and whoops and hollers filled the small room.

The old man waved a hand, quieting them. He scanned his audience, mischief lighting up his eyes.

Moira relaxed a mite, despite the less-than-warm welcome she had received from him mere moments earlier. Sinead spotted her across the room and headed toward her friend.

When the silence had stretched to his satisfaction, and the crowd seemed sufficiently bated, he began. "*An Grianan Aileach.*" It sounded like a title.

At once, Sinead's voice was in Moira's ear. "He's telling the story of the Grianan of Aileach. It's an ancient ring fort half a day's ride from here."

Moira nodded. She was completely captivated by the story, though she understood not a word. The crowd, equally drawn in, offered in unison boos and hisses, or alternately cheers and hoorahs. At the tale's end, the packed room exploded in applause and cheers. The dour-faced man, now bearing the slightest of grins, stood, offered a little bow, and hobbled back to his seat in the corner.

"Anois," Paddy called. "*Ceol!*"

As if from nowhere, all manner of instruments materialized. Moira counted three fiddles, two Irish flutes, a bodhrán, and a set of uilleann pipes. Hands clapped and feet tapped as the musicians played a heart-pumping set of reels and jigs. During a particularly rousing reel, driven by a strong bodhrán undertone, a lone figure hopped into the empty space in the middle of the floor. Moira was stunned to see Colm before her, his eyes closed, feet tapping furiously.

Colm's arms dangled loosely and a look of sheer bliss rested on his face. His feet shuffled in a blur with an occasional toe tap or heel scrape punctuating a phrase in the music. It had been ages since Moira had seen anyone perform a traditional *Sean Nós* dance, and she was drawn in heart and soul. The song finished and Colm ended his dance with a flourish, arms raised over his head in triumph. The crowd offered their appreciation for the show, and Moira joined in the applause.

When the hoopla settled once more, Paddy opened the floor for requests.

"We need a song!" a voice called from the back wall.

"Aye."

"G'on, now."

"Sing us a song, so."

The grocer raised both hands in surrender. "Okee, okee. A song youse want, a song ye'll get."

The crowd cheered in unison.

"But I doubt youse want a song sung by the likes o' me?"

"Nae!"

"Laird, help us, no."

"Who'll ye have, then?" he asked.

Various names were murmured from the crowd, none of which were familiar to Moira.

Then Colm lifted halfway out of his seat and called, "Sean McFadden, sing ye a song."

Moira's gaze flew to Sean, who was leaning up against the wall near the hearth, arms folded across his chest.

He shook his head in protest. But the crowd wouldn't back down. At last, he acquiesced and made his way to the center. Finding a spot in the midpoint of the floor, he settled himself, hands placed comfortably in his pockets, eyes closed, signaling his readiness to begin. The crowd fell silent.

Sean inhaled, and when the first note released into the air, Moira clutched her heart. His voice was like silk on velvet. Masculine yet without the gravelly quality so many men seemed to possess. The song, sung a cappella entirely in Gaelic, was melancholy and beautiful all at once. Moira ached at the sound of it. And never wanted the song to end.

Sudden pain shot through Moira's side, and she turned to the source. Sinead's elbow rammed repeatedly into Moira's ribs. "What?" she whispered to her friend, unable to keep the irritation from her voice.

"No wonder yer man is singin' this song." Her eyes sparkled with delight. "'Tis called '*Bean Dubh a' Ghleanna*—The Dark Woman of the Glen.'"

"It's lovely, but—"

"It's about a dark-haired lass so beautiful," Sinead said, "it makes a man lament. The man canna eat nor sleep until he sees her again. He watches his flocks in the day, but his thoughts are consumed only by her beauty. And although every lad from Donegal to Dublin tries to win her hand, he purposes to make her his bride."

Moira knitted her brows in confusion and stared at Sinead.

Sinead rolled her eyes and held up a tendril of Moira's black hair. "Don' ya see, Moira? He's singin' about ye!"

Moira turned her attention back to Sean. Sinead whispered the English translation of each line in her ear as he sang. Moira's heart quickened, wondering at her friend's prediction. Surely he wasn't singing about her? It was simply a traditional song to which Sean was partial. Wasn't it?

The warmth of his voice filled the air, and the entire crowd seemed just as enchanted as Moira. Heat rose up her neck and radiated to her face, setting her ears on fire.

Inside her, it was as if Colm's feet were dancing, setting her stomach in a delightful, terrifying whirl.

As Sean sang the last line of the song, he opened his eyes and looked at Moira, long and deep.

Sinead whispered the lyrics' final meaning: "'Hoping to win the dark maid's affection.'"

CHAPTER 27

When the music and stories paused for tea and cake, Sinead grabbed Moira by the arm and dragged her outside.

The night smelled like moss and ocean-dampened grasses. The chilled evening air filled every inch of her lungs, refreshing her from the stagnant, ale-infused sauna the house had become.

"Ye *canna* tell me he wasn't singin' to ye." Sinead pulled Moira down to sit on a rock wall.

"Sinead," Moira chided gently.

"No, really," Sinead insisted. "I've seen the way he looks at ye—and ye at him. Ye canna tell me there's not a spark there." She cocked an eyebrow at Moira.

"I won't deny he's very handsome. And kind. And incredibly strong. But he's given me no reason to believe he carries any real feelings for me."

"Oh, really?" Sinead scoffed. "Ya mean a heartfelt serenade in front o' the whole village isn't reason enough?"

Moira opened her mouth to retort, only to snap it shut again. She shrugged. "You don't *know* that he was singing about me, that's all."

"Whatever you say." Sinead slumped, clearly growing tired of arguing about it.

The pair sat in silence for a moment, enjoying the brisk-ness of the night. Inside, men bantered among themselves, women chattered happily between sips of tea and bites of cake. The occasional bleating of a sheep in the distance floated through the air. Moira thought for a moment this place could really be home but then remembered the recep-tion she'd received so far. It should have been a peaceful time, but inside Moira was in turmoil.

Despite the magical evening, the fact remained there was a secret looming over her, threatening her livelihood. After all, if the people of Ballymann couldn't trust her, how was she to ever earn the right to help shepherd their children? Out here in the quiet of night, away from the bustle of the crowd inside, it seemed the perfect time to broach the subject. She swallowed hard, attempting to bolster enough courage to ask Sinead about her mother.

Moira broke the silence and cleared her throat. "So, back in the Poisoned Glen, you said I should know more about Glenveagh. What did you mean?"

"Oh, nothing, really." Sinead's voice was light and breezy. "Just that I figured since yer mam had worked there all those years, you knew everythin'." She turned her gaze away, as if realizing she had said too much.

"Well, Mother never really talked about that part of her life. I vaguely recall her saying she had been a member of a household staff. But she never told me where, or what exactly she did." Moira hoped this would encourage Sinead to open up further about what she knew, but the girl simply sat staring blankly into the darkness. Moira continued. "I'd love to hear more about it though. Glenveagh Castle? It sounds utterly enchanting!"

Unable to contain herself, Sinead bubbled over with ex-citement. "Oh, 'tis grand, you can believe tha'. The gardens are so expansive, full of every color of flower you could imagine. And, wait 'til I tell ya, it's got a pool! That's right. It's right down there on the level with Loch Veagh, so you can sit in the pool and reach out and stick yer hands right in the lake."

"Oh, that does sound enchanting! So, my mother was on the household staff there?"

"Oh yes, she was one of their best. Second only to the head-mistress. At least, according to Mammy, anyway." Sinead's eyes rolled upward, as though playing back a conversation in her mind, and then she nodded as if to reassure herself she had remembered correctly. "In her final months at Glenveagh, she'd been promoted to head chambermaid. She was responsible for makin' sure wha'ever the visiting bigwigs needed in their rooms was provided quickly and efficiently."

Rather than being satiated, Moira's appetite for information was only further roused by Sinead's account. Why would Mother hide such things from her? Did she truly hide them, or simply fail to mention them? And how did Sinead know all of this? "Well, that's delightful. I'm so proud to hear she was so well respected. Here I was worried there might be something more sinister to the tale."

Sinead slid from the wall and paced back and forth in front of Moira, her hands bobbing up and down. She chewed her lip with such vigor Moira feared the girl might draw blood.

Sinead's nervous behavior confirmed Moira's suspicions, and fueled her to press further. "What is it, Sinead?"

The girl gave a quick but violent shake of her head.

"Please," Moira implored. "You know you can tell me anything. I promise not to be cross with you."

Sinead's eyes tracked to the open door of her bungalow. Inside, Mrs. McGonigle bustled about clearing teacups and plates of half-eaten cake. "Is it your mother? Are you worried she'll be upset if you tell me?"

Sinead's eyes fell to hers. They were glassy and wet, and her bottom lip trembled. She nodded ever so slightly.

Moira rose and clasped her friend's hands in her own. "Dear, sweet Sinead. I would never wish you trouble at home." She paused and wiped a tear from the girl's fleshy cheek. "But . . . I need to know what happened. Why is the whole of Ballymann treating me as if I'm unclean?" Moira's lip quivered now, and she searched Sinead's eyes through fresh tears of her own.

At Sinead's bidding, the pair increased their distance from the open door—and away from Mrs. McGonigle's ever-listening ears. Sinead wiped her cheeks with her apron, steadied herself with a breath, and began. "Moira, ye're not gonna like this. But, word 'round the parish is that yer mam—" Sinead looked past Moira into the darkness.

Moira squeezed her hand, willing her to continue.

"You see, folk say she had a . . . a moment of indiscretion with John Adair. He's the son of the family who owns Glenveagh."

Moira recoiled. "'Indiscretion'?"

Sinead nodded. "Someone discovered her in his chambers. With him."

Moira leaned against a rock wall and dropped her elbows to her knees. A thick, warm hand lay on her back and rubbed, but it imparted not even a modicum of comfort. "It can't be," Moira whispered. "It can't." She lifted her head and searched Sinead's eyes. She found no lie or embellishment. Sinead spoke truth.

"I'm sorry, Moira." Sinead pulled her into a tight hug. "But, ehm, there's more."

Moira pushed out of her embrace, shaking her head. "How can there be *more*?" As she heard the words coming from her mouth, a sickening feeling wormed into the depths of her heart. She pressed a hand to her belly, the realization of what Sinead would say dawning.

"When ye showed up here, Moira . . . ye're of the right age. And folk began to piece it together." She nibbled her fingernail. "Ya see, yer mam left Donegal in such a rush, and it was about that time it came to light of her . . . of what happened. The rumor mill was flyin' anyway. But when they saw yer face arrive in town, they knew it must be true."

Moira pressed her palms onto the top of the rock wall. Cold seeped up her skin, and the moss pressing against her skirt soaked it with dew. But she didn't care. Images flooded her mind of all the times she'd seen her mother in the wingback chair in their sitting room in Boston, Bible open across her lap—with the pages tattered and dog-eared from decades of use.

This can't be true. Bile rose to the back of her throat. She swallowed it down, the vile burn trailing all the way.

"I'm sorry, Moira. I wish it weren't true." Sinead's voice was thick with sorrow. "An' I'm sorry ya had to hear it from me." She offered a soft pat on Moira's shoulder, but when Moira gave no response, she walked away in silence, head and shoulders slumped low.

"I wish I'd never asked," Moira whispered to the night between soft, silent sobs.

CHAPTER 28

On Monday evening, Moira's head pounded as she trudged along the narrow side street leading away from the village center. If the main road had seemed little more than a back alley when she had arrived in Ballymann, this road—if it could even be called that—was naught more than a widened footpath.

The news from the previous night, still raw in her heart and mind, weighed her down in heavy shackles of dread and doubt. Surely Mother wouldn't be party to such a scandal?

Moira stooped and plucked a lone shamrock from the middle of the path, twirling it absently between her fingers. Studying its delicate leaves, she marveled at the tiny thing's tenacity and sturdiness, how it managed to grow in the last place it seemed to belong.

I know how you feel, wee thing.

As she rose again, the weight of her mother's history threatened to pull her down again. Much as it pained her to admit, the timing did seem to fit. And it would certainly explain why Mother had shared so little of her life here with Moira. And what about her dear father? She'd doted on him so—and he on her—before sickness had taken him from them far too soon. Was he even her real father? She shook her head, trying to dislodge the thoughts before they could take root.

"I refuse to believe it," she told the patchwork of fields surrounding her. She straightened her apron and forced her mind to focus on her errand.

It shouldn't be too much farther now. Little Aoife had given Moira the directions to Áedach's house. The lad had been away from school for a whole week now. Despite the glorious peace his absence provided, as his teacher it was Moira's responsibility to ensure her students were well educated. It was hard to educate them when they failed to show. Besides, getting a glimpse into his family life might provide some insight into how to handle his disruptive behavior.

Disruptive? Ha! Moira had long since realized his behavior had moved well beyond disruptive and bordered on violent.

She crested a hill. To her right towered the large oak tree Aoife had described. Standing a few feet from the side of the road, its roots poked up from underneath the rock wall that shared its space. This had to be the place.

Moira halted her steps and stared in disbelief. Surely this was not the boy's home?

The hovel of rocks stacked into a ramshackle structure stood—just barely—at the base of the tree. Shocks of thatch— probably taken from Sean and Colm's supply when their backs were turned—were stuffed, helter-skelter, between rocks and laid over the top for a makeshift roof. The foliage from the lofty oak no doubt provided even more coverage—in late spring and summer months, anyway. Today, though, the tree was bare.

Moira pressed the flat of her hand against her stomach. If this was his home, it was no wonder he looked and dressed the way he did. With careful steps she crossed the road, the shamrock in her fingers now forgotten and abandoned to the ground.

"Áedach?" Her voice quavered before threatening to disappear altogether. She didn't know if she wished he would answer or not. As she neared the wall, the stench of urine, smoke, and drink assaulted her. Reaching into the cuff of her sleeve, she retrieved her handkerchief. She didn't take time to admire the dainty needlepoint flowers her mother had embroidered on the corner, along with Moira's initials. Rather, she stuffed the cloth under her nose and climbed over the wall, taking care not to topple the stones that had surely withstood centuries of gales.

A length of bark slathered in tar was propped over the opening of the shanty. "Áedach," she called again. A low groan rumbled from inside. Was that human or animal?

Moira bit her lip and looked around to see if anyone else was nearby. How foolish she was to come alone! Even if there was no element of danger, it was inappropriate for a single lady to be in the home of a young man without a chaperone.

She had assumed his parents would be home, so impropriety hadn't crossed her mind. And if she was honest, she knew no one would have agreed to come with her. In fact, they likely would have attempted to dissuade Moira from coming at all—which was why she had asked a child for directions to this place.

There was naught to be done now, though, save press on. She had called his name twice, and he had answered—at least something had responded. If she left now without completing her errand, she feared he might think she was taunting him. Besides, her curiosity was piqued. She needed to see how the lad survived in such squalor.

Her trembling hand reached for the primitive door. Once more a groan emanated from within, followed by an alarming cough. All thoughts of propriety and danger flew from her mind, and Moira removed the door from its place and stepped inside, ducking to keep from disturbing the roof.

Her stomach lurched at the reek that welcomed her. She willed herself, and her lunch, stable. The room was dark, and for a moment blackness was all she could see. As the dismal picture came into view, she fought to keep at bay the tears welling.

A pitiful pile of ashes smoldered in one corner, the so-called wall behind it scorched black from years of daily fires, she assumed. Along the opposite wall, which consisted of the rock wall and trunk of the oak, Áedach lay on a pile of rubbish, dried grass, and seaweed.

He was curled in a ball, and even in the poor light Moira could see he was dreadfully pale. His body convulsed as a hacking cough sliced the air. With his feet bare and filthy, and his clothes thinned and torn, Moira now saw him for the child he truly was. Here, in this moment, he was no more a threat to her than a blind kitten. Even as she crouched inside the low shanty, she towered above him. Her state of power over him was not lost on her.

Moira knelt on the ground beside him and tried to ignore the dank liquid seeping through her skirts. She chose to believe it was merely earth damp and not something viler. She cocked her head to look square at his eyes. They were mere slits, not focused on anything in particular.

"Áedach," she whispered, "it's Miss Doherty. Can you hear me?"

The lad lay still, but a slight blink of his eyes caught Moira's attention. She rose quickly and poked her head out of the opening, once more surveying the landscape for anyone who might be of assistance. There was no one.

If only Ballymann boasted a doctor. Then I could turn the lad over to him and be done with it.

Alas, no doctor was to be had. Moira inwardly scolded herself for even getting into this situation in the first place.

There was no way to discern what sort of aid the lad required without first discovering the severity of his illness. She knelt at his side again. "I'm going to place my hand on your forehead." She paused, studying his grimy hair and dirty face, loath to bring herself to touch him. "I must see how high your temperature is."

Another pause. Then a blink.

She placed her hand across his forehead, and gasped. He was at least as hot as a fresh cup of tea, and his skin was dry as a bone. With her other hand she grasped Áedach's fingers, then his toes. Ice cold.

"How long have you been like this?" The concern she heard in her own voice surprised her. No blink followed the silence this time. "Have you been ill this whole week?" More stillness. She placed the palm of her hand on his chest. His breaths were shallow and labored. Harsh rattles accompanied each exhale.

Moira removed her cape and laid it across the boy. The danger of covering a fevered body with too many blankets sprang into her mind. As a child, she had heard stories of neighbors who had died from such treatment. However, the lad needed some kind of covering, or the elements would surely do him in.

"I'm going to go find some help."

Silence. A blink. His rib cage rose. She thought he might try to speak. Instead, another splitting cough broke the silence and violent convulsions rocked him. Moira's eyes burned. From tears, the stench, or shock she could not tell. She backed out of the shelter before hopping the wall and sprinting up the lane.

"I'll not be long before I return," she called over her shoulder. As she neared the main road, a vision of Áedach cornering her in the schoolroom flashed across her mind's eye. Her sprint slowed to a jog. The memory of his putrid breath on her face as he spoke his vile words snaked its way through her thoughts. Her jog slowed to a walk.

"Ye have no idea wha' kind o' power I hold over ye." His words echoed through the deepest recesses of her being. Her feet stilled and she stood static as a stone. She surveyed the rugged Atlantic before her. But she saw instead Áedach's eyes. Not the cloudy eyes she had observed today but the icy, ire-filled eyes from a week ago. Her body tensed at the mere thought of their last encounter, the fear strangling her once more.

She shuddered at the thought of his hands on her, his eyes looking over her like an animal to be tamed. He didn't deserve her mercy. He deserved to . . .

Moira clasped a hand over her mouth, terrified at the direction her thoughts were taking. Never before had she wished ill against another, yet the thought came so easily in regard to Áedach. She had truly feared for her safety that day alone with him in the schoolhouse. It was no secret the lad not only hated her but also wished to harm her—and wished it by his own hand. It would be unwise of her to help him return to health just so he could continue his quest. Would it not?

"God help me." She groaned, wrapping her arms around her trunk. Hugging against the cold, aye, but also holding back the anguish roiling within.

The clouds parted over the water and the sun gleamed over the lapping waves. But the sight did nothing to bolster her spirits. Guilt joined the cesspool of emotions as she turned for home. Áedach needed immediate aid, and she was the only one who could provide it—the only one yet aware—and likely the only one who would care.

But even her caring seemed far paler than it ought to have been.

CHAPTER 29

As she turned up the path to her door, Moira heard muffled voices coming from behind her house. She froze, her heart lodged in her throat. Instinct told her to run. Her feet, however, refused to move. Her main adversary lay helpless in a hovel half a mile away. Who else could it be?

Buach?

At that moment two heads—one topped with a tweed flat cap, the other a mop of chestnut brown hair—popped up over the ridge of her roof.

"Why, greetin's to ye, Miss Doherty," Colm called down.

"Are you alright?" Sean's brow furrowed. "Ya look as if you've seen a ghost."

A spark of anger kindled inside Moira at the fright they'd just given her, but it fizzled just as quickly as it had come, replaced by a tidal wave of relief to see her friends.

"Well, you lads did startle me." The words tumbled out of her, mixing with nervous laughter. "Whatever are you doing? The roof isn't leaking again, is it?"

Colm's sun-worn face crinkled with a smile. "No, no, she's all sound for ya, Miss. We simply like to check up a week or two after a job, jus' to make sure it's holdin' up well."

The two men worked their way down and soon appeared

around the north corner of the house. "I'm headin' home," Colm said. "You'll be along shortly, Sean?"

"Yes, sir."

"Could I make you a cup of tea?" Moira offered.

"I'd best not stay either." Sean met Moira's eyes. "Are ya sure you're alright? I get the feelin' there's something more than just a startle from two auld thatchers."

Oh, Sean, if only I could tell you.

Never had her heart ached so deeply for a sympathetic ear. Her visit with Áedach weighed on her already heavy heart. She wanted nothing more than to confide in Sean what she'd just seen, as well as what she'd learned about her mother, to talk through the possibilities and logic of it all. But she couldn't bear the thought of exposing her family's shame and chance seeing even a hint of disappointment in Sean's eyes.

She must have hesitated too long, because Sean stepped closer. "Come now, you know you can tell me anything." His eyes implored her to trust him. She longed to share her heart, bare her soul to him.

Not yet, Sean. It's too risky. She couldn't share the burden of her mother's indiscretions, but perhaps Sean could offer wisdom for her dilemma with Áedach. That would give reason enough for her fallen countenance and would likely appease his curiosity.

"I've learned that Áedach is quite ill. Gravely so, I fear." She didn't offer how she'd come to learn of the lad's condition. "No one else seems to notice his plight. Or indeed if they have taken notice, do not deign to care, nor offer any service to him."

"I see." He tugged at the hair on the crown of his head. "And is that what vexes you so?"

Moira shifted her weight. "Well, now that I know, am I not bound to action?" She searched his eyes, hoping for some wise word to set things right. Part of her hoped he would spur her to care for the lad. Part of her silently pleaded with him to say something that would release her conscience from such a duty.

"I think"—he worked the back of his neck and shook his head slowly—"I think . . . perhaps I am not the one to advise ya on such a matter." Irritation colored his voice. His lips formed a thin line, and his hand flopped to his side.

Was he irked with her, that she would seek such guidance from him? Was it his own lack of real authority on the matter? She suddenly regretted asking him at all.

"I see." She stepped closer to her door, but his hand caught her sleeve.

"I've wanted nothing more than to throttle the boy from the first time he dared show ye any fleck of disrespect." He released her sleeve and held his hands out, palms up, as if to convey his own confusion. "I fear that any advice I might give ya would serve my own interests more than his. But if he's as ill as you say . . ."

"Yes, well, thank you for your transparency, Mr. Mc-Fadden. If you'll excuse me, I've had a trying day." She opened the door and stepped over the threshold.

As she closed the door, Sean's voice wafted in its draft, "Good day, then."

The chalet seemed emptier and more silent than usual. She'd checked that the latch locked fully behind her. Áedach may be on his deathbed, but who knew what manner of folk were abroad in this place anymore? She hadn't seen Buach since their unpleasant encounter in Letterkenny. For all she knew he was lurking around the corner, sucking his tooth and waiting for the opportune moment to catch her unawares.

Moira went through the motions of stoking the fire and making a meal for herself. She worked over her lesson plans for the next day. It all felt like an exercise in futility. She despised the fact that her passion for teaching was being snuffed out by the swirling mix of confused feelings about helping her most troublesome student. A knock at the door sent her into the air, scattering the papers in her hands.

Using the door as a shield, she opened it just enough to see who was there. "Colm!" She swung the door wide and resisted the temptation to embrace the dear man. Her gaze then fell upon a lovely woman standing next to him.

Her hair, like tufts of spun cotton, was piled high upon her head. Her cheeks were plump and as rosy as currant jam. She smelled of cakes and rosewater, and the gentleness on her face filled Moira with such warmth she feared she might cry.

"Miss Doherty, this is the missus." Colm glanced at his wife and gave a playful wink. "Peg, I'd like ya to meet Moira Doherty."

Peg grabbed both Moira's hands and pulled her in to place a kiss on both cheeks. "It's truly a pleasure, dear. I've heard so much about ye already from me auld man here."

"The pleasure is all mine, Mrs. Sweeny."

"*Tsk!* Nuy, nuy, me name's Peg." She shook her head merrily, which set her hair wobbling like a plate of cream custard.

"Right. Peg it is, then. Please, do come in." The group made their way into the heart of the room. "Is there something I can help you with?"

Colm cleared his throat. "Well, I'm a bit embarrassed to say this to ye, but I canna help but give ye my two pence worth of advice."

Moira knitted her brows, confused. "On what subject?"

He removed his cap and spun it in his hands. "I swear to ye, I wasn't spyin' on youse. But I . . . I heard what ye said to Sean. About Áedach."

"Oh." Moira slumped onto the edge of her table.

He must think me cruel. Or daft. Or both.

"Ye're a kind lass, that much I can see straightaway," Colm said. "And I know ye must be truly torn. I know how the lad has been to ya."

You don't know the half of it.

"Ye need to ask yerself," he continued, "if you're truly willing to let another human being suffer 'cause of his wrongdoin's toward ye."

To hear it said plainly in that way sent a shock of remorse through her. Moira buried her face in her hands. Was she truly capable of turning her back on someone in need, no matter how vile? She believed not. But to think of extending mercy to the lad drove bile to the back of her throat, burning as fiercely as her heart. She'd had no trouble having compassion the moment she saw Áedach lying helpless and dying in that squalid hole. Now, though, helping him seemed an impossible task.

All she could see in this moment was what he had stolen from her. The innocence he had nearly ripped from her reputation, the steadfast trust in her own mother he had taken from her. Áedach had robbed her of everything that mattered. How was she supposed to throw all that aside, risking exposure to his illness, to help him?

Peg moved next to her. "Ya see, none of us desairves grace. That's why it's called grace." She ran a gentle hand over Moira's shoulder.

"I don't blame ye fer being hesitant to come to his aid," Colm said. "Just know that if ye decide to help, Peg and I will be there with ye, each step of the way. And iffen ye don't . . . we'll see to the lad."

Peg squeezed Moira's hand. "After all, we're God's children too."

The woman's words hung in the air for a moment before she bussed the top of Moira's head and the pair took their leave. *"We're God's children too."* The words echoed in Moira's mind.

"If I'm Your child, why are You allowing me to be in this situation?" She groaned the audible prayer when alone once again. When her prayer was met with silence—no sense of peace, no still, small voice in her spirit uttering an answer—she shoved thoughts of compassion and mercy out of her mind.

CHAPTER 30

Moira stirred the morning's dying embers, hoping to revive them enough to heat a pot of water. With the back of her hand she wiped beads of sweat from her forehead, then her upper lip. She pretended not to notice her hand quivering as it stoked the ashes with the poker she kept near the fireplace. She told herself everything was fine. When the cinders refused to cooperate, she slumped back onto her haunches, exasperated.

Everything was not fine, and the dream from which she'd awoken only magnified that fact. In the dream, she'd flashed from one scene to the next, starting with Áedach's face, pale and gaunt, staring into the distance. Suddenly there he was, strong and healthy as ever, pinning her to the desk at school with hand a poised over her chest. One after another the haunting scenes assaulted her slumbering mind, echoes of his maniacal laughter swimming in the background, when a new voice broke through the din.

"Father, forgive them; for they know not what they do."

Then all went black and silence settled over the dream world. A blinding flash broke the darkness, and before her was a hill, shadowed in the dusk of a storm-filled sky. Silhouettes of three crosses divided horizon from heavens, when the image of Áedach's face floated across the scene. That was the scene that startled Moira awake, drenched in sweat and panting.

As she sat now on the floor in front of the hearth, the early morning chill spreading as quickly as the heat from the hearth was fading, she knew the meaning of the dream. She knew none was worthy of grace; none able to earn through any scheme of man the salvation offered through the sacrifice of the cross. But what of the voice? Was it simply a reminder of Christ's unconditional love? Or was there more to it? Did Áedach not truly understand what he was doing? Was there more to the story than was apparent?

Grace and judgment parried in a cruel tug-of-war for Moira's heart. She desired above all else to love God well, and to serve Him the whole of her life. But could she do so if it required such sacrifice? She threw herself facedown on the floor and cried out to God.

"Help me, Father! Give me the strength to do what is right in Your eyes." She lay there, prostrate and praying, until the words would no longer come. Her sobs slowed and her breathing returned to a normal pace. She pushed herself to standing, resolve slowly edging into the place where anger tried so desperately to remain.

As she had been praying, the truth of what God was asking of her grew stronger. She was still angry at Áedach for what he had done to her. And uncertainty of his intentions once he regained his health still sat like a rock in the pit of her stomach. But she determined, insomuch as was in her power, to not withhold the same grace that had been offered her. It would take time for her feelings to catch up to her resolve, if they ever did.

Please God, let my heart not remain hardened.

The sun was just peeking over the top of Mount Errigal when Moira set out for the market to purchase some carrageen moss. She had learned from her mother that tea made from the dried seaweed could soothe sore throats, and a heated poultice of the plant laid across the chest could calm coughs. It would be easy enough to gather carrageen herself down on the shores of Ballymann, but she had neither the time nor patience to dry it. Her earlier visits to the McGonigles' market revealed she could fetch it already dried there, saving her both time and headache.

The enticing aroma of freshly baked brown bread and scones sent her stomach rumbling, even though she had only just finished her own breakfast.

"Hello? Sinead?" She wove between the flour sacks and barrels of produce, making her way to the back counter.

"Weel, if it isn't Moora Darrty!" Sinead came out from behind the counter and greeted Moira with a gentle embrace. "I was afraid ye'd never speak to me again after I said such awful t'ings about yer mam."

Moira winced. "I admit, it was quite painful to hear, but I hold you no more responsible than myself for such stories. You were only conveying what you'd heard."

Sinead's shoulders fell, and her whole body seemed relieved at Moira's words. "I'm so grateful, Moira. What can I do for ya?"

"I've come looking for some dried carrageen, and cheesecloth for a poultice."

Sinead's eyes widened, and she laid a hand on Moira's shoulder. "Ye're not ill, are ya? I'll do all I can ta help ya."

"No, no, I'm just fine." Moira chuckled, touched by her friend's concern. "One of my students has fallen precariously ill."

"Oh, gracious, that's a shame." Sinead quickly set about gathering the needed items. "I'll throw in some fresh lemons.

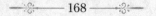

If ya plan to make a tea with the carrageen, lemon helps cut the bitterness." In no time at all, Sinead was back at Moira's side with the needed supplies, plus a small loaf of bread. "If ya need help, I can come with on yer errand. What are the child's symptoms?"

When Moira told her of the high fever, strident cough, and sallow skin, Sinead nearly dropped the goods in her hands. "God seeve us, it's back!"

Moira relieved her friend of the seaweed, lemons, and bread, lest they tumble to the floor. What on earth had the girl so shaken? "What's back? What do you mean?"

"Hardly two years back, a plague fell on this land like none have seen since the Great Famine." Fear clouded her eyes, and she paced back and forth as she spoke. "Folk say it was brought to our shores from the men who fought in the Great War. Others say 'twas the wrath of God. At any rate, it was awful. Countless died, and nothin' could bring any cure or relief." Sinead stopped her pacing and looked Moira straight in the eye. "Ya canna help the child, Moira. Ya canna. It's too dangerous fer yerself."

"But it seems like he has no one else to care for him. I can't just leave him to die." The conviction in her own voice surprised Moira, given she was still wrestling with taking action at all.

Sinead's eyes rolled upward as though searching her mind for information. Then she leveled her gaze back at Moira. When she spoke again, her voice was low and her speech slow and measured. "Just who is this child?"

Moira tried to think quickly, but her mind was like molasses on a cold day. What would her friend think of her bringing aid to her nemesis? Try as she might, she could not think of any reason to give an answer other than the truth. She heaved a sigh and gave her answer to Sinead's feet, too embarrassed to look her in the eye. "Áedach MacSuibhne."

Sinead snatched the bread and lemons from Moira's hands. "I'll not do a t'ing to help that scallywag. That lad's been naught but trouble for this village. If he's ill enough to pass from this world to the next, I say good riddance."

Moira fell back a step, shocked at her friend's vehement response—and sickened to see its similarity to that which was still searching to place roots in her own heart. "I don't believe that. I know the lad is troubled, but that's all the more reason he needs someone to show him kindness."

"*Wheesht!* Listen to ye, miss high and mighty! Well, ye do what ye will. But if ye're to be 'round the likes o' him, ye can stay away from the likes o' me."

Tears stung Moira's eyes as she searched for a response to the venomous change in Sinead's demeanor. "You can't mean that, Sinead."

"I can, an' I do." Sinead dropped the bread and lemons onto the counter and crossed her arms. "If ye're gonna risk yer life for some no-good thief like Áedach MacSuibhne, so be it. But ye won't be bringin' his illness 'round me, or this shop. So ye just do what ye must and be on yer way."

Moira laid the money for the carrageen and cheesecloth on the counter and left in silence. She had known people would likely disagree with her decision, but she had no idea it would alienate her from those she had come to love most. She couldn't deny still sharing some of Sinead's animosity toward Áedach but also could no longer deny her call to obedience. She lifted her chin, squared her shoulders, and set a determined pace out of the shop, ready to do what she knew she was meant to do.

CHAPTER 31

As she made her way to the narrow lane where Áedach lay waiting for help, Moira tried to rein in her thoughts. She passed the pub with its dirty windows and black smoke ever curling from the chimney skyward. She was passing the road that led to the parish church, gray and foreboding, when something nagged at her. She stopped and surveyed the land and sea surrounding her. All was quiet except for the bare gorse branches clacking in the brisk Atlantic wind. Something was missing.

She checked the items in her basket. Carrageen, cheesecloth, a jug of hot water, all tucked carefully within the folds of her apron, which served as a basket lining. All was as she had intended.

"If ye decide to help, Peg and I will be there with ye, each step of the way." Colm's words bounded into her mind like a spring lamb on a grassy hill.

"Thank you, Lord, for the reminder," she whispered, dismayed at how close she had come to repeating her mistake of tending to the young lad alone. Colm had once described where he lived—for giving the whereabouts of one's home seemed a required portion of an introductory conversation in Donegal.

"Over the hill beyond the center of town," he'd told her.

The hill wasn't far from her now. Its crest loomed on the near horizon, and she recognized it as the hill she had ascended on her first day exploring Ballymann.

The journey to the top was just as arduous as it had been the first time, and she was grateful for the downward slope on the other side. Another small road, not unlike the one where Áedach's hovel stood, peeked from behind a holly bush just as the hill flattened out briefly, before starting the ascent of yet another knoll. Thankful for the turn to flat ground, Moira started down the path.

Not more than fifty yards ahead, rising behind a hillock, Moira spotted one of the finest examples of a clean thatch she'd ever seen.

That must *be Colm's place.*

Her steps quickened, and she struggled to keep the basket level as she dashed toward the cottage.

She arrived at the Sweenys' door breathless but excited. Before she could knock on the post, the door swung open. "I was wonderin' when ye'd show." Peg smiled wide, her willowy hair swaying with her.

Moira couldn't hold back the nervous laugh that bubbled within. "Yes, well, I suppose I was a bit slow to come around." Heat crept up her cheeks.

"*Tsk, tsk!* The good Laird works with each of us in His oon way, in His oon time." She patted Moira's shoulder affectionately. "Now, just give me a wee sec and I'll be right as rain and ready to go." She ushered Moira inside and motioned for her to sit in a wooden chair near the door. Peg then scurried around the corner to what was obviously the kitchen, given the decadent scents wafting in her wake.

Humble but bright, the cottage was clean and inviting. Shame nipped at Moira. She hadn't envisioned Colm living in such a quaint and lovely home, let alone married to such a delightfully kind woman.

Maybe I'm the one who knows not what I do.

In a flash, Peg reappeared carrying a large basket. Rounded tops of brown bread peeped over the edge and the strong scent of fresh tea floated in on ringlets of steam. Tucked behind the bread was a stack of lemons, as well as other small bags and containers that were unfamiliar to Moira.

Peg deftly slung a cape across her shoulders with her free hand and nodded for Moira to open the door. The pair stepped out into the brisk spring morning and started for the main road.

"Wait! Wait, my dears!" Colm appeared from behind the house, winded and carrying a small whiskey jug. "Nothin' cures the ails of the Spanish Flu like a bit o' strong whiskey and ginger."

"Och, ya crazy auld man." Peg rolled her eyes, but she took the jug from her husband and pressed a kiss on his cheek.

Colm winked at his wife then turned to Moira. "I've sent Sean to the schoolhouse to tell your other students they can have the day off, Miss Doherty. Give 'em not a worry."

"Oh, thank you, Colm. I completely forgot about the school." A sheepish smile lifted the corners of her lips. "Some teacher, eh?"

Colm waved a hand. "Don't give it another thought. Ye've important work at hand."

After parting from Colm, the women walked in silence for a pace. Moira spoke first. "I can't thank you enough for coming with me, Peg. But . . . how did you know I would do it?"

The old woman turned her face to Moira, the unmistakable twinkle of kindness in her eye. "Ye're a fine lass, Moira. I knew ye'd eventually come around. And even if ya hadn't, I was prepared to visit the lad within the hour."

Peg smiled and Moira relaxed, feeling like she could trust the woman with her life.

"Ah, have ye seen our *halla* yet? There she is. Isn't she lovely?"

Moira followed the direction of Peg's outstretched finger. Her eyes finally fell on a long stone building, its roof thatched just as expertly as the Sweeny home. "My Colm thatched that, so he did." Pride shone on her face. "Along with the church, this is the heart and soul of Ballymann."

Moira slowed her pace as she approached the building with reverence. She pressed her hand on the wall, wishing the cold stones could share their memories. Had her mother rested her hand on this very spot? Moira's throat tightened at the thought of her mother, young and carefree, strolling here with her friends. "It's absolutely beautiful, Peg."

The woman smiled but seemed confused by Moira's intense reaction. "Come now, dear, we must be off. Poor Áedach has waited long enough, aye?"

It pained Moira to leave the hall so soon after discovering it. If she'd only continued on over the hill that first day, she would've stumbled upon the hall ages ago. Now she was finally here and had to leave before even getting to experience it. But she knew Peg was right.

Moira had selfishly let Áedach lay alone for a whole night before deciding to come to his aid. She wished she hadn't promised him that she would return soon. Perhaps the illness had distorted time, making the lad unaware of how long she had truly tarried.

The pair continued on the way toward their patient, silence lending a quieting calm to their journey. Moira knew it was a rare thing to be so comfortable with another human being when no words were being spoken. She tucked the sweet satisfaction away in her heart and smiled to herself as they turned onto the lane where Áedach lay waiting.

CHAPTER 32

It was eerily quiet when Moira and Peg reached the hovel. No hacking cough rent the air, no groans echoed the child's plight to the fields and rock walls. A sickening panic gripped Moira, and she suddenly wished she hadn't waited for her feelings to catch up with her mind.

"Oh, Peg, why did I delay? Pray that my fear and selfishness haven't cost the lad his life."

Peg offered a sympathetic glance and gestured to the door as if to say, "There's only one way to find out."

The stench was nigh unbearable when Peg removed the bark door from its resting place. Pressing her handkerchief to her nose, Moira ducked her head inside the dark room, all the while praying to find the lad alive.

Áedach looked as though he hadn't moved a muscle since Moira left him the evening before, and her ears rang from the silence. With reverent yet timid steps, Moira tiptoed next to him and slowly extended her hand to check his fever. Just before she touched his forehead, Áedach released a growling sigh. Moira screeched and fell back onto the dirt floor.

"Is ever'thing alright, dear?" Peg's voice called, muffled through her own kerchief.

"He's alive," Moira answered. She couldn't help but wonder if Áedach had done it on purpose. To put her in her place.

He lay still and silent once again. If it was a ruse, it was a good one.

"Áedach," she murmured, "I'm going to check your temperature. There's no need to fear."

The lad gave no answer, nor any indication that he either heard or understood what she'd said. His skin was gray. And even though his eyes were closed, Moira could see they were sunken, and purple shadows hung in crescents under them.

She extended her hand once again, this time reaching her mark. Though as dry as a snake's back, he registered even hotter than he had been before. "Peg!" Panicked, Moira called, "It's worse than I thought!"

In an instant, Peg was at her side, unpacking the goods from the basket.

The women abandoned their kerchiefs now. The reek was no less revolting, but both had need of their full capacities. Moira hastily unfolded a square of cheesecloth and poured some of the dry carrageen in the center. She then gathered the corners together and wrapped twine around them before tying the string tightly in a square knot. She placed the pouch into a bowl and poured some of the hot water from her basket onto it, letting it steep.

Peg rolled the lad so that he lay on his back and opened the front of his shirt down to his navel. The tenderness with which Peg worked struck Moira, and tears sprang to her eyes.

Easy, Moira Girl. Focus on the task at hand.

Peg readjusted the cape Moira had left with the lad and nodded at her. "Ready."

Retrieving the poultice from the bowl, Moira wrung the excess water from the bulbous pack and patted it around

Áedach's chest, covering him from shoulder to shoulder and from chin to navel, before setting the carrageen poultice in the center of his chest.

Peg worked deftly to assemble a tincture of the seaweed and hot water. She added a generous dollop of honey and a squeeze of lemon. She poured the liquid into the tip of a baby's bottle and carefully squeezed a few drops into his mouth.

His lips, chapped and peeling, were lifeless and still.

She turned his head to the side, though only slightly. "Ya don't want the *créatúr* ta choke, but we need the tincture ta drain down his throat."

Peg's aged and gentle hand stroked Áedach's hair tenderly, and she hummed a tune Moira couldn't place. As the sweet melody floated in the air, Peg gazed at the ailing boy as though he were her own child, no hint of disgust or judgment on her face.

No longer able to hold them at bay, Moira felt tears spill down her cheeks as she watched the tender scene.

The next half hour passed in much the same way. Peg sang comforting words, stroked Áedach's hair, and occasionally squeezed a few drops of tincture onto his parched tongue. Moira refreshed the poultice with water from the kettle and reapplied the healing herb between trips outside for kindling to feed the fire.

When the tincture was gone and all the heat from the kettle dissipated, the two women prepared to take their leave. There was nothing more they could do.

"Áedach, peata," Peg whispered into his ear, "Moira an' me must be off now. But we'll be back in an hour or two to check on ye."

He neither moved nor spoke, but Peg laid a hand upon his heart and whispered a blessing before gathering her basket and stepping out of doors.

Once outside and a distance from the hovel, Moira slumped against a sturdy oak and breathed in the crisp, fresh air. She smoothed her hair and pressed her kerchief to her face. Caring for the one who had made her short time in Ballymann so painful had not been nearly as difficult as she had anticipated. However, she also knew there was no way she could have done it with the deep tenderness and unconditional compassion with which Peg had cared for him. She raised her eyes to look at the woman standing a few feet away.

Peg's hands were pressed to the small of her back and she arched her chest toward the sky. When Peg straightened at last, she caught Moira watching her.

"What is it, dear?" She absently pressed the back of her hand to the younger woman's cheek, which was growing more flushed by the second.

"Thank you, Peg." The words threatened to catch in Moira's throat.

Peg flapped her hand as though Moira's thanks were a pesky fly buzzing around her face. "Och! Don't be silly."

"No, in earnest." Moira reached for the woman's hand. "I was determined to care for Áedach's health needs . . ." Her voice trailed off as she stared at her feet, scraping an arc in the dirt. "At least, I was after the Lord convinced me thus. But . . . well . . . I would have treated him, yes. I would have done all the same things you did today. But you moved with such compassion, such tenderness. *That* I could not have done on my own."

Peg smiled and patted Moira's hand.

"I don't know that I can say I've forgiven him for what he's done," Moira continued. "But watching you today planted a seed in my heart. A seed of compassion that makes me believe it could be possible . . . and makes me want to act in the same way you did, from now on."

"Oh, sweet Moira." Peg enveloped her in an embrace the likes of which Moira hadn't felt since she'd hugged her own mother. "Ye're a good girl, and ye have a good heart." She backed away and cupped Moira's face in her hands. "A good heart, indeed. The Laird is not finished with ye, dear."

The two stood, smiling at one another with glistening eyes, until Peg said, "Come on, now. Come home wit' me and let's have a cuppa and some stew before our patient has need of us again."

CHAPTER 33

The stew was thick and rich, with a pillowy mound of mashed potatoes spooned onto the center. Its warmth soothed Moira's body as well as her spirit. The pair ate in silence, both enjoying the respite from the dank hovel and the stress of caring for a dying patient. The ticking of the clock and the occasional clink of spoon against bowl were the only sounds, and neither woman seemed to mind.

Suddenly the door burst open and the hearty laughter of two work-tired men filled the air. Peg wiped her mouth, aimed a weary smile at her guest and then her husband, and rose from her seat. "*Fáilte abhaile*, love." She bussed Colm's cheek and took his coat.

Moira rose to greet the man of the house, who was still chuckling along with the mystery guest shadowed behind him. "Hello, Colm—" The words caught in her throat as the other man turned around. "And . . . Mr. McFadden, it's lovely to see you again." She hurried back to her seat, her cheeks burning. She hadn't seen Sean since their disagreement outside her chalet the day before, and the tension, thick as butter, enveloped them.

Sean cleared his throat. "Miss Doherty."

Peg arrived with two fresh, steaming bowls of stew, and the men took their places at the table.

Moira kept her eyes on her bowl, stirring more than eating, annoyed that Sean had robbed her of the appetite for such a delectable dinner.

"So." Colm broke the silence. "How's the patient?" All movement at the table froze, his question hanging in the air like Irish mist.

"Well," Peg ventured, "it doesna look good. The puir lad's temperature is as high as Errigal, and I canna believe that cough of his hasn't already split him in two."

Moira felt Sean's eyes boring into the top of her head, and she wished she could crawl into her bowl and hide under the mash.

"Patient?" Sean queried. "Are ye fine, upstanding ladies caring for one of Ballyman's ailing citizens?" His question was innocent enough, but his voice dripped with sarcasm. It was obvious he knew the pair were caring for Áedach, and he was clearly troubled about it.

Moira's eyes shot up to meet his. "Yes," she answered, a bit more sharply than she'd intended. "As I've told you already, young Áedach MacSuibhne has fallen deathly ill. Peg and I are working to ease his suffering as best we can."

Sean grunted in acknowledgment and shoved his spoon into his dish. He thrust a far-too-large bite into his mouth, sending broth spilling down his chin and onto the table. He wiped the mess with the back of his hand and continued eating.

Moira grimaced. His animal-like disregard for polite dinner decorum disgusted her. An inexplicable desire to goad him overwhelmed her. "Yes," she continued. "And we'll be going back after supper to see to his evening care and ablutions."

Sean's spoon stilled and his eyes slowly raised to meet hers.

Moira shifted uncomfortably in her seat, regretting her impulse to press into his obvious frustration. She was too far into the charade now though. She'd have to hold her ground.

"Well," Sean said at last, finally using his napkin to clean his hands and chin, "just ye be careful out there. It'll be dark soon and ya never know who is lurking in the shadows."

"Now, Sean," Peg crooned as she collected Moira's plate. "Ya know very well we'll be careful. There's no need to put the fear of God into the lass. The Laird has given her a task, and there's nothin' ye can do about it." She punctuated her statement with a stiff nod before heading to the kitchen.

Taking her cue, Moira joined Peg. The pair worked quickly to ready the basket of goods for their final visit to the patient for the night.

⁂

"'Nothin' ye can do about it'? *Humph!*" Sean's boot heels struck the ground in angry steps as he walked home. What was the lass thinking? What could possess her to go out of her way, risking her own health, to nurse the scourge of Ballymann to recovery?

"Sean . . . Sean!" Colm came running up the path, breathless.

Worry seized him, and Sean grasped the man's shoulders as soon as he reached him. "What is it? Is Moira alright?"

Colm stopped short. Even in the moonlight Sean could see the glint in his eyes.

"Aye, I imagine Miss Doherty is right as rain." He held up something in front of Sean. "Ya left in such a tizzy, ya forgot yer hat." A full grin split Colm's face and a hearty guffaw bellowed into the cold night air.

"Oh." Sean snatched the hat from Colm's hands and stuffed it on his head. "Thanks."

"Come now, lad." Colm's voice held no hint of judgment or joking. "What is it that vexes you so?"

Releasing a deep sigh, Sean folded his arms and leaned against the rock wall that lined the side of the street. "Does it not bother ya? Peg lookin' after that . . . that boyo?"

"No," Colm said without hesitation. "Why does it bother ye? No offense, lad, but what business is it of yourn?"

Sean took off his hat and shoved his hand through his hair. "It's not safe, man. Don't ya see? You know what the lad is capable of, how he's treated Moira."

Colm laughed. "Son, the boy is on his deathbed. What sinister deed do you imagine him committin' when he canna lift his own head?"

"That's not the point." A sheep bleated in the distance. "Oh, be quiet with ye!" Sean called into the darkness.

"There's no need beratin' one of God's créatúrs just because ye're upset at—and in love with—a pretty lass."

Sean's mouth fell open and he sputtered, "I . . . what . . . er . . ."

Colm remained silent and pinned Sean with his stare.

"I can't help it, Colm," he said. "I tried to warn her that it wasn't safe, but she just won't listen. It's infuriating!"

Colm's shoulders bounced as he raised a hand to level a steady slap on Sean's back. "Welcome to *na mná*, lad. Welcome to women." He chuckled some more, obviously delighted at his own joke. "In all seriousness, though, Peg was right—the Laird has given this task to Moira. And ye canna stand in her way of obeyin'."

Sean shook his head. "How do ya know it was the Laird, and not some stubborn idea she came up wit' on her own?"

"Ya know yerself the way Áedach has treated her. An' who's to say what else he's tried to do that she hasn't told us about? Would *ye* conjur such an idea if things were turned 'round?"

Sean's shoulders slumped. "My own reaction was to throttle the lad, and I said as much to Moira."

"I know. Ye forget, I heard."

Sean nodded.

"I think," Colm continued, "maybe yer upset more that she didna take yer advice than ye are that she's put herself in any danger."

He didn't want to give the auld man the satisfaction of agreeing with him, but in his heart, Sean knew Colm was right.

"Aye, maybe," Sean managed at length. "But it's not just for the sake of my own ego, ya know."

"Mm-hmm." Colm's head bobbed in the darkness.

"I just want what's best for Moira." Sean hoisted himself off the wall and paced in front of his mentor. "I just don't see how caring for that *rógaire* is what's best for her, command of the good Laird or not."

"Careful, Sean. Ye're standin' on shaky ground wit' that argument." Colm joined Sean on the road and squared himself so they were looking eye to eye. "Smack in the middle of what God is askin' is the best place for any of us to be. I know you want what's best for the lass, but I think yer confusin' the idea of best with the idea of safe."

The words struck Sean with such force he had to steady himself lest he stumble back from the blow. Had Colm always been so wise? Had Sean always been so selfish?

"Thanks, Colm." Sean extended his hand. "Good night."

Colm grasped his arm, holding just below the elbow. "*Oíche mhaith, a mhac.*"

CHAPTER 34

Moira pulled her cloak tighter around her neck and tucked her face against the biting cold. It was a bitter day, and the mist hanging in the air stung her cheeks as she hurried to the schoolhouse. Desperate for the respite of the fire that would soon be roaring in the school's hearth, she jogged the last few yards to the musty old building.

Once inside, she set to work stoking the leftover ashes, bringing the slumbering fire back to life. When was she last here? Days had blurred together, and Moira had been walking through life in a fog thicker than the one suspended outside. She remembered very little of the past week, save caring for Áedach and her dispute with Sean, no longer certain which vexed her more.

As the fire crackled to life, Moira backed up as close as prudence allowed. The heat radiated up her spine, warming her skirts and thawing her aching toes. She hoped it would dispel the mist that seemed to have taken up permanent residence in her mind as well.

Lord, give me strength.

The children would be arriving any moment, and she longed to be fully present, giving them the full of her energy and the attention they deserved.

Down the road, the church bells tolled the first note of their morning song. Moira planted a smile on her face, closed her eyes, and awaited the sound of shuffling feet scurrying up the path.

The bells rang out the final clang, but Moira still stood alone in the schoolroom. She waited. Minutes ticked by. It was typical for one, maybe two students to be tardy, but everyone? Something wasn't right.

She moved to the window, but there was too much condensation to see much of anything. Wiping the pane clear with her sleeve, she looked again. Not a soul could be seen on the path in either direction. Grabbing her cloak, she headed back out of doors.

The biting cold greeted her like a slap in the face. Nevertheless, she pulled the door closed and made her way to the middle of the street. Beyond the church, only a hawthorn tree could be seen on the horizon. As she looked toward town, the silhouette of a cart passed in the mist on the main road, but there were no children as far as the eye could see.

Moira counted on her fingers, reminding herself of the date. To her mind it was Friday, but perhaps in her state of mental fatigue more time had passed than she realized?

She made her way to the McGonigles' shop. A few folks milled about inside, availing themselves of the freshly baked scones or collecting their latest messages. She recognized a few from the Sunday night gathering, which now seemed a lifetime ago.

Mrs. McGonigle rounded the corner with an armload of bread, which she delivered to a waiting patron. The two carried on a brief conversation in Gaelic before the customer left and Mrs. McGonigle wiped her hands on her apron and turned to head back behind the counter.

"Good morning, Mrs. McGonigle."

"Miss Doherty." She gave a curt nod and busied herself moving jars from one shelf to the next.

"It's a soft day," Moira continued, using the phrase Bríd had taught her to refer to the veil of mist outside.

"That it is." Mrs. McGonigle kept her eyes on her task, rearranging the jars a few more times without looking up.

Moira shifted her feet. Why was Mrs. McGonigle being so aloof? She decided to press forward anyway, choosing to believe the woman was merely tired. "Would you be so kind as to tell me what day it is? I'm afraid I have my calendar all jumbled in my mind."

Mrs. McGonigle shot her a wary glance, her brows knitted together—in confusion or annoyance Moira couldn't discern. "'Tis Fridee, lass."

Moira chewed her fingernail. Friday? Then where were all the students? "Do you kno—"

"Is there somethin' I can get fer ya, lass? If not, I'm gonna have to ask ye to make room for the other customers."

Moira blinked hard. Just a week ago she was considered part of the family. What on earth had happened? "I'll take half a loaf of brown bread, please," she managed to say after an uncomfortable pause.

When Moira stepped to the counter to retrieve the bread, Mrs. McGonigle took a marked step backward, holding the rag over her mouth and nose.

More confused than ever, Moira thanked her for the bread, left her money on the counter, and made her way out into the frigid morning.

Perhaps I will find more warmth out there.

On the street, all manner of people milled about—all manner except children—braving the elements in order to take care of business. This sight no longer surprised Moira, as she had learned soon after arriving that if she waited only for good weather to accomplish a task, nothing would ever get done. She decided to circle back to the school in case the students had arrived in her absence. Moira hoped they would have a half-decent explanation for their tardiness.

The schoolhouse was dark and quiet, save for a slight orange glow that could be seen through the foggy windows. No children loitered. None came up the path. Utterly perplexed, Moira headed back to the main road to go home and drown her confusion in a nice hot cuppa.

Just as she turned the corner, sweet little Aoife came up the walk with her mother. Moira waved excitedly and hurried toward them.

"Aoife!" Moira stopped short in front of the pair and offered a smile. "Mrs. O'Sullivan, how do you do?"

Aoife smiled in return. "A Mhúinteoir!" She stepped out to hug Moira, but her mother grabbed her by the arm and pulled her back, forcing the girl to stand behind her.

"Marm." The woman's sharp voice was kitten-like compared with her glare. She snatched Aoife's hand and nearly dragged the girl across the street.

"Mrs. O'Sullivan? Is everything—"

"We're after bein' late, marm. Leave us be."

Moira couldn't be sure because of the mist, but she thought she saw tears sliding down Aoife's cheek as she offered a shy wave before her mother yanked her around, turning the child's back on Moira.

Moira's free hand slumped to her side and she took her frustration out on the ground with a stamp of her foot. What on earth was happening?

More than solitude and yet another cup of tea alone, Moira needed the company of a good friend. Peg was resting this morning before their planned trip that afternoon to check on Áedach, and Sinead would obviously not welcome her company. She hadn't the energy for the possible row a visit to Sean might spark—not to mention the impropriety of such a call. Her list of possible companions grew thin. Then, through the mist, a beacon of welcome flickered in the dusky light, much as it had the night she'd arrived.

Bríd! Of course! It had been forever since the two had shared a proper visit over a pot of tea. She started toward the guesthouse, her mouth already watering at the thought of Bríd's brown bread. As she raised her hand to knock on the door, her stomach sank.

I hope she'll welcome me.

Bolstering her courage with a deep breath of Irish mist, she knocked and waited.

The door swung open, and Bríd's eyes grew twice their size when she saw Moira. "Oh, peata!" She scooped Moira up in an embrace, the aroma of bacon and bread wafting from her curls. "How are ya, dear? It's been ages. Come in, pet, come in."

She grabbed Moira's hand and led her into the sitting room, where a roaring fire awaited. "How are ya, dear? How're the wee dotes down at the school? Is yer chalet holdin' up well in the spring gales? Wait, don't answer that. First, *cupán tae!*" She spun on her heel and bustled into the kitchen.

Moira helped herself to a seat by the fire—the same seat in which she'd sat her first stormy moments in Donegal. It felt like years since that night. What a comfort to be back.

Bríd burst back into the room with a tray loaded with her famous tea and biscuits and a few slices of brown bread still steaming from the oven. She poured tea into both cups, sat back, and released a contented sigh.

"Now, peata, tell me everything."

Moira sipped her tea and smiled. "Things are never boring in Ballymann, are they?"

Bríd cackled and slapped her knee. "I suppose you could say that. We may look like a sleepy auld village, but there's plenty o' drama to go 'round."

Moira meant to laugh, but it came out as an exhale through her nose that connoted derision more than delight. She regretted it immediately. "You could say that again." She helped herself to a slice of bread, giving herself time to formulate her next words. "One of my students has been ill."

Bríd nodded. "Áedach."

Moira wagged her head. Truly nothing was secret, was it? "Yes. Peg Sweeny and I have been looking after him. I honestly didn't want to. He's been such a bane for me, as you well know." She took another bite, savoring the buttery goodness.

"But ya couldn't verra well let the lad die, right?"

"Exactly!" A cloud of crumbs burst from her lips and she wiped them away, too keen to get her story out to be embarrassed. "Other than Colm, you seem to be the only one who understands that. Sinead McGonigle, who I thought was a good friend, has all but disowned me, and Sean"—she tossed her bread onto her plate—"eh, Mr. McFadden, was quite bothered by the whole notion. Both of them think me daft or naive."

Bríd reached across and patted Moira's arm. "The Laird said to love and pray for our enemies. He didna say 'twould be easy."

Tears threatened to spill into Moira's tea, and she bit her lip so hard trying to keep her composure she tasted blood. "Thank you for understanding," she said at last, her voice a scant whisper.

"Aw, peata, I know you've had a hard time of it since ya arrived here. But God didna bring ya here just to let ya fall. Trust Him and His ways."

"Thank you." Moira pulled a handkerchief from her sleeve and dabbed at her nose. "Maybe you can shed light on something else?"

"Of course, if I can."

"None of my students showed up for school today. Is it a holiday I don't know about?"

Bríd shifted in her seat and shook her head slightly.

"Oh." Moira drew the word out, gathering her thoughts and trying to decide what to ask next. "Almost everyone in town is giving me the cold shoulder. I saw one of my students today—the sweetest little girl—and her mother just about dragged her away from me as though I had the plague."

"Well . . . as far as they're concerned, ya do."

"What?" Moira clanked her teacup down harder than she intended. "What are you talking about? The plague?"

"Steady, lass." Bríd laid a soothing hand on her shoulder. "Have ya heard about the Spanish Flu epidemic that tore through here not too long ago?"

"Yes. Sinead said something about that. My neighbor succumbed to the dreadful disease as well. I hadn't realized it had been so bad everywhere."

"Ya have to understand, Moira, folk are still recovering from that. Not physically, of course, but emotionally. We lost thousands in County Donegal alone." She refilled their tea. "Families were torn apart when they lost husbands, wives, children. It was awful." Bríd's stare brought a poignant pause to her story. "And the death was only the half of it. The treatments were often worse than the illness itself as doctors reverted to the auld ways in a desperate attempt to bring some modicum of relief."

Moira's tea sat untouched, her bread forgotten. "That's terrible."

Bríd nodded, drawing a long drink of tea.

"But . . . what does that have to do with *me*?"

"Moira, dear, don't ya see? If Áedach is in as bad a way as folk say, it could mean the Spanish Flu has returned. You've been spending extended periods of time with the lad. Touching him. Cleaning him." She paused, her eyes searching Moira's. "They're terrified of it happenin' again. They won't do anything to risk exposin' their children."

Moira slumped in her chair, unable to hold back the tears any longer. "Those poor people." Her stomach churned. "I never dreamed that helping Áedach would put anyone but myself at risk."

"*Tsk!*" Bríd retrieved a fresh hankie from her own sleeve and offered it to Moira. "Listen, pet," she continued. "Ya have to do what the Laird directs ya to do. Ya also have to be willing to accept the consequences of yer obedience."

"That sounds funny, 'the consequences of your obedience.'" Moira offered a weak smile. "But I suppose you're right. I don't want to put anyone else at risk, but I can't ignore what God has clearly told me to do."

"So, it's decided then." Bríd raised her teacup high as though toasting. "Ye're to keep on doin' what the Laird told ya, and He'll bring the kiddies back when it's time. *Sláinte.*"

Moira followed suit, raised her cup, and finished the last of her tea with a confident gulp.

CHAPTER 35

The sun had just slipped below the horizon when Moira arrived at Peg's house. She could barely make out the glow from the windows in the murky dusk. As she approached, the terrible sound of coughing sprang from the bungalow. Fear paralyzed her as accusing thoughts accosted her at every turn.

Bríd was right, and now you've sent Peg to her death with your thoughtless plan. You're going to kill the whole village before this is all over. The children are going to get sick and parents will watch their babies die because of Áedach—because of you.

Moira stood outside the door, trembling and frozen with fear. How would she ever forgive herself if Peg succumbed to the same ailment as Áedach? She never would have been exposed if not for Moira's asking for help.

Finally, she could take the hacking, barking coughs no more, and Moira burst into the house, all thoughts of decorum abandoned out of concern for her friend.

"Peg? Peg?" Her calls sounded more like the screech of an eagle than the voice of a friend. Breathless, Moira ripped her damp cloak from her shoulders, her fingers aching with the cold—the same cold ache of dread strangling her heart at the thought of losing her new friend.

"Now, now." Colm appeared from around the corner.

"My Peg is a'right. She's not got what the lad has, so ye can breathe easy. Wish I could say the same fer her though."

"Are you sure she's alright, Colm? She sounds dreadful."

Colm's shoulders shook. "Yer right aboot that." He looked in the direction of the bedroom where Peg lay. "'Tis not the Spanish, Asian, Irish, or any other kind o' flu she has, I assure ye. It's the croup. She gets it with every spring damp."

Before she realized what she was doing, Moira wrapped the man in a hug. "Oh, thanks be to God."

Colm gently patted her back. "Yes, amen to that, miss. Amen to that." Then he tenderly grabbed her shoulders and leveled her straight again. "But just 'cause Peg is sick, that doesna mean young Áedach will go unattended this evening. A cold night like this, he has need of a good fire, broth, and a caring hand more than ever."

Moira furrowed her brow. She didn't disagree but didn't feel comfortable going alone, particularly in the dark.

"Come." Colm beckoned her farther inside. "Warm yerself by the fire and have a cuppa afore ye head out." He led her to an overstuffed wingback chair in front of the fire. A matching chair was opposite, and in it sat Sean.

"Moira." His eyes glowed in the firelight. They held an intensity she'd not seen before.

"Good evening, Mr. McFadden." She nodded and tried to smile politely. What was he doing here? Was he going to try to talk her out of helping again?

"I asked Sean to come here tonight." Colm pulled up a creepie between them. "'Tis clear Áedach needs nursin', perhaps tonight more than ever. I canna go because Peg needs me here. When her coughin' fits get goin', she needs me to help with the steam and such."

"I agreed to go with you," Sean added.

Moira's mouth fell open, and she rushed to shut it. "That's very kind of you, Mr. McFadden. Very kind indeed, but—"

"But nothin'," Colm interrupted. "Ye canna go alone, and no one else will go wit' ye. There's no impropriety to the two o' ye walkin' in public. An' Sean here'll stay on the side of the rock wall opposite the lad's place. He'll hold the torch and keep watch fer animals and the like. He won't breach the wall unless yer in trouble." He stared hard at Sean. "Right?"

Sean cleared his throat. "Em, yes. That's right." His posture softened and he slumped his elbows to his knees, his eyes boring into Moira's. "I was wrong to be so cross with you before, Moira." He took her hand in both of his. "Will you forgive me?"

Heat rose from her fingertips to the top of her head. Her heart beat so loudly in her ears she wasn't sure if he had said anything else. Next to her she could practically feel Colm grinning from ear to ear.

"Yes, Sean, I forgive you."

Sean. He couldn't remember the last time Moira had called him by his first name. A smile spread across his face. "Brilliant, lass." He gave her hand a gentle squeeze and, though it nearly killed him, slowly released it.

Colm smacked his hands together, jolting Sean out of his stupor. "Right, that's settled now, so it is." The old man rose and retrieved something from the mantel. "Peg'd had somethin' a little different in mind fer yer visit this eve, Moira. She hopes ye might be agreeable to carryin' out her plan?"

Moira straightened in her chair and brushed her hands across her skirts. "Yes, of course. What is it?"

"She has all the trimmings for yer poultices and tea and such as usual." He paused and looked slowly from Moira to Sean and back again. "After ye're done with yer medicinal ablutions, she thought ye might read a bit o' the Good Book to the lad." In a slow, reverent motion, he handed a small, black book to Moira. The cover was cracked and worn, the binding of the pages precariously thin.

Moira took the book from Colm as tenderly as if he were handing her a newborn babe. Her cheeks flushed, and she pulled the treasure close to her heart.

"'Tis not a real *Bíobla,* o'course. Ye'd need a horse and cart to drag the family Bible down the road. This here's an auld ledger that Peg took to writing passages and verses in." He shook his head and stared off in the distance, as though he were looking clear into the past. "She said she wanted a way to keep the Book close, so she could always hide it in her heart. It never leaves her apron pocket—except fer tonight."

Moira gasped. "I'd be honored."

A strange feeling welled up inside Sean as he watched Moira's face fill with awe as she thumbed tenderly through the pages. Had he ever held such respect for the Word of God? It had always been held in high regard, sure. But he strained to recall a time when it was as precious to him as it seemed to be to Moira in this moment. If his love for her wasn't cemented before, it was now. He loved the girl, heart and soul, and asked God to help him treasure his faith like she did.

"That's lovely, Colm, truly." Sean stood and headed to fetch his coat and Moira's cloak. "We'd best be off before time escapes any further."

Moira rose and placed a tender kiss on Colm's forehead.

Dismayed to find a lump forming in his throat, Sean had to look away.

"We'll take good care of Peg's book, Colm," Moira promised. "You just take good care of Peg."

Moira met Sean in the entryway and turned, allowing him to help her with her cloak. He placed it over her shoulders, resisting the urge to kiss the top of her head, her cheeks, her lips.

Steady now, lad. You have a job to do, and you won't disappoint the lass again.

"Shall we?" She looked up at him and pulled her cloak tight around her neck.

"Yes." He opened the door, welcoming the icy blast. "I believe we shall."

Chapter 36

The air between Moira and Sean wasn't awkward, as she'd anticipated, as they walked the road to Áedach's hovel. She wondered briefly what her mother would think of Sean. She hadn't expected to forgive him so quickly, but when she looked into his eyes and felt his hands engulfing hers, all frustration melted. She knew he had merely wanted to protect her. Truth be told, the sentiment only endeared him to her all the more.

"Thank you for coming tonight."

"Ye're quite welcome." He stopped walking and turned to face her, keeping an appropriate distance between them. "I am truly sorry for trying to stop ya. I shouldna have let my concern for you silence my compassion for someone in need. I didn't realize . . . I didn't realize what it meant to ya."

"In earnest, I had my own reservations about it. Resistance, you might say." She studied the outline of his face in the darkness, the firm line of his jaw softened by the mist and shadow. "What's done is done, and now we move forward. Yes?"

"Yes." His voice was thick, and he ran a hand through his hair.

She continued down the path, hoping to break the spell

JENNIFER DEIBEL

of longing he had seemed to place over her. She ached to
fall into his arms and let him promise her everything was
going to be alright. Never before had she felt such things
about any man. For any man. It both scared and delighted
her. What scared her most, perhaps, was the thought that
her growing affection for Sean would distract her from
what God had brought her here to do. She would care for
Áedach, yes, but surely there was more to why He brought
her so far from home.

At the same time, the idea of fulfilling her callings alongside a man like Sean filled her with giddy excitement and a
deep sense of contentment she could hardly contain. The
two schools of thought continued to war for her heart as
the pair carried on toward Áedach.

All was eerily silent when they arrived. Sean wedged the
flashlight in a hole in the wall and offered her his hand to
help her over.

"I'll be right out here if you need me."

Moira made her way to the makeshift door, rapped on
the stone beside it, and entered.

She made swift work of rekindling the fire, recalling her
first attempts to recycle embers in her cozy chalet. At the
time, she never believed she'd master the task, yet here
she was.

"How are we feeling today, Áedach?"

Again, the lad appeared not to have moved at all since
her last visit. Moira's coat still lay across him, but his breaths
seemed to come without quite as much work, which pleased
Moira greatly. He didn't fight her when she dropped the
tea and carrageen infusion into his mouth, nor when she
worked the poultice over his chest. Whether he was too weak
to protest, too unconscious to notice, or welcomed the aid
was unclear. But Moira was grateful for the ease of work.

"Now, Áedach, I thought I'd read a bit to you, if that's

alright?" She moved closer to the fire for the light, taking care not to get Peg's ledger too close to the flames. Unsure how to find any particular passage or verse, she opened to the first page, and her heart sank. It was all written in Irish. In the dim firelight, she noticed English words in the margins, scrawled as though written very quickly.

Clever, Peg. Thank you.

She ran her fingers over the words, wondering what had prompted Peg to begin this holy undertaking and why she had chosen to start with this particular passage.

How awful that I had not thought to bring God's Word to the boy.

Shame and embarrassment flooded her soul. The all-too-familiar guilt sidled up to her once again, whispering her failures and ripping holes in her faith that God could—or would—use someone like her.

There is therefore now no condemnation to them which are in Christ Jesus. The words floated into her heart like a cool breeze on a hot day.

Moira wasn't perfect. She probably should have thought about reading Scripture to her patient. However, Peg had, and now Moira was here, truth in hand, and she wasn't going to squander the opportunity any further.

Please, God, let Your words fall on open ears.

She cleared her throat and began, "'The Lord is my Shepherd; I shall not want.'" Her throat tightened and tears slid, unbidden, down her cheeks. How long had it been since she'd opened her own Bible? The words were fresh water to her weary soul. Taking a deep breath to steady herself, she continued.

"'He maketh me to lie down in green pastures: he leadeth me beside the still waters. He restoreth my soul: he leadeth me in the paths of righteousness for his name's sake. Yea, though I walk through the valley of the shadow of death, I will fear no evil: for thou art with me; thy rod and thy staff they comfort me. Thou preparest a table before me in the presence of mine enemies: thou anointest my head with oil; my cup runneth over. Surely goodness and mercy shall follow me all the days of my life: and I will dwell in the house of the LORD for ever.'"

Moira closed her eyes, letting the truth wash over her anew. She refreshed the poultice and set about a final round of ministrations for the night.

"You know, Áedach, it's all true. Everything I just read. You're in the valley of the shadow of death right now." She dipped the poultice in the water, squeezed out the excess, and began to pat again. "You may yet be on the brink. Only God knows for sure. But you don't have to fear the evil any longer. I don't know if you can hear me . . . but if you can, think on those things you've heard in the meantime until I return. Let Him comfort you."

She studied his closed, unmoving eyes. His chest rose and fell with greater ease, but his skin was still dreadfully hot and the color of ash.

Oh, Lord, let him be well—so he can know the truth.

It didn't take long for Moira to pack her things. She added more turf to the fire and tucked the coat around her patient. She stepped out the door, then paused and turned back.

"Good night, Áedach. And God bless you."

CHAPTER 37

The hour was late, and Moira's bones ached when she and Sean arrived back at Colm's to return the basket of medicinal items and Peg's beloved ledger. They'd paused their journey only long enough for Moira to thoroughly scrub her hands and forearms, at Sean's insistence.

After one knock, the door swung open and Colm stood before them, one eyebrow raised.

"Well, back so early, are ye? I didn't expect to see the likes o' ye again this night." His expression seemed a mix of doting father whose son had been out too late and genuine concern for the reason they'd been on a mission of mercy.

"We came to return your things . . . Peg's things." Moira held out the items.

"*Tsk, tsk!* Ye just hang on ta those, now, pet. It'll be a few days yet afore my Peg is ready to venture back into the world o' nursing, and ye don't want ta hafta be coming back here every day." He shook his head and gently pressed Moira's hands, and the items in them, toward her. "Now, ye've had a long evenin', I'd wager, and ye'll be needin' yer rest. I trust ye'll get the lass home safe?" He turned his gaze toward Sean.

"What? Oh, yes. I'll make sure Moira is home safe, and

then it's off to me own place. I've a full day of work tomorrow, and my master has no patience for lagging on the job." Sean winked at Colm. The interchange warmed Moira.

"Safe home to ye both." Colm tipped his cap. "I'll give yer love ta Peg."

Sean motioned to the road with a grand sweep of his arm. "After ye, m'lady."

"Why thank you kindly, good sir." She curtsied, and the pair started for her chalet. They walked along in silence. Every now and then Sean would take a breath as though he wanted to say something, but then he'd clamp his mouth shut and grimace slightly. Moira wouldn't have noticed if she hadn't been glancing his way every few steps.

He fixed his cap, dropped his hands to his sides, and worked the back of his neck before finally placing his hands firmly in his pockets.

"So . . . you believe the young man will survive?"

Moira chewed her lip. "As I said when we left him, his breathing was much less labored than before, but his fever is still quite high. As far as I can tell, he's still unconscious. I cannot know."

"Hmm. I heard you reading to him."

She nodded. "I read Psalm 23."

"I know."

"It's been far too long since I've spent any measure of time in the Scriptures," Moira confessed. "I think perhaps I drew more from it than he did."

"Well, I should hope so."

Moira gaped at him, chagrined. What was he implying with a statement like that? After all this, did he still think her a fool?

Sean held up his hands in surrender. "What with the lad bein' unconscious and all, I would hope you'd garner more wisdom from the Good Book than a man in a coma." His smile faded instantly. "I shouldna spoken that way. Áedach may not be a man of integrity, but neither am I, if I treat his suffering lightly."

They continued walking, caught in the somberness of what was not yet over.

At length, Sean said, "Well, here ye are, Miss. Ye're home."

Moira's heart sank. *Already?* "Yes, it appears I am." She turned to face Sean and waited until he looked straight into her eyes. "Thanks again for accompanying me tonight. It means a great deal to me."

His eyes locked on hers and they stood, silent and motionless, both barely breathing. "My pleasure." His voice was thick and rough, and it set Moira's spine tingling.

Sean took a step toward her.

Her heart quickened. She didn't know if she hoped or dreaded that he might kiss her.

Keeping his eyes locked on hers, he slowly leaned toward her. Moira's breath caught in her chest as heat flashed on her cheeks. She wanted to turn away, lest he see the desire in her eyes. But no matter how hard she tried, she couldn't tear her gaze from his. He bent at the waist, gently took her hand in his, and pressed his lips to the back.

Her head spun, and it took all her strength not to melt beneath his touch. He lingered there, his breath warm on her fingers, for just a second before straightening again and releasing her hand. "Good night, fair lady." He backed away with a few slow steps before turning and disappearing into the darkness.

Moira drew her hand to her face, pressing her own lips against the place where his had been mere moments before. The same hands that had served her perceived enemy, Áedach.

She had never been in love before but couldn't imagine a more euphoric feeling than this one. Though not ready to fully admit its depths, she knew in her heart she held more than admiration for Sean McFadden. She stood in the mist longer than was prudent, straining to follow his outline through the fog.

The warmth of the moment eventually faded, and a shiver shook her from her reverie. She went inside, secured the door, stoked the fire, and hung the kettle over the flames. Despite the exhaustion that clung to her bones, she knew sleep would not be swift in coming this night.

As she sipped her tea, she replayed the events of the night over and over again. She remembered the terror that had gripped her at the sound of Peg's cough. The honor that had welled in her heart when Colm handed her the ledger. The fresh sense of compassion as she read Scripture and prayed over Áedach. Her thoughts all swayed together until the entire evening was a swirl of emotions, sounds, and colors. And then. Then the moment that took her most by surprise and would take up residence in her heart as the highlight.

She shivered as she recalled the strength of her desire to feel Sean's kiss upon her lips. And how thoughtful of him to protect her honor—particularly given the current rumor surrounding her origins—by exercising restraint and offering a polite kiss to her hand.

Those were the thoughts that stayed in her mind as she drifted toward sleep—Sean's kindness, thoughtfulness, and the press of his kiss on her skin.

CHAPTER 38

Try as she might, Moira couldn't coax the smile from her face as she walked to the shop the next morning. Tempting though it was to hide and avoid those she knew took umbrage with her helping Áedach, obedience had to be her highest priority. So she walked in confidence, ready to face the "consequences of obedience," as Bríd so perfectly stated. Gratitude swelled for Bríd, who gave her a way to express what was happening in her relationships with those in Ballymann.

As though coordinating with her mood, the weather was bright and pleasant. The air still held a heavy chill, but gone was the mist and fog from the previous day, and the sun shone strong and clear. When she reached the entrance to the McGonigles' shop, Moira paused and took a deep breath, steeling her nerves for whatever assault might await her inside.

"God, give me strength." The prayer was audible only to herself. She entered, taking time to scan the shelves and produce for what she might need. Hushed voices wafted from the back of the store, the women clearly unaware she could hear them. She was eyeing a large tub of dried beans when a whispered phrase caught her attention.

"No right, I tell you." The voice was unfamiliar to Moira. "That lass has no right waltzin' in here, wit' her English an' her ignorance of the auld ways. Now she has the gall to be risking the health o' the whole o' Ballymann? And for what? A good-fer-nothin' scoundrel? *Tsk, tsk!* I don't understand why they would even allow her here to begin wit'."

The words hit Moira like a punch to the gut. Of course, she had questioned her own legitimacy as a replacement for the beloved teacher. But to hear it so bluntly, that the village likely shared such an opinion, caused her to question again what God was thinking when He led her here.

"Now, now." The second voice interrupted Moira's reverie. Mrs. McGonigle. "The gairl didn't know all o' this when she came. Sure, I doubt her mammy even told her why she left Ballymann. Moira's a sweet lass, make no mistake. She's in way over her head, but she's dug her own grave now, an' she'll have to live with the consequences of her choices."

Tears pooled in Moira's eyes, blurring her vision and clouding her thoughts. Until she'd heard her name, she could almost convince herself they might be talking about someone else. There was no denying it now though. She needed to escape. To get out of there before they discovered her and thought she was intentionally eavesdropping. In her haste, she backed into the barrel of dried beans, spilling them with a horrific crash all over the wooden floor.

"Och!" In an instant she was on her hands and knees, scrambling to gather the beans, which had scattered like a herd of cats in a room full of rocking chairs.

"Let me help you, miss." Two masculine hands brushed over hers as they worked to wrangle the wayward beans. Moira lifted her gaze, wiped her eyes with her apron to clear her vision, and found a pair of sapphire eyes staring back at her. A gleaming smile greeted her, along with a mop of perfectly coiffed jet-black hair. All except a wayward strand that insisted on hanging down the stranger's forehead, setting his eyes ablaze in a fire of azure. Her breath caught in her chest and she fell back onto her haunches.

When she attempted to express her gratitude, a jagged mixture of breath and spittle flung forth and landed squarely on the gentleman's nose. Mortified, Moira buried her face in her hands and her words finally materialized. "Oh my goodness, I'm dreadfully sorry." Fumbling with her sleeve, she produced her kerchief and offered it to him, dismayed to see her hand shaking like an oak leaf in a gale.

He accepted the offering and dabbed his face, chuckling. "Please." His voice was dark and smooth. "Don't worry another second about it. Ye're grand, I promise." He offered the used hankie back to Moira and extended his hand. "I'm Declan—Declan O'Malley."

Moira shook his hand, keenly aware every nerve in her body was awake and alive. His gaze drew her in like a hypnotist's watch, and she couldn't tear her attention away.

"And you are?" His brows arched high.

She blinked quickly and shook her head. "Moira." She stared at their hands, oscillating mindlessly up and down in an endless handshake. Yet she couldn't convince her hand to let go. "Moira Doherty. I'm the new teacher here in Ballymann."

"Ah, so ye're the fine lass I've been hearing so much about." His eyes sparkled, and Moira noticed a dimple on his cheek that melted her inside, even as her heart fell.

He's heard about me. Would she never be free of the rumor of her mother's indiscretion in this place?

"I'd heard they'd hired a lass from America," he continued. "I'd not heard she'd arrived though. I'm glad ye're here." He stopped shaking her hand and cupped it with both of his, his thumb gently stroking the back of it.

The action both delighted and unnerved her. Never before had a gentleman been so bold upon first meeting her, but the attention and sensation flooded her with warmth and a sense of importance. A man's touch had never had such an effect on her either—except for Sean's.

Sean! How could she be so foolish, letting a man she had barely met treat her with such familiarity, such audaciousness. Before she could wrangle her hand free of his, another voice entered the mix.

"O'Malley."

Moira and Declan turned in unison to see Sean standing in the entryway of the shop. "McFadden." Declan hopped to his feet and greeted Sean with an embrace and a manly slap on the back. "How are ya, ye auld"—the men glanced at Moira—"eh, ye auld *codger*?"

"I'm grand, now, can't complain." Though he was speaking to Declan, Sean's eyes bored into Moira's. "I didn't know ye were back in Gweedore."

"Well, you know how it is. You've got to get out of the rat race every now and then." Declan's distinct lack of accent stretched and smoothed his words. "I'd had enough of the barrister work for a while and needed to come home to good ol' Donegal for a spell."

"Aha. Well, glad to have ye back. I see ye've met Miss Doherty."

"Yes, Moira and I were just teaching these beans a lesson, weren't we, lass?"

Moira mustered a meek nod.

Sean's jaw worked back and forth, and the whole of his body was stiff as a board. "I can see that. I'll fetch a *scuab*." He headed for the back of the shop, then paused. He turned to Moira. "Declan an' I can take care o' this, Miss Doherty. Ye go ahead about yer business."

Moira hadn't procured any of the groceries for which she had ventured to the shop in the first place, but the look in

Sean's eye stopped her from arguing. "Good day to you both." She lifted the corners of her mouth in a shaky smile. As she turned to go, she nearly walked into Mrs. McGonigle and her conversation companion, who seemed to have witnessed the whole scene between her and Declan. Moira didn't recognize the strange woman. They both shot a glance at one another before mumbling a greeting to Moira. She nodded in return and exited.

Just before the door closed behind her, Moira heard the stranger stage whisper, "The apple don't fall tew far from the tree, now, does it?"

CHAPTER 39

"I'm tellin' ya, Colm, the man's trouble." Sean paced in front of his mentor's fireplace, the skin on the back of his neck raw from the near constant rubbing since he'd left the McGonigle's shop.

Colm patted the table with his meaty hand. "Come, lad." He waved Sean over. "Sit an' have yer tea."

Sean reached the table in two steps and flopped into a seat opposite the man. He took hold of his cup but had no stomach for tea. He slid the cup to the center of the table, splashing the milky liquid onto the wood. It pooled for a moment before soaking in, Sean watching it the whole time.

Colm's eyes were as wide as saucers. "Good grief, now I know 'tis serious if ye won't take yer tea!" A hearty laugh bubbled out of his mouth, and he gave Sean a playful nudge. But there was no laughing for Sean on this day.

"'Tis serious, man! O'Malley's no good, I'm tellin' ya. Ya know yourself what he was like as a boyo."

Colm nodded, pursing his lips in thought. "Aye." He drew a long drink of tea and sat back. "Declan had his fair share of wild oats to sow, but that doesna mean there's more left in his pouch."

Sean remained unconvinced.

Colm cocked an eyebrow. "So, ye're tellin' me that ye're the same lad ye were ten years back?"

Sean threw his hands up, exasperated. "C'mon, Colm, that's not fair and ye know it. 'Course I'm different. I've grown. Changed."

Colm nodded emphatically. "Agreed."

"I know what ye're tryin' to say, and I don't deny that the same could be true for Declan." Sean's hand went instinctively to the back of his neck. He winced and scratched his scalp instead. "It's just that men like him—men who treat women the way he did—don't change much in that regard. Not in my experience, at least."

Colm looked pensive, and he swigged the last of his tea. "Ya have a point there, lad. All I'm sayin' is ta watch and pray. The Laird can change even the coldest man's heart."

"*Humph!* He'd better watch his manners, that's all I have ta say." Sean shook his head. "The nairve of him callin' her Moira when they'd only just met." He slumped back into his chair, crossing his arms over his chest. "God help 'im if he so much as looks at her with disrespect."

Sean released a deep sigh. *If Declan O'Malley thinks he can win the heart of Moira Doherty without a fight, he's got another think comin'.*

❧❦☙

The dough was soft and warm in Moira's hands as she kneaded it again and again. How could she have been so stupid to allow herself to be part of such a display? There was no mistaking the hurt in Sean's eyes when he caught sight of her hand in Declan's.

There was also no denying that Declan had stirred something in her. And while she felt bad for injuring his pride, Sean had never made any proclamations of intention or interest of any kind. He'd been a gentleman and gone out of his way to help her. He'd kissed her hand. But could that account for more than a polite gesture? Had she made too much of it? Sean had never said . . .

I think he made his interest quite clear last night, Moira Girl. She brushed her fingers over the place where his lips had lingered and closed her eyes. But it was Declan's piercing blue eyes she saw in her mind. While true that she'd made no promise or commitment to Sean, she couldn't deny that she had very nearly proclaimed herself to love him less than twenty-four hours earlier.

Was this a test of the state of her heart? Moira felt petty and foolish to be so moved by a man she'd only just met, but the butterflies that still fluttered when she pictured the newcomer's face threatened to drown out all logic.

Not ready to forget her feelings for Sean too quickly, she purposed in her heart to focus her energy on nursing Áedach and Peg and meditating on the Scriptures she would read to them each day.

Lord, don't let my heart be distracted from what You've brought me here to do.

She formed the dough into a ball, cut an *X* in the top, and placed it in the oven.

And please give me wisdom with these two gentlemen, both of whom have managed to waltz their way into my heart too quickly.

<hr />

The bread was still steaming when Moira wrapped it in cheesecloth and started out for Peg's house. She wanted to check on her friend before making her way to Áedach's for the day's visit. While Peg recovered and Sean was busy with work, they'd all agreed Moira could tend to Áedach on her own during the day. And with the children all but forbidden to attend classes, Moira's days were her own. How long could that go on? How long before her job would be officially ripped from her and given to another?

As she walked along the hillside, the sea churned, swirling this way and that, much like her own thoughts.

She was so lost in reflection, she found herself outside Peg's door in what seemed an instant. Colm let her in and welcomed her with a fatherly kiss on the cheek. He gave her the prize of a bigger kiss on the cheek when she presented him with the freshly baked brown bread.

"Ah, ye're a dear, lass." He scurried into the kitchen with his treasure and reappeared just as quickly with a plate and a slab of butter. He motioned for her to join him at the table.

Moira sniggered into her hand as she watched Colm hack off a wedge of bread and slather it in the creamy butter, licking his lips like a child in a sweet shop.

"My Peg's the best cook in Gweedore." He sank his teeth into the bread and moaned in delight. "But since she's been under the weather, she's not been able ta cook, of course." Crumbs flew as he spoke. "And ya don't want me comin' anywhere near a cooktop. It's been near-moldy bread and whatever else I can scrounge together for the last few days."

"And how is our patient?" Moira interjected when he paused for another bite. "It's much quieter than it was last night. Has her cough settled down?"

"Aye. She's still sleepin' sound now." He wiped his mouth on his sleeve.

Moira grimaced, imagining the work it would be for Peg to get butter stains out of a linen shirt.

"T'anks be to God, her chest cleared along wit' the weather. I'd say another day or two an' she'll be right as rain."

Moira released a breath she hadn't realized she'd been holding. "Thank God, indeed!" Relief washed over her at the realization that Colm had been right in his diagnosis and that she hadn't brought Áedach's dreadful ailment into the Sweeny home.

"Well, enjoy the bread." She pressed fists firmly to her hips and gave him a playful scowl. "I expect you to share with Peg, you know?"

Colm's shoulders slumped and he pushed his lower lip out in a mocking pout. "Aw, do I hafta, marm?"

Hearty laughter enveloped them both as they made their way to the door. "Give my love to Peg, and let her know I'll be by again tomorrow to call on her."

"Will do, dear, will do." He opened the door for her. "Ye keep yer wits about ye, lass. Ya never know who ye might run into, an' who might try to run away wit' yer heart."

Moira laughed again, but one look at Colm's face told her he wasn't joking. She cleared her throat and straightened her stance. "I will, Colm. I promise." Turning to head for Áedach's, she couldn't help but wonder why he would make such a remark.

Did he know about Sean's innocent kiss to her hand? Surely word hadn't gotten around about Declan? "It's not like I did anything wrong." The rock walls were fine conversation partners these days. "He was the one who took my hand—I didn't pursue anything with the man. Besides, it was just a friendly handshake."

"I thought it was a rather friendly handshake myself."

Moira shrieked and jumped back. She'd been so busy talking to herself, she hadn't seen Declan leaning against the hawthorn tree on the corner leading to Áedach's road.

"Oh, good afternoon, Dec—eh, Mr. O'Malley." Her steps quickened, and she glanced to see if anyone else was in the vicinity.

"Aw, do call me Declan." He matched her pace, only walking backward. "Someone says 'Mr. O'Malley' and I look for my auld man." He flashed his dimple and Moira melted inside again.

Why did he have to be so disarmingly handsome? And charming? "Mr. O'Malley, we only just met this morning. I hardly think it appropriate for me to refer to you by your first name."

He spun to face forward, still matching her stride. "Have it your way. But mark my words, I'll have you saying my name before you know it."

She looked at the road ahead but could feel him staring at her. Heat stung her cheeks, and she bit her lip to keep from smiling under his gaze.

"So, where are you off to in such a hurry, *Miss* Doherty?" He leaned in as close to her ear as he could while keeping pace and whispered, "Or should I say 'Moira'?"

She stumbled at the warmth of his breath on her ear, and he deftly circled an arm around her waist to steady her.

"*Ahem,* Miss Doherty will suffice, thank you." She righted herself and stepped out of his embrace. "One of my students is quite ill and has no one to care for him. Peg Sweeny and I have been nursing him back to health. Unfortunately, she's fallen ill herself—not with the same ailment, thanks be to God—so I'm on my own for the next day or so." As soon as she'd said it, she wished she hadn't let Declan know she was going to be out here alone. His forward behavior, while somewhat enchanting, gave her pause.

"Well, I think what ye're doin's just wonderful." He slowed his pace and clasped his hands behind his back, as if to reassure her of his intentions. "Not many would give the time and energy to do that for someone who couldn't repay the kindness."

Moira's mouth opened slightly. "Repayment never entered my mind."

"Oh, no! I didn't mean to imply—"

She kept walking, eyes forward. "I just meant to say I had reservations about helping the lad, but I hadn't ever considered his ability to pay. Or repay."

"Well, like I said, I think it's admirable." Declan looked at her until she met his gaze. They smiled at one another, and the familiar heat returned to her cheeks.

Declan shifted his gaze forward and stopped. "Well, it's quite the small world here in Ballymann, isn't it?"

Moira followed his gaze.

Sean was leaning against the rock wall under Áedach's tree.

CHAPTER 40

Was this really happening for a second time? "Why hello, Mr. McFadden!" Moira said, grasping for words. "How lovely to see you!" Regret instantly filled her for not calling him Sean. "I was on my way here to care for Áedach when Mr. O'Malley met me on the road."

"Quite an extraordinary lass Ballymann has for a teacher, eh, McFadden?"

"Indeed." The familiar mixture of hurt and anger clouded Sean's eyes. "I was at Colm's earlier today and saw that Peg is still unwell. I thought ye might need my help again today wit' the boy."

"Yes, of course. Thank you, Sean." She nodded. "I was worried I'd be on my own this time."

"Well, now you have double the help!" Declan stepped forward until he was nearly toe-to-toe with Sean. The two men looked each other over for a moment, volumes spoken with their eyes.

"And you both have my thanks. Now, if you'll excuse me, I have a patient who needs tending." She made her way over the wall, which proved much more difficult without Sean's strong hand to help her, and went to see to Áedach.

The lad seemed much the same as he had the day before, and the day before that. Moira went through her routine as usual, straining to hear what might be transpiring on the other side of the wall. Would they resort to fisticuffs? Was she imagining it all, or did they seem to be challenging each other—over her?

If she was truly honest with herself, Sean's quiet way coupled with his boisterous sense of humor settled a peace over her like she'd never known. He truly seemed to care for her well-being, as well as her reputation. He knew she was concerned, given the uncertainties surrounding her mother, and he seemed to go out of his way to ensure propriety at all times. Even his display of affection—if that's truly what he'd intended it to be—was steeped in honor and consideration for her image in Ballymann.

But Declan. Moira couldn't deny his brazen flirtations left her more on the side of uncomfortable than cherished. But when he looked at her with those sapphire eyes, and smiled at her punctuated with that dimple, all thoughts of propriety, manners, and reputations vanished and all that was left was the beating of her heart. But what did that mean? If she truly loved Sean, she wouldn't have such intense feelings toward Declan. Would she?

"I never thought I'd say this, Áedach, but I envy you. Maybe I could sleep for a few weeks and wake up when this is all blown over, eh?"

Áedach lay, motionless, oblivious to the storm of emotions raging within Moira. Releasing a long sigh, she reached for her apron pocket and produced Peg's ledger. "Let's stay in Psalm 23 for a while, shall we?"

⚜

Sean eyed his childhood acquaintance who preened his hair like a dandy and resisted the urge to comment. Searching his mind for some topic of conversation, his thoughts turned to the unrest taking over the country.

"So, what news of the war?" he managed to ask at last.

Declan shrugged. "Things are progressing, so it would seem." His eyes darted nervously.

"From what I hear, things are quite desperate in Dublin."

Nervous laughter rumbled in Declan's throat. "That's one way to put it."

Interesting. "Is that why you decided to come home?"

Declan toggled his head back and forth and shrugged. His eyes scanned the horizon as if searching for a change in subject.

"Good grief, is she always in there this long?" Declan paced a groove in front of the rock wall.

"If ye have someplace ta be, by all means, go right ahead. I'm sure she'll understand."

Declan leveled a glare at Sean. "What is it with you and Moira, anyway? Is she promised to you?"

"It's Miss Doherty to you. And, no, we're not promised to each another—not that it's any of yer business anyway."

Declan grinned. Sean, willing himself to be the picture of confidence and calm, gripped the rock wall behind him until his knuckles turned white to keep from throttling the man where he stood. He refused to give Declan the satisfaction of knowing he'd gotten under his skin.

"It's decided, then." Declan stroked his chin and slowed his pacing until he stood directly in front of Sean. "May the best man win."

Before Sean could respond, the door to Áedach's hovel opened and out came Moira, squinting against the light. "You're both still here, I see. Thank you for your services standing guard. The patient is much the same, and if you both don't mind, I'll be off to put my feet up and have a cup of tea."

"I'll walk you home," both men offered in unison.

Moira's eyes darted between them. Behind him Sean

heard Declan chuckle. Declan pushed past Sean and reached across the wall, sweeping Moira over it before either one had a chance to protest.

"I didn't want you to trip on that lovely dress." Declan offered her the crook of his arm.

Sean's fingers curled into a ball, and his teeth clenched so tight his head hurt.

Moira stood, motionless, looking from Sean to Declan and back to Sean. Though he wanted nothing more than to sweep Moira up in his own arms and ask her to be his for all time, he didn't want to put any undue pressure on the lass. Sean bowed slightly at the waist and gestured toward Declan. "After you, Miss."

A look of confusion flashed across Moira's face. Then she pursed her lips, setting her jaw, and stepped toward Declan. She took his arm with a confidence Sean had never seen from her before. Was she cross with him? Was she flaunting Declan's attentions?

The three walked up the lane, making their way to the main road that cut through the heart of Ballymann. Ahead of Sean, Declan prattled on about goodness knows what, while every once in a while, Moira would glance over her shoulder at Sean. When she saw him looking at her, she would straighten her posture and hang on Declan's every word.

As they neared the main road, the ugly words Sean had heard said about Moira in the shop that morning echoed in his mind. If Moira was seen walking into town with not one but two single men of eligible age without a proper chaperone, the tongues of Ballymann wouldn't stop wagging until the rapture. He wanted nothing more than to stay with them and keep his eye on Declan, to ensure he treated Moira with the respect she deserved, but he couldn't bear the thought that he could possibly cause her reputation any further damage.

Sean cleared his throat. "I'll be takin' my leave here. I trust you'll see Miss Doherty safely home?" His eyes bored into Declan's, daring him to even think of laying a finger on her.

"Yes, of course. Good day, McFadden," Declan said, returning the sharp gaze.

Moira's brows knitted together, then arched. "Are you sure you don't want to come along? You're most welcome."

I want nothing more, lass. "No, thanks. I'm to call in on our last thatch repair to see how it's holdin' up."

She nodded and offered a sad-looking smile, before turning toward Declan. A thousand swords pierced Sean's heart as he watched her take the man's arm, her smile widening when she looked at his face.

CHAPTER 41

Moira pushed aside the twinge of guilt for not insisting Sean join them and focused her full attention on Declan, who was regaling her with the tale of how he became a barrister in Dublin.

"It's quite rare for someone from a little village in the Gaeltacht to be accepted to practice law at such a prestigious firm. But when I showed up to be interviewed, they liked what they saw." He glanced at her out of the corner of his eye.

Was he checking for her reaction? Her approval? "That's fascinating, Mr. O'Malley."

Declan feigned a cough into his hand that sounded remarkably like "Declan."

She swatted his arm in mock discipline. "You're awful, Mr. O'Malley!"

"Hopefully that's not such a bad thing?" He stopped walking and steadied his gaze upon hers.

Moira's heart thumped wildly in her chest, and she fought to find the right words. *How does one answer a question like that?*

He released her arm and offered a shallow bow. "I don't mean to press. I just like to joke, that's all. Shall we continue?" He gestured along the path and the pair fell into step again. "So, tell me—what convinced a young American girl like yourself to pull up stakes and move halfway across the world to Ballymann, of all places? Why not Paris? Or Vienna?"

Her lips parted in a grin. "Paris and Vienna didn't ask." Bubbly laughter rolled off her tongue. "In all honesty, though, I couldn't not come. I love teaching. I love seeing that moment when everything falls into place and a pupil suddenly understands a concept they've been struggling with. I love seeing the world through fresh eyes every day. It's my calling, teaching. How could I not do it? Plus, it's the last thing my mother asked me to do before she"— Moira swallowed—"before she passed."

Declan's eyes were wide, and the corners of his mouth drew downward. Clearly he was impressed with her passion and sense of duty. "Well, that makes perfect sense, Miss Doherty. Especially the more I get to know you. And I'm sorry to hear about your mother. But you missed half the question."

Moira furrowed her brow.

"Why Ballymann?"

She sighed wistfully. "It's the halla."

Now Declan's brow creased.

Moira read the confusion covering his face and couldn't help but laugh. "Okay, not *just* the halla. I grew up on the noisy streets of Boston, listening to Mother's stories about good ol' Ballymann and her beloved Ireland."

Understanding dawned in Declan's eyes. "That explains it. It always comes back to the mammy." They laughed again. "But tell me more about the halla. Why are you so drawn to it?"

"Every few months, our Boston neighborhood—which is mainly filled with other Irish immigrants—would hold a traditional céilí. They were the highlights of my year. No sooner would one céilí finish before I began counting the days to the next one." She looked at Declan but couldn't read what he thought, so she continued. "Each and every time the festival ended, Mother would get a far-off look in her eye and say with a sigh, 'Moira, darlin', it was a lovely dance, wasn't it?' 'Yes, Mother,' I'd say. And she'd always respond, 'Ah, but there's nothing like a dance in Donegal.'"

Declan smirked. "Really? She loved the musty auld hall with the stale smell of stout and sweat wafting from decades-old woolen jumpers?"

Beginning to feel a bit foolish for waxing so poetic, she decided to try once more to help him understand. "I never heard much about my mother's life here in Donegal, but what stories I did hear always surrounded the céilí. She would tell me tales of how Paddy Blue-socks had one too many pints, or how Father O'Friel tripped during his solo Sean Nós dancing. But my favorite stories were the ones she would tell about the old halla. She'd talk about how everyone in town would gather on cold nights and heat up the thatched building with their dancing, laughter, and craic. I always dreamed of one day seeing the place for myself, but never dared to believe I actually would."

"So, what did you think?"

"What did I think about what?"

Declan held his hands out, palms up, and bobbed his head as if that would coax an answer from her. "About this mystical halla when you finally stepped foot inside! Was it everything you'd dreamed it would be?"

The only thing that masked her ire at his sarcasm was the embarrassment flooding her as she was forced to confess. "Well . . . I haven't actually seen it yet."

Declan guffawed and slapped his knee. "What? You must be joking."

She chewed her nail before answering. "I'd been so busy when I first arrived, and I didn't know where it was. Then time got away and . . ." She was about to detail the difficulties she'd encountered, but something nagged inside not to say anything. "And life got full."

Declan shook his head. "I don't mean to poke fun. Truly, I don't." He shrugged. "I thought with how important it was to you, that would've been one of the first things you'd have done when you arrived, that's all."

"Oh!" She hopped and clasped her hands together as the memory dawned on her. "I've seen the outside, actually."

He looked at her in confusion.

"One day, Peg and I passed by it on our way from her house to Áedach's, but we hadn't time to stop in. But don't you worry, I'll get there." She chewed her lip. "Eventually."

He smiled at her with a twinkle in his eye, and Moira could almost see the wheels in his mind turning. "Yes, you will, Miss Doherty. You will indeed."

"You make it sound so ominous, Mr. O'Malley." She chuckled coyly.

"Not ominous. But we can't have Ballymann's finest teacher go without fulfilling her lifelong dream. And you know the Paddy's Day céilí's coming up soon." He arched his brows and flashed his dimple.

She clasped her hands behind her back, digging her fingernails into her skin trying to rein her thoughts in beneath his handsome gaze. "Ah, yes. Then I do believe you're right. I'll see the halla in all her Paddy's Day glory before we know it." She looked over her shoulder and realized they were standing at the path to her door. "Well, Mr. O'Malley," she said, "thank you for accompanying me home. I wish you a good afternoon." Then she turned on her heel and hurried for the door before he could attempt to grab her hand again as he had done that morning.

"Good night," he said.

She turned and offered a slight wave to him from the doorway, and as the door was closing Declan mouthed a single word.

"Moira."

CHAPTER 42

Moira was delighted to see Peg in such good form the next afternoon. Having dropped by again before heading to Aédach's, she found Peg sitting in her chair near the fire, poring over a tattered copy of the Bible. Colm had been right—the book was massive.

"Thank God you're doing so well." She bussed the top of her friend's head. "How's the cough?"

"*Tsk!*" Peg batted her hand through the air. "Ya shouldna be fretting over an auld biddy like me when ya have a whole schoolful o' wee ones that need lookin' after."

Colm chuckled in the corner as he spread a thick slab of butter on a chunk of the brown bread Moira had brought. "Ah, c'mon, *a Stoir*," he crooned. "Ya know she's only askin' 'cause she loves ye."

Moira's heart skipped at the word "love." She hadn't realized it before, but Colm was right. She loved this dear couple almost as much as she'd loved her own parents. They'd taken her under their wings, lavished the love of a parent upon her, and guided her in the fear and admonition of the Lord. Suddenly overcome with emotion, she rose and stoked the fire, hoping to keep at bay the tears that threatened to spill down her cheeks.

"Aye, love, aye." Peg reached out and squeezed Moira's hand. "She's a good girl, our Moira."

The two women locked eyes, and in that moment, Moira knew they were forever bonded in a special sort of kinship forged through the fires of hardship and spiritual connection.

"Her cough is fine, by the way," Colm called through a mouthful of crumbs. "I'd say by tomorrow she'll be right as rain."

"I'm glad to hear it!" Moira lowered herself onto the wing-back chair opposite her friend. "It will be nice to have your company again tending to Áedach—once you feel strong enough, of course."

"Aye." Peg nodded. "I'm looking forward to that as weel, peata. How is the lad, anyway?"

Moira shrugged. "It's difficult to say, really. His temperature seems to have stabilized somewhat, but he still hasn't roused. And then there's that terrible cough."

"The poor créatúr." A slow, heavy sigh eased from the woman's lips. "All we can do is keep on wit' what we know and keep layin' him at the Laird's feet."

"Amen." More crumbs accompanied Colm's fist on the tabletop.

"Well said, dear friend." Moira gave Peg's hand another squeeze. "Speaking of, I'd best be off. I'm hoping to get home a bit earlier this time and enjoy a nice, quiet evening in front of the fire."

Colm saw her to the door, and she pulled her cloak tight around her neck as she headed for the main road. Thoughts, prayers, doubts, and worries swirled through her heart and mind as she walked. Prayers for Áedach, prayers for herself, worries about her mother's secret, and doubts about her own reputation vied for her heart's attention.

Just as she rounded the corner onto Áedach's road, a large blur landed at her feet with a thud. Jumping back with a start, she stumbled, dropping her basket, its contents scattering on the road.

"Oh, Moi—Miss Doherty." A strong hand grasped hers. "I'm so sorry! I didn't mean to frighten you so."

Moira looked up to see Declan's eyes, swimming with concern and remorse, staring back at her. She swiped the hair from her forehead with her free hand. "Why, Mr. O'Malley, whatever were you doing?"

He placed his other hand beneath her elbow, steadying her. Moira tried to ignore the feel of his touch.

"I . . . I just . . ." His eyes fell to his feet and he offered a sheepish shrug. "I just wanted to surprise you, that's all."

She didn't know whether to laugh or slap the man. "Well, I'd say you succeeded."

Nervous laughter enveloped them both. Declan gathered her things from the road while she brushed the dirt and moss from her skirts.

"I truly am sorry." He handed her the basket. "I just wanted to ask you something."

"What did you want to ask?" Glory be, he was handsome.

"I know you're off to tend to Áedach." He paused while she nodded. "And I'll leave you to do just that. But I wanted to ask if you'd meet me here, right at this spot, this time tomorrow?"

She stared at him and raised her eyebrows.

"Maybe not this exact spot." He eyed the ground where she'd dropped the basket. "But here at the corner. I promise, no tricks or jokes this time. I have a surprise for you."

Curiosity mingled with uncertainty at his request. She rearranged the items in her basket. "I don't know."

"Aw, say you will, Miss Doherty?" He removed his cap and bowed deeply at the waist.

Curiosity and unease played a nauseating game of tug-of-war within her. She had to admit the possibilities of what his surprise could be were intriguing. But then there was also the nagging sense of apprehension she'd felt during her previous encounters with him. Although he had toned down his forward behavior. *Ach!* How far her mind could wander!

"Please?" He looked up at her and grinned.

How could she resist that smile? His giddy, boyish delight tipped the scales in favor of her curiosity. "Oh, alright, Mr. O'Malley." She dipped a curtsy. "I'll meet you here this time on the morrow."

Declan clapped his hands together. "Lovely. Perfect. Until then, Miss Doherty." He bowed once more before stepping aside to let her on her way.

CHAPTER 43

Billowy clouds decorated a cornflower sky while myriad questions swirled in Moira's mind. Ignoring the slight disquiet gnawing at her gut, she wondered anew at what surprise Declan might have in store. It delighted her that he would go to any such lengths. She also noted that Sean had orchestrated no such gesture, grand or small.

Yes, Sean had happened to be there for some of the more harrowing experiences Moira had been through in Ballymann, but that was more by sheer happenstance than his own design. Besides, it would be rude of her not to at least see what Declan's surprise was.

Footfalls on the path behind her broke through Moira's thoughts. Smiling to herself, she turned on her heel. "You couldn't wait until tomorr—" But no one was there. She scanned the horizon, examining each rock and tree but found nothing but God's nature. Sweat prickled her palms and she swallowed the lump rising in her throat. Though she was nearly at her destination, the ailing boy's hovel would offer little protection from anyone who might be about with sinister intentions. Her pace quickened, and she surprised herself with the speed at which she hopped the wall.

Blood rushed in her ears, every leaf rustling in the breeze.

Taunting her. Even her own footsteps haunted her, tricking her senses into believing a predator was just within reach. Bothering not with the formality of knocking, she thrust the lean-to door open and ducked inside.

Her breath fighting to escape her lungs, she hunched behind the door and watched through the cracks in its bark for any sign of her follower. When no one appeared after a moment or two, the pounding in her ears subsided and her breathing slowed. She exhaled a sigh of relief and chided her imagination. Wiping the sweat from her brow with the back of her hand, she turned to tend to her patient.

A shriek escaped her lips, and she fell back against the wall. There sat Áedach, awake, fully alert, and leaning up against the corner.

The pallor of his skin and labored breaths told her he was not yet well but improving.

"Áedach." Moira's parched tongue could barely eke out his name. She swallowed hard and plastered a smile on her face. "It's good to see you awake—you gave us quite the fright, you know?"

He opened his mouth to reply, but instead of words a splitting cough broke the silence between them. Moira rushed to his side and offered him a sip of tea from her flask. Between rasps, he eyed the flask warily before searching her face.

"It's only tea, I assure you." She offered it again.

Taking the container, he lifted it to his nose and sniffed. When it smelled innocent enough, he shrugged and braved a small sip. In a flash he upended the beaker and chugged heartily.

Moira grabbed his hands, lowering them to his chest. "Easy, lad, easy. You mustn't drink too much too quickly. I know you're parched, but small sips every few minutes is best or your stomach will distend."

He glowered at her but obeyed, raising the drink to his lips again, this time taking just a nip. Moments passed without another word spoken.

Moira searched her mind for what to say. Did he know why she was here? Did he remember how she'd left him for so long the first night she'd found him here? Did he mean to harm her?

"How are you feeling?" she asked at last.

He grunted. "Like I fell off the top o' Mount Errigal."

"I don't doubt that." Stirring the fire back to life, she sighed deeply. "You were quite ill, Áedach. We thought we were going to lose you."

"'We?'" His lip curled up at the corner.

She busied herself looking through her basket of goods, trying to shake the memory of Áedach's body pressed up against hers when he threatened her at the schoolhouse. "Mrs. Sweeny and I have been treating you. Though I have to say, we didn't hold out much hope for you at first."

"Auld Lady Sweeny, eh?" He shook his head in surprise and attempted a sarcastic chuckle, but it sent another ripple of hacking coughs through his body, and he had to take another swig of tea to settle it once again.

"You've been unconscious for over a week, lad. You need to take things slowly and rest as much as you can."

"A week!" He mashed his eyes with the heel of each hand, as though that would cause him to wake up in a different reality. "I'd o' never dreamed I'd be nursed back to health by the likes o' ye." He shook his head again and raked a hand through his matted hair.

"Well, I never dreamed I'd be nursing the likes of you back to health either." Her hand flew to her mouth. "I'm very sorry. I shouldn't have said that."

He waved a dismissive hand.

Moira rolled her lips between her teeth while she visually

inspected her patient. Clearly his chest still ailed him greatly and needed continued treatment with the poultices. She had no way, however, of knowing if his fever had broken without a proper examination. Caring for the boy when he was unconscious and on the brink of death was one thing. Touching him and being in such close quarters while he was awake was quite another. Though clearly in a weakened state, he was still Áedach, and as far as Moira knew he still held the same ill will toward her as he had a fortnight ago.

The Lord had called her to care for the lad, hadn't He? Surely that meant whether he was awake or not. She whispered a prayer for strength and scooted closer to her patient, but she left a foot between them—for propriety's sake as well as to ease any uncertainty he might hold for her intentions.

"Áedach, I'm happy to see you awake and talking, but you're plainly far from fully recovered. I need to see if your temperature has come down. And you need a poultice treatment."

He shifted uncomfortably and smoothed his hands over his tattered clothes. At length he nodded and averted his gaze from hers.

She laid a shaky hand upon his forehead, relieved to discover the searing heat she'd felt from him thus far was gone. "You've still a fever, but it's lower than it was, thanks be to God."

Heat rushed to her cheeks as she opened his shirt to apply the poultice. Having him awake for the treatments was proving far more awkward than she had expected. After patting his chest thoroughly with the herbs, she placed the poultice in the center of his sternum.

He looked from the poultice to her and back. "What now?"

"Well, um—" Now it was her turn to shift nervously.

"What is it, so? Yer face is the color o' summer berries. Wha' else must ya do?"

"In order to get the full benefits, the herbs must sit on your chest for a good while. I'll refresh it with hot water a few times in the process."

"So . . . we just sit 'ere?"

"Yes. Usually, though—" Her voice trailed off. She needn't have been so sheepish.

"Wha'? Just say it, woman!"

"Usually, while the herbs do their work, I read aloud to you. From the Scriptures."

Áedach pursed his lips and lines creased his brow, showing his confusion.

Moira produced Peg's notebook, wagging it in her hand. "I've been reading the Bible to you. God's Word?" His blank stare spoke volumes. She searched her mind for the Gaelic word—she'd heard Peg and Colm use it before. At long last it came to her. "Bíobla. Am I saying that right? I've been reading from the Bíobla."

Recognition dawned on his face before his eyes clouded and he sank back against the wall once more. "Do wha' ya like."

"We've read quite a lot in the Psalms, but I've also read some from the book of John—eh, that's *Eoin*, I believe?" She looked to him for confirmation but found only a blank stare and furrowed brow. She cleared her throat and read, "'For God so loved the world, that he gave his only begotten Son, that whosoever believeth in him should not perish, but have everlasting life.'" She lifted the poultice from his chest, dipped it in the hot water, squeezed out the excess with her free hand, and placed it back on his chest. "'For God sent not his Son into the world to condemn the world; but that the world through him might be saved. He that believeth on him is not condemned: but he that believeth not is condemned already, because he hath not believed on the name of the only begotten Son of God.'"

"*Humph.*" Áedach shifted, clearly uncomfortable. She jolted when he snatched the poultice from his chest, flinging it so it landed in the bowl with a plop. Clutching his shirt around himself, he turned away from her.

Staring at Áedach's back, the clear path of his spine protruding beneath his rag of a shirt, Moira silently gathered her things to go. She pulled her cape—which lay in a heap at his feet—up to cover his body. After a final stoke of the fire to be sure it wouldn't go out prematurely, she turned toward the door. As she pushed it open, Áedach stirred.

"Ye'll come again *amárach*, won't ye, Miss?"

Moira smiled. "Of course."

CHAPTER 44

The brisk air refreshed Moira as she twisted and stretched, relieving her back from the ache of crouching in that small space for so long. Rather than getting easier with time, it seemed the aches built one upon the other so each visit was more stiffening than the last. Moira was too grateful, however, to pay much mind to her aching back. Grateful that her patient was on the mend. Grateful that he didn't seem to mind her tending him, and grateful that he hadn't tried to harm her while she was there. Perhaps that for which she was most grateful, though, was the chance to share with him—albeit briefly and somewhat begrudgingly on his behalf—that he was loved by God no matter what.

"Let him hear it, Lord." She echoed her heart's cry. "Let him truly know that he is loved."

And let me hear it too. The reality of her own shortcomings washed over her anew, and her heart swelled even further at realizing God's grace.

Somewhere across the wall, the sound of footsteps returned. Moira's pulse quickened, and she ran her hand along the back of her neck, coaxing the hairs standing on end back into their place. A scan of the fields surrounding her revealed nothing, and the dimming light of dusk offered no help. Would that it were July rather than early March and the sun would lend its light well close to midnight. Alas, it was sinking into its watery bed at five o'clock.

She continued down the road, anxious to reach the village center and the opportunity for more people milling about. The footsteps grew louder behind her, picking up speed. Moira started to run but stepped on the hem of her dress, causing her to splay her hands on the road to keep from falling completely. By the time she righted herself, the footsteps were nearly upon her. She chose to face her foe.

She spun about on one heel and her hand flew to her chest. "Sinead! You gave me such a fright!" Laughter bubbled up and she brushed the dirt and pebbles from her hands. "Why didn't you call out to me?" Moira reached out to hug her friend. Sinead recoiled from her touch.

Surely she's not still cross with me for tending to Áedach?

Sinead pierced Moira with her gaze. "I see ye're followin' in yer mammy's footsteps, so ya are." Disgust covered her face, and she crossed her arms over her chest.

"Whatever do you mean?" Moira combed her thoughts, trying to reconcile what exactly Sinead could mean by such a remark.

Judgment and disdain dripped from the laugh that rolled off Sinead's tongue. "Ye were in there an awful lang time, Moira dearie." She looked Moira up and down. "In a single lad's shanty, alone? Ye were certainly in there lang enough for—" Her eyes narrowed into slits. "Just how exactly are ya nursin' puir Áedach back to health, eh?"

The accusation hit Moira like a slap in the face. "How dare you! How could you think I would ever do such a thing?" Hands shaking, Moira smoothed a hank of hair from her face. "If you'd have listened more closely, you'd have known the extent of my nursing duties was the application

of an herbal poultice and reading from the Good Book."
Bile swirled at the back of her throat.

"So ya say." Sinead circled Moira slowly. "All I know is
Ballymann's teacher spent an extended amount of time
alone with one of her male pupils. It seems to me, Moira
Darrty, perhaps the rumors about yer mammy weren't so
unfounded 'tall."

Moira gasped, gripping the handle of her basket tightly
to keep from pummeling Sinead where she stood. Splin-
ters from the basket pricked her skin. "Say what you will,
Sinead, but you know I would never dream of such a thing."
Tears stung her eyes, but she continued. "Think back to
our time together in our better days—days not so long ago.
You know me."

"Turns out I don' know ye as well as I thought I did. I
wonder how the good folk of Ballymann would feel about
this turn o' events? I'd venture ta guess they wouldn't want
such a filthy *tart* fillin' the wee minds of Gweedore's best
an' brightest."

Stunned, Moira turned in silence and walked toward the
town. Did Sinead really believe Moira to be so indiscreet?
Surely others would believe the truth of what she was doing
with Áedach. But what if they didn't?

"Don' think I won't say anythin'," Sinead called after her.
"Ye watch yerself, Moira Darrty. Watch yerself, an' watch
yer back."

How had her life come to this? In Ireland barely a month
and she had already been avoiding shopping at the market
in order to escape the whispers and stares. But with her
supplies running low, she knew she would have to face the
McGonigles sometime. "One of the joys of small-town living," she muttered to the emptiness. "Only one place from
which to buy your groceries."

"You know, they say talkin' to yerself is either a sign of

brilliance or insanity." Sean was leaning against the rock wall at the corner of the main road. His legs stretched long in front of him, crossed at the ankles. His arms overlapped at his chest, and a playful smile was on his lips. How good it was to see him. How safe.

She offered him a weak smile. "I sure feel like I'm losing my mind today."

Concern flashed across his face and he rose to his feet. "Is everythin' alright?" He glanced down the road behind her, the muscle in his jaw working back and forth. "Did somethin' happen with Áedach?" Ruddy stubble peeked out along his jawline. His green eyes were as clear as the reflection of spring hills in a calm lake. How could she have forgotten how handsome he was?

She shook her head. "No, no, nothing like that." She heaved a sigh and rested against the wall. "I just am wondering what the point of it all is."

His brow furrowed. "Go on."

"Why on earth would God bring me here, if I was just going to be run out of town on a rail?" A tear slid down her cheek. Sean gently wiped it away. She relished the feel of his skin on hers.

"I'm so sorry." His voice was thick with emotion. "I don't know what plan God had for bringin' ya here, Moira. But I'm sure glad He did."

She met his gaze.

"I don't pretend to be an expert in the ways of the Almighty." He dropped his hand and sat next to her on the wall. "An' I know I don't read the Book as much as I should. But I do know God is doing something in you, Moira. Your heart has changed. Whatever it is He's doin' in you through your work with Áedach, and fighting against the darkness that's pressing in on you—I just can't imagine He would waste any of that. You're a different woman than the one

I met only weeks ago," he continued. "He's changing you . . . and watching that unfold has changed me. If me drawing nearer to God is the only good thing that comes out of Him bringing you to Ballymann, I'd say He worked a miracle through you."

Tears flowed freely now, and Moira made no attempt to hide them. How foolish she'd been, lured by Declan because of his smooth words and those striking eyes. Such wisdom and depth flowed through Sean, and she held no doubts that he ever wanted any less than what was best for her.

She placed her hand on his, the skin rough and calloused under her fingers, but it bothered her not at all. "Thank you, Sean." Her eyes searched his, willing him to hear all that she couldn't bring herself to say. "Truly."

He nodded slightly and gave her fingers a tender squeeze.

They stood there together for a moment, volumes being spoken in the silence between them. In the distance a sheep bleated, and the church bells began to ring.

"I'd best be off." Her voice was barely above a whisper.

"Good night, Moira." He released her hand, and she instantly missed the warmth of his touch.

Her heart ached to leave his side, and as she walked home, she committed to meet Declan on the morrow—but only to tell him her heart belonged to another.

CHAPTER 45

Moira's heart thumped against her chest as she made her way to the agreed-upon meeting place. *Lord, give me strength.* She held no concern of being drawn back in by Declan's charms—God had opened her eyes to the truth about her affection for Sean. Rather, she concerned herself with being direct enough to communicate clearly that she had no intentions of continuing any kind of relationship with him.

As she approached the corner, her heart sank. Declan wasn't there. Turning about, she looked for his silhouette on the horizon, but not a soul was present.

A rustling on the stone wall drew her attention. Under a loose rock, one end flapping in the breeze, was a paper. On it was only her name and an arrow, pointing north. Retrieving the paper, she peered up the road. When she saw no one on the path ahead, an argument waged within her.

If she followed his instructions, he might think her interested in pursuing more than the polite, congenial acquaintance of two members of the community. However, if she tarried, she might miss the chance to speak what was on her mind—and the urgency with which to do it.

Gripping the paper in her hand, she set her face to the

north and stepped out in faith, trusting God to work in the less-than-ideal circumstances.

Once at the top of the hill upon which she'd stood and surveyed her new home on her first day in Ballymann, she discovered another paper flapping at her, this one stuck to a gorse bush, directing her down the other side of the hill. She continued, finding a new paper every few yards, until finally she reached the junction with the road that led to Colm and Peg's house. Fighting the urge to turn right and flee to the warmth and solace of her friends' good company and hospitality, she searched for another paper to guide her next steps.

To her left stood the town halla, the one place she'd longed to explore since the day she'd arrived. All at once, Declan appeared from around the corner of the building.

"Surprise!" He held a bunch of wildflowers and sea grasses in his hand, his dimple flashing at her.

"Good morning; Mr. O'Malley." Moira dipped the smallest of curtsies. "I was beginning to wonder if I was ever going to find you." Instantly, regret flooded her for making a remark that could easily be interpreted differently than she'd intended.

"I was just wondering the same thing." He closed the distance between them and extended the flowers to her. "I feared you'd changed your mind."

She reluctantly took them from his hand.

Declan reached over and pushed the door of the halla open. "I can't wait for you to see this, Moi—Miss Doherty."

"Mr. O'Malley." She cleared her throat. "I must speak with you."

"Of course, of course!" He hopped over the threshold and beckoned her inside. "Let's talk in here where we'll be out of the elements."

Moira hesitated. Glancing inside the thatched building,

she could see he'd brought lanterns. Shadows and light danced upon the walls and all the stories her mother had told flooded her mind. The need to see inside overcame her, and she stepped through the doorway.

The sight stole her breath as she scanned the room. On the far-left wall stood a fireplace. No fire crackled in its hearth now, but she could almost feel the warmth that radiated from it during the céilí celebrations. The musty aroma of the ancient thatch wafted from above. In the corners and along each wall, bales of hay provided makeshift seats for partygoers in need of a rest. She ran her fingers along the roughhewn stones that made up the wall. If only those stones could talk!

"D'you like it?"

"It's . . . it's extraordinary."

She felt Declan's warmth from behind, and he placed his hands upon her shoulders. "I hoped you'd love it," he whispered in her ear and grazed his lips on her cheek.

She jumped away from his grasp and absently wiped the place his lips had been. "Mr. O'Malley, whatever are you thinking?"

"I'm thinking you're beautiful, and lovely, and . . . soft." He took a step toward her.

She held up her arm, palm extended. "Stop right there." Her legs shook beneath her. "I fear I might have given you the wrong impression, Mr. O'Malley. I met you today only to tell you"—she swallowed hard, building her courage—"to tell you I cannot pursue a friendship with you. It isn't proper."

"Proper?" He laughed. "What's so improper? Besides, it's not so much friendship I'm looking for." Desire swam in his eyes, and Moira wished he wasn't between her and the door.

"That, sir," she continued, "is exactly my point. I have no

intentions of pursuing any kind of relationship with you. Friendship or otherwise."

"You can't mean that." His voice dripped with desperation. "I saw the way you looked at me, flirted with me. I know how you feel about me, Moira."

"No, Mr. O'Malley, you don't." Her heart raced. She had to find a way to get out of there. She took a step toward the exit, but Declan slid in front of her. He reached back with his right leg and kicked the door shut with a sickening thud.

"You little tease. Don't pretend that you don't want me." He stepped closer. Instinctively she moved backward, away from him, until he had her pressed up against the wall.

"Please, you don't want to do this." Her voice shook, and his face blurred through her tears.

"Oh, yes, I do." He pressed his mouth against hers. He released her only to take a breath and kissed her again. Hard. So hard she tasted blood. She struggled against him, but the more she fought, the harder he pressed. He pulled away just far enough to look at her face. His eyes were filled with a vacant, angry blaze that terrified Moira to her core. "I know who you are. I know who your mother was. And I know you take after her in more ways than one."

"No!" She shook her head violently. "No, it's not true. None of it. Please!"

He grabbed a handful of her hair and shoved her face toward his, kissing her harder than before. With his other hand he groped and grabbed where and what he pleased. She managed to wriggle her face free of his and screamed.

Furious, he grabbed a fresh handful of hair and threw her to the ground. "Quiet, woman!"

Pain shot through her head as it hit against a rock that must have crumbled from the fireplace to the floor long ago. Warmth pooled under her head.

Desperately she clawed the ground, trying to escape. But

he sat upon her and his mouth found hers again and again. Then her neck. Her ear. He grasped the neckline of her dress and ripped the fabric.

No, God, please! Someone help!

Her kicks and punches only seemed to goad him further until finally, he managed to pin her arms above her head with one of his hands while the other tore the remainder of her dress.

Her vision blurred and began to darken. Somewhere in the distance a shout floated on the air, sounding far away and close by all at once.

The room spun and suddenly she was free of Declan's weight. But everything faded to black and silence.

CHAPTER 46

Sean draped his coat over Moira, averting his eyes from her bruised flesh. "Colm, is he awake?" Sean shook his right hand a few times, trying to quell the throbbing in his knuckles from the punch he'd served to Declan's jaw. The lad lay on the ground where he'd fallen.

"Nae, lad, the brute's out cold." Anger registered on the old man's face, but pride shone in his gray eyes. "Ye see to Miss Doherty—take her over to me missus. I'll make sure this one doesna move."

Sean scooped Moira's limp body in his arms. Her black hair was matted to the back of her head, but warmth from the blood seeping from the gash still trickled down his elbow.

Lord, have mercy on her. Save her.

Taking care not to press on any wounds, he sidled out the door and hurried to the Sweeny home.

"Peg! Peg!"

The door flew open. "*Oh, Mhaidean!* What's happened?" She rushed to Sean's side and brushed the hair from Moira's forehead with a tender hand, then lifted one of the girl's eyelids with her thumb. "Bring her inside. Ye can lay her on me bed."

Sean obeyed, turning sideways as he crossed the threshold

so as not to catch Moira's foot or her head on the door-frame. He made his way to the back room and laid Moira as gently as he could on the ticking, rearranging his coat to ensure her modesty. Blood—Moira's blood—slicked across his palm. Hair and dirt studded the crimson stain. Unbidden, trembles overcame his body, and his stomach roiled, threatening to deposit his breakfast on the floor.

"Oh, peata." Peg's warm hand circled on his back. "There's some hot water on the stove. Go clean up and help yerself to a cuppa tea. I'll see to Moira now."

Sean stared at the older woman, her face blurred through his tears. "But Moira . . ." He extended his hand toward her, then withdrew it quickly. "She's hurt. She's so very hurt."

"She's in good hands now, love. It wouldn't be proper for you to tend to her in this state."

Sean nodded absently.

"There's a good lad. Get cleaned up, have yer cuppa, and then ye can tell me what's happened." She gave his shoulder a compassionate squeeze and led him out of the room, closing the door behind him.

Sean stared at his hands, covered in Moira's blood, knuckles burning, and rage boiling in his heart. Stomping to the kitchen, he grabbed the pot of nearly steaming water from the stove and poured it over his hands, ignoring the searing heat as it washed the blood of the woman he loved from his hands. Through the window above the washbasin, he could see the thatched roof of the halla. He stared hard at it as he scrubbed, his thoughts scattering this way and that.

He slapped his hands on his breeches and stormed out the door.

"Declan!" His voice thick with rage, he called the name again. Sean kicked the halla door open. "Declan O'Malley!"

Declan was propped up against a pile of hay, chin dropped to his chest, obviously still unconscious. Colm had tied Declan's hands behind his back, and Sean relaxed some knowing the brute was subdued. One benefit of a lifetime of thatching was Colm's ability to tie knots sure not to come undone in a hurry. "Ye're a good man, Colm."

Colm nodded, arms crossed tightly over his chest.

"Oy!" Sean kicked Declan's foot, pushing down the rising desire to pummel the man where he lay.

Declan stirred and moaned. Sean reached down and grabbed his face, shaking it violently. "Oy! Come on now, man." He punctuated his words with a smart slap across Declan's stubbled face.

Declan's head bobbed from side to side before raising up to look at Sean. He clenched his eyes shut then open a few times and worked his jaw back and forth, wincing in pain. "What's the meaning of all this?"

Incredulous, Sean paced in front of his prisoner's feet. "The meaning? You abused a chaste and righteous young woman, ya *chancer*. You're lucky I didn't kill you then and there."

Declan sneered. "You've got it all wrong, lad." He licked his lips. "She lured me here and tried to seduce me. You should've seen the ways she tried to entice me." A guttural laugh rattled his chest.

Sean's fingers balled into a fist then opened, again and again.

"When I resisted, she went insane and attacked me."

Sean lunged toward him, but Colm caught him before he reached his target. "'Tis not the time nor place, lad."

Sean shot a glare at the old man. "Ya can't be serious?"

"He'll stand before the *Gardaí* for his crime." Colm laid a strong hand on Sean's shoulder. "Don't heap guilt upon yourself by acting unwisely. Ye saved the gairl's life, and you did right by her and yerself with what you did. Any more, though, and ye'll be in the wrong as well."

"Aye," Sean growled, clenching his teeth so hard his jaw ached. "You can spin yer lies all ya want, Declan, but Colm and I know what we saw. And any man can look at the state o' that poor girl's body—" His voice caught in his throat. "Everyone will know what you did, and no one will buy that load of malarkey you're sellin'."

He reached down and grabbed Declan by the elbow, yanking him to his feet. Together, Sean and Colm dragged the prisoner to the Gardaí house.

⁕⁕⁕

When Sean and Colm burst through the Gardaí door with Declan, Tom Duffy scrambled to his feet behind his large desk.

"*Cad a tharla?*" The officer yanked his waistcoat into place. "What's all this?"

Sean pushed his way past him and thrust Declan into the holding cell, slamming the door with a clang. "This . . . this rake is after assaultin' Miss Doherty." He paced the room, breathless.

Duffy's eyebrows shot up, and he looked hard at Declan, who slumped onto a creepie in the corner of the cell, looking neither guilty nor innocent. "Tell me exactly what's happened."

Sean smoothed his hair back and splayed his hands on the desk. "Colm and I were heading out for a thatching repair when we heard a commotion in the halla. At first all we could hear was scuffling and muffled voices. Then we heard a scream—a female scream. A . . . terrified scream." He rolled his lips between his teeth and took a deep breath, fighting to keep his rage in check. "We burst into the halla to find—" He closed his eyes and waited for the lump to leave his throat. "We found yer man there tryin' to have his way with Miss Doherty. She was bleeding from her head, and barely conscious. He'd ripped her dress from her—it's still on the floor of the halla. I pulled him off her and gave him a right hook across the jaw."

Duffy rubbed his fingers across his jowls before resting them on his plump belly. He turned to Declan. "Was that the way of it?"

Declan shrugged, a smirk playing on his lips. "You know how these young, single teachers are, Duff. She lured me there and tried to seduce me."

The officer's brow furrowed, and he scooted up close to Sean. "Are ya sure it was as you say? You know, Miss Doherty's been said to—"

Colm raised his palm up, signaling Duffy to say nothing more. He stepped closer to the officer and looked him in the eye. "We've known each other a long time, Tom. All our lives, aye?"

"Aye."

"God as my witness, it happened just as young Sean here told ye. O'Malley assaulted that poor lass, and I won't stand here an' let ye use gossip to make an innocent gairl account-able for an attack that nearly stole her life. She lies in my house now, unconscious."

Duffy looked back at Declan, who turned his palms up toward the ceiling as if to say, "You can't blame me for try-ing."

"Colm, of all the folk in Ballymann, I trust ye more than any—other than Father McGowan, o'course."

Colm nodded.

"I'll give yer wife some time to tend to the lass's medical needs, and then I'll need to talk to her meself."

"Anything ya need." Colm shook Duffy's hand.

Sean nodded at the officer and leveled another glare at Declan before turning to head out the door and back to Moira.

CHAPTER 47

A dull ache throbbed in Moira's head, turning her stomach with each beat of her heart. The aroma of fresh bread and tea hung in the air, and muted voices floated from somewhere in the distance. As she opened her eyes, blurred lines and hazy light swam in her vision. When she raised her hand to her face, it seemed to weigh a thousand pounds. Her muscles screamed with each movement.

Her vision finally clearing, panic seized her. This was not her home. Where was she? Whose voices was she hearing? Without warning, images flashed across her mind—Declan's face shoved against hers. His body hovering over hers. The weight of him pressed down on her. Her heart raced, and she curled over the side of the bed just in time to get sick in a bowl that rested on a creepie.

The door eased open, and a wash of warmth and light flooded the room. "Oh, peata, ye're awake." Peg's soothing hand brushed Moira's hair from her face as she finished emptying her stomach. Though embarrassed at her state, Moira was grateful for her friend's presence.

"Just take it easy," Peg crooned. "Ye'll be wantin' to go slow now at first."

Gingerly, Moira pushed against the side of the bed to sit up. The throbbing in her head instantly intensified, and she lay back down. Every muscle in her body ached, and her legs felt as if they'd been ripped from her torso.

"Peg? What happened? How did I get here?"

Peg's eyes, filled with compassion, looked over her face. She offered a sad smile. "Sean and Colm brought ye here. Ye were attacked, peata. In the halla. D'ye have any memory of it?"

Declan's stubbled face and the stench of his breath flashed in her memory. She turned her face to the wall. "Yes, yes I do. I'd hoped it was a nightmare." A few tears slid down her cheeks, wetting the pillowcase beneath her. Sean and Colm had seen her . . . like that?

"Oh, dearie." Peg stroked her hand. "I'm so very sorry. This should never have happened to ye."

"No, it shouldn't have." Though she wanted nothing more than to hide away from the world forever, Moira forced herself to turn and look at Peg. "I never should have gone in there with him, Peg. I was so foolish."

"If ya don't mind me askin', love, why did ye?"

Heat burned behind Moira's eyes, and she licked her lips while she searched for just how much to tell her friend. "Decl—er—Mr. O'Malley had asked me to meet him at the corner of Áedach's road. He had a surprise for me."

Confusion flashed on Peg's face, but she nodded, encouraging Moira to continue.

"At first I was flattered, you know? He'd been so charming."

Peg tipped her head to the side, eyes narrowed, obviously not sharing Moira's original opinion.

"But," Moira continued, "as the time drew near, I realized something. I saw how foolish I was being and decided I needed to make it clear I wasn't interested in anyone except . . . That I wasn't interested in a friendship or anything else with him." She shuddered. "Not wanting to appear rude,

I met him there to tell him that I no longer wanted his company, because my heart belongs to—"

Sean knocked on the doorframe and entered the room. Moira clamped her mouth closed and searched for what she could say next.

"I'm so glad to see ya awake, Miss Doherty." Sean's green eyes bore into hers.

She dipped her head. "Thank you, Mr. McFadden." Did he know all that had happened? Surely he'd never accept her now that . . . now that she had been attacked in such an intimate way.

"Moira was just telling me how she had come to be in the halla with Mr. O'Malley." Peg looked from Sean back to Moira. "You were saying he'd asked you to meet him, because he had a surprise for you. And you'd agreed only to tell him, what, my dear?"

Moira wished the bed would open up and swallow her whole. Must Sean stay for this part of the story? When he pulled a chair from the hallway and took a seat next to Peg, Moira knew there was no escaping it. As mortifying as it was to admit her foolishness, she didn't have to admit to them why she didn't want to pursue Declan's friendship any longer.

She cleared her throat. "That I no longer wished to keep his company." She picked at a loose thread in the blanket. "When I got to the corner where we were supposed to meet, I found a slip of paper with my name on it and an arrow pointing north."

"And you followed it?" Sean's voice cracked with disbelief.

She looked away from his intense gaze. "Yes, I did. I see now how foolish it was of me, but I truly just wanted to say my piece to him and be done with it."

"It's alright, peata." Peg patted her hand and offered Sean a sidelong glance. "Go on."

"The night Mr. O'Malley walked me home—after you left us, Sean, after we'd been to Áedach's house—I had told him how I'd longed to see the halla. I thought he'd wanted to . . . to make a dream come true for me. I was so very wrong."

Peg and Sean sat silent, waiting for her to continue.

"I was wary at first, but when I got a glimpse from the doorway, I couldn't help but go inside. I'd waited my whole life to see it. Once inside, however, Declan got angry when I told him I didn't want to see him any longer, and he—" Moira stopped her story there, wishing to leave the shameful details unspoken.

"Well," Peg said at length, "ye're right that ye shouldna gone inside there with him—with any man—alone. But that doesna mean you desairved what he did to ye. Thanks be to God, Colm and Sean came along when they did before—"

Moira's breath caught in her chest, and she clutched the bedcovers to her neck. She remembered falling, hitting her head, blacking out. Had Declan not then run off, stopped his attack?

Sean's face reddened and he worked his hat between his hands. "Aye, we heard ye scream and rushed in. I pulled him off o' ye."

Then he knows? Sean knows the depth of my shame? No wonder his eyes held such anger. *There's no hiding the truth from him now, and he certainly won't want a woman who's been ravaged.*

"I'm quite tired," she managed at last. "Thank you both for your visit. And thank you, Mr. McFadden, for your help. I do believe you saved my life." She gingerly turned on her side to face the wall again, fighting to keep the sobs from rocking her body until she knew she was alone.

"I'll come back in a wee while with some broth and tea for ye." Peg kissed her temple and quit the room.

"Just rest now." Sean's voice was thick—with emotion or anger, Moira couldn't tell. "We need you well. All of us."

The door closed, and all the tears and shame she'd been holding in burst forth in wracking sobs that sent excruciating pain through her entire being. She welcomed the pain. It was the payment for the foolishness that had cost her the love of a good man. And very nearly her life.

CHAPTER 48

Moira awoke to the sound of the door scraping open and the soothing scent of tea arriving just ahead of Peg, who set a tray of tea and brown bread on a small table and took the seat next to the bed.

"How're ya feeling, love?" Peg poured a steaming cup. Moira watched the steam float and swirl until it disappeared long before reaching the thatched ceiling.

"I'm alright." Moira sighed. "My body will heal, but I'm not so sure about my pride. How could I have been so foolish, Peg?"

"*Tsk!* Ya need to give yerself the same grace ye've shown to yer patient doon the road." She handed the cup to Moira. "Ye were only tryin' to do right by yerself and Mr. O'Malley. Ye couldn't have known what he was plannin' to do."

"I should've known better." She sipped the hot tea, letting its comforting warmth soothe her body and spirit. "I just . . . it's that halla. I've dreamed of seeing it ever since Mother first told me the stories about the dances when I was a little girl."

"I know." Peg nodded. "Nostalgia can be a powerful draw. But there's no sense in beatin' yerself up over something tha' canna be changed now. Ye need to focus on getting better and getting back to what the Laird has for ya to do here."

Moira laughed the doubtful scoff of one no longer sure of the truth.

"You listen to me, Moira Doherty. God didna bring ye here only to abandon ye now. I don't know why He allowed what happened to ye, but I know He doesna waste a thing. Don't let this harden yer heart. Let Him use this to heal you more deeply than ye ever thought possible."

Use this to heal? She nodded at Peg but questioned in her heart what possible good could come out of losing everything she held dear.

"Now, ya just rest, eat yer broth, and drink yer tea. We'll have ye right as rain afore too long. We don't want Áedach floundering out there on his own, do we?"

"Áedach!" Moira threw the covers from the bed. "I told him I'd be back."

Peg eased Moira back onto the bed. "It's alright, pet, it's alright. Bríd looked after ye while Colm and I saw to Áedach these last few days."

"Days?" The room began to spin.

"Ye were asleep for two days after the attack. Just rest now."

Two days? Nothing in her world made sense any longer. Thank God for good folk like Bríd, Peg, and Colm. Moira ached at the idea of Áedach waiting for her, wondering if she'd abandoned him like everyone else.

She relaxed at the thought that Colm and Peg were sure to continue to care for the lad with compassion and kindness, just as she would. And they could definitely be counted upon to continue reading Scripture to him.

Open his heart to You, Lord. Her eyelids grew heavy, and the room began to fade. *Let Áedach know You. Save him. And save me.*

Sean paced in front of the Sweenys' fireplace, his cup of tea long forgotten on the table. Duffy had gone into Moira's room an hour ago. How much more could there be to tell? It had been nearly a week since the attack, and Sean had only seen Moira in fleeting glimpses. When he tried to speak with her, she kept her answers short and void of detail, and would then require a nap, which cut their conversations even shorter.

He wanted nothing more than to sweep her up in his arms and promise to protect her for the rest of his life, but she seemed bent on keeping him at arm's length. Of course, he knew she would need time to heal—emotionally as much as physically—and he was willing to wait as long as it took. But having her push him away was killing him more and more each day.

"Sit doon and drink yer tea, lad." Colm was buttering his third piece of bread. "Ye're makin' even the mice nairvous."

Sean gestured toward the room. "How long is Duffy going to take in there? Surely he has enough evidence to convict O'Malley?"

Colm shrugged and wiped his mouth with the back of his hand. "These things are quite delicate, ya know. There's nothin' more ye can do but wait."

Resigned to his fate, Sean sat at the table and took a sip of his now-tepid tea before pushing the cup and saucer away from him. He jumped to his feet at the sound of the bedroom door opening and Duffy's feet scuffing the hallway.

"'Tis done." Duffy eyed the teapot and slices of brown bread on the table.

"Ye'll have a cuppa before ye go, aye?" Colm was already pouring the tea.

"Ye're a good man yerself, Colm." Duffy licked his lips and accepted the cup.

"So?" Sean wanted to shake answers out of the officer.

Duffy looked at Sean from the corner of his eye, then he finished his tea in one go. He raised his eyebrows, questioning.

"Do ye have enough to convict O'Malley?" Sean asked.

Duffy set his mouth in a firm line and nodded. "Aye, we do. From the looks o' the bruising on Miss Doherty, 'tis clear she was on the defensive."

Sean combed his fingers through his hair. At least the cur would pay for his crime. "Thank you, Officer."

Duffy helped himself to a slice of brown bread and saluted Sean and Colm with it before taking his leave.

Sean pressed his palms into the table and hung his head. As glad as he was Declan was going to suffer the consequences of his actions, there was still nothing Sean could do to stave off the pain and humiliation Moira endured.

Another scuff in the hallway caught his attention. He looked up to see Moira standing in the doorway. Her skin was pale, and dark circles shadowed her eyes. A large bruise covered most of what showed of her left arm, and her thick black hair was plaited over her shoulder, keeping it away from the wound on the back side of her head, no doubt.

Peg came sweeping around the corner behind her. "Look who wanted to venture into the land o' the livin'!"

With careful steps, Moira made her way to one of the chairs in front of the fire, wincing as she lowered herself to sit. "I couldn't have my gracious hosts thinking me rude, now, could I?" Despite the pain evidenced by the deepened lines around her face, her eyes maintained a hint of humor, or perhaps mere civility.

"Welcome back." Sean clasped his hands behind his back

to keep from reaching out to stroke the top of her head, or wrapping her into an embrace.

Moira nodded and offered a polite smile, her gaze lingering on his face for only a moment before turning to the fire.

Peg patted Sean on the shoulder as she passed by and whispered, "Give her some time. She'll come 'round."

He sighed. "I'm so very glad to see you on the mend, Miss Doherty. I must be off to see to our customers. I leave ye in the good care of our friends here."

"Thank you, Mr. McFadden." She barely glanced his way. "Good day to you."

Sean quit the room, welcoming the cold sting of the March morning air and vowing to do whatever it took to keep from losing Moira's heart for good.

CHAPTER 49

Moira stared at the doorway Sean exited through as though she could watch him disappear over the hill.

Forgive me, Sean. Don't give up on me yet.

"Now, peata, ye'll have some broth." Peg handed the steaming bowl to Moira. Compassion and kindness shone in her eyes, as always. "Would ye like a report on how yer own patient fares?"

After taking a moment to savor the rich, comforting liquid, Moira set her spoon down eagerly. "Oh, yes, please, Peg. How is Áedach?"

"The lad continues to improve." Peg lowered herself into the chair across from Moira. "A slight fever's still on him and the cough lingers, but his face isn't so wan and he's taken some broth and tea."

Relief washed over Moira. "Thanks be to God."

"Indeed!" Colm agreed from the table behind her.

"Ya havna heard the best part." A grin spread across the older woman's face. "I was in such a state of concern over ye a couple days past, that I saw to his ablutions and treatments and bade him farewell. He stopped me afore I could get out the door. You won't believe what he asked me." Peg paused for dramatic effect.

Moira leaned forward in her chair, ignoring the ache in her hips. "What? What did he ask?"

"He looked right at me and he says, 'Will ye not read ta me from the Bíobla, Mrs. Sweeny?'" Peg cackled and slapped her knee. "Can ye believe that?"

Tears sprang to Moira's eyes and she bowed her head in awe. "The Lord is willing that none should perish. Thank You, God."

"Well said, peata." Peg patted Moira's hand tenderly. "There's one more thing."

Moira raised her eyes to meet Peg's, lifting her brows in question.

"The lad's been askin' fer ye," Colm said through a cloud of crumbs.

"Me?" Moira spun about in her chair and winced from the shooting pain in her head. "Whatever does he want with me?"

"He wouldna say," Colm continued, circling around to stand in front of her. "I've made it clear that it would be a wee while afore ye could make the journey there—but I've only told him that ye're unwell, not *why* ye're unwell. But when ye feel up to it, Peg and me'll go wit' ye."

Moira sank back into the chair, her tea and broth forgotten. Questions swirled in her mind. If the lad had been asking to be read to from the Bible, surely his reasons for wanting to see her wouldn't be sinister in nature. It was hard for Moira to imagine Áedach preferring her care over Peg's—Peg had such a gentle and nurturing way about her, as Moira had been blessed to experience firsthand.

For a brief moment, she entertained the idea of venturing out to Áedach's that afternoon, but when she rose to return to her bed, the throbbing in her head and aching in her joints convinced her to wait.

Once back in bed, Moira slid Peg's ledger from the bedside table and thumbed the pages. How kind of Peg to leave it with her. She opened to the book of John, where she'd left off with Áedach, and continued reading.

"For God sent not his Son into the world to condemn the world; but that the world through him might be saved." Fresh tears stung her eyes. Wasn't she condemned already? Condemned to a life defending against rumors and whispers dragging her character and that of her mother through the mud. Condemned to live with the physical and emotional scars of her foolish behavior. Condemned to lose the man she loved because she was conned by a handsome face and a beguiling smile. She read the words again.

"For God sent not his Son into the world to condemn the world: but that the world through him might be saved. He that believeth on him is not condemned." Peg entered the room with Moira's forgotten broth and a fresh pot of tea. She sat on the edge of the bed and glanced at the verses Moira was pondering. She reached up with a tender hand, rough and calloused from a lifetime of service in her home, and wiped tears from Moira's cheeks.

"'Tis a powerful idea, aye?"

Moira nodded.

"I remember when it first dawned on me what God was truly sayin'," Peg continued. "It doesna matter what the world says I am. It doesna matter even what I believe myself to be—and I have some dark thoughts when it comes to me own heart, to be sure. If I believe in the Laird Jesus Christ, and what He did fer me, I canna be condemned."

Moira picked at a fingernail.

Peg hooked a finger under Moira's chin and raised her face to look at her with the tenderness of a mother. "I know ye feel responsible for what happened, but ye canna live in defeat. Ye love the Laird, and ye follow hard after Him.

Not a man on earth can condemn ye. Besides, no woman desairves what happened to ye."

Moira wasn't entirely convinced, but as she looked at Peg and the sincerity shining in her eyes, gratitude washed over her for this unexpected friendship. "Thank you."

CHAPTER 50

Moira squinted as she stepped out in the bright sunlight. After so long indoors, she greeted the fresh air like an old friend. Most of the pain had subsided, and the gash in her head no longer throbbed with each movement. Occasional flashes still haunted her memory with images she'd rather forget, but even those were coming with less frequency and intensity.

Peg's arm linked through hers, and Colm tipped his hat at the women. "Shall we?" His eyes sparkled in the bright March sun.

The air still held a bit of a chill, but the harshness of winter had mostly departed. Moira's heart felt light for the first time in weeks.

"After you, m'lord." Moira curtsied dramatically. The trio laughed and set off toward Áedach's.

As they passed the halla, Moira paused. It didn't look near as dark or foreboding as it had in her dreams of late. A gaggle of women buzzed about the place, hanging window boxes and sweeping leaves.

Peg patted Moira's hand. "They're startin' preparations for the grand Paddy's Day céilí."

Moira nodded.

"Ye don't have to go, ya know, peata. I know the halla holds dark memories for ye."

"Indeed it does." Moira heaved a sigh. "At the same time, I've dreamed of dancing at a céilí in that halla since I was a little girl. I pray God gives me the strength to attend." She looked down at the traveling dress she'd worn the first day she rode into town. It was faded and the cuffs were fraying. It was her only gown now. The one Declan had torn asunder was beyond repair—or so Peg had said. Not that she could bring herself to wear it again anyway.

Moira's heart sank at the thought of attending the céilí in so drab a garment, but her gratitude to God for sparing her life outweighed the disappointment—most of the time.

The trio reached Áedach's hovel. The door was open and smoke circled up from the entrance. Moira knocked on a stone near the door. "May I come in?"

"Aye, Miss. Please do," Áedach said from within.

Moira looked from Peg to Colm and back.

"We'll wait out here for a few minutes." Colm took hold of Peg's hand. "But we're only a step away should ye need us."

Moira nodded and ducked inside.

Áedach was sitting up. More color filled his face than she'd seen even before he'd fallen ill. A small fire crackled in the corner, and Moira's cloak—which had remained with the lad since her first visit—was folded neatly by the door. The odor of sick and sweat had wafted away through the open door, for which Moira was exceedingly grateful.

"Áedach." Moira smiled. "You look so well! I'm happy to see you up and with such color to your cheeks."

Áedach tried to hide a grin and looked at his bare feet, which he then tucked up underneath himself.

"Colm and Peg said that you'd asked for me?"

He cleared his throat. "Aye, marm." He drew swirls in

the dirt floor with his fingertip. "I just . . . I wanted to say t'anks. Yas didn't have to do what ye done. Especially after the way I treated ye."

At a loss for words, Moira nodded. "It was my honor."

"Why?"

Moira jumped at the intensity of his voice.

"Why'd ye do it, like? Ye could've just let me be. Let me . . . die. Why'd ye go out o' yer way to care for me?"

Moira shifted into a more comfortable position, crossing her legs beneath her. "It's quite simple, really. God told me to."

Creases spread across his forehead. "Wha'?"

Moira laughed. "You did treat me horribly, Áedach. I won't be shy in saying so. I'd also be lying if I said I wasn't tempted to leave you here on your own. But God"—she paused, choosing her next words carefully—"He reminded me that none of us are perfect. The Bible says all have done wrong, or we've left good undone. But He forgives us and loves us just the same. My heart was just as dark as yours when I . . . hesitated to help you in your time of need."

Moira squeezed her eyes tight, the pain and disgrace striking anew at how close she'd come to playing such a key part in a young man's death. "Don't you see, Áedach? God has been so generous with His love and mercy for me, I couldn't help but extend the same to you."

Áedach pursed his lips and nodded, staring a thousand miles away. "I canna say I totally understand, Miss." He shrugged. "But I'm grateful. And . . . I'm sorry."

Colm poked his head in the door. "Are we interruptin'?"

Moira laughed. "Not at all, Colm. Come in."

Colm ducked inside while Peg poked her head in the door, holding a packet wrapped in muslin cloth and tied with a string. "Just a wee somethin' for the lad, now he's feelin' better." A broad smile graced Peg's face.

Áedach's eyes widened, and he pointed to his chest. "Fer me?"

"Aye, lad." Colm laughed. "We canna have ye fallin' ill again after these women worked so hard ta nurse ye back to health."

Slowly, as if in a stupor, Áedach untied the string and opened the cloth packet. The muslin was that of a new shirt. It was wrapped around a new pair of breeches and a hearty woolen jumper, the same fleecy white color as the lambs dotting the Donegal hillsides. His jaw fell open. "*Gabh raibh mile maith agaibh*." He ran his fingers over the soft fabrics. "I've never had the likes o' these in my life. I don't desairve such a gift."

Colm chuckled. "It's a grand good thing the Laird doesna give any of us what we really desairve."

Moira fought to keep her own composure. How did Colm and Peg afford such a lavish gift?

"Come now, let's give the lad some privacy to dress." Peg motioned for Moira and Colm to join her out of doors.

Once out in the cool breeze, Moira gaped at her friends, her hands spread wide. "How on earth?"

The couple shared an endearing glance and burst into laughter. "I've been knitting that jumper for Colm for months. When we learned of Áedach's condition, and certainly after we'd visited, we both knew that jumper was meant for the lad. The rest of the clothes were bartered for easily enough."

"Yet another benefit o' my trade." Colm rocked on his heels, grinning from ear to ear.

"You two never cease to amaze me." Moira shook her head.

The door scraped open, and Áedach cleared his throat. He stooped through the door, squinting and raising his hand to block the sunlight. After a few weeks in that dark hovel, Moira could only imagine the shock of stepping outside. He stood for a moment, hunched with a hand over his face. When he finally straightened, blinking, he held his hands out. "Well, what d'ye t'ink?"

Peg clasped her hands over her mouth and fawned over the lad. "Don't ye look *breá*!"

Áedach's cheeks reddened.

"Oh!" Colm jumped. "I nearly forgot." He grabbed his satchel and pulled out a pair of shoes. The leather was slightly faded, but the soles and laces were in good condition. "They're nothin' fancy, but they'll keep yer *cosa* dry."

Reluctantly, Áedach reached out for the shoes. He turned them over and over in his hands before leaning against the wall to slip them on. The thin leather reached up over his ankles and hugged his feet as he tied them snugly. He sniffled and ran the back of his hand across his nose. "I've no way to repay ye."

"Och!" Colm waved a meaty hand through the air. "'Tis a gift, lad!"

Áedach shook his head. "I just wish—oh wait." He ducked back inside, and in a flash returned with a small paper in his hand. He held it up for the group to see. Intricate swirls and knots filled the page. "It's nuttin', really." He shifted his feet back and forth. "Just a bit o' doodles with the burnt end of a twig. I saw them on a rock once and just copied them down from memory when I was alone."

Moira, Colm, and Peg moved closer to get a better look. A spiral swirl filled each corner of the paper, and a knot of three unbroken triangles filled the center.

Peg smiled. "'Tis the trinity knot. How fitting."

Moira gingerly ran her finger over the knot representing the Father, Son, and Holy Spirit, taking care not to smudge the drawing. "It's lovely, Áedach."

"'Tis my gift to ye." He shrugged. "After all ye've done, it's the least I can do."

Colm gave Áedach's shoulder a fatherly squeeze. "Ya don't owe us a thing, lad. But if ye do nothing else but spread this kind o' love to others, I'll be happy."

Áedach smiled and offered his hand to Colm, who shook it heartily.

Peg wrapped an arm around Moira's shoulders and squeezed.

What a mighty God You are.

CHAPTER 51

It was the first real spring-like day of the year, and Ballymann shone like a new ha'penny. The gales had retreated back over the mountains, leaving in their stead a gentle breeze that set the budding flowers swaying.

Moira had never seen so many people bustling about the village center. Folk lingered in doorways and strolled in the streets. Instead of people rushing from this place to that, faces down against the wind, smiles greeted every passerby and laughter floated through the air. Life had returned to the seaside village, and with it the joy that had been tucked away to endure the long, dark months of winter.

Ignoring the stares at her fading bruises and hushed voices whispering of her suspected character flaws, Moira smiled at the whole of the town as she made her way to help with the preparations for the upcoming Paddy's Day celebration.

Despite the gleesome weather, apprehension niggled at Moira. She'd not returned to the halla since that horrible day, and the haunting memories threatened to keep her away for good. But if she did that, she'd be allowing Declan to steal an even deeper part of her. The idea of redemption spurred her on toward the building, praying for strength all the way.

However, when she arrived at the halla, she gasped at the sights that greeted her. The walls, freshly whitewashed, gleamed in the spring sunshine. Window boxes overflowed with flowers of every color. It was as if the halla itself had washed itself clean from the horrific events and offered Moira the chance to do the same. Colm and Sean perched at the top of the roof, cleaning up the thatch and patching any weak spots. Peg came bustling around the corner, chatting away with Bríd. Both women carried wide baskets full of flowers.

"Moira, *beag*!" Bríd all but dropped her basket and ran to embrace Moira. She cupped Moira's face in her hands. "How are ya, dear? Peg's told me ye've had a rough time of it."

Moira smiled. "Yes, I'm fine now, thanks. It's so wonderful to see you."

"What d'ye think of our wee halla here? Isn't she lovely?"

Moira looked over the building once more, the renewed exterior mirroring the renewing God was doing in her own heart. "Yes, yes she is."

In the distance, Moira caught a glimpse of a strikingly elegant woman. Her lavender gown flowed flawlessly to the ground, and her silvery hair was piled in an intricate weave of plaits on her head.

"That's Lady Williams," Bríd whispered in her ear. "The widow of one of the great landlords of Donegal. Sent here from Britain, they ruled their tenants with great kindness—something that canna be said for all the landlords we've seen. Wonder why she's out today? We rarely catch a glimpse of the woman."

"At one point, way back when yer mam was still here, the Lady claimed her daughter was promised to marry John Adair—son of Cornelia Wadsworth, owner of Glenveagh

Castle," Peg added. "But we never saw or heard any evidence to that. The man only visited a handful of times during his summer holidays from his studies abroad."

Moira nodded, keeping her eyes on the beautiful older woman in the distance.

Bríd's eyes clouded. "Yer mammy met him once. When she worked at the castle."

Moira and Peg looked at Bríd, bewilderment painted on their faces.

Bríd waved her hand as though swatting the memory away like a fly and then linked her arm in Moira's. The three women headed around the side of the building to fill the window boxes and planters lining the walls on the ground. All the while Moira felt Lady Williams's eyes boring into the back of her head.

As the women worked, they chatted about the weather and the upcoming celebrations, before circling back to the weather. It seemed no matter if the weather was horrid or beautiful, the Irish could talk of little else. With the laughter of her friends echoing in her ears, Moira became keenly aware all other talking and movement had ceased.

Following the gaze of the rest of the crowd, Moira saw Áedach shuffling up the road, proudly wearing his new togs. As he approached the halla, one mother quietly nudged her daughter behind her. Others watched in silence, falling back a step or two, scowls darkening their faces. Without a word, Áedach smiled and dipped his head toward Moira and her friends, picked up a broom that had been abandoned on the ground, and began sweeping the path leading to the halla's door.

Moira and Peg looked at each other, eyebrows raised, smiles playing at the corners of their lips. Bríd, unaware of all that had transpired between the lad and Moira and the Sweenys, took a protective stance in front of Moira.

"It's alright, Bríd." Moira laughed. She stepped out from around the corner and walked right up to the lad. "Good morning, Áedach." She smiled warmly at him.

Whispers rippled throughout the crowd. Moira couldn't hear everything that was said, but she could hear enough. *Brazen. Hussy. Tairt.*

In thee, Lord, do I trust. I am not afraid. What can man do to me?

"It's good of you to come." She smiled as sweetly as she was able.

Áedach looked around and hung his head. "Ye don't hafta talk wit' me, Miss. I know what folk t'ink o' me."

"*Seafóid!*" She waved her hand through the air as she practiced the Irish word for *nonsense* Colm had taught her.

Áedach's eyebrows shot up and his mouth fell open. The two burst into laughter. "Aye, Miss." He bobbed his head. "I just wanted ta help. After all the trouble I caused, it seems only right." He shrugged and continued sweeping.

"You're a good lad." She patted his shoulder and turned back toward her flowers just as Peg was approaching.

"Good morn', lad." Peg smiled and placed a motherly hand on the boy's shoulder. A new wave of whispers rippled through the bystanders, though not a single foul sentiment was uttered. "Keep up the good work." She patted his shoulder and turned back to her own duties.

As though Peg's example defused the anger of the crowd, each one resumed their work. Some nodded slightly to Áedach, some merely softened their expressions as they picked up their spades or paintbrushes or sacks of spuds.

Moira stole a glance at the roof just in time to see Colm wink down at Peg, and Peg blow a sly kiss to her husband. Sean stood, silhouetted by the sun behind him, looking down at Moira. One hand rested on his hip, the other draped over the tall handle of his spade. With his face shrouded in shadow, Moira couldn't read his expression, but his stance looked to be one of dismay. Was he cross with her for interacting with Áedach in public? It seemed every move she made only served to drive him further away.

Even as her heart ached to call him down and talk through the chasm that stretched between them, she offered a polite nod and returned to helping Peg and Bríd plant the last of the flowers.

⁂

Sean shook his head in disbelief, watching Moira engage Áedach in conversation in front of half the village.

Even after all she's been through, compassion reigns supreme.

She had looked up at him, and their eyes had locked, but the smile on his face seemed to make little impression on her. A sadness filled her eyes that cut Sean to the core, and he stood atop that thatched roof wondering what he'd done to distance her so.

"She's a remarkable lass." Colm stood next to him, hand on his shoulder.

"Aye." Sean watched her take her place with Peg and Bríd and continue planting flowers, working the dirt with her lithe fingers, using as much care with the tender shoots as he'd seen her use with everyone who'd crossed her path. "That she is." Sean felt Colm's stare, and he turned to meet it.

A playful smile tickled the corners of Colm's mouth. "There's more work to be done, lad."

More work than you know, man. God, give me wisdom.

CHAPTER 52

Whispered voices carried on the breeze as Moira made her way to Áedach's home later that afternoon. Clear skies stretched overhead, but the air held more bite as the sun hung low over the horizon. "I won't be long," Moira had told Peg as she departed from the halla. "I just want to see how he fares after a full day of activity."

As she approached, the voices grew louder.

"Ye've got it all wrong, it's not like that 'tall!" Áedach's voice was laced with intensity.

"Bah!" The second voice was familiar, but Moira couldn't attach a name to it. "She is as I say, lad. She's a disgrace, an' she comes from disgrace. Stick wit' the plan!"

Moira ducked behind the large oak tree, guilt nagging the pit of her stomach for eavesdropping.

"I . . . I can't! She's been so kind to me. If ye'd just listen," Áedach pleaded.

"No!" The second man's raspy voice echoed through the valley. "Keep to the plan. I'll not say it again. That woman runnin' her mouth ruined my life. We will—we must—devastate her."

"But, Uncle!"

The door swung open and Moira ducked below the wall.

Peeking through an opening between the stones, she could see the hunched silhouette of an old man shuffling out of the hovel and heading farther out into the field. He turned back to Áedach. "Ye know yer task. Set yer tongue a'waggin'."

The last of the fading sunlight illuminated the man's wrinkled face, a wayward tooth protruding from his lips.

Buach! Moira clamped a hand over her mouth to keep from gasping aloud. *Buach is Áedach's uncle?*

So many questions crowded Moira's mind, she didn't know which one to give attention to first. She crouched there in the dirt, cold creeping onto her back from the stones behind her, and waited until the door scuffed closed again. Careful not to alert Áedach to her presence, she rose, brushed the dirt from her skirts, and fled.

Buach's words reverberated in her mind. *We must devastate her. Stick to the plan. Ye know yer task.* If not for Áedach's argument of the woman's kindness, they could have been talking about anyone. Moira knew, though, she and Peg were the only ones to show any modicum of kindness to the lad. The conspirators meant to devastate one of them, and given Moira's history with Buach, she could only guess the woman they had been discussing was her.

Anger burned as she realized that Buach, being the lad's uncle, likely knew of his condition and had done nothing. How could he allow a member of his own family, a child no less, to live in such poverty?

Valid questions, Moira Girl, but you have more pressing matters at present.

A brief thought scuttled across her mind to keep this information to herself, to handle it on her own. She dismissed it just as quickly as it had come, with a shake of her head. *God has given you good friends here for a reason.* She made her way back to Peg and Colm's. The place was like a second home to her now, and she felt just as welcome there as at her own mother's house.

Peg answered the door and invited her in. "Back so soon? Have a seat by the fire, pet. I'll fetch the tea."

In a moment Peg was back with her trademark tray of tea and brown bread. "Now, tell me what has yer face so clouded with concern." She took the seat across from Moira.

Moira told her of the conversation she'd overheard between Áedach and Buach. "I know it was wrong of me to listen in." She chewed her lip. "But when I heard what they were saying, it was like I was frozen."

Peg nodded. "'Tis quite disturbing, what ye've heard." She stirred the milk into her tea. "I've no idea what on earth Buach could mean by 'devastate her.' But I think it's safe ta say that ye will go no place alone."

Moira sank back into the chair. She hated the thought of troubling someone to chaperone her everywhere she went. But there was no arguing the fact that it was a bad idea for her to walk around Ballymann on her own, not knowing what Buach had in mind—or what Áedach had agreed to do.

"Colm will see ye home this evenin', and I'm sure between him and Sean we can work out havin' someone by yer side in yer comin' and goin'."

"I'm not so sure Mr. McFadden will be so open to the idea." Moira rose and circled the room. "Ever since the attack, he's been . . . different."

"Can ye blame him, love? He was worried sick over ye for days. It was nearly as traumatic for him to come across ye in such a state as it was fer ye."

Moira stopped pacing and looked at her friend. Could that really be what it was? She hadn't considered that finding her there—bloodied, unconscious, clothes torn asunder—would trouble Sean so. Could it be he wasn't cross with her at all? She tucked hope down in her heart, afraid to let it take root too deeply. She could not bear to let hope bloom only to have it uprooted once more.

Footsteps sounded at the door, then it swung open. "Well, hello, Miss Doherty! I didn't know we were expectin' ye today." Colm planted a tender kiss on her cheek. "I'm happy ta see ye."

"Colm, dear, would ye be so kind as to see our wee lass home?" Peg filled Colm in on the latest details. Anger clouded his eyes with each word.

"Miss Doherty, ye have my word. Ye'll not walk one step alone until we've reached the bottom o' this."

Moira smiled, once again overcome with gratitude for such undeserved blessings.

CHAPTER 53

The red door at the teacher's chalet stared down at Sean once again. It seemed ages ago that he last stood on this doorstep, awaiting Moira's answer. When the door swung open, Sean was struck by the sadness in her eyes, but her smile at his greeting brightened the dreary day. "Peg's waitin' for ye down at the halla."

Moira stepped outside. "Thank you, Mr. McFadden. It's good of you to take time away from your work to accompany me."

Weary of the formalities, Sean longed to shake free of them and return to the comfortable banter they'd enjoyed only weeks ago. The pair walked in uncomfortable silence as far as the market. When he could no longer stand it, Sean broke the quiet. "So, how are ya doing?"

She smiled at him briefly—a tired smile pushed up by the bottom lip, gone as quickly as it appeared. "I'm just fine, thank you."

Frustration burned in Sean's belly. Would she never open up to him? Did she no longer trust him? Perhaps she was now distrusting of all men. After the ordeal she had survived, who could blame her? Refusing to let her endure alone whatever mixture of emotions was sure to be churning within, Sean stopped and placed a hand on her shoulder. He waited until her eyes met his and held them there. He searched her face, struck once again by her beauty—a beauty only enhanced by the grace of her character. "No, really. How are ya doing, Moira?"

For a brief moment, she covered his hand with hers and he reveled in the cool touch of her skin before she removed her hand and clasped it daintily in her other. Her head dropped and she studied her fingers.

"It is good of you to ask." She met his gaze once more. "Truth be told, I'm weary. And I worry, though I try not to because the Lord is so very clear how He feels about worry. But I don't understand why any of this is happening, and I don't know how to guard myself against an enemy I can barely see."

He offered her the crook of his elbow, and after a pause, she accepted it. They fell into step again. Resisting the impulse to envelop her hand in his as they walked, he said, "Ye'll not face it alone, that I can promise ye." He looked down at her profile, awed how such strength could be housed in so delicate a vessel. "Seen or unseen, I will always guard against anyone who means you harm."

Her hand tightened in the crook of his arm. "Thank you."

Peg and Colm were waiting outside the halla as Sean and Moira approached. Peg greeted them both with a warm embrace and a kiss on each cheek.

"We'll take it from here, Sean. There's only a few more things need doin' afore the big party tomorrow."

Sean smiled at Moira and tipped his cap. "Until next time."

Moira tipped her head and matched his smile. "Indeed. Thanks again, Mr. McFadden."

As he turned to go, he couldn't help but notice her gaze linger on him longer than he'd seen in weeks.

The sun rode low on the horizon that evening, and the familiar Donegal chill had returned to the air. The preparations for the celebration complete, Peg and Moira walked in step with one another toward the chalet. Moira tugged her wrap tighter around herself and shivered.

"Oh, dear," Peg said, "where's your scarf?"

Moira felt about her neck. "Oh, sugar, I draped it on the windowsill at the halla when we were working."

"No matter. No one will bother it overnight. Ye can fetch it in the morning."

Moira considered it for a moment and nodded.

"Are ye lookin' forward to the céilí, pet?"

"I am." Moira released a sigh.

"What is it, then?"

"I feel terribly shallow, but I'm just a bit disappointed that I'll have to wear this dress." She ran her hands over the faded skirt. "I had hoped to have made my other dress by now, but with all that's gone on, it's still unfinished. Now with only a day before the party, I've no time."

Peg nodded, a smile playing on her lips. "Aye, 'tis a shame. But fear not, lass. No gown, no matter how tattered or frayed, could quell your beauty." She gave Moira's cheek a motherly pat before taking her leave at the path to Moira's door.

Lord, help me be content with that which You've already blessed me.

She opened the door to her chalet and froze. Her heart raced and the breath caught in her chest. On her table sat a large white box. It was certainly not there when she left. Remembering the eggshells and Buach's threatening words to Áedach, fear gripped her. In desperation, she called Peg back.

Peg came, breathless, running up the hill to her door. "What is it, pet? Are ye alright?"

Moira extended a shaky finger toward the box, unable to form words.

Peg pushed past Moira and entered the house. She checked every corner and shadow for potential intruders, but Moira noticed a hint of a smile on the woman's lips.

"'Tis all safe, my dear." Peg motioned her into the kitchen and began stoking the fire. "Come see what awaits ye."

With timid steps, Moira approached the table and reached out, hands trembling, to lift the lid from its place. Once removed, the lid fell to the floor as Moira clapped both hands over her mouth. Freshly pressed and neatly folded, the blue dress from O'Toole's Textiles stared up at her. She ran her hands over the bodice, the velvet smooth like butter on a summer's day. With great care, she lifted the dress out of the box and ran a hand along the sleeve, fingering the delicate peach lace at the cuff.

"Peg! What have you done?"

Peg held her hands up, palms out in protest. "Wasna me, peata." She shrugged and moved closer to join Moira in admiring the gorgeous gown. "It seems someone wants ye to be the belle o' the ball on Paddy's Day." She chuckled and wrapped an arm around Moira's shoulders.

Carefully returning the dress to the box, Moira struggled to rein in her emotions. "Oh, Peg." She retrieved a handkerchief from her sleeve and wiped the tears from her cheeks. "It's too grand a gift. However am I supposed to accept it?"

Peg lifted her shoulders, her face alight with mischief. "'Twould be a great insult to refuse such a generous gesture. Besides, ya canna return a gift when ye've no idea whence it came." With a flourish, Peg whisked the dress from the box and hung it in the press, leaving the door open to allow it to air.

Moira stared at the dress in disbelief, her mind reeling with possibilities of who could've lavished such a gift upon her. Áedach had spoken of wanting to repay her kindness, but he had no means of purchasing such a gown. Even if he'd managed to scrape the money together, how would he have gotten to Letterkenny and back? No, it couldn't have been him.

Peg had already denied it, and with how she and Colm hadn't shied away from claiming responsibility for Áedach's new clothes, Moira had no reason not to believe her. Perhaps Peg had mentioned to Bríd how much Moira had gone on about the gown in weeks past? The only other people who knew about it were the McGonigles—highly unlikely given Moira's latest encounter with her once-close friend. Other than the McGonigles, the only other person . . .

Moira's breath caught as the realization hit her.

Sean.

CHAPTER 54

Sleep eluded Moira. She rolled from her box bed and opened the door to her press. There hung the blue velvet dress, its fibers shimmering in the moonlight from the window. Recalling how beautiful she'd felt when she tried it on at the shop, how perfectly it had hugged her body, and the look in Sean's eyes when he saw her wearing it, her stomach fluttered. Heat pricked her cheeks as she allowed her mind to ponder how he might react.

Imagining him requesting the honor of a dance, Moira lowered into a deep curtsy. Never mind she was barefoot in her nightdress, she twirled and swayed a waltz with her imaginary hero right there in her bedchamber, while images of the halla aglow in firelight and the company of good folk danced in her mind's eye.

Her reverie was cut short when the church bells began to toll. Judging by the depth of darkness and the height of the moon, it couldn't have been any later than ten o'clock. Shouts arose on the street outside her door, and the sound of feet slapping the road in haste beckoned her to the window. Men of all ages fled hither and yon, some carrying buckets, others shouting orders in Irish. Moira grabbed her robe, tied the belt hastily around her waist, and hurried outside.

An orange glow lit the horizon while the activity in the

streets reached a frenetic pace. Moira hastened to join a group of women gathered on the footpath. "What is it? What's happened?"

The women stared ahead at the growing glow, not looking to see who had asked the questions. One woman who bounced a sleeping baby on her hip mumbled something in Irish. Crackling and popping sounds floated on the air, while another woman translated. "'Tis a fire. I've not gone down to see, but only one t'ing could burn like that."

"The halla," the other women replied in unison.

Moira gasped. "The halla?" She grabbed a handful of her robe skirts and sprinted down the road, paying no mind to her instructions to go nowhere alone. Buach would have to be daft—daft and very bold, indeed—to try anything with so many people about.

Horses, carts, and people littered the street. Moira darted as carefully as she could among them, desperate to reach the halla. She had to see for herself.

Please, God, not the halla.

The glow on the horizon grew as she neared. Watching for any sign of the fire dying, Moira's focus stayed on the halla and not on the street in front of her. Her shoulder ached. She'd knocked over someone else in the crowd.

Mortified, Moira uttered an apology and reached down to help the woman. When she was on her feet again, the woman cleared the hair from her face. It was Sinead.

"Oh, friend, I'm terribly sorry. Isn't it awful? What shall we do?"

Sinead glared at Moira. "Ye shall not do a t'ing. That halla belongs to Ballymann and her people. Not transients of low moral character." Sinead turned on her heel and ran toward the market.

As much as she'd like to make amends, Moira couldn't force Sinead to believe her any more than she could force the sun to shine. More pressing matters demanded her attention anyhow. Gathering her thoughts, and her skirts, she hurried to the halla. Men were scattered about, shouting orders and gathering myriad supplies. A chain of farmers, weavers, shepherds, and others stretched from the halla down to the sea, passing buckets back and forth, the first man in the line tossing water onto the building before sending the empty bucket back again.

Moira sank onto a boulder at the corner of the road to Peg's house. Flames licked the sky and poured from the windows. The valiant efforts of the townsmen seemed futile against such a blaze. Through her tears, Moira made out Sean's silhouette at the front of the line of men. *Of course he would be first in line to help.*

She hadn't meant to distract him, but when he caught sight of her through the hazy glow, Sean handed his bucket to the man behind him and made his way over to her.

"Ya shouldn't be here. 'Tisn't safe."

Moira looked at his face. Fatigue and heartbreak were written all over it. Soot streaked across his forehead and down one cheek. She fought the urge to smooth it away with her hand. "I had to see." She eyed the flames once more. "How can I help?"

Sean looked back at the building and shook his head. "'Tis done now, lass. Naught more we can do but try and douse the flames. That thatch on the roof is so dry, it won't go out in a hurry. And you've seen the bales inside lining the walls. They make fine seats for tired dancers on a cold night, but unfortunately they also make great kindling."

"What a shame." Moira laid a hand on his arm. "I never would have dreamed a stone building could burn so."

"Aye," Sean said. He looked at Moira, and it seemed as if he wanted to say something more, but Peg's voice ripped through the night air.

"Colm!" She screamed. "Colm!" She lunged toward the building, but Sean caught her in his arms.

"No, no one's inside." He turned and squinted at the windows. The roof groaned and a loud crack split the sky.

"He said . . . he said he was going to check one more thing." Peg beat Sean's chest with her fists. "He said somethin' wasna sittin' right with him and he had to go check on the halla. Colm!"

As if in response to her screams, the roof groaned again before collapsing completely into the building. Flames shot into the night sky. Peg crumpled to the ground, a guttural cry unlike any Moira had ever heard piercing the air.

She wrapped her arms around Peg and nodded to Sean. "Go!"

Sean ran to the other men. "Colm Sweeny's inside, lads. Let's go! Move it! Get that water over here! You—head over there." Sean continued to call out orders while the men went into swift action. Bríd and some other women from the village gathered around Peg and Moira. Bríd's prayers mixed with the cacophony as others wept openly. Still others could do nothing but stand and watch, mouths agape. Peg's wails echoed on through the night.

CHAPTER 55

The sky faded from slate to black, and the only sounds were the rustling of the Atlantic waves down below, the occasional crack and pop of the blackened remains of the halla, and Peg's cries, which had dwindled from gut-wrenching wails to exhaustion-laced whimpers.

Moira sat, arms still wrapped tightly around her friend, rocking back and forth like her mother had done so often for her as a little girl. Oblivious to any chill in the air, Moira stared as the smoke reduced to wisps and curls and ascended to the heavens. Footfalls on the road drew her attention. Sean approached.

He laid a tender hand on her shoulder. "Why don't ya take Peg back to her house. Give her some dry clothes and a hot cuppa. The lads and I will begin the search, now the flames have died down."

Moira bobbed her head slightly and looped her arms under Peg's shoulders. "Come on, let's get you warm and dry."

Peg's face shot up to Moira's as though she meant to protest. Instead, she crumpled, and a fresh spate of tears spilled onto her cheeks and splashed down the front of her wrinkled dress.

Her body numb, Moira held the weight of her friend as they shuffled the few hundred yards to the Sweeny home. Inside, the house was eerily silent. A plate of crumbs and a half-drunk cup of tea sat at Colm's place at the table—evidence of his late-night snack abandoned to see to the halla. Moira turned Peg's shoulders as they passed the sitting room, discreetly averting the woman's gaze from the sight.

Peg slumped down to sit on the bed, her gaze glued to the floor, her mind obviously elsewhere. Moira searched through the wardrobe and settled on a dark brown dress rather than the traditional black of mourning. *They may yet find him alive. Please, Lord, let it be so.*

She dressed her friend in silence as tears slid ceaselessly down Peg's cheeks. Once the buttons were fastened and dry stockings in place, Moira eased her to lie down on the bed, pulling up a quilt to cover her—the same quilt that had comforted Moira as she recovered from the attack. "Just rest. I'll put the kettle on."

In a stupor, Moira shuffled into the kitchen, set the kettle to boil on the stove, and arranged the tea tray as thoughtfully as she'd seen Peg do so many times. *How did this happen? What was Colm doing there? This can't be real.* The whistle broke through her thoughts, and she poured the steaming water into the teapot, watching as it turned golden brown when it hit the tea.

She carried the tray to the room where Peg lay, the soft breathing and slow rise and fall of her shoulders indicating sleep had mercifully fallen upon her. Leaving the tray on the creepie next to the bed and setting the fire in the fireplace to rights, she slipped the door closed and made her way to the sitting room.

A knock at the front door broke her reverie. Bríd stood in the doorway holding Moira's faded traveling frock. "I thought ye might need somethin' other than your *gúna oiche* to wear."

Moira looked down at her damp, soiled robe and night-gown. "Oh, thank you, Bríd. It wouldn't do for me to carry on like this, would it?"

Bríd shook her head with a sad chuckle.

"Will you stay for tea?"

"I won't, peata, but thanks." Bríd was already turning to go. "There's loads more to be taken care of in town."

"Of course." Moira waved her friend off, closed the door, and made her way to the sitting room, where she hastily changed her dress. She stood in the middle of the room and turned about, unsure what to do next.

Unable to bring herself to clear Colm's dishes, she slid into the upholstered chair and absently poked at the fire with a stick. Memories swirled like a gale around her—Colm standing at her door with Sean, hat in hand, eyeing the tea cakes on the table behind her. His weathered eyes winking down at his wife. His fatherly hand placed firmly on Sean's shoulder.

The door scuffed open, pale early-morning light spilled onto the floor, and Sean's form filled the entryway. She raised hopeful eyes to his, dismayed to see him covered in soot. There was gut-wrenching sadness in his eyes. She raised her eyebrows. *Is there any hope?*

Sean's head fell forward, his eyes on his feet, and he shook his head so slightly she almost missed it. Sean's knees buckled, and a cry welled up and out of him as his face collapsed.

Moira flew over and caught him before his knees hit the ground, easing him to the floor. She held him close and stroked his head. "Shh, shh," she crooned in his ear. "I'm . . . I'm so sorry."

Sobs rocked their bodies as they mourned their friend,

their father figure. "I should've been there," Sean whispered. "I should've saved him."

Moira could only wag her head over and over. Clasping handfuls of his shirt as she held him and sobbed.

❧

Limbs aching as she stretched, Moira did her best to ignore the dull throbbing in her forehead—a side effect of crying for hours. The warmth of the turf fire kissed her face, and she was surprised to find a plaid draped across her and a pillow under her head.

"I couldn't bring myself to disturb ye." Sean was seated at the far side of the table, as far as he could get from her.

Moira rubbed her eyes and stood, folding the plaid neatly and draping it across a chair. "My apologies for falling asleep." She smoothed her hair down. "Have you heard anything from Peg?"

His gaze turned toward the room where Peg slept, and he shook his head. "I believe she's still asleep." He rose to his feet, the chair scraping against the floor, and made quickly for the door. "I must go and see about arrangements for Colm's—" His voice broke. Clearing his throat and straightening his posture, he continued. "I must see that everythin' is in order. Bring Peg down to the halla in half an hour's time. She'll want ta escort her husband home."

Home? Whyever would they bring the body here? Her furrowed brow must've communicated her confusion.

"For the wake," Sean explained. "He'll lay in repose here before he's laid to final rest."

Moira swallowed the lump in her throat. "Of course."

Sean quit the house, the loud thud of the closing door punctuating their grief.

How hard this must be for him. Lord, grant him peace.

After tidying what few things were out of place and splashing some water on her cheeks, Moira went to see Peg.

She knocked softly with the knuckle of her pointer finger and eased the door open. "Are you awake?" She peered around the door. Peg sat in bed, leaning against the headboard. Her eyes were red and swollen, her cheeks chapped from hours of weeping. "Oh, Peg." Moira swept to the bed and wrapped her arms around her, both women crying anew. After a moment, Moira fetched a clean handkerchief from the press and handed it to the new widow.

Peg dabbed her face and took a deep breath to quell the sobs. "Thank you, peata," she whispered.

"Em, Peg." Moira cleared her throat. "Sean was just here. They'll be ready for you down at the halla soon. To . . . walk . . . to bring Colm home."

Peg's watery eyes studied Moira's hands. "Aye."

"Shall I fetch your mourning gown?"

Peg nodded. Moira retrieved the black muslin dress from its hanger and proceeded to prepare it—opening the buttons, unlacing the bodice. Peg's hand stilled hers. Their eyes met and with a squeeze of her hand, Peg communicated what she could not voice.

"Of course." Moira brushed a kiss to her cheek. "I'll give you some privacy."

Not ten minutes later, Peg joined Moira at the hearth. Moira whispered a prayer for strength and led Peg to the door. As they ventured out, three of Peg's neighbors approached.

"We'll see to everythin', love."

Moira recognized one woman as young Aoife's mother. The other women, none of whom were familiar to Moira, nodded in agreement. One, a stout woman with hair the color of copper, reached out and squeezed Peg's hand before heading into the house.

Peg and Moira walked in silence toward the halla. As they approached the crossroads, Moira's jaw fell open and Peg pressed her handkerchief to her mouth. Dozens of people lined both sides of the road. Some held flowers, others candles. Men had removed their flat caps and held them over their hearts in respect.

When they reached the main road, Ballymann's residents lined the streets in both directions as far as the eye could see. An uilleann piper played a mournful tune as Sean, the priest, Paddy, and another man carried Colm's body on a makeshift stretcher out of the halla. Since it was draped in white canvas, it was easy to pretend someone else lay underneath. But the evidence of the far-reaching impact of Colm's kindness, compassion, and goodness stretched along the streets of all of Ballymann. There was no denying it—Colm Sweeny was dead.

Moira studied the faces of those she knew. Grief and anger were etched on the lines of Sean's face, but he carried himself with the pride and dignity befitting his mentor. Peg stood straight and tall, chin lifted, though trembling.

Oh, Peg, you need not be strong. There's no shame in grief.

Every eye followed Colm, and as the pallbearers passed Moira and Peg, the crowd turned in unison. On a hill in the distance, Moira caught a glimpse of Lady Williams. She stood, skirts rustling in the breeze, with a smirk on her face. Her eyes seemed to scan the crowd, and when they met Moira's, what looked like shock registered on the woman's face. Lady Williams looked from Moira to Colm's body and back again. Moira furrowed her brow, confused.

Focus, Moira Girl. 'Tis Peg who needs you now.

With slow, marked steps, Peg led the town to bring Colm home one last time.

CHAPTER 56

The Sweeny house was awash with candlelight when Moira entered behind Peg. The neighbor women had lit hundreds of candles, many of which stood in the back bedroom. The linens were stripped, and white cloth covered the heather mattress. Moira watched in awe as the evening unfolded.

Peg took her place by the fire—the seat of honor, as it were. Would that this honor could pass from her. The three women Moira had met on their way out followed Sean and the others as they carried Colm's body into the room. They laid the stretcher on the ground and the men carefully lifted him onto the bed. Moira started to enter the room, but Sean held his hand up to her. He and the other men slipped from the room and closed the door. Sean pulled Moira aside.

"Ye'll want to stay out here," he whispered.

Moira furrowed her brow. "Can I not help?"

"'Tis tradition for the neighbor women to wash and prepare the body." He looked toward the door and his eyes darkened. "Ye'll not want to see Colm in that state, Moira. He'd want you to remember him as he was."

Moira pressed a hand to her mouth, fresh tears pooling in her eyes.

"There are other things I must attend to." Sean's expression softened. "I am sorry." He briefly laid a tender hand on Moira's shoulder.

Assuring him she would be fine, she sent him to see to his duties. So many traditions and customs of which she was unaware. It was like a well-choreographed dance, each person knowing their part, each step familiar to them. Everyone but Moira. She did her best to be useful, making sure there was always water in the kettle and a fire in the hearth.

All the mirrors had been covered, and the clocks were stopped, showing the hour at which Colm passed. Peg sat, stoic, in her chair and graciously received the endless stream of mourners.

Without the benefit of the clock, it was impossible to track how much time had passed. It seemed hours before the door to Colm's room opened and the three neighbor women emerged, faces somber. One by one they presented themselves in front of Peg. They shook her hand, kissed her cheek, and murmured the traditional Irish sympathies: *ní maith liom do trioblóide*—"I don't like your trouble."

Once the women had all greeted her, Peg stood and squared her shoulders. She extended a hand to Moira, who grasped it immediately. The pair walked slowly to the room where Colm lay.

Soft candlelight cast shadows on the walls. The women had done a fine job of preparing the room, so it was tasteful and beautiful. Crisp white linen adorned with black ribbons was draped across the body, and several pipes and dishes of tobacco and snuff were placed strategically around the room.

Peg clutched Moira's hand so hard her nails dug into skin, but Moira remained still. Despite Peg's obvious grief, no tears fell as she stood by the side of the man she loved. After a moment, Peg leaned over and kissed the linen over

Colm's forehead. She whispered an endearment meant only for his ears, then gently touched her forehead, belly button, left shoulder, then right. "Amen," she whispered and turned to Moira, giving her a slight nod.

Moira took a moment to whisper a prayer of thanks for Colm and all he had done for her. She laid her hand upon his shoulder and dropped her head as she prayed. Sensing the presence of others in the room, Moira lifted her eyes and turned to join Peg at the door. A steady stream of men filed in and uttered their respects to Colm before taking a puff or two from one of the pipes in the room.

Moira followed Peg back to the sitting room, where Aoife's mother, the copper-haired woman, and the other neighbor were setting out glasses of *poitín*, pints of ale, and trays piled high with brown bread, cakes, and biscuits. Donations from the townsfolk, Moira assumed. In the corner, the mournful whine of the uilleann pipes whirred, and a fiddler tuned his strings. Another gentleman produced a bodhrán as visitors and mourners filled every nook and cranny of the house.

Still, Peg sat in her chair, ever the gracious hostess, even in her grief. But it was Peg's dry eyes that gave Moira the most pause. She vowed to keep a close eye on her friend and not let her succumb to the numbing effects of grief.

❦

The somewhat boisterous conversations filling the house fell to an abrupt silence. Whispers and murmurs floated to the rafters. Moira, sensing someone behind her, turned around.

Lady Williams's lithe figure loomed over her. A good head taller than Moira, the woman was foreboding indeed. Up close, the lines and creases on her face indicated she was far more advanced in years than Moira had believed. A stern expression was plastered on her face, and she looked Moira over for a long while before finally speaking.

"Good day, Miss Doherty."

Moira curtsied nervously. "Good day, Lady Williams."

"I did not expect to see you today. Not . . . here, anyway."

Moira racked her brain for what sort of meaning the Lady held by that statement. Unable to find any she merely uttered, "Yes, Lady Williams."

Looking over Moira's head toward the table laden with drink, Lady Williams sniffed and stepped past her, heading for one of the other women of Ballymann with whom to converse.

Utterly confounded by the encounter, Moira reclaimed the seat across from Peg, whose face briefly registered the same confusion before returning to the somber countenance of a widow at the wake of her husband.

As the day wore on, more people filled the house, spilling outside and milling about the fields surrounding them, despite the damp, dreary weather. Music poured forth ceaselessly from the group in the corner, each musician breaking as needed for a drink or breath of fresh air.

No one spoke a word to Moira, though plenty shot dirty looks her way as they whispered with Lady Williams across the room. Some made a wide berth around her as they shuffled through the house, while others managed a *tsk, tsk* with a twitch of their noses as they passed.

Throughout the day as Moira passed through the hall to refill the kettle or fetch another tray from the kitchen, she noticed that a woman from the area was always seated in a chair at the foot of the bed where Colm lay. Though not always the same woman, someone consistently occupied that seat—it was always a woman, and never Peg. Men filed through, doffed their caps, bowed their heads, and dutifully puffed from a pipe, yet there a woman sat. Moira assumed it was yet another custom she wasn't used to.

As evening approached, the crowd dwindled, but more people than Moira expected lingered. When the *angelus*—the countrywide ringing of the church bells to call people to prayer—rang at six o'clock, Sinead and her parents arrived, bearing armloads of fresh-baked scones and bread, and a fresh barrel of poitín.

Moira stepped toward Sinead, who pursed her lips and turned in the opposite direction. Mrs. McGonigle offered a curt nod before greeting Peg and then heading in to pay her respects to Colm. Paddy made his way to a group of men congregated in the kitchen. Moira tried to ignore the hurt she felt at Sinead's continued disdain, but each new shun was like lemon juice in a fresh wound.

When the night had well fallen, and the candles dripped from their stands, a familiar scuffling made its way into the house, and a recognizable *tsk, tsk* caused the hair on the back of Moira's neck to stand up. She turned and fell back a step as her worst nightmare appeared in the doorway.

Buach.

CHAPTER 57

Buach approached Peg, hat gripped in his hands so tightly Moira thought he might soon rip it in two. "It canna be true." His voice was thinner than ever, and it held a quaver that suggested tears were not far away.

Peg leveled a measured gaze at him but said nothing.

Buach lifted her fingers and brushed them with a kiss, murmuring the traditional sympathies before raising himself to stand as straight as he could. He avoided Moira's gaze altogether, but when he caught Lady Williams's eye, he flicked his head, motioning her aside.

With the grace of a swan on water, Lady Williams made her way to the hallway with Buach struggling to keep up behind her. After a moment, heated whispers could be heard, but Moira found it impossible to discern whether they were speaking in Irish or English, let alone what they might be saying.

"*Stad!*" Buach's raspy voice sliced the air.

Lady Williams reappeared in the sitting room, her cheeks flushed. The same stern expression resided on her face but fear now clouded her eyes. Behind her, Buach shuffled toward the room where Colm lay in repose. Curious, Moira slipped in behind him.

For a long while, Buach stood silent over the body, his

hands twisting and untwisting his hat again and again, as though wringing water from a rag. Warmth grew near on Moira's back, and without looking she knew Sean stood behind her.

"Has he said anythin'?"

Moira shook her head, keeping her eyes on the old man.

All at once, Buach collapsed in a heap on the floor, sobs filling the air. His shoulders shook and unintelligible words poured from his mouth along with his wails.

"*Logh dom! Logh dom!*" he cried again and again.

Moira glanced over her shoulder at Sean. His brows drew together. Confusion swam in his eyes.

"What is it?" Moira kept her voice a mere whisper.

"He's asking . . . for forgiveness." Sean's eyes met hers, then they both looked back at Buach. He was still balled up on the floor, one hand clutching the hem of the burial cloth draped over Colm's body.

Lady Williams pushed past the onlookers crowding the door and stood over him. "There, there." Her voice was flat and devoid of all emotion. "Come now, let's get you some fresh air."

Buach straightened but remained on his knees. "I'm sorry. I'm so sorry. Peg, *tá brón orm!*" He looked straight at Moira. "Tá brón orm. Tá brón orm."

Moira pressed her lips together and took a step toward him. Before she could get closer, Lady Willams took his arm and pulled him to his feet.

"Pull yourself together, man," she hissed in his ear, loud enough that the others could hear.

He sniffled loudly, wiped a dirty sleeve across his face, and yanked his other arm from her grasp.

Lady Williams jutted her chin in the air and with dainty yet hurried steps, left the room. Buach started to follow suit, but Sean grabbed him by the arm.

"Let's have a wee chat, auld man." Sean dragged Buach into the kitchen and all but threw him into a wooden chair near the fireplace. "What's all this about?"

Buach hung his head, chin trembling. He wagged his head but stayed silent.

"Speak, man!" Sean bent over to meet Buach's eyes. "Did ye start that fire?"

Buach's gaze flew up to meet Sean's. "Nae! Nae! I didna touch the halla!"

Sean straightened and crossed his arms over his chest. "So you say." He started to pace the room.

Moira watched, biting her lip to keep her tears at bay. What was happening?

Suddenly the crowd behind her parted, and Peg slid past Moira and into the kitchen. Men removed their caps and bowed slightly at the waist.

"Buach O'Boyle." They were the first words Peg had spoken in hours. "I know ye loved my Colm. We all did."

A robust chorus of ayes and hear, hears burst forth from the crowd.

"But 'tis also no saicrit that there are others here who were closer ta him than the likes o' ye." She paused. "So what is it ye're so terribly sorry fer?"

The old man shook his head, swiping his nose with his sleeve again. "I canna. I canna."

"You can't *what*?" Sean crouched low, forcing him to speak face-to-face.

"We t'ought . . ." He glanced around the room, seeming to rest his eyes on the crowd in general. "We t'ought it was ye in the halla, not Colm."

Voices rippled through the crowd, and a sickening feeling floated to the back of her throat. *We?*

"Ye thought it was me?" Sean pointed to his own chest.

"Nae." Buach buried his face in his hands.

"Then who, man? Speak!" Sean gripped the old man by the shoulders and shook him until his teeth chattered.

Moira laid a hand on Sean's back. "Sean, please."

Sean's trembling slowed, and he turned to look at her. She shook her head ever so slightly, and Sean took a measured step backward. "If not me," Sean asked through clenched teeth, "then just who did you think it was?"

"We t'ought it was ye." A crooked finger raised in the air. "Miss Doherty. The teacher."

Gasps filled the crowded room, and Moira stumbled backward. A pair of unseen hands caught and steadied her. She didn't look back to see who it was. She only righted herself and stared at Buach in disbelief.

CHAPTER 58

Sean watched in horror as the color drained from Moira's face. He scanned the kitchen for another chair. Someone read his thoughts and handed him one from across the room. He set it behind Moira and eased her to sit, then he turned his attention back to Buach.

"Ye're not makin' any sense, auld man." Sean resisted the urge to shake him again.

"We were aimin' fer the teacher." Buach nodded in Moira's direction. "If I'd o' t'ought fer one second we'd hurt Colm . . ." His face screwed up, causing his wayward tooth to protrude even farther, as new tears poured down his cheeks. "I'm so sorry, Peg. Please, ye must fergive me."

A hand on his arm drew Sean's attention away from Buach. "But why? Why did you seek to harm me?" Moira's strained voice was almost more than Sean could bear.

She stepped forward, recognition registering in her eyes. "'That woman running her mouth,'" she said softly before crouching to look Buach in the eye. "Were you talking about my mother? Did she do something to you?"

Buach's gaze dropped to the floor. "Aye."

"But why? Why treat me so poorly?" Moira asked.

"Because you deserved it," answered a voice from the doorway.

Confusion twisted Moira's face as Lady Williams entered the room.

"Explain yerself, madam," Sean said.

"Because of you." Lady Williams sniffed at Moira in contempt. "Because of your tart of a mother, my daughter was overlooked to marry John Adair."

Moira looked confused as she rose from her crouch. "I beg your pardon, milady, but I fail to see how something my mother did to Buach twenty years ago would be an obstacle to your dauther's marriage, nor how it warrants harm to me."

Lady Williams sighed and moved closer to Moira. Her bony hands rested on her hips. "Your mother was a housemaid at Glenveagh Castle for the Adair family. Their son, John, only visited during his holidays from university. He and my daughter had supped at the Adair table on many occasions, and it was said that he was going to propose to my Grainne at summer's end that year."

Sean noticed a few women rolling their eyes, but they seemed too interested in this latest twist of gossip to protest. He knew this story as well. Lady Williams had made no secret of the supposed impending engagement, but it had been widely disputed by those who would have been more privy to such information.

Moira crossed her arms over her chest. "And my mother's position as a housemaid factors into this how?"

"She was caught in quite the compromising situation with John." Lady Williams looked around the room, as if to survey the response to this accusation. When shock failed to register with the crowd, she continued, "A short time thereafter, your mother fled in her disgrace to America, while John was forced to leave Gweedore forever to avoid the shame that hussy had brought upon his household. He never again returned to Glenveagh, and my daughter lost the wealthiest marriage prospect she'd had."

A heavy silence filled the room as the crowd mulled over Lady Willams's story, each person presumably trying to connect the dots between her, the Adairs, and Moira.

Moira's eyes widened. "You . . . you blame me for Mr. Adair not marrying your daughter?"

"Don't you see?" The woman's voice rose far louder than was prudent for a lady. "*You* are the fruit of the sordid affair. It is because of you that Noreen fled, bringing further shame upon the Adair name. You were the catalyst for the rejection that befell my family. Someone had to pay. And with your mother off in America, your arrival was the perfect opportunity to avenge my family's honor."

Moira's jaw fell open, disbelief coloring her face. She wavered as though she was going to faint. Sean placed his hand between her shoulders to steady her.

"Tell them, Buach." Lady Williams's voice was thick with desperation. "You're the one who discovered the affair. Tell them!"

Only then did Buach drop his hands from his face. "Nae! Nae!" He cried and waved his hands frantically in the air. "It was all a lie!"

"What?" Fire ignited Lady Williams's eyes before she could regain her composure. "But you said—"

"I know what I said," he spat out. "An' I'm tellin' ye, 'twas a lie."

"Yer lie cost my husband his life. Ye'd best tell the truth now." Peg's voice was cool, but her fists were clenched tightly at her sides.

Buach heaved a sigh, stood, and turned his face to the fireplace. "What ye said about Noreen workin' at Glenveagh is true." He placed a hand on the mantel. "I was workin' there as well. In the stables."

"Aye, go on," Sean said when Buach paused longer than he had patience for.

"Noreen had caught me stealin' some o' Master Adair's silver. I'd hide it in my waistcoat a piece at a time. Anyhow, when she discovered me with it, I begged her not ta go ta the aut'orities." He shrugged and turned his back to the fire, keeping his gaze on the ground. "When she reported my crime, o'course I lost my position. I'd never work in Gweedore again."

"But why turn your venom on me?" Moira was steadier on her feet now, her palms turned up in question.

"Because of yer mammy, I lost everyt'ing. When she left for America soon after, I saw me chance. I told folk she had to flee because she'd been gettin' up close an' pairsonal wit' John Adair and ran away to America when she found herself to be in the family way."

"You fool!" Lady Williams hissed. "How dare you drag me into your charade!"

"Whan ye showed up, Miss Doherty, I saw my chance to get back at yer mother in me own way." Buach's red eyes turned at Peg. "I never dreamed it would end up hurtin' the best man Ballymann has e'er seen."

"Ye still haven't explained the fire." Sean placed a firm hand on Buach's shoulder and pressed him back into the seat.

"Aye." Buach shook his head. "Because of the story I told all those years ago, I knew Lady Williams was just as cross wit' Noreen as me. When we'd heard Moira was goin' to be helpin' wit' the readyin' of the halla, we saw our chance."

"*You* were supposed to be the one in that godforsaken halla," Lady Williams hissed at Moira. "I should've checked to be certain, but when I heard movement inside, I assumed it was you. After all, your scarf was draped through the window."

"I'm sorry," Buach cried again. "If 'tweren't fer my wag-gin' tongue spinnin' yarns, none o' this woulda happened. I just wanted Noreen ta feel the pain she put on me."

"Yer own daft behavior is what hurt ye, auld man." Sean grabbed his arm, pulling Buach to his feet. "Yer all-forsaken pride was willing to take the life of an innocent girl to keep up appearances on a rumor ye started over twenty years ago."

"The Gardaí'll deal with the pair o' ye." Sean nodded at a few of the men and they sprang to action. Two grasped Lady Williams and another pair took Buach by the arms as they led them outside. As they passed through the crowd, some spat on their faces, others called out foul insults.

"Wait," Peg yelled. She approached Buach until she was standing nose to nose with him.

"Let 'im have it!" called a voice from the crowd.

"Pummel 'im!" came another.

"Buach." Peg held her head high, though her chin trembled. Moira stepped up beside her and slipped a hand through her elbow. "I . . . I forgive you. And may God have mercy on yer soul. And on ye, Lady Williams."

Gasps and murmurs rippled through the crowd as Peg nodded at the men to take the culprits away.

CHAPTER 59

When the guilty parties had been escorted outside, the crowd seemed to lose interest and dispersed—the events of the night sure to be fodder for stories told around the fire for years to come. A few women mumbled admiration to Peg as they made their way back to the table, to sit vigil with Colm, or to head home to their own children.

"Oh, Peg." Moira lay a hand on Peg's shoulder and guided her back to the fire. "I don't know what to say."

What a senseless loss. Colm's absence would be felt by the community for decades. And for what? To save face over a crime committed and reported long ago? Lady Williams's grievances were moot, knowing John Adair's lack of return had nothing to do with Noreen O'Connell Doherty.

"Rest assured," Sean was saying when Moira came out of her reverie, "Buach and Lady—though I hate to refer to her as such—Williams will be dealt with swiftly and harshly. Duffy can hardly ignore their confessions, especially with so many witnesses who heard them."

Moira sank into the chair across from Peg and stared into the fire. "'Tis my fault." She shook her head. "Had I never come here, none of this would have happened."

"Seafóid!" Peg leaned forward and clasped Moira's hand. "The Laird brought you here. Of that I have no doubt. Ye are as much to blame for what happened to my dearest Colm as ye are for the tide comin' and goin' each day."

"But, Peg—"

"Nae." Peg cut Moira's protest short. "Colm loved to serve ye. He loved servin' the whole of Ballymann. Sure, he'd said something wasna right. He had a hunch somethin' was out o' sorts. That's why he went to the halla last night. He was always watchin' out for folk in this town. He'd hate to see ye blamin' yerself for somethin' ye didna do."

Moira squeezed Peg's hand, the lump in her throat holding back any words she might attempt to say.

Peg returned the squeeze, then rose and bussed the top of Moira's head. "Now, if ye'll excuse me, I'd like to sit with my husband."

Out of respect, Moira stood. As she turned to the hallway, Sinead entered from outside, her cheeks stained with tears. "Oh Moira, can ya ever forgive me?"

Moira rushed over and embraced her friend.

"I shoulda known," Sinead said between sobs. "I shoulda known it wasna true. I've been so awful to ye."

"Aye, you have been." Moira braced Sinead's shoulders and eased her back to look in her face. "Had you but asked, I could have told you the truth. In fact, I *did* tell you."

"I know." Sinead's gaze fell to the floor. "Folk were sayin' so many t'ings, and when I saw ye come out of Áedach's place alone, my imagination went wanderin'."

Moira sighed and grabbed Sinead's hands. "If Peg can forgive those who hurt her poor Colm, and the Lord can forgive me for all I've done wrong, I suppose I can forgive you." She looked hard at Sinead's face before breaking into a smile and gathering her friend in a warm embrace.

From the back of the house, a mournful groan filled the air. It sounded so near a howl, Moira looked about to see if it was an animal.

"Peg's begun the *caoineadh*." Sinead's eyes swam with compassion.

Moira furrowed her brow.

"The keening . . . her official mourning," Sinead clarified.

"I must say, I'm relieved to hear her cry."

Sean and Sinead looked at her as though she had two heads. Moira looked from Sean to Sinead and back again. "She'd been so . . . calm. I was worried that she was slipping away from us."

"Once again ye're unfamiliar with our ways, Miss Darrty," Sinead said in a mocking scold. "Once the body arrives at the wake house, there can be no cryin' 'til the deceased has been properly prepared, or ye risk attractin' bad spirits into the home."

Moira grimaced. "But the women finished preparing things hours ago."

"Aye." Sean motioned for the trio to take a seat at the table. "Sometimes the widow—or widower—chooses to wait until the first night to begin keening. Just to be safe."

The copper-haired woman appeared in the doorway, a glass of poitín in hand. She raised it aloft and began to recite a poem. All in Irish, Moira only caught a word here or there, but as she spoke, and Peg's keening mingled with the mournful words, heads bowed throughout the house. When the woman finished, each person raised his or her glass in silent toast to Colm and drank.

One after another, women stood and recited poems or sang a mournful tune. When the songs were finally done, the poitín low, and the mourners sufficiently cried out, each took their leave, one by one. Only the three neighbor women remained with Moira, Sinead, and Sean throughout the night. Colm was never left alone, and Peg continued her keening long into the morning.

The sun was just beginning to peek over the Donegal hills when Moira left the Sweeny house. She needed fresh air and water on her face. She needed time to think and pray before returning to Peg's for the procession to the church. As she trudged home, memories of Colm and Peg washed over her.

If not for Colm, her chalet would be in shambles, and she likely would not have met Peg. Without Peg, she wouldn't have had the courage to continue looking after Áedach. Her feet stilled.

Where was Áedach? She'd not seen him since he arrived to help with the Paddy's Day preparations at the halla. *Except for the conversation you eavesdropped on at his hovel that night.* Buach had ordered the lad to "keep to the plan."

Did Áedach know of Buach and Lady Williams's plans to kill her? Had he run away when he learned of the fire? She made a mental note to stop by his hovel after the funeral to see the lad and how he fared. But she purposed not to go alone.

A gust of frigid, salty air woke Moira from her thoughts like a slap to the face. She looked about, realizing she'd walked right past her chalet and was nearly as far as the guesthouse. A heavy slate sky hung overhead. Nature itself was in mourning, it would seem. The street was unusually empty, and no figures could be seen in the windows of the pub.

Moira crossed the road and wandered down the path leading toward the ocean until she came to the rock she had sat upon her first day in Ballymann. Very little, if anything, had changed since she was last there. Yet everything had changed. *She* had changed.

Gathering her skirts around her, she sat on the rock and

once again closed her eyes. Sea grass rustled and tickled her legs. Waves crashed upon the rocky shore, singing their own doleful ballad. Her spirit was raw and worn, her heart broken at the loss and deception she'd suffered at the hands of her fellow community members. Wanting to pray, needing to pray, her words were sorely lacking. No matter how hard she tried, no eloquent phrases conjured in her heart, and no utterances lifted from her spirit to the Lord.

Come to me, ye who are weary. And I will give you rest.

The familiar promise from Scripture whispered deep in her heart and soothed like water in a parched land. Rather than force some contrived prayer or attempt to appear holier than she was, she allowed herself to simply rest in the presence of the One who had brought her here.

At length, the weight lightened. Her breaths came easier. *Don't let this be wasted, Lord. Redeem these evil days and restore the hope of those who have none.* She opened her eyes, finding the world just as she'd left it when first she sat upon the rock. Her heart was still heavy. Grief still surrounded her like a shroud. But the despair had lifted.

In Him, there was never a promise of no grief on this side of heaven, but there was always the promise of joy. And she would await that day with a hopeful heart.

CHAPTER 60

Music and laughter greeted Moira when she returned to the
Sweeny house. She felt refreshed from her time of reflection, and a smile lit her face, despite the grief still gripping
her heart. So many friends, neighbors, and even people
from neighboring villages filled the house, Moira could
hardly fit inside the door.

Sinead met her and pulled her into the throng, placing
a kiss on each cheek when she finally got close enough.
"Wha' d'ye think? Quite the party, aye?"

"Quite!" Moira laughed. "I thought this was a funeral."

"Oh aye, 'tis!" Sinead bobbed in time with the lively reel
pulsing from the sitting room. "Give me an Irish wake over
an' Irish weddin' any day!"

Moira's eyes grew wide. "Truly?"

"Oh, aye! The wake is a celebration. O'course folk are sad
and there are tears and all that. But they send their loved
one off wit' joy and gratitude for a life well lived. And we
celebrate tha' we got to be a part of it—even if it was over
too soon."

"And the wedding?" Moira couldn't imagine a funeral
being more joyful than a wedding.

"Oh, there's love and happiness and all." Sinead rolled

her eyes. "But we take our marriage vows very serious, like. It's a happy occasion but very somber."

Moira nodded, then caught sight of Peg. She greeted her with a hug and offered her condolences once again.

Peg's eyes were red and black shadows grew beneath them, but she bore a smile. "My Colm woulda loved this, ya know?" She looked around, tears pooling again.

"I know." Moira took Peg's hand in hers and squeezed.

Just then, the door to the room where Colm lay in repose opened. The three neighbor women emerged from the room and led the crowd outside. Peg stood next to the outside door, Moira next to her. With slow, even steps, Sean and the three men from the day before carried Colm's body out of the house. Once outside, their pace quickened greatly. The musicians fell in line behind the men, Peg behind them, and the rest of the crowd followed.

The journey, though only to the next road over, was an arduous one. The crowd continued their songs and stories as they walked, but Moira struggled to keep pace. Why didn't they use a cart to carry the body to the church and gravesite? Her breaths came in ragged puffs as she purposed to stay with the group.

Sinead glanced at her, a knowing smile on her lips. "If ye think this part's bad," Sinead spoke into Moira's ear as though reading her thoughts, "wait 'til the walk to the *reilig*." She gestured across the main road toward the ocean. The gray spires and Celtic crosses of the graveyard jutted into the air. How had Moira never noticed it before?

Not located next to the church where Moira had expected, the cemetery was on a hillock right by the ocean. Moira could see the narrow footpath that zigzagged around the bottom and wound its way upward. She couldn't fathom having to carry a coffin on such a path.

When the party finally reached the church, they were

greeted by the priest, his face solemn and his few wispy hairs flapping in the wind. He led the congregation inside, and the service began.

Though lasting only three quarters of an hour, the ceremony was lovelier than Moira had imagined—despite not being able to understand any of it because every word was in Irish. Moira was moved, once again, by the depth of care that surrounded Peg and the strength of heart Peg displayed. Though she knew the days and weeks to come would be the real test for Peg, Moira couldn't help but feel with such a support system in place, her friend would be alright.

⁂

As they huffed along to the graveyard, Moira's feet stepped over and around stones and roots that jutted out of the rutted pathway that was barely wide enough for three people across. *No wonder they don't use a horse and cart.*

When they finally reached the top of the hillock, Moira sucked in a breath. Áedach stood by the open grave, his hair whipping wildly in the wind that had picked up during the service.

The congregation murmured and two men went around the back of two large gravestones and grabbed the lad, holding his arms behind his back. "What did ye know of yer uncle's plans?" one of them growled.

"Nothing! Not until it was all over, anyway."

"Lads." The priest laid a hand on each of the men's shoulders. "'Tis not the time."

Both men scowled at Áedach but let him go with a shove, nearly knocking him into the grave. When he regained his balance, he backed out of sight.

The graveside service consisted of lowering the coffin into the ground and laying two spades in the shape of a cross on the lid.

"In case they're wrong and Colm wakes up, he can dig himself out," Sinead whispered. Moira shuddered at the thought.

More prayers were said and blessings spoken, before each of the parishioners, starting with Peg, dropped a handful of dirt into the chasm. The congregation then snaked its way back down the hill and the men headed for the pub, while most of the women went to their own homes. It was time now for the widow to have her privacy.

"Ye'll come home with me, aye?" Peg looked at Moira and Sean in turn.

Privacy of her choosing. "Of course," they agreed.

"And bring the lad." Peg nodded to a tall *cairn* with a statue on top, behind which they could just see Áedach's hair flapping in the wind.

Chapter 61

Moira set about making the tea and Sean gathered enough chairs for all of them to sit by the fire. With the tea properly served and their fingers and toes beginning to thaw after the hours spent out of doors, Sean turned his attention to Áedach.

"Now, lad," Sean said, "none of us here hold any fault against ye for what took place. But 'twould serve you well to be forthcoming with anything you know."

Áedach shifted in his seat and looked nervously at each of them.

Moira reached out and patted his hand. "It's alright, Áedach. You're safe here."

Sean couldn't tear his eyes from Moira and the way she cared for the lad. The poor creature was scared half out of his wits. Compassion radiated on her face, and though Sean knew she was exhausted, she somehow poured the same level of energy into caring for him as she had caring for Peg the night before. And for Áedach the weeks he lay dying in his hovel. And for her students each day she'd been charged with their care. Whatever doubts could have remained in his heart about his love for Moira vanished in that moment. Sean blinked hard to keep the tears at bay. *Focus, man. 'Tis not the time, nor place.* He glanced at her face once more. *But it will be soon.*

"Go on, now. Let's hear it." Sean willed his voice to be calm and soothing.

"Whan ye first arrived, Miss Doherty, Uncle Buach pulled me aside." Áedach swallowed hard. "I'd not seen him in a long while . . . not since the night he first introduced me to the poitín."

Sean ground his teeth. Just like that snake of a man to hook a child on drink. He nodded to encourage the lad to continue.

"He told me the story of how he'd caught yer mammy with that fella over at Glenveagh." He leaned his head toward Moira. "An' how ye'd come to make sure he'd paid fer his crime. But he told me he hadna done it—that yer mammy had lied about that to keep him quiet about her romancin' yer man Adair."

"Is that why you were so angry with me?" Moira's face was the picture of calm as she questioned him.

He nodded. "Aye, marm. And I'm verra sorry. Had I known—"

"No need, lad. You couldn't have known your uncle was lying."

"Anyway," Áedach continued, "Uncle said I needed ta make sure ye didna cause any trouble, and to threaten to spill yer saicrit if ye did."

"'Set yer tongue a'waggin','" Moira whispered, staring a million miles away.

"Well, yeah." Áedach looked surprised. "Tha's exactly wha' he said. But I had no idea he was plottin' ta harm ye. I know I done some things ta ye, Miss, that desairves punishment far worse than ye've ever given me."

"Yes, you were rather hateful." There was a twinkle in Moira's eye, despite her firm tone of voice. "But I figured a long illness that nearly killed you tamed you some." She

winked at him, and the first smile Sean had ever seen on
Áedach's face shone brightly.

"Aye." The boy nodded. "But that's not really why I came
today."

Every eye was trained even harder on the lad. "Well," Peg
said slowly, "why did ye come, then?"

Áedach rose and paced the room. "Ye and Colm were so
good ta me. I didna set that fire, but I didna stop it either.
I know ye have no wee ones ta continue lookin' after ye
now that Colm's gone. I came to offer my services, such as
they are."

Peg pressed a hand to her mouth, stood, and enveloped
the boy in an embrace. "I'd be honored to have ye look
after me, Áedach."

"I'd only ask one t'ing in return, if I could be so bold?"
His face turned crimson.

Peg's brow furrowed slightly. "What might that be, lad?"

"I only ask that ye and Miss Doherty—if she's willin'—
keep reading to me from the Bíobla." He ducked his head
and chewed his thumbnail nervously.

Sean, mouth agape, looked from the lad to Peg to Moira
and back before the room erupted in laughter.

"I think I speak for all of us," Moira said, "when I say that
we can definitely do that."

"Amen!" Peg looked to the ceiling, hands clasped and
fingers laced together.

"Only if I can join too," Sean said as he laid a hand on
Áedach's shoulder.

"That settles it," Moira said. "Weekly prayer and Bible
reading at the Sweeny house."

The group cheered before a revered silence settled over
them. As Sean studied each of their faces, awe washed over
him, and he was humbled that such beauty could come
from such darkness.

Chapter 62

More than a week had passed since Colm's funeral, and Moira had just spent the first night in her own home since the fire. She had been staying with Peg, keeping watch over her, cooking, and cleaning up after the wake. She was willing to stay as long as Peg needed. Moira had planned to stay longer. In fact, she had not wanted to leave the Sweeny house, but Peg insisted.

"I've got to start living life again sooner or later," she'd told Moira. "Besides, I won't be alone once Sean and Áedach finish building my caretaker's chalet in the back."

With the truth about Moira's past now out in the open, the people of Ballymann finally seemed to be warming to her. Many stopped and chatted with her in the shop, and she heard from many parents that the children were looking forward to returning to school.

Sitting now in the quiet morning light of her own home, with no school day ahead of her, Moira dropped to her knees. "Lord, I never would have dreamed You would bring about such beauty and redemption from the ashes. Thank You for the miracle You've worked in Áedach's life, and forgive me for when I've doubted You. Help me live a life worthy of that to which You've called me."

She continued in that posture of prayer, soaking in the presence of the Almighty. The clock ticked away on the mantel, but she had no inkling of how much time had passed. If it weren't for the knock at the door, Moira felt she could have passed the entire day there in prayer.

She answered the knock and was surprised to see Sinead at her door, smiling like a giddy child on Christmas morning. "Good morning, Sinead. What brings you by this fine morn?"

A hearty laugh bubbled up and Sinead wagged her head. "Doncha know it's no longer morning when midday has passed?"

Moira's brows raised. "Surely it isn't midday yet?"

"Nearly one o' the clock!"

Moira stepped back, allowing Sinead into the house.

"I've come ta request the honor of yer presence."

Moira sat at her table and motioned for Sinead to do the same. "I'm sorry?"

Her boisterous laughter was contagious, and before long both women were cackling, though Moira didn't quite know why. When the laughter died down, both sighed deeply. Moira placed a hand on Sinead's. "Oh how I've missed you, friend."

"Aye." Sinead nodded. "And I, ye." Sinead squeezed Moira's hand. "Now, that's enough o' that. There's not much time."

"Not much time for what?" Moira asked.

"I was sent to bid ye come at two o' the clock. And ye've been requested to wear yer new frock." Sinead nodded, satisfied that she'd delivered her full message.

"Two o'clock? Where? Who's inviting me?"

Sinead wagged a finger. "*Tsk, tsk, tsk!* Just get on yer fancy dress, I'll help ye with yer hair, we'll pinch up some color in those cheeks, and ye'll be ready in time. Aye?"

Moira shook her head, curious what in the world could

be happening. However, it was clear Sinead was going to offer no further information. She retrieved the dress from her press, and Sinead squealed from across the room.

"Oh, Moira, I didn't know that was yer new dress!" She clapped her hands and jumped up and down in place. "Where did ye get it?"

"From O'Tooles," Moira teased.

"Och!" Sinead swatted the air. "I know *tha'*! But how?"

Moira shrugged. "It was left here on my table as a surprise. I was meant to wear it to the Paddy's Day céilí, but then—" Her countenance fell.

Sinead crossed herself and then kissed her thumb. "Aye, was a sad Paddy's Day fer us all. I can't remember ever hearing about a time when all festivities were canceled."

The friends clasped hands, letting the gravity of the moment settle on them once more. Sinead was the first to break the silence. "We'd best get ye dressed, love."

The girls worked in tandem getting Moira out of her faded traveling frock and lacing and buttoning up her new velvet gown. When Sinead tied the strings of the apron around her waist, Moira looked down at herself and ran her hands over the rich fabric.

"I can still hardly believe it's mine."

"Let's see to those locks, aye?" Sinead worked Moira's hair into an intricate weave of plaits and curls. When she placed Moira in front of the looking glass, Moira could hardly believe her eyes. She turned toward her friend, whose eyes were teeming with joy.

"It's nearly two o' the clock, dearie. Ye best be on yer way."

"But *where* am I going?"

Sinead pressed her lips together and moved to the door, opening it for her friend. When Moira stepped out, her mouth fell open at the sight that greeted her. As far as the eye could see, men, women, and children—her precious students—lined the street. As Moira stepped onto the foot-path, Aoife ran up, threw her arms around her waist, and squeezed.

"I knew you'd stay!" She handed Moira a single flower, grabbed her hand, and led her down the street. One by one, each person handed her a flower and offered a curtsy or bow. Every now and then, one of her students would run up and join them, or someone would call out a greeting on the breeze.

Tears of joy pooled in her eyes as Moira realized she had done it—she had saved her mother. Not her mother's life but her legacy. Understanding bloomed like a daffodil in spring, and Moira finally realized why God had brought her to this place.

As they walked, Moira assumed this was the village's way of welcoming her back to the school, so she started to turn down that road. But Aoife tugged at her hand. "No, Miss, *this* way. Toward the halla!"

❧

Sean's heart pounded in his chest and blood rushed in his ears. He paced back and forth, wearing a path in the freshly swept dirt floor of the halla. The community had worked all week to clear the rubble from the fire because of their excitement to help Sean execute his plan.

A commotion outside drew his attention. Children squealed, footsteps filled the road, and the murmur of a crowd grew louder. He stepped outside, shading his eyes against the sun with his hands, and grinned.

Moira, surrounded by a throng of skipping, laughing children, made her way down the street. Flowers overflowed from her hands, and joy radiated from her face as she greeted each member of the community in turn. Someone leaned in and said something in her ear. She just laughed, shrugged, gestured "I don't know," and continued down the road. His heart swelled at the sight of her in her new gown.

He had taken great pains to get to Letterkenny and back in time to surprise her with it before St. Patrick's Day. He'd scraped together every extra shilling and worked some odd jobs for various folks around town to earn the price of it. Seeing her in it now, with her face shining and eyes glistening, took his breath away.

"Miss Doherty, look!" Aoife pointed right at Sean.

Moira's gaze followed the direction of the girl's finger until her eyes fell on him. She stopped, brought a hand to her mouth, and laughed. Resisting the impulse to run like a spring lamb and scoop her up into his arms, Sean merely extended a hand and beckoned her: *Come.*

Chapter 63

Moira's pulse raced and a fresh spate of tears sprang to her eyes as she took in the sight of Sean standing in front of the halla, hand extended to her. A deeper sense of love for him welled within her, and she ran until she reached him. Her arms full of flowers from the townsfolk, she had no free hand with which to accept his. She looked around until her eyes fell upon Aoife.

As if on cue, Aoife darted over and held her arms out. "I'll hold yer flowers for ye, Miss."

"Thank you very much, my dear." Moira leaned over and deposited her veritable garden into the girl's waiting arms. After brushing the leaves from her sleeves, she laid her hand in Sean's. "Good afternoon, Mr. McFadden."

Sean curled his fingers around hers, and her heart fluttered at the warmth of his touch.

Leaning over, he pressed his lips ever so lightly to her fingers. "Miss Doherty, ya look a dream." Playful mischief brightened his eyes and he nodded toward the door. "Shall we?"

Moira merely nodded, then looked back over her shoulder at the crowd. Peg stood there, tears shining in her eyes. She nodded and blew a kiss to Moira.

Moira turned back to Sean and smiled. "I believe we shall."

He led her into the old building, and Moira's breath caught yet again. The afternoon light poured in through the open roof, and candles lined the walls, filled the fireplace, and lined the stone mantel. Though the crowd pressed around the building, poking their faces in the windows and the doorway, the sounds of the throng faded, and Moira's attention fixed on Sean as he walked her throughout the halla.

"Here," he said, taking her to the far back corner, "is where Paddy McGonigle, and his father before him, would serve the ale. Next to him, here, Father O'Friel kept a close eye on his flock." He leaned in so close his lips brushed her ear as he whispered, "When he wasn't entertaining the crowd with his Sean Nós dances, anyway."

Moira giggled and placed a hand on his arm. Her other hand was still safely tucked in his as he continued the grand tour of the open room. She studied his face, the strong cut of his jaw, and the slight shadow of an afternoon beard. His green eyes shone with love for this place and her people as he retold many of the same stories Moira had heard from her own mother. Standing here now, surrounded by the people she loved, Moira appreciated the tales even more. It was as though all who'd gone before were there with them, enjoying the delight of this moment.

Even a building can be redeemed. The fear and pain she'd experienced at the hand of her attacker could have left a stain on her heart and the building itself, but it had all been burned clean in the fire. It held no threat. Only the wonder of hope.

"And over here," Sean continued, leading her to the far opposite corner. "This was Noreen O'Connell's favorite spot, so I've heard. It was in this corner she would sit and chat with her friends before leaping to the floor for her dances." He let go of her hand, as though he knew she'd want to fully experience this sacred place.

Moira could envision her mother, young and carefree, laughing and dancing the night away. She ran her hand along the wall, as though she might feel her mother's hand through the years. What a gift Sean had given her.

"Moira Doherty?"

Moira turned at his voice.

"May I have this dance?"

From the door, musicians began to play a slow, melodic waltz. Sean bowed deeply, then rose to meet her gaze as he extended his hand.

"I'd be honored, Sean McFadden." She curtsied and placed her hand in his once more. He pulled her close, wrapping his other arm around her waist, and let the music sweep them away.

As they twirled and swayed together, Sean's eyes never left hers until he leaned in close and whispered in her ear, "I love you, Moira."

In that moment, they could have been flying and she wouldn't have known it. Moira closed her eyes and laid her head on his chest. The scent of cotton and heather was embedded in her memory as uniquely his. When the music faded, they stood together, fingers laced, holding one another for a long moment until Moira finally lifted her head and gazed deep into his eyes.

"I love you too."

He inclined his head toward hers and smoothed a tender hand over her hair. His lips hovered just a breath away from hers while his eyes traced the contours of her face. Pulling her closer still, he whispered, "Say it again."

Moira's breath stilled in her chest. She caressed his cheek with trembling fingers, her eyes searching his. "I love you, Sean McFadden."

His green eyes lit up, and a smile curled on his lips. "Dance with me. Forever?"

She returned his smile and nodded.

He lowered his mouth. Softly at first, he pressed his lips to hers. When she wrapped her arms around him, he pulled his face away to look at her once more. Moira caressed his hair and pulled his face close. Their lips met again, the kiss deepening. Moira relished all that words could not convey. There in the warmth of his kiss and the tenderness of his embrace, she knew she'd found her true home.

"Yeeoo!" a voice howled in the distance. The musicians struck up a lively reel. The couple laughed and Sean whisked Moira away, hopping and spinning about the halla. Moira knew her mother had been right all along.

Pulling Sean to a stop, she planted another kiss on his mouth. "Ah, my love, there truly is nothing like a dance in Donegal."

CONTINUE READING FOR AN EXCERPT
FROM **JENNIFER DEIBEL**'S NEXT

Sweeping Irish

Romance

CHAPTER 1

No one ever tells the truth about love.

The stories and fables paint a glowing portrait of valiant acts and enduring romance. Love, it is said, is the most powerful force in the world.

Stephen Jennings knew better.

He watched the pair from behind the polished glass case as they huddled together, giggling and fawning over one another.

"This one here, lad." The gangly man gestured at the display. "We'll take it."

The rusty-haired lass swooned. "Oh, Charlie, do ya mean it? In earnest? Oh!" She squealed and threw her arms around her beau's neck.

"Very good, sir." Stephen removed the silver ring from the case and buffed it carefully with a polishing cloth. He started with the hands that encircled the heart, then moved to the crown that topped the design. How many times had he recounted the tale of the Claddagh? More than he cared to count. With the ring sufficiently shined, he handed it to the gentleman.

Fingers trembling, the man took the ring. A foolish school-boy grin spread across his face. His lass fanned herself, still giggling. The man glanced at Stephen out of the corner of his eye.

Oh no. No. Not here.

The man sank to one knee. "Maggie, you know I love you—"

Maggie erupted into hysterics. Stephen gritted his teeth, jaw aching from the pressure, and pasted on his best smile—though he feared it came across as more of a grimace.

"You know I love you," the man said again. "And I couldna wait another second before askin' ye . . . will ye marry me?"

Unintelligible sounds gurgled from Maggie's lips as she yanked him off the floor and kissed him hard before holding out a trembling hand.

"Is that . . . is that a yes?" The man's puppy-dog expression rivaled that of any begging canine in the alleys.

Good heavens, man, are ye daft?

"Oh, aye, Charles! Yes! Yes! A thousand times, yes!"

"I love you!" they said in unison.

Stephen had seen what "love" could do. Not even a mother's love—which is said to be the most powerful—could protect his own beloved mum from leaving this world while bringing Stephen into it. And the glassy-eyed, giddy type of love the couple before him now displayed had certainly not served any grander purpose than deluded self-fulfillment. How could they be so blind?

Charles slipped the ring on Maggie's finger and presented her hand to Stephen. "Is it on properly?"

Stephen cleared his throat. "Aye, that's right. The tip of the heart points in, toward her own heart, if she's spoken for." He looked between the two, who only had eyes for one another. "And it seems she is most certainly spoken for." Though he tried to soften it, his voice sounded flatter than it should have. After all, the store needed this sale. He pasted another smile on his face. "*Comhghairdeas.*"

Charles looked at him now. "*Go raibh míle maith agat.* A million thanks." He handed the payment to Stephen and guided his bride-to-be out of the shop.

Stephen watched them leave, resisting the urge to rush and slam the door behind them. *Fools.*

"I canna do this anymore." He dropped his head. His knuckles were white, and the edges of the case dug into the heels of his hands. He slapped his palm onto the wood beam that anchored it to the wall.

It was bad enough he was the only one who seemed to understand the truth of it, but his family made their living peddling the idea and legend of love. Salt in an ever-open wound. How could no one else see? Love was a myth. A crutch. And he couldn't be part of flogging the lie any longer. He rubbed his hand over his head, down his face, then pulled a piece of paper from his trouser pocket.

He read the words he already knew by heart.

Dear Mr. Jennings,

We are delighted to accept you as an apprentice at Sánchez Iron and Masonry Works. Your family's skill with design and craftsmanship is well known. We look forward to adding your expertise to our repertoire. Once you have acquired the necessary funds for your move, please let us know and we will make your lodgings ready.

Sincerely,
Roman Sánchez

Eyeing the door to the shop, Stephen could no longer deny the inevitable. *It's time.* Father would be devastated, but the thought of staying here, hocking jewelry, and reliving his family's legacy day in and day out was enough to bolster his courage to share his plans to leave.

Replacing the letter in his pocket, he turned to search for his father. But before he could take a step, the back door of the showroom opened and his father escorted someone inside. "Ah, Stephen, there's a good lad. I've someone I want ye to meet." Seamus's eyes carried more spark than usual, and there was a bounce in his step that Stephen hadn't seen in ages.

Stephen turned his attention to his father's guest. Standing arm in arm with his father was a strikingly beautiful woman. Her golden hair twisted on top of her head in an intricate weave of braids and coils that fell around her shoulders in soft curls. Blue eyes pinned Stephen where he stood, and soft dimples accented her rosy cheeks as she smiled at him. She was beautiful, aye, but something about her seemed . . . amiss. Her dress was too fine. Her posture, too straight. He'd been around the store long enough to know a beautiful face and beguiling smile meant nothing. The most striking face could hide the blackest heart. What was this lass's secret? Still, Stephen's heart thudded unnaturally against his chest.

"Stephen, my boy, this is Miss Annabeth De Lacy." Seamus beamed.

Stephen shook himself from his thoughts and turned his eyes sharply to his father. "De Lacy? As in—"

"How do you do?" Annabeth interrupted him and extended her left hand, fingers daintily dangling down.

Stephen looked from Annabeth to his father and back. "De Lacy?" He practically spat the name out.

"That's right," she said, hand still extended. She lifted her chin. "My father, Lord De Lacy, is the new landlord for this parish." She cleared her throat and gave her hand a slight twitch.

Seamus continued to beam, then frowned and jerked his head slightly in the direction of the woman. "Where're yer manners, lad?"

Making no attempt to mask his irritation at his father for bringing a British courtier into the shop, he stepped forward, grasped her fingertips, and wagged her hand briefly before dropping his arm back to his side. "Miss." He nodded curtly. "Father? A word?"

Ignoring his son's agitation, Seamus made an announcement. "Lady De Lacy is to be your apprentice." He puffed out his chest so proudly the buttons practically popped off his waistcoat.

"Appr—my what?"

"Just what I said. Lady De Lacy here is to be your apprentice. Ye're to show her the way of things. Ensure she knows the legend of the Claddagh, show her how to make the rings. She's quite an accomplished artist." He winked at Annabeth, and she rewarded him with a pearly-white grin.

"Please, call me Anna."

An apprentice? What was the old man thinking? Sure, it could work to Stephen's advantage if there were someone capable of staying on when he left. But a woman? And a *British* woman, no less? He crossed his arms over his chest, cleared his throat, and said through gritted teeth, "Father. May I please have a word?"

"Och!" Seamus waved a dismissive hand, then patted Annabeth's. "I'll only be a wee minute, lass. Take a look around the shop, so."

Father and son stepped out of earshot of their new guest. "What's the meaning of this?" Stephen asked.

"Now, now. It's not as bad as ye think." A hint of resignation flickered in the old man's eye.

"Is tha' so?" Stephen's jaw ached.

Seamus pressed his lips into a thin line and shrugged.

"And what about Tommy, huh? After what they—"

Seamus lifted a silent hand. He stared hard into Stephen's eyes for a long moment before answering. "No matter what has happened in the past, this is our present right now. You're going to do this." He paused. "I need you to do this."

"Father, have you gone mad?"

"Mad? Have you seen the lass?" He chuckled and winked at Stephen.

"Be serious, man!"

"Serious, ye say? How's this for serious?" Seamus glanced over his shoulder then continued, "The British government has sent us lowly Irishman a new landlord. I don't know if ye'd noticed, but the last one they sent us was a real saint." Sarcasm laced the old man's voice.

"True."

"Well, that shiny new landlord has requested we apprentice his daughter. It's a mite out of the ordinary, I'll grant you, but I'm not quite in the mood to cross the Brits at this stage." Footsteps punctuated his point as a unit of soldiers marched past the shop. Whether they were Irish or British troops was impossible to tell.

Stephen sighed as an unwelcome shiver traversed his spine. The old codger had a point, much as he hated to admit it. "Fine, we need to stay in their good graces—if they even have any. But why me? The pair of ye seem to get on just fine. Why can't ya teach her yerself?"

"In case ya haven't noticed, lad, I'm no spring chicken." He stretched his arms out to accentuate his point. "I'm gettin' too auld to even be running the shop, let alone teachin' another wee one. I was going to talk to ya about it anyway, but when Lord De Lacy approached me last week, it was mere confirmation. It's time, boy."

"Time?" Stephen's brow furrowed. "Time for what, Da?"

Seamus rolled his lips between his teeth and stared at the ground for an uncomfortable length of time. Finally, he cleared his throat and said, "It's time for you to take over. You're a better jewel smith than I ever was, and you've a smart head for business on yer shoulders. That last bout with the fever I had over the winter is what clinched it. The shop . . . she's yours." Seamus pulled a handkerchief from his waistcoat pocket and swiped at his eyes. "Come now, lad, help your apprentice settle in and learn the shop."

Glossary of Terms

amárach—[uh-MAH-rugh]—tomorrow

a Mhúinteoir—[uh WOON-chorr]—teacher, when addressing them directly

angelus—[ANE-geh-luss]—the national call to prayer in Ireland; church bells ring at noon and six in the evening

a thaisce—[uh HASH-kee]—a term of endearment, used when speaking to someone (not about them)

amadán—[AH-mah-donn]—idiot

anois—[eh-NISH]—now

babaí—[BAH-bee]—baby; young one

beag—[BYUG]—little

Bíobla—[BEEB-luh]—Bible

bodhrán—[BOW-ronn]—a traditional Irish drum

breá—[BRAW]—handsome

cad a tharla?—[CAD uh HARR-luh]—what happened?

caoineadh—[KEEN-cheh]—keening; grieving

céilí—[KAY-lee]—a party with music, dancing, and often storytelling *ceol*—[KYOHL]—music

cosa—[CUHSS-ee]—feet

craic—[CRACK]—fun, good times; often, but not always, involving music

créatúr—[KRAY-tur]—creature; often used as a term of endearment for an infant

Día dhuit—[JEE-uh DITCH]—a common formal greeting in Irish Gaelic

fáilte abhaile—[FALL-chuh uh-WAHL-yuh]—welcome home

Feabhra—[FOW-ruh]—February

footed—used to describe when turf is stacked on its end, typically to let it dry further

go raibh míle maith agaibh—[guh ruh MEE-luh MY uh-GEE]—Thank you very much, to more than one person

Gaeilge—[GAY-lih-guh]—Gaelic/Irish

gardaí—[garr-DEE]—police

grá mo chroí—[GHRA MOE CHREE]—love of my heart

gúna oiche—[GOO-nuh EE-huh]—nightdress

halla—hall

logh dom—[LOWG dumm]—forgive me

muinteoir—[MOON-chorr]—teacher

ní maith liom do trioblóide—[NEE MAH luhm do TRUH-bluh-juh]—traditional Irish sympathy greeting; literally "I don't like your trouble."

oh, Mhaidean—[oh WHY-jahn]—an exclamation of dismay; literally "Oh, Virgin!" referring to the Virgin Mary

oíche mhaith, a mhac—[EE-huh WAH uh WAHK]—good night, son

peat—[PEET]—a type of moss, found on the bog, used as solid fuel; also called *turf*

peata—[PA-the]—pet; a term of endearment

poitín—[PAH-cheen]—Irish moonshine

rógaire—[ROH-gerd-uh]—rogue

scuab—[SKOO-uhb]—broom

seafóid—[SHAH-fooj]—nonsense

seanchaí—[SHAWN-hee]—a storyteller

sean nós—[SHAWN OHS]—a form of traditional Irish danc-
    ing or singing

shillelagh—[shih-LAY-lee]—a traditional Irish club or walk-
    ing stick

sláinte—[SLAHN-chuh]—an Irish toast of blessings and
    health

stad—[STAHD]—stop

tá brón orm—[taw brone OR-uhm]—I'm sorry

tá sé ceart go leor, gach duine! Tá sí go álainn!—[taw shay cart
    go lore gak DINN-yuh! Taw shee go HAW-linn]—It's
    okay, everyone! She's lovely!

uilleann pipes—[UHL-uhn PIPES]—the Irish form of bag-
    pipes, played by pumping a bag using one's elbow rather
    than blowing into a mouthpiece

Author's Note

Thank you, dear reader, for journeying with me to Bally-mann. Though a fictional place, it was deeply inspired and influenced by the tiny seaside village my family and I lived in for two years: Derrybeg, County Donegal. I hope this incredible land and her people have found their way into your heart as they have mine. I had the honor and bless-ing of living in Ireland for a total of almost six years, and I always say my heart was born there and I never truly found it until we moved to Ireland.

A few of the places in this book are real. The Poisoned Glen with the roofless church was a favorite exploring spot for us. The Central Bar in Letterkenny is real and is still there. In fact, that is where I, much like Moira, ate my first real Irish meal—except for Bríd's cooking, of course! O'Toole's is also a real store located on the high street of Letterkenny. Glenveagh Castle is real, as is the Adair family. However, to my knowledge, John Adair was never promised in marriage to anyone in Donegal. And while British land-lords ruled Donegal for ages, to my knowledge there was never a Lady Williams.

Bríd Martin is loosely based on a delightful woman named Maire who runs Teac Campbell Guesthouse in Bunbeg, County Donegal. She is an amazing cook and an incredibly kind, welcoming woman who never stops running.

Irish Gaelic is the first and daily language of the thousands of people who live along the west coast of Ireland in pockets called Gaeltachts, where the language is protected. We became comfortably conversational in this beautiful ancient language. If you'd like to hear me speaking the beautiful language, as well as hear the two songs referenced in the story—"An Bheán Dubh na Ghleanna" and the Ballyeamon Cradle Song—you can find videos on the *A Dance in Donegal* board on my Pinterest page (https://pin.it/ytzhv2tfzuilyk).

ACKNOWLEDGMENTS

I almost don't know where to start. This book has been a labor of love years in the making. First and foremost, I must thank God for His infinite kindness in allowing me to tell stories and realize this dream.

Secondly, to my incredible husband, Seth. You always work to make my dreams come true—you have from the very beginning. Thank you for supporting and championing me. Thank you for keeping me grounded and holding me accountable to meeting my goals when my confidence faltered. I cannot fathom a person I'd want to journey this life with more.

To my kids—Hannah, Cailyn, and Isaac—thank you for being my biggest cheerleaders and for being willing to talk out story ideas and eat sandwiches for dinner way more often than you really wanted to. I can't imagine life without you, and I'm so honored to be your mom. Let this book be a reminder that it's never too late to chase your dreams.

Thank you to my mom, Bonnie Martin, for reading every chapter as it was written, rewritten, and rewritten again. Thank you for cheering me on, giving me honest feedback, and being just as excited as I was each step of the way. To my dad, Jerry Martin, thank you for the gift of my faith and showing me from an early age what a godly man looks like.

To my Irish friends—Debra and Brian O'Gibne, Deirdre Forristal, Donal and Linda O'Donnell, Mart O'Donnell, Rick Russell, and the gang at Builín Blásta Café—thank you for being our second family. For welcoming us into your homes and lives; helping us learn the language and culture; celebrating holidays, birthdays, and births with us; and grieving with us through incredibly difficult times. You were the best part of Ireland, and I miss you so deeply that my heart aches every day.

My writers group gals—Liz Johnson, Lindsay Harrell, Sara Carrington, Tina Radcliffe, Erin McFarland, Ruth Douthitt, and Rhia Adley—thank you for providing listening ears, words of wisdom, and shoulders to cry on. You ladies gave me strength and courage when I wanted to give up. Thank you for the gift of your friendship.

And to all my friends who've cheered me on along the way—Charity Verlander, Stacy Dyck, Christen Krumm, Donna Carlson, Rachel Fordham, Jocelyn Green, Sarah Sundin, and the incredible Palmer Small Group—my heart is forever grateful for you.

Jaimie Jo Wright and Tricia Goyer—thank you for believing in me, investing in me, and championing me. I for sure would not be here without your kindness and support.

To Chad Segersten—my principal when I was going through the process of signing the contract for this book—your support, encouragement, and flexibility will forever be in my heart. Not a day goes by when I don't think of you, your leadership, and your excitement on my behalf. May you rest in peace.

To my amazing agent, Cynthia Ruchti. What can I say? Only God could orchestrate the string of events that brought us together in this working relationship. Thank you for believing in me, for loving my characters as much as I do, and for your prayers, guidance, and wisdom.

Finally, thank you to my wonderful editors, Rachel McRae and Robin Turici, and the team at Revell. Words cannot express how grateful I am for you, your expertise, and your excitement to bring *A Dance in Donegal* to the world. Thank you for taking a chance on me.

Jennifer Deibel is a middle school teacher and coffee lover. She believes no one should be alone on their faith journey, and through her writing she aims to redefine home through the lens of culture, history, and family. After nearly a decade of living in Ireland and Austria, Jennifer now lives in Arizona with her husband and their three children.

Meet *Jennifer*

Find Jennifer Online at
JENNIFERDEIBEL.COM

and sign up for her newsletter to get the latest news and special updates delivered directly to your inbox.

Follow Jennifer on social media!

 JenniferDeibelAuthor   🐦 ThisGalsJourney   📷 jenniferdeibel_author